P9-DEU-825

ZANESVILLE

ZANESVILLE

A NOVEL

Kris Saknussemm

VILLARD ⓥ NEW YORK

This is a work of fiction. Names, characters, places, and incidents are the products
of the author's imagination or are used fictitiously. Any resemblance to actual
events, locales, or persons, living or dead, is entirely coincidental.

A Villard Books Trade Paperback Original

Copyright © 2005 by Kris Saknussemm

All rights reserved.

Published in the United States by Villard Books, an imprint of The Random House
Publishing Group, a division of Random House, Inc., New York.

VILLARD and "V" CIRCLED Design are registered trademarks of
Random House, Inc.

Grateful acknowledgment is made to the following for permission
to reprint previously published material:

Marge Crumbaker: Excerpt from "Boot Hill" by Marge Crumbaker and
Pat Wilson. Reprinted by permission of Marge Crumbaker.

Edward B. Marks Music Company: Excerpt from "Bat Out of Hell" by
James Steinman. Reprinted by permission of Edward B. Marks Music Company.

Hal Leonard Corporation: Excerpt from "Dust in the Wind" by Kerry Livgren.
Copyright © 1977, 1978 EMI Blackwood Music Inc. and Don Kirshner
Music Inc. All rights reserved. International Copyright Secured. Reprinted by
permission of Hal Leonard Corporation on behalf of EMI Blackwood Music Inc.

Sony/ATV Music Publishing: Excerpts from "I Am the Walrus" by John Lennon
and Paul McCartney. Copyright © 1967 (renewed) by Sony/ATV Tunes LLC.
All rights administered by Sony/ATV Music Publishing, 8 Music Square West,
Nashville, TN 37203. All rights reserved. Used by permission.

Universal Music Publishing Group: Excerpt from "Wichita Lineman" by
Jimmy Webb. Copyright © 1968, 1996 by Universal-Polygram International
Publishing, Inc./ASCAP. International Copyright Secured. All rights reserved.
Reprinted by permission of Universal Music Publishing Group.

Warner Bros. Publications U.S. Inc.: Excerpt from "Here Comes Peter
Cottontail" by Steve Nelson and Walter Rollins. Copyright © 1950
(Renewed) Chappell & Co. (ASCAP). All rights reserved.
Reprinted by permission of Warner Bros. Publications U.S. Inc.

ISBN 0-8129-7416-6

Printed in the United States of America

www.villard.com

2 4 6 8 9 7 5 3 1

Book design by Simon M. Sullivan

For Matt Bialer
rabbi, amigo, co-conspirator

Acknowledgments

My loudest thanks go to my agent, Matt Bialer. Matt, along with his assistant, Cheryl Capitani, provided invaluable editorial recommendations and continuous personal bolstering. Thanks too to Anna Bierhaus for her support—and to Paul Witcover, who provided astute criticism at just the right time.

I am fortunate to have a sharp and adventurous editor in Chris Schluep. To Chris, Bruce Tracy, Dan Menaker, and Gina Centrello, thank you for taking a chance on me.

Over the years of rejection, several dedicated editors of literary journals have supported my work. I would like to thank in particular Jodi Daynard and Joshua Cohen of the *Boston Review,* Howard Junker of ZYZZYVA, Robert Fogarty of *The Antioch Review,* James McKinley and Robert Stewart of *New Letters,* Richard Newman of *River Styx,* Paula Deitz of *The Hudson Review,* the editors of *In Posse Review* and the Web del Sol team, and Roderick Clark of *Rosebud.*

If there is a heaven, I'm sure it must be very much like the MacDowell Colony. The colony's generosity, hospitality, and emotional reinforcement mean more to me than I can say. So too with the Squaw Valley Community of Writers.

On the personal front, I am grateful to my business partner, David Hobby, who not only lent his design expertise to the book's website but has given me years of friendship, good advice, and much-needed tolerance—along with teaching me the survival value of optimism through the courage of his fight with cancer. Pete Walsh is my Web wizard and has been a huge help in so many ways.

Just before the book contract was issued I went through an ugly divorce. Jeff Maynard and Zoe Hebdon, Glenys Johnson, and Janet, Vytas, and Alexis Didelis stood by me in a very crazy time. My oldest and best friend, Philip Abrams, and my loyal sister June, along with her husband, Ken, and daughter, Janie, could not have been more supportive. To my lovely Karen, who knows what lies ahead?

Finally, I would like to thank my mother, Ellen Kester, a tireless teacher and inspirer of young people for more than fifty years, including me. To all these collaborators, my deepest gratitude.

KS

Man is a god in ruins.
—Ralph Waldo Emerson

My Life Is Wind

Eighteen thirty-eight. A time of transmogrification in America. Across the South the sweat and blood of black people turns into white cotton. A part of Mexico, which had turned into the Republic of Texas, will turn into the United States, which will turn into war. Fifteen thousand Cherokee endure the eight-hundred-mile Trail of Tears to Oklahoma, while in New York State an arithmetically inclined devout farmer named William Miller predicts the world will end in five years.

It is out of this whirlwind that one of the most neglected geniuses in history appears:

LLOYD MEADHORN SITTURD, born to Hephaestus Sitturd, a blacksmith and frustrated inventor with Shawnee blood (reputedly related to the great chief Tecumseh), and Rapture Meadhorn, the Gullah-speaking daughter of a freed Cumberland Island slave and a Kentucky mountain "granny woman."

Conceived on the great Serpent Mound in Adams County, Ohio, Lloyd is born in the town of Zanesville. His twin sister, Lodema, is dead at birth. At the time, his father, a reluctant believer in William Miller's advent movement, is building a "Time Ark" to shield the family from the effects of the end of the world, while Rapture is pioneering the use of marijuana in the treatment of dementia and terminal illnesses.

Lloyd is an inventive prodigy. By age four he is making miniature airships and writing secret books in his own invisible ink. At five he designs and builds a fully operational mechanical beaver.

Following the Millerites' Great Disappointment, when the world does not end, Hephaestus moves his family from Ohio and takes up a desolate farm property he inherits in Dustdevil, Texas. There, on the Fourth of July, while young Lloyd is tending the shrine he has created in his dead twin's memory, a tornado whisks the boy away. He is gone for twenty minutes—and returns to the exact same spot. When asked what transpired while he was in the whirlwind, Lloyd says he communed with the spirit of his dead sister, who imparted to him knowledge of a higher order of evolutionary development. The story is dismissed as childish fancy, but one aspect of it rings incontrovertibly true—his prodigious inventive gifts are heightened further.

It is his technological wizardry that later underlies the North's victory in the Civil War—an outcome that would've been achieved much earlier had his ideas been followed more faithfully. (His strategy for the Battle of Shiloh involved introducing organic mescaline into the Confederate water supply.)

Following the war, he experiments with new theories and methods of camouflage, hypnotism and accelerated learning, calculating and translating machines, new kinds of prosthetic devices, the use of organic drugs to treat mental illness, radical surgical procedures, early cinematography, psychical research, and weather control. His brilliance is undermined only by a pathological disrespect for follow-through, a voracious sexual appetite, and a lingering sense of guilt and loss over his dead twin sister. These demons drive and derail him, as his fortunes rise and fall— from the towering heights of wealth (at one point he maintains schools of Falconry and Dream Interpretation at his estate Labyrinthia, between the Black Hills and the Badlands of South Dakota) to absinthe-soaked orgies in seedy Manhattan hotels.

His greatest commercial success is the grand amusement park known as Macropotamia, built at the convergence of the three rivers in Pittsburgh. It is here, long before Brooklyn's famous Luna Park, that the world's first true roller coaster debuts—an unprecedented achievement for its time. (It was Sitturd who coined the phrase "Must be 42 inches tall to ride.") Sitturd calls the attraction—modeled on a tornado—"Lodemania," but later changes its name to "The Rapture" following Mark Twain's description of it as "a religious experience" (while strongly discouraging tobacco chewing).

Twain's assessment proves prophetic, for large numbers of patrons begin reporting spiritual visions while riding The Rapture, a phenomenon that deeply worries and aggravates religious leaders. Tension surrounding the roller coaster finally culminates in a controversial incident involving three young schoolgirls, which forces the ride's closure. Accidents and attacks on other attractions follow.

Destroyed by a suspicious fire, Macropotamia dwindles into legend. Sitturd travels under various aliases and eventually becomes a recluse, concentrating on breeding experiments and research into what today we would call artificial intelligence and robotics. Rumors regarding his investigations and achievements are rife within the Pinkertons and the Secret Service, leading to legendary claims that one of his "creations" was the real assassin of President McKinley at the Pan-American Exposition in Buffalo in 1901, the event that led to the presidency of Theodore Roosevelt, a former neighbor and friend of Sitturd's back in South Dakota days.

Weary and embittered, Sitturd retires to Dustdevil, Texas, the scene of his earlier experience with the whirlwind. There he rebuilds the shrine to his sister and begins a community dedicated to the lost principles of what he terms the American Spiritual Promise. He adopts no name for his followers, but people of all races are welcome—and it is interesting to note that he also refers to "all" sexes. It is unclear whether the latter remark metaphorically includes homosexuality or anticipates biotechnological variations. Another alternative is that Sitturd is so addled by a lifetime of drugs, he doesn't know what he is saying. In any case, sexual relations are open, constant, and, in the eyes of conservative neighbors, depraved. To add further insult, Sitturd's collective sweeps blue-ribbon honors at the state fair for the quality of their produce and livestock, not to mention the fact that they supply all their own electrical power with Sitturd's unique double-helix windmills, which he calls "Turbinators."

During a swimming party and poetry reading, which is later described as a "pagan ritual with satanic overtones," a vigilante force attacks the compound, sets fire to buildings, and attempts to lynch Sitturd from one of his own windmills. Fear, more than common sense or decency, keeps the murder from reaching its conclusion, but the shock of the attack and the threat of further raids drives off most of the commune's members. Later, the rest of the barns are burned, along with Sitturd's laboratory, the library, and the experimental crop fields. The trout and eel ponds are limed, the pigshit engines ignited, and the windmills pulled down by draft horses. Sitturd is left alone and old in the wreck of the last standing farmhouse.

Then on the Fourth of July, 1913, a little after midday, a tornado of blood-red dust sweeps through the remains of the community and siphons up every remaining stick of timber and page of book. Lloyd Meadhorn Sitturd is never heard from again, leaving behind only the shrine to his dead sister with the inscription . . .

THE HIDDEN MAY BE SEEKING
AND THE MISSING MAY RETURN

PART 1

Afraid on Arrival

Every child begins the world again.
—HENRY DAVID THOREAU

CHAPTER I

Fort Thoreau

He crashed back into himself and felt the Easter evening damp. Dolls and chains hung in ritual fashion from the branches surrounding him, and through the knife-hacked oak trees he could make out great luminous spires and domes, and older, grim, but luxuriant blocks of apartments sealed with steel-plate louvers as if against attack. Beside these rose skeletal scaffoldings on which, judging from the hives of lights, whole families perched on open-air platforms while resourceful or desperate individuals dangled in slings and sacks suspended from guy wires.

Across the sky, as though projected from behind the sulfur-tinged clouds, flashed pictograms and iridescent banks of hypertext. The word VITESSA was repeated often . . . and slogans like EFRAM-ZEV . . . THE RIGHT MOOD AT THE RIGHT TIME. He felt hypnotized by the messages, information raining down like some new kind of radiation. Then there were streams of news images and giant flickering headlines . . . AL-WAQIʿA STILL A THREAT . . . VOYANCY LINKS NOW HALF-PRICE . . .

He'd been standing there for a long time, he thought, having woken suddenly by the fountain, amazed to find that his hair was long and so blond it almost seemed to glow in the dark. It reminded him of a childhood story but he couldn't pin it down. Then he realized that of much greater concern was that he couldn't remember where he was. It was a park of some kind, a vast shadowy garden in some siren-filled city. But which one?

He heard a voice . . . garbled and yet unnaturally clear, seeming to come from inside his head. *I'll take Manhattan.* It was a man's voice, both far away and far too close.

What did that mean . . . to *take* Manhattan? He tried to shake himself out of his haze. Something terrible had happened. Drugs, head injury. "I don't remember my name!" he said aloud, and felt his heart pound at the implication. Even his clothes seemed strange . . . navy cotton drawstring pants, Guatemalan slip-ons, a T-shirt that said I'VE BEEN TO WALL DRUG, and a cream-colored windbreaker with a logo on the chest that showed a wheelbarrow with flames rising out of it. Judging from the grime and odor he might have been sleeping in the bushes for several nights. But Manhattan meant New York, that much he did think was right. Was that where he was? All he could bring to mind was waking with a start with some intuition of danger. Then he heard what he couldn't decide was the same voice or another and glanced around frantically. It said, *For I came down from heaven, not to do mine will, but the will of him who sent me.*

Shit, he thought. I'm hallucinating. Then a sudden deep sense of alarm brought his whole being alive. There was another sound in the outer darkness. Someone or something was approaching. Seeking him out. *Clip clop* came the echoes that his hyperanxious ears filtered out . . . from the tunnel. He hid behind the bushes behind the fountain. His vision seemed to blur and his head filled with static. He waited, muscles cramping.

Out of the black maw they emerged at last, one on a large chestnut horse, the other on a bay. The horses were shielded with synthetic face and chestplates, while the riders wore old-fashioned

NYPD uniforms. When the figures stopped, he could see that they didn't have faces. Just flat sheets with scanner slits. Up close, in the sodium lights, the scan masks were scraped and cloudy. From the south came bursts of gunfire and thudding low-frequency music, but here it was quiet enough to hear their echolocation sonar. His heart bounced as he smelled the tense, strangely sweet animal scent of the horses. At last a flare of static passed between the two mounted shapes. Then, just as they'd appeared, they moved on, the horses' hooves striking the asphalt with a timeless Roman rhythm, their imposing silhouettes fading into the trees.

The moment they were past, from behind one of the spray-painted boulders, a figure wrapped in matte-black cable tape wearing an NV helmet leapt out. "Yer ass is lucky," the shadow said, grabbing one of his hands in a neoprene fighting glove—weaving through a labyrinth of stripped cars and barbed-wire effigies. They looked like origami contrasted with the turrets rising above the park, armorguard facets gleaming like reptilian crystals. "Hurry," his guide called out. "Meter says you gonna have a meltdown."

The darkness became a membrane of endlessly falling slow-motion snow, only the flakes were like glass faces, painfully intricate but beautiful to behold. "This way!" the figure called, and it was like stepping through a wall of cool white light. Suddenly, all around were people. He felt a dart of warmth hit his arm. Then he fell, and he seemed to keep falling, or rising, as if he'd been taken up inside a whirlwind, faces and disintegrated memories orbiting around him. A *whirlwind*, he remembered. *I came here by whirlwind.*

When at last the spinning stopped, the bodies and the faces had stabilized, and standing over him was a large black woman who, as his eyes began to focus, he came to see was in fact a man, wearing makeup, an aqua wig, and a long African-style robe over sheepskin boots from which a Beretta Cheetah was just visible.

"We've given you some ZENO," the vision informed him. "Try not to move fast."

He was lying in a tent on an old cot. Candles glowed. Through a gelpane window he could see people passing between radomes and tepees. He heard an accordion and smelled marsala. Sparks rose from oil drums.

"Yo," a voice behind him said, and he saw it was the tape-mailed figure who'd found him minus the night-vision helmet—a Puerto Rican girl of about sixteen with a pigskin face graft that suggested a dark market burn ward.

"Who are you?" the large black woman/man asked.

He tried to focus. He couldn't get over his long blond hair. There wasn't an ounce of fat on him and yet for all the hardness of muscle, his skin was smooth. Except for the terrible burning he felt now on his back. That's what made me black out, he realized. Pain. Pain from the skin of my back. There was something there but he couldn't bring himself to think of it. Voices rustled in his brain . . . *Last hope . . . Psyche War . . .* beneath the sadness of a blues guitar drifting in on the night wind from somewhere far away—or deeper inside himself.

"Do you know who you are?" the large black woman/man repeated, but he couldn't answer. Who were these people and what did they want? Where had he been going when he fell out of the whirlwind?

To meet someone, he thought. To find someone. There's somewhere I have to be. *There's someone I have to be.*

"That's all right," the dark-skinned giant said. "Let's start with where you are. You're in New York City. In a part of Central Park that no one but us knows exists. We call it Fort Thoreau. It's a kind of sanctuary. We refer to ourselves as the Satyagrahi, and I'm Aretha Nightingale."

So saying, the speaker brought over a psykter of purified water and poured a cup for him, carefully considering the man's white-blond hair and tomorrow-staring eyes. There was something intriguingly familiar and at the same time deeply foreign about this night visitor. He was of average height and certainly less than average weight, but he radiated a presence that filled the tent.

The man drank some water and said, "You're a—"

"A drag queen? That's right, honey, I am!"

In fact the speaker looked like a former linebacker trying very hard to imitate some forgotten disco singer like Donna Summer.

"Used to be a lawyer. Lead counsel for the largest insurance company in the world. Lived a few blocks away. Of course I had to keep my private life secret. Then one day I saw I had to get out of the limo and back behind the mule. But that's another story. That's my story. Tinkerbell says the Securitors let you skiddo."

"Who's Tinkerbell?'

"Me." The PR girl winked, laser-edging a frozen-forged Gerber blade.

"Is someone after you?" Aretha asked, noticing again how long and blond the odd man's hair was, how outwardly strained and yet internally resilient he appeared.

"I don't know . . . I can't . . ."

Aretha picked up a detector and ran it over him. The device recorded an electromagnetic disturbance of an unknown kind.

"So do you have *any* idea who you are?"

"N-no. I . . . don't . . . ," the man said, staring around at the walls of the tent, which he saw through the gloom were decorated with chintzy Chinese fans, kimonos, and ostrich feathers.

"And you don't know how you got here?" Aretha prodded.

The blond man thought for a minute. Beyond the crazy idea of falling out of a whirlwind all he remembered was staring at the syringes in the fountain and then being seized with a scorching pain across his back. "No," he said finally. "I only remember the things on horses."

"We're going to give you a bioscan," Aretha announced. "The psychometer that Tink had shorted out on you. You had a brainwave reading that we've never seen before. Makes Saint Anthony's Syndrome and Pandora withdrawal look like an attack of the jitters. Is there anything else that comes to mind . . . right this minute?"

"A song," the blond man replied, trying to focus. *"I am a lineman for the county and I drive the main road . . . searching in the sun for another overload . . . I hear you singing in the wires . . . I can hear you through the whine . . . and the Wichita Lineman . . . is still on the line!"*

There was a moment of silence, then into the tent charged a thin young man with tall straight spines of hair. "What in hell was that?"

"What happened?" Aretha asked, coming alive with a jolt. "Where did you come from, Broadband?"

"That was a full-force jam!" the young man announced. "Almost blew Heimdall's signal guard on the entire compound!"

"Did you *do* something?" Aretha asked the man with the long blond hair.

"I sang . . . a bit of a song," he answered.

"Did you hear him, Tink?"

"No." The burned girl shrugged, sheathing her knife. "Must be trippin'."

"Well, whatever it was, don't do it again," Broadband pleaded. "We can't do a shakedown tonight."

"All right, Broadband." Aretha nodded. "We're cool, here."

The kid with the spiky hair stomped out and Tinkerbell followed, baffled.

"Well!" said Aretha, applying more lipstick. "That puts a *whole* new light on things. You may not know who you are, but I'd bet my wig that some interesting people do. Y'all wouldn't mine stripping down, would you, honey?"

"Why?" the man demanded, and Aretha caught the coiled-to-strike glitter of adrenal cortex.

"Because we've got a lot at stake here," the drag queen snapped, pressing the STRESS button to alert Flip Flop and Tolstoy. "This isn't a health resort, it's the last resort for a lot of people. Now strip down and let me look you over."

The blond man got up from the cot and yanked off his clothes. The skin of his back ached. Seconds later he was naked, facing Aretha, whose mouth was open wide.

Tinkerbell burst back into the tent carrying supplies. "Ooh, shit!" the girl cried, gawking and covering her eyes at the same time. "That's—"

"*Way* too much of a good thing," Aretha finished for her. "And I think we should leave it right there. Now turn around, baby, and let me see what *other* surprises you've got. You sure could use a sleeve for that one!"

He pivoted slowly, but even so, he felt his penis flop against his lower thigh with a meatiness that revolted him. My God, he thought, looking down. I'm some sort of freak. How can my own body feel so alien?

Then Aretha saw the scarring on his back. "Jesus . . . that's . . . !"

"Painful," the blond man said.

"But it—it's old!" Aretha cried, looking closer. "Do you know what it says?"

"FATHER FORGIVE THEM *F* . . . It's the third *F* that hurts the most."

He could see the letters burning in the air before him, clearer and sharper than the words he'd seen in the sky.

"Shit!" exhaled the drag queen. "I want to run some medical tests on you—and then for you to consult Dr. Zumwohl."

Aretha handed him a clean Lucron tracksuit and a faded Fordham University sweatshirt and they left him alone to dress. After he'd pulled on the tracksuit and sweatshirt another teenage girl came into the tent. Her face was painted in a tribal fashion and seemed to sparkle.

"My name is Ouija," she said. "Have something to eat."

His head throbbed. She produced an unmarked tin of food. When she opened the lid, he saw tiny hammerhead sharks, perfectly proportioned and densely packed. He picked one out and swallowed it whole. It had a savory, oily taste and made him thirsty. He ate several more with krispbread and had another gulp of water.

He kept hearing voices in his head. One was like a talkback radio personality. The others were vague and friendly, like old people telling stories on a porch, but he couldn't understand what they were saying. He plucked a couple more hammerheads out of the tin and devoured them. Aretha returned and led him through the door of the tent.

The scene outside resembled an army field hospital set up in the middle of a gathering of religious pilgrims and a derelict carnival. The darkness was disrupted by torches, campfires and garish neon signs in the shapes of martini glasses, dancing girls and blinking sombreros. Pole-mounted solar modules rose above tents and rigifoam Quonset huts, although there were other more permanent structures, including an IRT train car and a series of ferroconcrete pillboxes, some covered with hubcaps and pizza pans, all laced with cables and wires from which dangled paper lanterns, inflatable Statues of Liberty, and stuffed King Kongs. People of all ages and colors regarded him curiously, peering up from simmering pots of matzo ball soup or Brazilian black beans. Several had improvised prosthetics, baroque lobster arms or carbon fiber legs blinking with fairy lights.

"GlimmerPoodle," Aretha remarked, pointing to two muscled women, one bald and white, the other white-haired and black. "And that's Framegrabber and Little Pigeon. Hey, Ten Beers—how's that implant?"

Some people Aretha introduced more ceremoniously, as if they were tribal elders—Yankee Boy and Lady Manhattan, a palsied Jewish couple in their nineties wearing New York Rangers jerseys—and an obese black man called Friar Tuck, who seemed intent on organizing a softball game. Other people leered out of the firelit dark with damaged faces and misshapen limbs. Babies cried.

"Who are they?" the blond man asked, pointing to four straining men hitched to an old Central Park horse carriage loaded with Indian children.

"They're former McDonald's board members. Penitents now. Took massive payouts when the Vitessa Cultporation turned McDonald's into McTavish's."

"I don't know what you mean," the uninvited guest said. His mind felt moist and blank, as if he belonged to another world.

"I rather envy you if you've forgotten Vitessa, even for a moment," Aretha said. "But it will come back to you. They're the most powerful conglomerate in the world. A political party. A religion. What they don't control they're trying to—and we're trying to fight them."

The blond man's eyes picked out an Amazonian boy with a weeping facial sore. The child had a dead squirrel draped over his shoulder and held a blowgun fashioned from an aluminum tent pole. "You're trying to fight them?" he asked.

"Us. And others like us," Aretha answered defensively. "You'll remember all of this. McDonald's was a powerful corporate organism once, but like Disney and Coca-Cola and Microsoft, it got blind sided by the Vitessa Cultporation, which on the whim of Wynn Fencer introduced McTavish's in its place."

The names wrinkled up only shadows and whispers in his brain.

"Fencer conquered cyberneering, genetainment, and neurotecture," Aretha continued. "So he said, 'Let's take the world's most uninspired cuisine and make it obsessively popular.' Overnight the haggis replaced the hamburger."

"What's a haggis?" the blond man asked, sucking in the scene with his eyes. The chicken coops and intensive garden terraces— miniature rice paddies constructed from tanks and troughs.

"It's a sheep stomach, honey. With your choice of filling."

"That sounds disgusting!"

"A demonstration of power."

"And who's that lady?" the stranger queried, pointing to a graying woman in a vampire-black robe struggling under a yoke of heavy buckets. Being near these people seemed to ease the searing pain in his back.

"Beulah Schwartzchild, the Supreme Court Justice and World Court Representative who cast the deciding vote that allowed Vitessa to unify their subsidiaries to become what they are today."

"What's she lugging? Why doesn't someone help her?"

"She's a garbage collector and she works alone. By her own choosing she works—always wearing the judicial robe she disgraced."

The woman stumbled, the buckets slopping over. The blond man moved to help. Her clothes reeked. Her hair was matted and streaked with gray. Gently he raised her up and righted the stinking buckets.

"That's not done!" a man with a respirator gargled from a salt-eaten Winnebago.

"I thought you said you helped people," the blond man flashed, watching as the sad woman shouldered the yoke again and staggered off.

"There are certain rules and ways here," Aretha Nightingale replied. "Beulah gave up her wealth and position of her own accord. She's free to go at any time."

"Where would she go?" the blond man asked as she disappeared between a dented pretzel wagon and a cannibalized Dodge Viper.

Aretha wasn't sure how to answer and was relieved when they arrived at a large military-style tent. Inside, a woman with long dark hair and very red lips greeted them. High up on her exposed left breast was a tattoo of the Mandelbrot Set.

"This is Natassia," the head of the Satyagrahi announced.

The interior of the polymer shell was devoted to a formidable computer apparatus and a collection of what appeared to be medical imaging equipment. Everything was scientifically pristine except for one shelf on which sat a lilac-colored latex vibrator and a half-empty bottle of Brandy and Benedictine.

"Let me see your hands," Aretha directed.

The man's skin was remarkably smooth. One at a time, his hands were placed on an I-Dentiscanner. Next, the dark woman with the fiery lips wheeled over an Iriscanner and eased the man's face into the positioning frame. Her skin gave off a piquant jalapeño fragrance. She noticed a profound swelling in his groin. "Just keep your eyes open and relax," she said.

"We're also going to photoscan the scar on your back," Aretha said.

The skinny man called Broadband stuck his head in. Gamelan music wafted in through the slit. "You're cool to run now."

"All right." Aretha nodded to Natassia.

The blond man took off his sweatshirt. The woman resolved the scans and entered them, and they turned to face the main monitor. Seconds later, across the screen, stark white letters marched in high-resolution certainty . . . IDENTITY WITHHELD . . . SECURITY STATUS . . . CLEAR.

"Your identity's password-protected," said Aretha. "Go up a level, Nasty."

The woman chafed at the nickname but executed the request.

IDENTITY WITHHELD . . . SECURITY STATUS . . . CLEAR.

"Try the next level," said Aretha.

The same words flashed up. CLEAR . . .

"What about Information Sensitive?"

"Shit," Natassia whistled as once more the words appeared. "What now?"

"Time's running out on the link. Try Unlimited Access."

The Tele-Path drive gave a deep, wearied whir. Twenty-five seconds. Thirty. A minute.

"Five seconds!" Broadband yelled from outside.

The screen fevered white, then seemed to black out entirely—and then one by one the letters glowed . . . C L E A R . . .

"Shut it down!" Aretha commanded, and Natassia disconned. But even with the link closed, the letters remained on screen, as cold and unequivocal as absolute zero.

"Well," said Aretha, gaping at the screen—then at the blond man's mutilation. "We've just found out that you're a very important person."

"How so?"

"Your identity's secret and you've got Master Access."

"I don't understand," the blond man said.

"You could walk into the Vitessalith in Minneapolis or any of the international headquarters. Same at the Pentagon. Efram-Zev Pharmaceuticals."

"But I can't remember my name."

Aretha stared again at the single white word on the screen and then the cruelly gouged words on the man's back. "Until you do—we'll call you—*Clearfather*."

"Clear . . . Father?"

"That'll do for now. But I'd bet that you have a password, maybe even a series of passwords that can make that access dance its ass off."

"But I can't remember them," the blond man sighed, rubbing his forehead. "Just bits of songs. One song."

"Don't sing it. Just say it—as flatly as you can. Wait! Nasty, get Broadband and Heimdall in here."

Natassia went out and returned with the spike-haired youth from before and an older man who had no ears. Where his ears were supposed to be there were two input portholes of molded dermplex and veranium, channeled into cochlear implants.

"Broadband you met. This is Heimdall," Aretha said. "Director of our network's security. Listen to this, you two. Go ahead, brother. Speak slowly."

"*I am . . . the very model . . . of a modern major general . . . I've information vegetable . . . animal and mineral,*" the blond man recited.

Silence gripped the tent. Then Heimdall sagged to his knees, shouting, "Bad data!"

Aretha flinched. "What did you hear, Nasty?"

"Something about Tutankhamen hunting a golden hippopotamus identified with the evil god Set."

"That's odd," said Aretha. "What about you, Broadband?"

"Quand nous ne sommes plus enfants, nous sommes déjà morts," Broadband answered and burst into a fit of dribbling laughter.

"Damn!" cried Aretha. "Nasty, get some of the Pythagorean complex—and some hot cocoa!"

"Make a mistake with the sacred and you get scared!" the earless man screamed.

"It's all right!" Aretha soothed. "Just stay calm."

Fortunately the cocoa came quickly. And the doses of the antihysteric. Ten minutes later Broadband remembered that he didn't speak French. Heimdall, too, began to settle, and his speech patterns and breathing returned to normal.

"Neurostealth programming," the earless one pronounced when he'd fully recovered. "Cryptolinguistic. Where did you pick it up?"

"I—h-have no idea," Clearfather stammered. Truly this world was mad.

Aretha, who had a sharp eye for shifts in mood, made sure Clearfather had plenty of cocoa. Whoever the blond man was, he wasn't like any of the other subterraneans or spies the Satyagrahi had seen before.

"Time for Dr. Zumwohl. The medication we gave you is wearing off."

"Aretha, you didn't say what you heard," Natassia remarked as the drag queen stepped to the zippered door.

"I heard the words, 'Strive to lead back the god within you to the Divine in the Universe,'" the former lawyer replied. "And it freaked me right out."

CHAPTER 2

Organ Donor

The part of the "sanctuary" they entered was filled with more deformed and technologically mingled people.

"Almost there," Aretha said, glad that Flip Flop and Tolstoy were close behind.

They passed two young Ethiopian boys guarding a farm of dough-boy swimming pools, one of which Clearfather saw was writhing with eels while another appeared to be brimming with freshwater crocodiles not much bigger than sardines. An enormous dog hauled itself out of the dark and grunted.

"Big Bwoy!" the drag queen bellowed at the beast, an ancient Rott-weiler whose head was embedded in a full-skull muzzle.

One of the creature's front paws had been replaced by a pick-and-place robot's end effector unit, while its back legs were engineered into a frame with wheels that came from an old golf buggy. Clear-father knelt down and was stroking the drool-slick jowls through the muzzle when a thin white man covered in Christmas tree tinsel and wearing a piece of headgear fashioned out of an antique lottery ball cage (complete with several old ivory lottery balls still bouncing around inside) rushed up and hollered, "Lucky! Lucky! Lucky! Everybody makes their own!"

"You've been warned about this monster, Grody!" Aretha chided.

"Haven't had the draw yet, haven't had the draw yet!" Grody squealed, dancing about so that the balls clacked in the cage.

Clearfather noticed that the man's hat, if *hat* was the right word, drew some oblique inspiration from the dog's muzzle. "What's the draw for?"

"Lucky, lucky, lucky . . . everyone makes their own!" Grody replied and shook himself so that his tinsel rustled and the balls pinged against the wires.

"You'll notice that the balls don't have numbers," Aretha whispered. "You wouldn't believe it now but they say Grody used to be a very fine neurochemist once, until he got hooked on the so-called intelligence enhancers."

"He loves that dog," Clearfather said as the thin man, still clacking and rustling, made his way into the shadows with Big Bwoy squeaking along on his back wheels.

"Come," Aretha said. "Time to meet Dr. Zumwohl."

They were at the doors of an ambulance that had been fished out of the Harlem River. The vehicle was rusted and bullet-fatigued, but it had been imaginatively patched up and the roofline featured an expensive oyster-shell satellite dish and exquisite TWIN-link componentry.

"What's in here?" Clearfather asked.

"A world of knowledge," Aretha replied. "And a lot of silly ideas. Like Grody's hat—it's a lottery. But we may find out how to treat you."

Aretha directed him to lie down on the couch he found inside and began attaching dermatrodes to his head. On the ceiling above he noticed a sign that said IN CASE OF EMERGENCY YOU WILL BE RETURNED TO YOUR BODY.

"Is it going to hurt?" he asked.

"This'll help the hurt, child. Just relax. I'll send someone when you're done."

At first nothing happened. Then gradually he had a peaceful but vivid sensation that the ambulance was filling with water and that he was floating. Then the floating became horizontal motion. His speed increased and he began to spin, faster and steeper, until he felt himself stretch and then explode, pieces of shattered being drifting down through black diamond air, becoming a jigsaw puzzle, which came alive. It was a picture of him walking. Down a narrow catwalk he seemed to glide, until he was on a stage, facing a tiny old woman with huge thick spectacles.

"I am Doktor Zooomvalll . . . ," the woman said, rising to her feet. She began to radiate. Then, to his further surprise, she seemed to divide. Out of her body came other bodies—eidolons—incredibly detailed holograms of the great psychiatrists and neurological explorers of history: William James, Freud, Adler, Jung, Szondi, Skinner, Pavlov, Luria. Every theoretical school and research approach was represented, from clinicians and counselors to hardware people like J. V. Brady, who made a career out of giving peptic ulcers to monkeys. One by one they appeared . . . Delgado, Reich, Rorschach, Stekel, Broca, Hess, Olds, Penfield . . . and when the Auditorium was full, Clearfather felt a thread of light reach out from each of the eidolons. Then the questions came at him like drops of rain running down a wire.

Aretha headed to the Information Station to see if the bioscans had turned up anything on his physical history. Finderz Keeperz, the head of cyberintelligence, was climbing out of the DataCube when the drag queen entered. Though he was afflicted with pituitary dwarfism (the result of his mother's use of anti-aging drugs), the diminutive hacker's oversized cranium housed a powerful brain.

He was dressed in a white safari suit made from a cloned paper mothwing fabric that he'd convinced himself made him look taller.

On his feet were the same pair of children's Nikes he'd bought in an Athlete's Foot store in Times Square just before his arrest for cyberespionage had forced him underground and into the ranks of the Satyagrahi. Up and down both stunted arms he sported the collection of Canal Street watches he used to monitor the fragile time distortion that the Mirror Field inflicted on Fort Thoreau, the counterperception barrier that kept the activities of the Satyagrahi hidden from the world outside—but that the little genius secretly believed might be altering the psychology of the community in unknown, potentially dangerous ways.

"Any deets on the meat?" Aretha inquired.

Finderz stepped free of the DataCube, the three-dimensional cybersystem they'd pirated from Vitessa that allowed full cognitive immersion.

"Initial indications are the body's in perfect health and has been dead for thirty years," he replied. "Subject born No Name Versteckt at a public trauma ward in Pittsburgh in 1979. Mother a teenage hooker. Get this! His schlong was mistaken by the attending ED as a vestigial growth, possibly an atrophied twin."

"Sounds like our boy all right," Aretha agreed. "What gives?"

"Damned if I know." The dwarf shrugged. "Momma goes on to marry one Joseph Sitio, twenty years older. Defrocked priest no less. Gives the boy his surname and the Christian name of Paul. Paul turns six, momma dies falling down stairs. Lives for the next two years with his loving stepfather. Then in June 1987 he's found on the steps of a Catholic church, bleeding from the rectum—tooth marks on his penis and a bit of artwork on his back that the county medical examiner describes as 'methodically savage.'"

"Let me guess?" Aretha grimaced. "A biblical quotation?"

"Gets worse. He's hospitalized throughout the next year, during which time he gets taken in by foster parents. Seems to have been going fine with attendance at school—but in 1992 he's sent off to the Muskrat Cove Home for Boys, where a year later something bad enough happens to get him transferred to Lovell. Released in 1999 just prior to the facility closing. Spends a month at a transition house—then out into the walk-on-the-wild side west of Pre Quake LA. Ends up in the Anaconda Room, a live-sex webcam joint. Performances hourly."

"You have to admire that." Aretha tried to smile.

"The Japanese patrons sure did," Finderz confirmed. "Along with his female performers. There he was spotted by a producer for the lead in an erotic art flick called *Priapus*. Even got his costar a role. They got married before the filming started but on the honeymoon in Vegas she OD'd. Paul was treated for severe depression at the Engelbert Humperdinck Center and then began a new phase."

"Let me guess . . . a country singer?"

"Close. Joined a Seventh Day Adventist church, then a Burn Again firewalking congregation in the Mojave. Over the next few years he tries Breatharians, Scientology, the Rosicrucians, Amway."

"A promiscuous searcher," Aretha remarked.

"Then he moves to Texas, changes his name, and founds his own cult called—"

"Wait a minute!" Aretha cried. "I remember them! He—he—was Hosanna? *That's* why he looks familiar. But you can't be serious!"

"Yes indeed, Hosanna Freed. He and a hundred other people, mostly women, formed a community called The Kingdom of Joy. Interestingly enough, the actual land the cult took over was the site of a similar movement back in the early twentieth century, founded by the neglected genius Lloyd Meadhorn Sitturd."

"I've never heard of him," Aretha said.

"That's because he's neglected," the dwarf replied. "But his community was attacked in the same way Paul's—or Hosanna's—was."

"Holy shit!" Aretha crowed. "Hosanna was worshiped as a fertility god! Wasn't he reputedly so virile, the pharmaceuticals panicked? The Christian Right feared that he actually had God on his side!"

"Or in his pants," Finderz replied. "They even joined forces with the radical feminists. Federal authorities launched an assault on the compound. Hosanna and the thirteen Wives of the Inner Circle dug in at the base of the Sacred Obelisk as the ATF and Homeland Security boys unloaded. He took thirty-seven rounds of Penetrator ammunition and was still alive when the medevac chopper landed."

"Christ, that's scary." Aretha whistled.

"Even weirder is that all the women were pregnant. With boys."

"And they all went down in that same blaze of stupidity!"

"All but one. Twelve of the babies' bodies were recovered. Either Momma Thirteen went AWOL in the firefight or they harvested the fetus from the corpse," Finderz said. "And don't forget that the official report says his corpse was cremated intact, but a CNN reporter took a photograph of the body before it was burned, which showed that the famous penis had been surgically removed."

"That's just ghoulish!" groaned Aretha. "But what does it mean? What are we talking now? Are we saying we've got a corpse—missing a cock—that's supposedly cremated—and we're thinking that this same body is walking around Central Park all these years later—without having aged—repaired as far as the bullet wounds go?"

"Plus, according to you, the severed organ is back in position."

"And judging by his reaction to Natassia, operational."

"There's also a missing baby unaccounted for. One of thirteen sons. And possibly a mother. Oh, and there's one more thing."

"Good God, what?"

"This information. It's got expertise. Vitessa code. But wiggly. The sole reason I could trace it was because I slipped in on that righteous access our new friend has. Connects back to one Julian Dingler."

"Who in the hell is that?"

"Vitessa Intelligent House Services of all things. Based in Pittsburgh, funnily enough," the dwarf answered. "No photogram on file."

"All right," said Aretha with a shrug of bewilderment. "Am I right in thinking that the most likely explanation for our unexpected guest is that his body was regenerated from the amputated penis that's been preserved—presumably by whoever cut it off in the first place?"

"Maybe, baby. There's just one problem with that theory," Finderz pointed out. "It's not possible for regen tissue to express acquired features like his scarring."

A shadow passed over Aretha's face. "No, it's not. But there's another explanation."

"You mean someone did that to him *again*? Why would any outfit with such slick technology go in for the Black Magic trip of that scarring?"

"You've got me," Aretha confessed. "It's disturbing any way you look at it. But we need to cover our tracks. What's the best way to destabilize this data?"

"We need THE ENTOMOLOGIST."

"Cyberconstructs shouldn't have so much absence of personality." The drag queen shivered.

"At least he works for us," Finderz remarked, entering the request.

Up out of the transparent depths of the DataCube appeared a huge numinous face obscured by the netting on a helmet that resembled a beekeeper's hat. Just visible through the mesh was the glinting suggestion of wire-rimmed spectacles. The voice was soft and cloying—the tone of a man who's forever rubbing his hands together.

"What would you like, my friendss? You have a requesst?"

"We want you to eliminate some information and to disable any recovery. No Search and Dismay. We want FUBAR," Finderz directed.

"Ooh," said the face. "Elimmminate. Dissssable. So aggresssive."

"File code coming now," Finderz said, transloading.

"Yess, I ssee," said THE ENTOMOLOGIST. "You have exccccelled yoursself, my friend. You had ssome help, I think?"

"Never mind," clipped Aretha. "How do we do it? Send in a virus?"

"Thiss is a more advancced form of information than what you are ussed to, my friendss."

The netting of THE ENTOMOLOGIST's helmet became a matrix of intricate fishing flies.

"What are those?" Aretha gasped.

"Beautieees, my friendss. Beautieees I have made. You see, the inforganism that you sseek to ssubvert musst firsst be tempted, it musst be lured. It musst be caught. We are going *fishhhing*."

"Shit," Finderz marveled. "Those are—"

"Lovely little bootsstrap constructs dessigned to imitate a ccertain priority enhancccement coding. Given the profile in question, I think we shhould try a niicce tasty . . . Jeruuuu-salem Cricket!"

At the first level of magnification the lure resembled a miniature grasshopper made of amber gelatin and laser-thin slices of black bamboo. As the magnification increased, the tissue revealed ever-finer layers of quicksilver information built around malignant microcode, rendered on the 3-D screen as a hidden barbed hook.

"Vvery lovely, yess? Oh yess, my friendss. No one will ever find what you accesssssed," THE ENTOMOLOGIST whispered soothingly, and the netted face dissolved into formlessness within the Cube, the glimmer of the wire-rimmed spectacles fading out last.

CHAPTER 3

Zugzwang

With Clearfather resting after his Zumwohl "consultation," Aretha transloaded the analysis for review in his
tent. The summary was frequently delivered by Dr. Zumwohl herself, which Aretha found annoying. Multiculturalism was a fine
thing—understanding that stubby little Germanic hologram was another matter. But considering that any of the constructs, from Jean
Piaget to John Lilly, was available to deliver the evaluation, the drag
queen was surprised when a vulturine African American in an army
uniform appeared on screen.

"Do I know you?" Aretha asked. "You're—"

"I'm Major Henry Flipper Rickerburn," the image replied.

"Flipper? What sort of name is that?"

"I'm named after Henry O. Flipper, the first African American to
graduate from West Point and a lieutenant in the Tenth Cavalry."

"Oh. Are you a psychiatrist or a neurologist?" Aretha asked.

"I graduated from West Point and Duke," the Major boomed. "I
was one of the first African Americans to hold a senior medical position in the U.S. Army. I have conducted major studies on the long-
term effects of clandestine work on intelligence operatives. I have

been in combat and in private practice. I died in 1998 and I'm still going strong! What have you done with your life?"

Aretha was put out by this response but managed some restraint. Even Jung, who could get a little rhapsodic, never got personal. Most of them had the kind of creepy detachment of Roger Sperry, the neuroinvestigator who was fond of cutting the brain stems in cats.

"On what basis are you representing the findings?" the Satyagrahi leader asked.

"I have the most extensive military and covert operation experience," the Major replied, puffing out his decorated chest. "Tonight's interloper is deeply encrypted. We have only vague suggestions of his capabilities. But they all cause concern."

"For instance?"

"He recognized Mahler's Fifth Symphony in a single line of music. He also seems to know every note of *Bat Out of Hell* by Meat Loaf. He's fluent in Sanskrit, Pali, Chinese, Hebrew, Greek, Latin, and Arabic. The languages, these coding systems, are completely transparent to him."

"But his memory—"

"His operating system can't locate the files. He doesn't know they're there."

"A stranger to himself," Aretha pondered.

"Quite literally. And you have to wonder why. His resting alpha rhythms far exceed the most intense grand mal seizure."

"Any memories emerge?"

"He quoted Plutarch: 'He who denies the Demons, denies providence, and breaks the chain that unites the world to the throne of God.'"

"So what's the bottom line? Is he—human? Some new kind of AI?"

"We believe he could be a weapon of mass instruction. The one point everyone agreed on is that he's bigger than we are."

"Bigger than the Auditorium?" Aretha gasped.

"More complex," the Major said. "Greater capacity. Much greater speed."

"But he can't even remember his name!"

"He may be in a neutral state awaiting activation. He may be damaged. In either case he's outside our ability to treat or safely contain. That's why we sent in an investigative reconnaissance unit."

"You sent in a psych probe? On whose authority?"

"Mine," the Major replied. "Our first probe was a construct called the Corps of Discovery—a low-signature insert into the cerebral cortex with a brief to map sites of unusual activity or apparent damage."

"The first probe!"

"It vanished without a trace."

"So you sent out a search party to look for the posse?" Aretha fumed.

"The second probe targeted the cerebellum."

"You were trying to take motor control!"

"Of a potentially hostile invader! Probe Two was destroyed. It was worse than an interferon attack. Heinously effective."

"Surely that constitutes self-defense of the most basic kind?" Aretha croaked. "You'd better not tell me any more such actions were taken!"

"What did you expect?" foamed the Major. "He presented as a fortress. *He's* even locked out. We responded as a military investigative unit!"

"Listen!" Aretha demanded, glaring at the screen. "You give me the full breakdown on that third probe or you'll be banished from the Auditorium. You and your wire-splicer friends—you're worse than anything Vitessa has to throw at us."

The second the words were spoken, a cold fear gripped the drag queen. The Major's demeanor, the radical and aggressive plan undertaken without authority—there had been near security breaches in the past, but nothing like this. This struck at the very heart of their technology. Only the Mirror Field, the hazing system that kept Fort Thoreau invisible to the outside world, was more sophisticated. It was said that Parousia Head herself had set it up, after she'd stolen the equations from the Vitessa R&D division that she'd headed. *Demiurgent,* PrimalWhisper, Itchy Logic—the names and hints of her exploits had entered the realms of legend at the same time that the technical achievements she was involved with had turned mythology into reality. The Mirror Field proved this minute-to-minute. Now, if they'd been infiltrated, what hope did the Satyagrahi have?

"Tell me about the third probe."

The Major's face seemed to contort the very monitor.

"It's a stealth combat unit, targeting the hypothalamus," the construct admitted finally. "Its mission is to exploit key drives like sex—then to work though the limbic system to take control of fear and anger. It disappeared without any confirmation signal but it's more robust than the other two."

"What's the life span? How does it disband?"

"It doesn't."

"Do you mean to tell me it's—"

"Ultimately cancerous."

"Cancerous," Aretha replied in a slow stinging whisper. "Right. One last thing. If his mind's encrypted and he's as powerful as you fear—how could you get *any* info?"

"There was only one way," the Major answered.

"What did you give him?" Aretha hissed.

"Tiresias."

"You madmen!"

"He's dangerous!" the Major replied. "His more or less immunity to the Tiresias proves that!"

"You should know, if anyone does, Tiresias can have major time delays in its impact. Goddamn you!" Aretha cried, losing control.

The Major looked as if he was going to say something, but Aretha shut down the program and hotlined Finderz. "Quarantine Dr. Zumwohl immediately—there's been contamination. And don't tell anyone outside MedTeam and CyberIT."

"But the Zumwohl recommendations impact on every psych consult we have," Finderz whined.

"Damage-control your ass off!" Aretha replied and flung his aqua wig at the wall of his tent.

The arrival of this prodigy threatened all that they'd worked for—particularly after the ominous pathology that Dr. Zumwohl had just demonstrated. Now the strange pilgrim was on the verge of a psychic crisis. Tiresias was one of the most interesting and dangerous drugs ever synthesized. For a very few people, secure and open in mind and spirit, Tiresias acted as a lens, focusing brainwave energy to laser strength. But for those who suffered from depression or psychosis, Tiresias could have catastrophic consequences. For someone like Clearfather—and it was hard for Aretha at that moment to think of anyone like Clearfather—the reaction could be horrific. With the heightening power of Tiresias, his mind might be powerful enough to reverse the polarity of the Mirror Field. He could be a weapon of fearsome psychological and physical force.

We can't let all our work be destroyed, even for humane reasons, Aretha thought. But that would mean sending Clearfather off. Did they have that right? And where would they send him? Where *could* they send him? The drag queen wished Parousia Head were there. Only two nights before he'd heard the younger people arguing that she didn't really exist. If she'd ever existed at all, they said, she must be dead or in prison now. Just when they needed her most. He put on Miles Davis's *Someday My Prince Will Come* and sipped some cocoa. Then he hotlined Finderz.

"I'm damage-controlling!" Keeperz insisted.

"Keep doing that," Aretha directed, "but check with MedTeam about the most reliable antidote to a Tiresias mindstorm."

"Oh, sure!" the flustered datavar grumped. "Anything else?"

"Yes, I want all the Strategists at IQ-HQ in fifteen minutes. We've got an armed, unguided missile stuck in the launch tube!"

Aretha disconned and put on his fluorescent pink wig. He found Clearfather in a hammock in the Post Anesthesia Recovery wing of Fort Thoreau's surgical facility.

"How do you feel? Aretha asked.

"Tired," Clearfather answered. "But I'm remembering some things."

"Such as?"

"A man in a radio station. And Uncle Waldo. He worked on a hundred jigsaw puzzles at the same time—and Aunt Vivian—she liked crossword puzzles. But I don't remember their faces."

"Anything else?"

"A boy . . . in a bathroom . . . with his pants down."

The image filled him with a sense of horror and disgust.

"You're worried about the results of your tests—" Aretha said.

"*You're* worried about them," Clearfather corrected. "You're afraid of them. And me. You're going to send me away."

"There are a lot of issues involved," Aretha hedged. "This is a resistance movement. We've been very trusting."

"Who are you resisting?" Clearfather asked, swinging the hammock.

"The Vitessa Cultporation for a start."

"So why do I have to leave? There are a lot of people here who are damaged or in need," Clearfather replied.

"Sometimes we have to make hard decisions. But I'm reluctant to make this decision on my own. So we're going to seek advice."

"Aren't you in charge?" Clearfather asked.

"I wouldn't put it so hierarchically," Aretha replied.

"Who is?"

"Parousia Head. The most wanted person in the world. A master hacker and alchemist of R and D."

"Am I going to meet her?" Clearfather asked.

"I've never met her," Aretha answered.

"Then how do you know she exists?"

"If she didn't exist, the authorities wouldn't be so concerned about her."

"That's an interesting argument. If you fear something enough, it must be real."

"I hadn't thought of it like that." Aretha smiled in spite of himself. "Come on. We're going to consult the III Chings. Are you all right to walk?"

"I'd better be—if I'm leaving soon," Clearfather replied.

Aretha winced and led him outside to a cement bunker. They passed a tent in which a group of catatonics were being rolled around by people in jumpsuits.

"Deconditioning. For those who suffer from overexposure—to get them back into their bodies and interactions with other people," Aretha told him. "Tinkerbell started there. She'd scored a Voyancy connection when she was tricking and disappeared into her own head. She has media flashbacks now—but who doesn't?"

"Maybe that's my problem," Clearfather said.

If only, Aretha thought as they went down inside the bunker.

"These are the III Chings," he announced, pointing to a diaphanous enclosure in the center of the basement. Inside the silky veiling, lying side by side in hospital beds, Clearfather saw three Chinese men. Each was attached to an intravenous drip and a bioscan monitor, but they were all connected to each other via dermatrodes that, in the hybrid lighting, seemed to cover them like a web.

"Who are they?" he asked.

"Identical lab triplets. In one of the strikes during the Holy War, the clinic where they were being studied was infiltrated with a nerve agent. Parousia Head rescued them a few years back, so the story goes. They've been in a coma almost their whole lives—a single shared reality."

"They don't look like they've ever gotten out of bed!"

"They haven't. All they do is dream. But we consult them on all important decisions."

"You ask three little men who are basically the same man, who've been asleep for years, for advice?"

Aretha ignored the question and asked aloud in a precise voice, "Should we allow Clearfather to remain with us?"

A moment later the silence was broken by a *rat-a-tat-tat,* and out of a printer popped a slip of paper. Aretha plucked it from the perforator and handed it to Clearfather.

"The price the dragonfly pays for its mobility is that it cannot fold its wings. What sort of answer is that? You might as well flip a coin. Let's try another one. Will I get my memory back?"

"No," Aretha said. "One question." But before he could lead Clearfather away, the printer replied.

"All right," Aretha agreed—and was just about to read it when Natassia rushed down the steps.

"I've got a line on what you heard when Clearfather spoke before," she said. "You know Old Fernley? Used to be a philosophy professor at NYU. He said those were the last words of Plotinus, the most important of the Neoplatonists."

"Thanks, Nasty." Aretha waved, slipping the second message in his pocket.

Tolstoy and Flip Flop took Clearfather to Recreation, which was housed in the IRT car. Tinkerbell and Ripcord stood on guard out of sight.

"All right." Aretha clapped, stepping into the rigifoam wigwam that served as Situation Room. "Clearfather, as you probably know, is not some schmuck off the street. One scenario is that he's a high-powered AI embedded in a flesh-and-blood matrix based on a cult leader murdered by the Feds thirty years ago. During his psych exam with Dr. Zumwohl, he was given a unit of Tiresias. He was also injected with three mind probes. One was destroyed on insertion; the other two haven't been heard from. This unauthorized behavior raises serious questions about the integrity of Dr. Z. Whether the Auditorium can be examined and repaired is a question for later. The point is, our security may have been breached. We have to adopt lockdown procedures across all operations. Second, we have to decide what to do with Clearfather. We may be at risk from external forces for harboring him—but even if we aren't, he's a psychic time bomb that's ticking as we speak. My view is that despite any desire on our parts to care for him, we aren't capable of managing the risk. I've consulted the III Chings and their advice supports this."

"What did they say?" inquired Dr. Quail, former head of Neurology at Bellevue.

"'The price the dragonfly pays for its mobility is that it cannot fold its wings.'"

"That's pretty conclusive," Broadband agreed.

"But this is too significant a decision for us all not to have our say, so I want to go around the room, starting with you, Heimdall."

Heimdall went to pull on an earlobe and then remembered he didn't have one. "I'd like to see him stay. If it could be harnessed—imagine the juju!"

Aretha nodded to Broadband, whose stalks of hair vibrated like antennae. "We can't handle the learning curve. Too dangerous."

"I hate to agree," Finderz said, shaking his great head. "But we've got a responsibility to what's gone before."

"All strangers come from Zeus," Natassia flared. "Besides, AIs don't get hard-ons! One way or another he was brought to us."

Lila Crashcart spoke next, her voice quivering. "The psychic energy reading for the compound has more than doubled in the last two hours. In another two hours the Field will start to feel the effects—and in two more hours—who knows?"

Dr. Quail somberly completed the circle. "We can't predict how the Tiresias will affect him. He may have a mindstorm, he may not. The only treatment now is to administer a nepenthe-related drug. We've recently acquired an Efram-Zev product called Oblivion.6. It will buy the maximum amount of time—it may even counteract the Tiresias entirely. We can be confident that we're not sending into the world anything more dangerous than what we took in."

"Is Clearfather at risk?" Aretha asked.

"He may never regain his memory. He may lose critical functionality."

"So he'll end up a toast head? Shit, we're real heroes!" Natassia coughed.

"Chill, Nasty," Aretha commanded. "No one feels good about this."

"We certainly don't," said Dr. Quail, speaking for the MedTeam. "But I believe that Oblivion.6 will decrease the threat with the minimum harm. There's a very strong chance that he will be no more amnesiac than he is now."

"Why can't we dope him up and see him through the crisis as we've done with hundreds of others?" Natassia complained.

"Your objection is noted," Aretha said sourly. "Dr. Quail, you and Lila get on the countertreatment now. Clearfather will leave tonight. Where do we send him?"

Finderz cleared his throat. "The logical destination is Pittsburgh."

"Pittsburgh!" Heimdall blurted. "How inhumane is that!"

"He has history in Pittsburgh," explained the dwarf. "Or his body does. And he may very well have a current connection. Julian Dingler, a Vitessa R and D guy there, may know quite a bit about all this. I say we should send him to Dingler."

"Jesus!" Natassia yelped. "We're going to FedEx him to Vitessa!"

"I somehow doubt that Dingler's role in this is Vitessa-approved," Finderz replied. "He might even be secretly on our side, or at least working for some other resistance cell. In any case we need to flush him out. To me this has the signs of a Minotaur project—some secret weapons/Overman op that's gone Bush. I have a feeling Wynn Fencer doesn't even know about it. Either way, we're in a zugzwang position."

"What's that?" Aretha asked.

"A chess term. It means being forced to make a move even though it's to one's disadvantage. If we keep him on, we put everything at risk. If we send him away, we may lose a great asset. It's a lose–lose situation, but the latter option's the safer."

"What if Vitessa doesn't have anything to do with him?" Broadband asked.

"If the truth of Clearfather's story lies outside Vitessa's involvement and he withstands the Tiresias, then Pittsburgh is the best place for him to start trying to piece the puzzle together," Finderz answered.

"Providing his brain isn't melted rubber," Natassia scoffed.

"What about Texas?" Aretha wondered. "That's another reference point."

"A hamlet called Dustdevil. That's where the original body was killed," Finderz informed the group. "It seems a bad trip to send him back there."

"Yeah, but Pittsburgh wasn't any picnic for him, either," Aretha noted.

"No," Finderz agreed. "But it was where the original body life began—and it's also the origin of the most recent external interest. I think the combination of those two makes it the most compelling choice."

"What other reference points do we have?" Natassia asked.

"In his earlier incarnation he was born and abused in Pittsburgh —institutionalized throughout his teen years nearby. He became a porn star in what was, before Bigfoot, the City of Angels—and then was hospitalized in old Las Vegas, where his first wife died of an OD. He later transformed himself into a cult leader in Texas, where many commune members including himself were eventually massacred by the ATF and Homeland Security."

"What a life!" the dark woman lamented. "I say if you're going to send him to Pittsburgh, let him know about those other places. Give him the whole story—tell him everything we know. We owe him that."

"Let's not forget that we don't *know* any of this for certain," Aretha countered. "We suspect. Second, we can't say what he'll remember when he comes down off the drugs. But there is a larger issue. By giving him the synopsis of his past life, we may be dooming him in part to repeat it."

"All right, what about this," Broadband interjected. "What if we alter his appearance and send him along via Greyhound? There won't be anywhere near as much scrutiny as at the airports. If we've got a Jiminee Kricket on him we'll be able to track him and see what happens. We've got a bunch of American Safari passes. All I have to do is hack in and activate one in his name. On the back of every pass is a map of the United States. We mark on it those places you've mentioned and leave it up to him and to chance what he makes of it."

"How cowardly is that!" Natassia blurted.

"No," Aretha argued. "There's sense there."

"What about LA?" Heimdall said. "Can't send him there anymore."

"LosVegas will have to do. So, it's settled. Anyone disagree?" Aretha called, and only Natassia did. "All right," said the drag queen. "Broadband, round up Go-Go and Hermes. We'll need to organize clothes, food, money, the bus pass—and a haircut. Finderz, we'll need instructions about Dingler. And don't forget that Clearfather may not remember any of this when he gets to Pittsburgh."

Aretha felt in the pocket of his robe and found the second of the III Ching's prophecies. *A cockroach can live without its head for nine days.*

"What's that?" Finderz asked.

"Nothing," Aretha snapped. "I'll get Tink and Ripcord ready to ride as backup."

CHAPTER 4

Good to Go

The Strategists and team leaders worked with precision as Clearfather struggled in the throes of the conflicting drugs—Tiresias stimulating electrical storms throughout his brain, countermanded by the obscuring mist of Oblivion.6. During the power surges a multiplicity of images flared. He saw a bathroom lit by candles—then a terrible light that made him gag—women holding hands around a needle of stone and a boy crying in a mirror—shattered by bullets—one of the shards stabbing him in the back. Then he was in a chair and someone was cutting his hair, dirty blond silk falling in his lap in the mercury vapor half-light.

"Where's Go-Go the Eskimo?" he heard Aretha call, looking more like a former Princeton linebacker than a drag queen, despite the Day-Glo wig.

Clearfather was sorry to see his hair drop. Then he was led to another tent and given underwear, socks, woollene jeans and a Pendleton shirt, Red Wing boots and a musty St. Vincent de Paul peacoat plus a shoulder bag. Natassia was crying, and someone they called Go-Go the Eskimo or the Gator Girl arrived, a woman of about eighteen or twenty, as pale as toilet porcelain, with two fried-egg eyes. She was joined by an Afro-American boy of about ten or eleven, who was even paler than she was.

"You're sending me off with a couple of kids?" Clearfather asked Aretha.

"Go-Go's forgotten more about the layout of this city than any civil engineer, fireman, cop, or comtrol wizard ever knew," Aretha announced. "She freed the GATORS."

"Who are the gators?"

"Guided Automatic Tactical Operation Response Systems. Robot units designed to deal with toxic disasters and terrorist crises. Always handy to have friends in low places."

"Psych level is still rising—but slowing," Lila reported.

"And who's he?" Clearfather asked, pointing to the spirit-white black boy.

"Hermes is an albino," Aretha said. "He beat fully envenomed security and communed with the master Subway System grid. He knows every inch and chaining code—every signal light. But he doesn't talk."

"Tell the III Chings that there are no llamas in the Bahamas." Clearfather giggled.

"Find Finderz. And where are the rest of the supplies?" Aretha called, fearing that Clearfather's brain might turn to mucus before making the Port Authority.

"I'm coming!" hollered the dwarf. "A nice set of instructions for Clearfather—and a private I-gram off to Dingler."

"This paper's blank," Aretha said, examining the note.

"It won't be in a few hours' time," Keeperz answered. "Delay-action ink in case anybody swoops on him straight up."

"What did you say to Dingler?"

"*Visitor arriving. Has information vegetable, animal, and mineral.* I signed it *The Wichita Lineman*. Then I bounced it off a couple of satellites. THE ENTOMOLOGIST gave it what he called 'the scent of the hive.'"

"Ticket's all set," Broadband reported. "What's wrong with Nasty?"

Aretha turned to see that Natassia was down on her knees trying to hold Clearfather's hand in an act of supplication.

Clearfather stroked his head and, as he did, all his remaining hair fell out. "No!" Natassia cried, clutching at the hair, trying to give it back to him—stuffing it in his pockets—then clasping his knees and burying her face against his thighs.

"Old Mrs. Rushcutter had a rough-cut punt. Not a punt-cut rough, but a rough-cut punt," the now bald Clearfather cackled.

"He doesn't know what he's saying!" Aretha insisted, thankful to see Dr. Quail approaching with another dose of Oblivion.6.

"How can he ever know what he's saying after what we've done to him?" Natassia shouted—peeled away by Quail's assistants.

They rolled out a motorcycle sidecar bolted into a sled-frame mounted on PowerMountain® tires. There was a small step behind for the driver to stand on. Go-Go reappeared leading a motley pack of dogs. Two of the mongrels had lost all their hair and were battling a rampant fungal infection. Some were missing snippets of ears or an eye. One had a bionic leg; another had five legs. Then there were two dogs that looked fit but wild, big muscular wolves from another time and place—the woods of Maine or the steppes of Asia—all of them straining at their thick black Hemlar straps. The egg-eyed girl hitched the panting dogs into the sled harness. Clearfather felt a wave of feedback slosh through his head.

"Here's a little smash'n'grab," the drag queen said. "I'm sorry we couldn't arrange a credit card for you but we need more time for that. This is a note for later. And this is a bus ticket good for unlimited travel for three months. What name did you use, B?"

"Elijah Clearfather," Broadband replied. "Thought it had a nice ring."

"Where am I going?" Clearfather asked. "Why can't I stay here?"

"Go-Go and Hermes will get you to the Port Authority," Aretha continued with great effort. "Do *not* speak to anyone you don't have to."

Ouija appeared, carrying a supply of food and drink provisions that she stuffed in his bag, followed by Grody clacking and shimmering and Big Bwoy squeaking along behind—excited by the other dogs.

"Lucky! Lucky! Lucky!" Grody croaked, and then—as if concentrating very hard—he bowed the caged helmet full of rattling balls and said, "You pick . . ."

Clearfather eventually reached into the wire basket on the man's head and plucked out one of the blank spheres. It felt as smooth as a stale gumball. He put the ball in his pocket. Go-Go strapped on a motorcycle helmet with an American flag painted on it and motioned for Clearfather to climb in the egg. Tinkerbell and the man called Ripcord were topping up the oil in the forks of two superlight Kawasakis when young Hermes growled up on a graphite framed Husqvarna. On his back was what had once been a Miroku shotgun, which someone had taken interesting liberties with.

"Are they coming, too?" Clearfather asked, pointing to Tinkerbell and Ripcord.

"Always have a decoy and a backup plan if you can," Aretha replied. "We don't have a backup plan, but we got us some badass decoys. And just as well, Sawbuck says there's lots of action tonight."

Friar Tuck pulled back a section of trodden turf to reveal a large set of utility doors leading to a jeep-width concrete ramp. Tinkerbell wore on her left thigh a .45 Adder that she'd boiled in a phosphate solution to obtain a poisonous green corrosion-resistant finish, while Ripcord, whose eyes now had a luminous amphetamine sheen, waved a Schaurig machine pistol that gave off a pheromonal whiff of gun lubricant. All of them goggled up except for Go-Go, whose bugged-out eyes seemed beyond electron-stimulated assistance.

"All right," said Aretha. "This is goodbye, Clearfather."

Tinkerbell and Ripcord roared out like muzzlefire and Go-Go whipped up the dogs, which were happy to be under way.

"Close the doors!" Aretha called after they'd disappeared. "Everyone to combat-ready positions. All you in CyberIT—get your ears to the grindstone! And you, Little Man, tell Broadband to power up the GATORS."

"Don't crucify yourself, Big Girl," Finderz consoled. "Everybody here's guilty of something. Cocoa in my tent?"

"Guilty?" Aretha muttered, grateful now for any distraction. "I thought you were just a Caltech prankster who got in Dutch with de guvment."

"Dutch, huh? I'd be doing twenty-five-to-life at Marion. Somehow I don't think I'm going to get that Nob Head Prize that Momma dreamed of," Finderz replied.

"Well, let's not dwell on the past," the drag queen said with a sigh as they reached the dwarf's tent. "I want you to find out all you can about those probes. We may have had to send Clearfather away, but we aren't just going to abandon him."

"I'm on the case." Finderz nodded, putting milk on a Bunsen burner. "But that stealth unit's bad business. Developed for the Holy War. The motto of the designers was that none of their probes was ever MIA, they were NYA—Not Yet Arrived. But THE ENTOMOLOGIST and I will find a way to flush it out."

"Heaven help us if he ever goes against us," Aretha said.

"His eccentricity may be the best defense against infiltration," Finderz asserted. "I think that was another of Parousia Head's great insights. The Rickerburn construct might've flipped because it was too rigid. Spiral minds are harder to twist."

"Do you think we'll ever see her . . . ," Aretha was musing. "I was going to say *again*. But you haven't ever met her, either, have you?"

"Nope." Finderz shook his bulbous head, handing Aretha a mug. "But I can feel her presence in the tech. The coding . . . it's like Bach. I don't believe she's just a myth—but I can see why people do."

"It comes down to faith," Aretha said.

"It's a fine line between inspiration and delusion and this whole place is balanced right on the fucking edge," the dwarf agreed. "But here's something I am sure of. You know those relatives Clearfather was talking about? Well, Aunt Vivian was the name of a project that Ronwell Seward was involved with before Vitessa."

"Ronwell Seward . . . now, there's a name I haven't heard in a while. What did he end up calling himself? Stinky Wiggler?"

"That's right. Good old Stinky Wiggler. Another neglected genius. Along with Parousia, he'd be the climax mind of our time—if he hadn't lost his."

"Imagine what would've happened if those two had ever joined forces," Aretha enthused. "He disappeared, didn't he?"

"We may hear from him yet. In the meantime, 'Aunt Vivian' was a project that concentrated on real-time continuous and sponta-neous encryption. Very edgy for its day. Refers back to Prohibition-Era Seattle. A woman broadcast secret messages to smugglers on her radio program *Aunt Vivian's Bedtime Stories for Youngsters.*"

"What do you think that means for Clearfather?"

"No idea. But I'm glad we've got a tracking device on him."

"Well, I hope for his sake Aunt Vivian turns out to be a nice old woman who can make a good cup of cocoa," Aretha said.

CHAPTER 5

Deadland Running

The cage fighting, cantor singing, vindaloo—everything stopped as the high-pitched droning grew louder and the insidious tom-tom network pounded out its call to arms and, in some cases, claws. The cacophony drove the Fort Thoreau dogs wild, echoing off the blackened brick archways and tiled caverns beneath the megalopolis—a Neolithic delirium of Japanese cartoons, Mexican ghost murals, and Mandarin death slogans.

Through the agony in his head, Clearfather glimpsed mazes of ramps and planks thrusting out and falling away into untold darknesses, as if some fiendish network of pharaohs' tombs were simultaneously being constructed and excavated. He seemed to see everything through a grid of plasma tinged a nauseous methyl violet. Mummy-like shadows gesticulated, ravaged old women swathed in cellophane and crumbling *New York Post*s . . . hooded figures celebrating bizarre jackhammer rites. Frying offal, octane, cordite—bodies soaked in kerosene and set alight to keep them from the rats, some of the chem-fed mutants reaching the size of pit bulls—this was what the subway-sewer-and-maintenance tunnels had devolved into, an archaeological nightmare where the withered and the larval writhed side by side and totemic dream societies turned themselves into hybrids of flesh and machine while being preyed upon by the gangs that warred for turf and tissue.

This was also where Clearfather and his escort now faced a gauntlet that was closing on them like a fist. The Satyagrahi dogs groaned with dismay as the evil throbbing grew in intensity. Go-Go whipped them up through another tunnel lined with dripping pipes. On and on through the intestinal labyrinth the girl steered the mongrels until they swept through an intersection of conduits and switching terminals and Clearfather saw Ripcord's crumpled bike—the Schaurig smashed in a pool of blood. Go-Go ducked just in time beneath a line of piranha wire stretched across the passage. A human hand and a Browning automatic lay on the ground. From out of the dark, Tinkerbell laid down rubber. The bald man turned and saw Hermes roar in from the western tunnel. All around them wailed and pulsed the raucous jeering of plastic horns and drums.

"They got Rippy," Clearfather heard Go-Go call.

"I know." Tinkerbell gestured with the Adder. "He didn't go quiet!"

"We gotta take 111 and then run the subway to the sewers."

"Shit," Tinkerbell gritted. "Trains don't eat you, zombies'll get you in the drains."

"The GATORS are on the move," Go-Go answered.

"All right," Tinkerbell said. "I'll draw as much heat as I can."

She let out a war whoop, skidding past a stripped Yellow Cab with a burned corpse still clinging to the wheel, an old-style cell phone stuck to its head. Hermes revved off south and Go-Go whistled up the team and took off after him, the eyes of the two wolves shining in the dark. It seemed to Clearfather that he could see their eyes gleaming as if he were out in front of them, his mind surging forward out of his body—beyond the sled—beyond the barricades of shopping carts and baby carriages.

Through the rubble around them and the dry ice and barbed-wire misery in his mind he took in the shrapnel of images. Psych ward rejects armored in hubcaps and stop signs. Lab abominations with the jaws of anglerfish huddled around steam grates. Steroid-gorged weight lifters naked except for hard hats and G-strings, pumping iron in grottoes of sputtering neon.

But it was not these overtly gruesome visions that wormed their way deepest into his consciousness. It was the little girl without legs, rolling herself along inside a studded BFGoodrich snow tire. And still the dogs pulled on and the hunters closed.

AK-47 fire tore the air in Tinkerbell's direction. It came from an acetylene-torched chicane of butcher's racks and grappling hooks. A shotgun blasted and a body rolled underneath—the dogs and the tires crushing it without swerving—then a rush of wind and dust hit Clearfather in the face—trash and fresher air roaring past as if a valve had opened. He saw the tracks of the subway trains—his mind moving out in front of the sled again and back behind into darkness—the different drugs in his system peaking—the scar on his back burning. Go-Go lashed the dogs forward down the service path beside the rails, every six hundred feet a blue light and another emergency station—behind them an express train bearing down. In the headlight he picked out four ferals on MX bikes. One of them sported a helmet-mounted turbine-driven Black Swarm unit ready to spew a horizontal rain of steel.

The driverless southbound was almost upon them—Clearfather heard a scream. "Yee-ahhh!" Go-Go brayed, driving the sled into another passageway—and down—the dogs floundering through a sewer, the chemical burning of the disinfectants and the industrial cleaners worse than the shit and body scum.

Out of the dark he saw red laser sights bloom over the tunnel walls. Five Jet Skis came rooster-tailing around a bend. Hermes farted out a fatboy canister of mustard gas that sent the flank ski plowing into the wedge. A flametrail of wreckage ripped between the walls, but the other skiers sliced through—the nearest one shouting, "GATORS!"

Up out of the mouth of one of the other tunnels there appeared a smooth dark metal-skinned amphibious robot on all-terrain tractor tires. It churned through the sludge, cutting between the dogsled and Hermes. The gangbangers let loose with what they had but the GATOR drove them back down the tunnel. The dogs heaved up into a drier passageway, a potassium glow revealing arms hanging from ventilation grilles, the smooth floor strewn with cartridge casings.

They switched between tunnels, occasionally catching sight of Hermes and Tinkerbell. Clearfather noticed that the dogs nearest to him were tiring. He could smell their exhaustion. *I must pull them,* he thought. *I must pull them.* Barking crazily, the team renewed its attack from the rear, the five-legger spurring on the hairless ruin in front of her. It was only because of this sudden burst they weren't all taken down in a hail of metal—for coming up behind them again was the feral with the Black Swarm, this time joined by an unholy alliance tattooed with the warpaint of skeletons.

Go-Go knew what would happen. They'd eat the dogs and rape her. Or maybe they'd rape the dogs and eat her. Hermes's bike took a hit and the albino cartwheeled off—landing in Clearfather's lap. The impact knocked the money Aretha had given him out of the peacoat. The cash blew back into the tunnel. "Mister," Go-Go yelled to Clearfather. "You got any ideas, now's the fuckin' time!"

The voice reached him through a firecloud. He hadn't seen the money fall from the sled into the darkness behind. He was aware only of the stunned flesh cradled in his arms and the fear-for-life smell of the dogs. Then the Swarm turbine whined behind them and he found that he was singing . . .

> *Like a bat out of Hell*
> *I'll be gone when the morning comes . . .*
> *When the night is over . . . like a bat out of Hell*
> *I'll be gone, gone, gone . . .*

Go-Go heard the whir of the weapon's motor and braced to be ripped apart . . . so when the dogs didn't disintegrate and the pain didn't come, she glanced back over her shoulder to see a wall of ammo chasing the sled but never gaining. Gradually the angry cloud of bullets lost all momentum and fell to the ground as harmlessly as thimbles and confetti while the incredulous skeleton men blazed through. Holy shit, Go-Go thought. "That was good, mister . . . you know any more?"

Clearfather looked down out of the acid mist in his mind at the boy he held. Then the deep anguish came. Go-Go watched in shock as her passenger's back burst into flame—which she hosed down with the mini fire extinguisher she carried—but not before the terrible heat shot through her. Then she felt unaccountably cool. She looked behind to see how close their pursuers were now, and all of the figures began to destabilize. They were no longer painted up as skeletons, they *were* skeletons. Their machines seemed to petrify and fade, their forms dwindling into disembodied tattoos that disappeared like gunsmoke, leaving behind a litter of flesh-piercing jewelry like savage party favors.

Onward the dogs pulled and no gun barrages could be heard—all the way to 42nd Street. Not a single lurker or malingero. No Hyena Men, no Curare Girls. Just an eerie quiet—except for a lone motorcycle. Hermes had regained consciousness by the time they arrived. A bad knock to the head, but when he climbed out of the eggshell Go-Go noted no major bleeding or penetrative wounds. What was even more surprising was that the scorch marks on Clearfather's peacoat weren't there.

"How'd jew do that?" she asked, but Clearfather didn't respond.

Motherfuckin' hallucination, she thought. But the approaching cycle was real. On it was Tinkerbell, with an impact-expanding blowgun dart embedded in her helmet and the blood rose of a .32 wound blossoming under a pressure pack smashed tight to her leg.

"Where'd they all go? Ain't none of those sonsabitches back there!"
Clearfather clambered out of the shell and collapsed.

"Damn!" Tink spat. "He ain't gonna make it solo. You take him up.
Put on these shades. People will think he's doped."

They came up in an alley off Eighth Avenue. Go-Go, who hadn't
been aboveground outside Fort Thoreau since being taken in by the
Satyagrahi, led Clearfather staggering past the dai pai dongs into the
Port Authority, her eyes bugging out behind Tinkerbell's malachite-
tinted shades.

"Gate Six," she said, looking at the screen. "Leaving in two minutes." She found his pass and gave it to the Ticketrix for scanning,
then stuffed it back in his pocket.

Clearfather turned away into the confusion among the sanghyang
trance dancers and the flattened chickens. An eidolon of Trinidad
Slade, the six-foot-six black hypermodel, strutted naked with an
ocelot, advertising Debauchery perfume. He stepped through her
into the cold and climbed on the bus, a nostalgized Scenicruiser. He
made his way toward the back and found the last empty seat.

"Welcome to Greyhound America!" the bus announced. "Tonight
we'll be traveling along the Greyhound Northern Automated Navigation Corridor. Please note that for your safety secure-cam units
may be monitoring activity in the main cabin area and a Beagle sensor is installed in the restroom. Now sit back, relax, and away we go
Greyhound!"

Clearfather felt the vibration of the engine as the remote-piloted
vehicle lumbered out of the loading bay. Then he saw the figure—a
young black boy with a ghost-pale face and hair. The boy held up his
hand as the Scenicruiser rumbled by, the colossal eidolons of Times
Square behind him, snowing static and the dense disorienting
prisms of short-term information known as "chrome noise."

PART 2

Continental Soldier

Madness is something rare in individuals—
but in groups, parties, peoples, ages, it is the rule.
—Friedrich Nietzsche

CHAPTER I

A Quaker State of Mind

A city trembling like a mirage . . . each of the skyscrapers a cyclone . . . ceaselessly whirling but perfectly stationary . . . and in the center of the helices . . . luminous elevators flashing at the speed of thought.

He woke alone in a seat on a Greyhound without a driver in the dark of an early morning. His head felt as if it had been recently shaved. He heard someone mention Bethlehem. Then a woman spoke of Pittsburgh.

He checked his pockets and found an American Safari pass in the name of Elijah Clearfather, a blank piece of paper, a small ivory ball, and a fistful of blond hair. No money—but a pack containing food supplies and a bottle of liquid. The hair matched the down on his arms—but he couldn't figure out why he'd have some in his pockets. The little ivory ball he didn't have any idea about, and the paper was as blank as his memory. He scrunched the paper up and stuck it between the seats. Except for the city of cyclones in his dream all he could think of was a silver spoon from the Pan-American Exposition in Buffalo in 1901. I must've been drugged, he concluded. He looked at the bus pass again. There was a map on the back with a large chunk of California missing and the words AMERICA—WHAT A GREAT DESTI-NATION! Someone had starred PITTSBURGH, a point near Amarillo with a handwritten name above it that read DUSTDEVIL, TX . . . and some screwball place called LOSVEGAS, which was on what appeared to be the new West Coast. He didn't think the writing was his. He tried to recall any connections he might have with these places, but none came. The one thing that came to mind beyond the cyclones and the spoon was the image of a young boy bent over a toilet. The boy was naked and there were candles lit. Then he saw a flashlight beam stabbing and probing through metal cots. The images gave him a choking sense of fear and shame. Have I committed a terrible crime? he wondered. And how could I have gone my whole life with a name like Elijah Clearfather and not remember it? He stared out through the safety glass, trying to make sense of what was happening.

Giant eidolons loomed above the interstate—holograms the size of buildings that were dimensionally rich and yet transparent. This is insane, he thought, as a towering Scotsman threatened to lift up his kilt and then waved at the bus with a lewd leer. How can people deal with things like *that*? But from the behavior of his fellow passengers these characters were an expected albeit annoying part of the mediascape, and indeed there was something so absurd about them, they seemed to blend into the passing scene despite their behemoth proportions. The voices and visions in his head were not so easily accommodated. Fragments of music, pain . . . things out of dreams. From out of the haze there would appear some incredibly complex image, like an entire wall of mathematical formulae distilled to a single hieroglyph . . . then poof.

He turned his attention outward trying to pick out anything familiar, but all he could make out was an intermittent radiance promoting something called WigWam Jackpots and a strobing sign announcing that the largest Howard Johnson's on earth was two minutes away. Where once had been steel mills, coal mines, and before that miles of forests, there was now a smear of icicle-like buildings—refreshment stations, casinos, refugee camps, gated communities, and Time Havens, where people banded together to live in accordance with the technology and morality of earlier periods.

Once past the HoJo driving rain set in, slowing progress. Two razor-scalped girls with clock-face tattoos jabbered and pointed to him. He got the impression they'd been listening to him when he'd been asleep. I wish I knew what I'd been saying, he thought. There was a long delay at the Harrisburg checkpoint (when had checkpoints come about?). Outside the window, quasar screens advertised a local firing range and the opening of a new ChildRite Nurturing Center, alongside an old-fashioned peeling billboard that was blank except for the words . . .

EVERYTHING YOU HOPE TO KEEP FOR THE JOURNEY YOU MUST LOSE ALONG THE WAY.

—*Stinky Wiggler*

A blast of static filled his head—and he heard the words *Welcome to Hermetic Canyon, Self Dakota.* He blinked and the billboard was gone, as if it had never been there. What did that mean? Stinky Wiggler was an even more remarkable name than Elijah Clearfather. And what was Hermetic Canyon? Where was Self Dakota? His back started to burn. When we get to Pittsburgh, I'll see a doctor, he said to himself. I have to see a doctor.

Out on the interstate, a suicide truck bomb slowed progress further. The sun came up but the sky stayed a dead-fish gray. They passed another of the fossilized billboards.

THERE'S NOTHING LIKE THE GENTLE, REASSURING SOUND OF A CIVILIZATION FALLING DOWN AROUND YOU.

—*Stinky Wiggler*

This time Clearfather heard singing in Latin—then a blues guitar. He saw images of cliffs and crags as if on another planet. Once again the billboard seemed to melt away into the warped rainbow of signs and fuel stations. He felt as if he were in the wrong body or tuned in to someone else's broadcast. But after the rush of sound and light, clarity came. And hunger. He pawed through his pack. He found a tin full of perfect little rainbow trout. A vial contained a murky liquid that tasted like celery.

The bus came in via an automated guard station on the Penn Lincoln Parkway. Soweto bars and karaoke clubs swept past as the tired spires of Steel Plaza rose in the shadows of the regional Vitessalith, the Chung Center, and the Bank of Bahrain. Down on the river floated a ragged fleet of dhows and a graffiti-covered gunboat flying Hyundai colors. The bus wished them all a "Happy Pennsylvania Morning" and started giving instructions about Quaker State connections. Clearfather headed tentatively into the station, wondering if someone was there to meet him—or capture him.

CHAPTER 2

Addicted to Strangers

Inside the depot, everything smelled of curry and bleach. He glanced around expectantly but no one caught his eye. Except for a Harijan buffing the floor—a base-level sanitation and observation robot. He was surprised by the exoskeletal creature, or rather machine, but he knew intuitively that it wasn't unusual or out of place. There was something about the way it seemed to fade into the linoleum and molded plastic of its surroundings. Even the clapped-out Nicaraguan mopping up in front of the Chinese menu screen for Starbucks didn't meld as completely.

To one side there was a cordoned-off area reserved for WOMEN & CHILDREN sponsored by ChildRite Nurturing Centers, a name he remembered from the interstate. The area was guarded by two brilliantly colored eidolons whose heads would've brushed the acoustic panels in the ceiling had they been solid. One was a voluptuous female orangutan as orange as cream of tomato soup. She was decked out in a tiara of wildflowers and a skirt of tropical green leaves, and haloed by repeating bursts of hypertext like talking rain. Clearfather couldn't tell if other people could see these words or not. They said things like QUEEN UBBA DUBBA and offered advice or made pronouncements such as BE KIND TO OTHER CREATURES and NATURE IS ONLY NATURAL.

Her equally overstated colleague was a drake, as in a male duck, between ten and twelve feet tall depending on how he moved or craned his neck, which he seemed to do with compulsive frequency. He was dressed in a prim sweater vest under the type of beige corduroy jacket that elementary schoolteachers once wore back when men were allowed near children. But his overall coloration was the deep shade of blue that a leaky pen leaves in a pocket—with a beak that was such an extreme yellow it shone like gold bullion. Hypertext flickered about him, too, in time with his irritating neck spasms. These messages said things like DOOLEY and BE NICE, PLEASE!

Clearfather couldn't recall any characters called Ubba Dubba or Dooley Duck but, judging from the reactions of the other people, they were known and even loved celebrities who appeared to be on the ChildRite payroll, so to speak. There was something distressing about seeing such large cartoonish things interacting with people and furniture so casually, particularly when the characters blurred together or the asthmatic boy with the face mask would run through them and they'd giggle or wince, the electric intensity of their hues fading out for a moment before they regained full resolution.

No one seemed to be waiting for him or watching him. As anxious as he felt, he waited and still no one made any move, so he decided to go to the restroom and check out his back. But he didn't see any signs for the restrooms, so he went over to the robot cleaner to ask for directions. "Excuse me," he said to the Harijan.

The sanitation unit regarded him with what was at first trepidation and then a dawning alarm tinged with enthusiasm. Then it spoke with a voice that made him think of a praying mantis. But he couldn't understand because a heavyset Securitor packed into riot pads blustered over and snarled, "Get away from that thing! Don't you know the rules?"

"I'm sorry," said Clearfather. "I want to know where the restrooms are."

"Listen," continued the Securitor, brandishing a stun gun. "What have you done?"

"I don't know what you mean," Clearfather answered, turning to see that the Harijan's pneumatic limbs had bent so that it appeared to be performing some sort of obeisance.

"All right!" the Securitor demanded, deactivating it. "Let's see some ID!"

Clearfather showed him his bus pass.

"What about your implant, smart-ass?"

"Implant?" Clearfather asked, looking blank.

"Your *Resident* ID system," the Securitor sneered.

The confusion was resolved when, in one continuous motion, the Securitor holstered his weapon, grabbed Clearfather's right hand, and tugged it toward him—then ripped up a Velcro patch in his vest to reveal a small plasma screen against which he laid Clearfather's hand with practiced accuracy. Clearfather heard a hum and the Securitor stopped. A moment later the guard seemed to find himself again—embarrassed—apologetic.

"I'm very sorry . . . sir," he said, snapping off every awkward word. "I'm so very . . . *sorry* to have . . . inconvenienced you . . . ," he mumbled. "There aren't enough signs. I'll make a full report. We'll action it. I can't tell you how sorry I am about this—misunderstanding."

"But where's the john?"

"Oh! Right . . . this way. You see?" The Securitor pointed. He reactivated the Harijan, which straightened up and resumed buffing, and then drifted over to the cordoned-off area and plopped down beside Queen Ubba Dubba.

Clearfather went to the men's room, which was crowded given the rest of the station. The security cameras had been plastered over with wet paper towels. There were two men in one stall and a man and a woman in another. Under the sinks a man who would've weighed less than a hundred pounds lay asleep or blacked out. Clearfather stepped up to one of the urinals. He was surprised at the size of his penis. My memory really is in trouble if I forgot about this, he realized. Then he turned and noticed that he'd attracted attention.

It was a teenage white boy. He had the telltale mark of the surgical brain implant that Clearfather had seen on some of the other people. His clothes were expensive but filthy. His face was effeminate—his lips injected with collagen. He had a fashion blue picture lens showing a Madonna and Child and the unmistakable signs of drug abuse in his other bloodshot hazel eye.

"That's the biggest dick I've ever seen, mister . . ."

Clearfather felt a powerful sense of loathing. It angered him to be looked at like that—and yet it brought to mind again the scene of the boy in the bathroom.

"What's wrong with you?" he demanded. "Don't you know better than to talk to strangers that way?"

"He's addicted to strangers," the man under the sinks groaned, and rolled out from underneath the plumbing.

Clearfather was surprised to see that the floorsleeper was so infested with head lice, the invaders were visible. "What do you mean?" he asked.

"God, fuck me harder!" Clearfather heard the woman shout.

"He's a Pandora addict," the licer coughed, bringing up an oyster slick of mucus that slithered down the drain.

"I don't know what you're saying," Clearfather said as the woman orgasmed.

"He needs sex like a junkie. They gotta get it or they'll blow their brains."

"C'mon, mister," the boy wheedled.

A woman emerged from the stall, panties around her wrist, with a face that resembled a warthog. A disheveled deaf-mute shuffled out of the stall after her. He looked at Clearfather and pressed his key-pad.

C Ar E TO M aK E . . . A D O nA TiON . . . ????

Clearfather touched the blurry cathode screen, and the man's face spasmed.

##¤♂ ♀☺♠♣♫ ♥♪√%&%$$!!!!дΔΩ‡њ+++??

"He didn't get that excited with me," the woman smirked. "You the one with the big dick? Give us a look."

Clearfather was getting upset. All he wanted to do was to inspect his back in privacy. "Listen," he said. "All of you get out of here."

The lice head snickered. The kid continued whining while the facially disadvantaged woman sniffed her panties and then slipped them back on. "Oh, Mr. Big Dick wants us out, huh? Well, who are you?"

"I'm not a pheasant plucker, I'm the Pheasant Plucker's son, but I'll keep on plucking pheasants till the Pheasant Plucker comes," Clearfather replied—and was taken aback at the vehemence of his assertion, without understanding what it meant or why he'd said it. The effect on the occupants of the restroom, however, was instantaneous. They all left.

Perplexed, he stripped off his peacoat and shirt and tried to examine his back in the mirror. He saw primitive letters cut into his skin with a box cutter and a soldering iron, or maybe acid. FATHER FORGIVE THEM *F.*

He put his clothes back on.

"All right," he said, to the bald stranger who stared back at him. "Let's try to find out why in hell we're here."

CHAPTER 3

Big Duck Demands Dick

He crossed the depot waiting for someone to make a move. No one did. The thought of hauling himself off to a hospital frightened him, so he leaned on a railing watching images on a series of liquidplex cubes that rotated like a dissolving and re-forming compound eye and kept referring to something called TWIN. There was something that called itself a Voyancy Terminal beside the system, which he supposed allowed a more personal hook-up to the images, although the service obviously wasn't free because there was a screen that blinked LOG ON CREDIT DETAILS and a glowing hand, which judging from his experience with the Securitor he guessed was designed to validate security or credit status.

There'd been another explosion . . . in Washington. An eidolon of a media personality called Vinata Nidhu appeared in the viewing area. In an anglicized subcontinent accent, she announced, ". . . *Yet another Tactical Despair explosion has rocked the nation this morning, demolishing the Aeronautics wing of the Smithsonian Institution . . .*"

In the air around her, silvery hypertext invited him to CHOOSE THE WARDROBE AND PRESENTER STYLE YOU PREFER . . . These offers were followed by a flurry of Chinese ideograms. Then the woman looked at Clearfather and said "Hablo español . . . Falo portugues . . . Je parle français . . ." Other kinds of characters flowed around her. Indonesian, Korean—the movement was disorienting. Then she vanished. It made him reconsider the hallucinations he'd been having. But it got him curious. He didn't have the physical portal that he saw on some people or the more common little boxes that linked into the headsets and glasses, so he didn't know what would happen, but he went over to the terminal, placed his hand on the glowing outline, and waited. Vinata Nidhu reappeared but not at full clarity as she had before. Hypertext streamed in—watery and radiant. "How do you want to see me?" the woman asked.

"Clearly," he answered.

The transparent woman shook her head, and a series of text options flickered before him. HETERO. GAY. PROFESSIONAL. PROVOCATIVE. SUBMISSIVE. DOMINANT. INTELLECTUAL.

"What are you now?" he asked, feeling a little foolish to be talking to this phantom—until he noticed a bag lady deep in discussion with Dooley Duck.

"Hetero-Professional," Vinata Nidhu sniffed and made one of those dismissive hand gestures as if to say, *Isn't it obvious?*

"Let's try Hetero-Provocative," Clearfather answered.

"Direct connections are aromatic," she informed him. "And private," she added. "Monsoon and Kalimpong Orchid are popular fragrances."

It struck him funny. This wasn't a newsreader so much as a table dancer you put inside your head. "Where are you coming from?" he asked.

"Informationally I'm based at a news desk in Chicago, but I'm visually generated from TWIN Central in Minneapolis," Vinata answered.

Clearfather noticed that a couple of drunks had slunk in to get warm. One of the men was tall and reddened, with a crooked frame that resembled a shillelagh. The other was all nose hair with the disintegrating squatness of a stubbed-out cigar. They tried to carry themselves like executives but about them both was the smell of protein excretion mingled with sour white sherry and a broad-spectrum disinfectant.

"I want to see you naked," Clearfather said. The broken-down men looked so forlorn, maybe a beautiful naked woman would cheer them up.

The eidolon looked at him for a moment and then said, "Nudity is not one of the public platform options."

"I'm not a pheasant plucker, I'm the Pheasant Plucker's son, but I'll keep on plucking pheasants till the Pheasant Plucker comes," he replied.

Vinata Nidhu disappeared but a moment later faded back in with amazing clarity—naked except for her gold necklace from which dangled a tiny Shiva. She had a more Dravidian sheen to her skin now. Her nipples were so dark they were almost purple. After all the goings-on that had been going on, lust surged through him, although he knew that the image before him was just that. Still, her frank and graceful nudity was impossible to ignore. Even Ubba Dubba and Dooley Duck became curious.

Queen Ubba Dubba's voice sampled Whoopi Goldberg and David Attenborough, the host of pre-TWIN BBC natural history documentaries. The mix was disconcerting although it researched well. Dooley Duck's vocalfile was based on the late actor Kevin Costner, although his character was paranoid—the result of the head of script development having had a bipolar breakdown.

"She's naked!" Dooley squawked. "That's like one of my worst dreams. Exposed. Bare. Vulnerable."

"Earth spirit. Goddess of love," Ubba Dubba intoned.

"Hey!" one of the other Securitors shouted. "You can't have nudie news presenters in here! Get that thing off the public broadcast area."

"I don't know how to do that," Clearfather said. "And I've got to go."

"I'm coming, too," Vinata said.

Clearfather stepped out of the viewing area—followed by the three eidolons: a naked goddess off the wall of a Hindu temple, a rotund ecofeminist orangutan, and a giant blue duck with psychological problems.

"Where are you taking them?" the Securitor called.

"I'm not taking them," Clearfather said. "They're just following me." And as he said this he saw that several people were following him, too.

"Come, children," Ubba Dubba enjoined them. "Let us all be naked as we were in the Great Forest at the beginning of time." And so saying, the queen of conservation slipped out of her green finery, which dissolved like hypertext, and stood, long-armed and hairy-breasted, like an overweight redhead with hormonal issues and a fund of gentle wisdom.

"W-w-hoa!" stammered Dooley, doing his trademark neck roll. "This is like . . . I can't be naked. W-w-hoa!"

"You *are* naked, Dooley," Ubba Dubba remarked. "Except for your jacket and that little vest you wear, which frankly doesn't suit you."

"You don't like my vest?" The duck shuddered. "I'm standing here on the edge of a full-blown *episode* . . . and you're saying you don't like my vest . . . and that other than that . . . I'm *naked*?"

"Hey, Dooley," one of the drunks called. "Take off that coat and faggy vest!"

"This is a nightmare!" Dooley wailed—and then brightened. "I'm not naked the way she's naked," he said, pointing to Vinata Nidhu.

"No," agreed Ubba Dubba. "You're missing some bits."

"W-hhhhhattttt?" the huge blue eidolon cried, and the look of dawning insight and panic in his eyes was hilarious and pathetic all at once.

"Hey, duck!" the other drunk called. "Show us your cock!"

"Dooley! Dooley! Dooley!" someone else chanted.

"You're saying . . . ," Dooley gasped. "That I'm a duck . . . without a dick?"

The huge blue duck's eyes blurred and burned, and for a moment he seemed to pixilate. Then he re-formed with a look of acute, miserable comprehension.

"I see it all now!" he cried. "*That's* why I'm allowed around children! I'm a genitally disadvantaged male! Oh, the shame! The shame!"

"Maybe it's not too late to change," Vinata suggested.

"Change is the only certainty," Ubba Dubba announced.

"It's all just hit me," the duck sobbed. "I've woken up to the truth. I don't think I can go on."

"What matters is the future," Ubba Dubba stated regally.

Clearfather had his hand in his pocket, fingering the curious ivory ball.

"Maybe you could get them—whoever made you up—to give you some new equipment . . . ," he suggested, noticing that the crowd was beginning to grow.

"Yeah, make 'em give you a dong!" the drunks hollered in unison.

"Fuck a duck! Fuck a duck!"

The rising uproar was too much for Greyhound. Securitors equipped with stun weapons swarmed. Everything seemed to break apart in Clearfather's head. He had to get out of there. One of the Securitors gassed a young street woman and he managed to slip out a side door while Dooley frantically rolled his neck, promising the panic-stricken group he was going to demand a rewrite and a re-rendering.

"Yeay, Dooley!" came the cries echoing behind in the station.

"Fuck a duck! Fuck a duck!"

CHAPTER 4

Allegheny Banger

Whiffs of ganja and tortillas . . . methane-green letters rotating atop a Vietnamese market . . . MERCY HOSPITAL, MONTEFIORE HOSPITAL, AND ST. FRANCIS MEDICAL CENTER ARE CLOSED TO PATIENTS WHO DO NOT HOLD A VITESSA CARD. ALLEGHENY GENERAL AND WEST PENN ARE ACCEPTING ONLY MAJOR TRAUMA CASES. PUBLIC DRUG TRIAGES ARE OFFERED TODAY IN THE FOLLOWING LOCA-TIONS: SASSAFRAS WAY ON POLISH HILL, PANTHER HOLLOW LAKE IN SCHENLEY PARK . . .

Maybe seeing a doctor isn't going to be so easy, he realized. Then again maybe all he'd have to do is give the Pheasant Plucker speech. He had no idea why people reacted the way they did or where the words had come from. He was shuffling down Liberty Avenue con-templating the problem when he spotted the two drunks.

"Hey," Clearfather said. "You know where I could get some food . . . free?"

"Breakfast at the Wieviel Organ Clinic in the Strip District is good. You can watch the towboats while they check your scans."

"What do have to give them in return?" he asked.

"You don't give 'em nothin'!" the squat, hairy one coughed. "At least not if you can help it . . . although, say . . . maybe you got somethin' to sell. You in good health?"

"You mean they want the organs . . . now?"

The drunks roared with laughter at this question.

"And there's Ghost Meat down there," the short one squeaked.

"Shush, Klein, he's looking for breakfast."

"What's ghost meat?" Clearfather asked.

"You don't want to know, chief," the lean, crooked drunk said. "Just look out for the Big Kidney. The whole operation's not exactly legal but it's AMA-run. Even the river pirates don't fuck with the AMA. Drift on down that way . . . past the markets."

Clearfather waved goodbye. He noticed quite a bit of anti-Islamic graffiti and signs for something called Al-Waqi'a, which had all been attacked. He was becoming more certain that he had been in Pittsburgh. But long ago . . . in the distant past. He remembered that the original *Night of the Living Dead* had been filmed in the city . . . and that it was Andy Warhol's hometown. Images of slagheaps and a Catholic church came to mind. But what did it mean now? He figured food would help.

Both the Allegheny and the Monongahela were choked with tugs and junks, dhows, floating casinos, and any number of barges stacked high with shipping containers like colored shoe boxes, the residents ascending and descending on a cat's cradle of Tyrolean systems. He kept walking.

There were still anthrax warnings up in the Strip District, and the coffee bars and trendy restaurants had closed. The wholesale markets had started up again, though, defended against beggars and marauders by drone Securitors and pig-killing dogs. On the fringe of the loading docks there was a sprawl of Pakistani and Serbo-Croatian food stands just beginning to open, and down in the rubble of lost nightclubs a family of Kyrgyzstanis offering sour horse's milk and Chinese vendors preparing monkey brains in rice wine.

At last he spotted an inflated red kidney the size of a GMC pickup floating above what looked like the remains of a warehouse. Emanating from the facility was a confusing aroma of latex, formalin, and Jimmy Dean Maple Sausage Waffles. An LED sign read FREE BREAKFAST FOR ORGAN VENDORS.

He had to walk through a Geigerscan to get in, then a man in a uniform ran a handheld over him while a stone-faced guard looked on. They waved him through an air lock. A faint buzzer sounded, and the inner door opened. A Malaysian woman in a white pantsuit ushered him into a waiting area overseen by a large smiling plasmagram of someone called "DR. HUGH WIEVIEL". Underneath his face was a hyperblurb that read: ORGAN SELLING IMMORAL? WHO SAYS? REMEMBER *EVIL* IS *LIVE* SPELLED BACKWARD. *Rejuv-E-Nation is the solution. We're not asking for your soul, we just want you to use your brain—if you have an organ to sell, speak to us for the best deal.*

Two men and a woman all wearing white lab coats appeared.

"I'm Dr. Miedo, formerly of Lima," the first man introduced himself, and from between cane-white dental caps a pungent spearmint-flavored toothpick stabbed out like a dart.

"And I'm Dr. Pinjrapol, formerly of Calcutta," the woman announced, sniffing loudly. Her hands looked like they came from another body and showed signs of a ruby-tinted rash between the fingers.

"And I'm Dr. Shecanguan," the Chinese man said and blinked his heavily lidded amber eyes.

"Where are you formerly of?" Clearfather asked.

"Most recently, Planned Parenthood down the street," the man hissed.

"You're here for a *free* breakfast, aren't you?" Dr. Miedo smiled, ejecting and retracting his toothpick.

Dr. Pinjrapol clapped her hands, and Clearfather was escorted by two nurses through a curtain. "An excellent-looking specimen," she confirmed.

"Yes," nodded Dr. Miedo. "We'll give our friend Mr. Brand first option. See what he's willing to pay for a nice healthy liver."

"Oh, yes!" hissed Dr. Shecanguan.

The nurses led Clearfather through a barrage of testing stations, then at last out to the balcony of what had once been a posh marina restaurant, enclosed now in a see-through tent looking out at the river. A short palsied man trembled up to him.

"The m-maple s-sausages are g-gone. A-all w-we have is the Al-allegheny b-banger. A de-delishioussss b-blood s-sausage—v-very nuu-trish-us. "

"A blood . . . sausage!" Clearfather grouched.

"What seems to be the problem, Torgal?" Dr. Shecanguan queried, sliding in through the plastic wall. "Behave yourself or there will be no medication."

Torgal trembled away so violently it looked like he might shake apart.

"Now," blinked Dr. Shecanguan. "Your test results are outstanding. How about putting off that breakfast and prepping for surgery? We have several buyers lined up. Would you be interested in selling a liver or a heart?"

"A liver . . . *a* heart? You have *one* liver and *one* heart," Clearfather replied.

"Exactly." Dr. Shecanguan smiled, showing teeth like old mahjongg tiles. "Which is why, if they are healthy and genetically sound, they are worth a good deal. We ensure that the fee is paid to the beneficiary of your choice."

"You think I want to die . . . to sell my organs for money? That's crazy!"

"Oh, don't be so hasty," Dr. Shecanguan insisted, patting his hand and pouring him a cup of coffee from a thermex jug.

Clearfather was about to take a sip of the coffee when he noticed Torgal peeking out of the kitchen. The poor man was shaking so badly, Clearfather found his own hand trembling and ended up sloshing coffee in Dr. Shecanguan's lap.

"I'm sorry!" he cried.

Torgal wobbled over carrying a sponge that had been soaked in very cold water, and when he applied it to Dr. Shecanguan's groin, it elicited another outcry and sent the doctor scurrying back into the clinic.

"D-don't d-drink the c-coffee!" Torgal sputtered. "It's . . . d-drugged! Q-quick!"

He dragged Clearfather into the kitchen and shoved open a sticky fire door that led to an alley. Clearfather took off before he could even think to ask any questions.

"Torgal." Dr. Shecanguan blinked, entering the kitchen wearing clean trousers a moment later. "You *really* shouldn't have let him go. We'd just negotiated a wonderful price for his organs."

"I . . . I'm . . . s-sorry . . . b-but . . ."

"Hush, Torgal," hissed the doctor as he produced a loaded syringe gun. "Now, we've promised Mr. Brand a liver. And we always deliver."

CHAPTER 5

Son and Shadow

Aretha Nightingale sat in his tent nursing a cup of cocoa and a guilt complex that even his psychedelic geisha wig couldn't alleviate. The Kricket they'd hidden on Clearfather was working, and Broadband had reported that the stranger had made it safely to Pittsburgh. The Oblivion.6 had prevented a mindstorm, but what other damage it had caused was unknown. The drag queen tried to imagine what state Clearfather was in and what he would make of the letter instructing him to call on Julian Dingler—not knowing that it had been discarded.

He noticed that the trees that had seemed so tight and greedy the day before were budding now. Grody's jonquils had come up overnight. The moods around Fort Thoreau had also improved. Who- or whatever Clearfather was, his coming hadn't destroyed them. And their decision not to take him in hadn't destroyed him. Not yet anyway. But the strange pilgrim had certainly stirred up strange thoughts.

Ever since the drag queen had come out and changed his name from Denzel Fiske to Aretha Nightingale, there'd been no looking back—especially not after he'd been recruited by the Satyagrahi.

From that time until Clearfather arrived, Aretha had blocked out much of his private history. He knew that his wife, Eartha, probably didn't want to see him again. But his son, Minson, was another story. Especially if the boy, who was now a man, knew the truth.

Minson Fiske, who'd once played the French horn at Juilliard, had abandoned New York and a professional music career to become a social worker in Fort Lauderdale, where he'd not only outed himself—he'd taken up boxing of all things—but also proved himself so good, he'd become a gay icon and then a national celebrity after knocking out the Reverend Stubby Kenwick, one of TWIN's top Christian Entertainment stars, during a charity brawl at Miami's Jackie Gleason Theater of the Performing Arts. Stubby woke up to discover he'd lost several million brain cells, twenty-two rating points, and all of his self-respect. Meanwhile Minson Fiske became a star overnight, donating his winnings to AIDS.2 benefits. Since then he'd signed with Avalanche O'Flaherty, who'd teed up the so called Fight for Life stunt with Xerxes "Corpse Maker" McCallum in the new Sun Kingdom in LosVegas, the megalopolis that combined the remains of Los Angeles and Las Vegas after the giant earthquake known as Bigfoot.

In his new post-Clearfather mood, Aretha had to admit he was proud. His son was doing what he hadn't been able to do himself until he was almost dead—being true to himself and an inspiration to others. But then to have the balls to get in the ring with Xerxes McCallum, a Congo-black bonebreaker from the slaughterhouse side of Kansas City, the world's highest-paid athlete! Forty-five bouts, forty-five KOs, and three deaths!

Aretha was afraid and excited for his son as he'd never been for himself. What a thing it would be to see the Fight in person! But it was an insane idea. There was too much work and responsibility here. Too many people dependent on his leadership. Oh, but what a moment! Of course Minson was likely to be knocked senseless in the first five seconds. He could be brain-damaged for life—he could die. But maybe not. Maybe not! Either way, it was a father's responsibility to be there. Wasn't it? Even if the father was a drag queen.

The idea rushed like wildfire through his mind. A secret op. To slip out of Fort Thoreau, travel to Nevadafornia and see the Fight! He might be banished from the Satyagrahi. He might never get to meet Parousia Head. He might be captured by Vitessa or arrested by the Feds—pretty much the same thing. But it all seemed worth it if he could see his son again (and maybe do just a little bit of shopping).

Aretha set out to see the dwarf. But when he arrived at the Information Station, the Cube was empty.

Aretha logged on to Finderz's thinkstation with the master password *placebo domino*. Not even the dwarf had that key.

In the dwarf's WIP file, Aretha noticed the letter to Julian Dingler that Finderz had drafted for Clearfather, but not the communication that had been sent to Dingler. That seemed odd. He'd have to raise the issue with Keeperz. In the meantime he summoned THE ENTOMOLOGIST.

Up out of the cyberdark the netted face formed. "Good morning, my friend," the soft voice oozed. "More fisshhing perhapsss?"

Aretha shivered. "Do you know what happened to a message Finderz sent last night to Pittsburgh? A coded message to Vitessa."

"I know nothing of ssucch a messsage," the soft voice answered.

Finderz had said THE ENTOMOLOGIST was one of their stronger assets. If he was twisted, all of Fort Thoreau was in jeopardy. The drag queen dispatched THE ENTOMOLOGIST back to cyberdarkness and resolved to speak to the dwarf the very first moment they had alone.

CHAPTER 6

The Whispering Cage

The experience at the organ clinic killed Clearfather's appetite. For the next couple of hours he wandered through the vaccinators and legal advice terminals, trying to steer clear of the quarantined areas. Something terrible had happened . . . maybe lots of terrible things. The name Vitessa rang bells, but what was Al-Waqi'a? And what were the little patches that people wore on their skin? When he looked at them closely, he saw that they had an almost living sheen—ultrafine microcircuits suspended in some form of skin-sensitive glycerine. He sensed that there was something individual about each one and yet they were all linked, like pieces in a huge jigsaw.

For a while he sat watching the Allegheny, fondling the little ivory ball in his pocket. He contemplated tossing it into the river but couldn't bring himself to do so. Instead he flung the soft wheat of his hair. He tried to concentrate on a plan. How was he going to get money? Who or what was he there to find? The problem was that every few minutes he'd hear voices. Sometimes they were like angels singing hymns or voices in an unknown language that made him think of Indians and buffalo . . . wind in tall grass. Other times they were like frenetic insects. Roaches on aluminum foil. He caught the phrases *level upon level . . . chain reaction . . . the Holy Ghost in the machine . . .*

Maybe I'm a schizophrenic, he thought. I just need some medication.

If so, he wasn't alone. He noticed many people wandering around talking to themselves. More people than he thought there should've been. That was another puzzle. The checkpoints, the eidolons, the Securitors, the talk of the Holy War and the disaster in LA—the Voyants and TWIN, which he'd worked out stood for The World Integrated Network—the number of damaged people—everything made him feel as if he'd been asleep for a long time. It was as if everyone who could afford it now was on psychoactive medication. An epidemic of mental illness had taken hold of America and possibly the world. The trouble was, it didn't explain the bizarre effect he had. In moments of clarity, I can project and control, he thought.

He glanced up at an ad for the Christian Investment Fund. It was an eidolon of Jesus saying, *"For I came down from heaven, not to do mine will, but the will of him who sent me."* It reminded him of his map. Perhaps *I'm* being projected and controlled, he thought, just like the eidolons. And like Dooley Duck and friends, I've somehow broken free.

He was just starting to unpack this possibility when he found himself confronted with another of the old-fashioned billboards.

MAKE A MISTAKE WITH THE SACRED AND YOU GET SCARED.
—*Stinky Wiggler*

This one was at ground level so he walked up to it to see if he could touch it, but the moment he did, it disappeared. Before, when he'd seen the signs, they'd triggered a flurry in his head. This time there was a parade of grainy images that wrinkled like photographs in a fire. A man outside a radio station. A circle of women kneeling around a pillar. Then the boy in the bathroom—and a Catholic church. He had a misty recollection of an Aunt Vivian and Uncle Waldo. But they were without faces. They gave him a sense of warmth and hope—and yet of sadness. He felt the letters engraved in his back come alive with heat, and it was all he could do not to fall to the pavement. Then he looked down the street and saw a real Catholic church. St. Aloysius.

The empty sanctuary was echoey and cavernous, as if built to contain the largest of the eidolons he'd seen, but old and grim even where daylight seeped through the stained-glass panels, all grimed with a layer of dust so that they seemed more like grafittied monitor screens than leadlight windows. A row of candles burned. In the corner, the confessional chamber. Like a Voyancy Terminal. In a small chapel alcove was a mural of Jesus with the words HE THAT LOSETH HIS LIFE FOR MY SAKE SHALL FIND IT. An eidolon console flickered out the stories of St. Nicholas of Tolentino, the noble pro tector of children, followed by a feature on Clare of Assisi, patron saint of television. A priest approached.

He was stiff and creaky, smooth and indefinite of face. His breath had a scent of raisins. "Welcome to Saint Aloysius," he breathed. "I'm Father Dominic. Are you all right?"

"I came in . . . to seek . . . guidance . . . ," Clearfather said.

"Well, I'm sorry that VatiCom is down at the moment so the Pope isn't here. We had a lightning strike last night. But . . ."

"The Pope?"

"The Apotheosis. The eidolonic presence. We're having technical difficulties after the storm, but we expect to be back online soon. Could I be of assistance? Or would you like to just sit and pray?"

Clearfather felt a searing pain in his back and saw again the image of the boy in the bathroom mirror, candles glowing. Then the flashlight that made him choke. The raisiny smell was very strong now and the burning in his back so bright he could see the letters before him.

"Come," whispered Father Dominic, noticing his distress. "Into the confessional booth."

In addition to the priest's discomfort in speaking face-to-face with strangers off the street, he liked showing off the confessional booth, with its mesh grille made of pressed zinc. The metalwork had such a delicate and almost moist quality, it made Father Dominic imagine that it retained the voices that passed through and, if stroked with the right touch, might reproduce those hushed admissions.

"How long since your last confession?" the priest asked when they were settled. The privacy and the scent of the pressed metal enlivened him.

"I don't know. I'm not sure I'm even Catholic. But I'm having visions and hearing voices," said Clearfather. "I see a young boy. Candles . . . and a mirror."

Just to describe it sullied him.

"Is the boy naked?" Father Dominic asked.

"What? Yes. Well, he's bent over a toilet or the counter in a bathroom. I'm afraid this is something I've done. A ritual."

"Tell me about the boy," came the priest's soft voice through the grate.

"His buttocks are arched."

"And is his skin smooth?"

"What?"

"I mean . . . are there signs of violence?"

"N-no," Clearfather stammered and he caught again the scent of raisins, a hint of corruption like halitosis and rosewater.

"How do you feel when you are with him?"

"I don't know if I have been with him! I don't know who he is or where he is!"

"But you want him."

"No! I don't like little boys. Are you listening to me?" Suddenly the priest's hoarse breathing made Clearfather think that the old man was listening too closely.

"You know what I think?"

"No!" the priest gurgled. "I haven't!"

"You're lying," Clearfather said, and he imagined he could feel the old man's soul, tumorous and ulcerated, smushing through the grate like some dank cheese.

"Who . . . who are you?" the old man gasped.

Clearfather swallowed hard, fighting back the sickness he felt in his gut. And he heard, like a voice reverberating through the sanctuary, but inside his own head . . . *a Man of Storms* . . .

"Who . . . who are you?" the old priest cried again, the tremor in his tone rising.

"I'm not a pheasant plucker, I'm the Pheasant Plucker's son, but I'll keep on plucking pheasants till the Pheasant Plucker comes."

The priest choked and laid his head against the mesh. "Father forgive me . . . I dream about it like you do. We are the same."

"No!" sighed Clearfather. "We're not. I don't know how it works . . . but those dreams aren't mine! But you, Father—as if you deserve that name!"

The quotation scraped into his back burned like magnesium.

"I know!" the old priest shrieked into his trembling hands. "But it's not just me! There are many—and they really do things! All the time! I only have evil *dreams*."

Clearfather retched and stomped out of the box, smashing the door on his side behind him. Outside, the air was full of grit and ethanol but now it seemed refreshing. A troop of Hare Krishnas paraded past. He fell in behind them and followed their chanting and drumming to the next street, where his head started to clear and the wicked burning on his back began to ease.

Father Dominic checked his pulse and waited until he was sure the man was gone. Then he heard a sound between a whisper and a snap. He moved to open the panel in the chamber but the door wouldn't open. He had to stay calm, compose himself. The dreams of the boys—they'd misled him. He prayed under his breath and then had to inch closer to the grate. He had the funny feeling that the confession box was getting smaller. He dabbed the moisture from his brow. His hands were shaking. The door wouldn't open. He called out. The air was as thick as old velvet. How could the box shrink? This is crazy, he thought. But he couldn't shake the idea that the space was contracting. He found it hard to breathe. There was no room! But it couldn't be. This is what comes of listening to people unburden their hearts and open their heads. It was just a moment of weakness—not like years and years of actual . . .

Oh, my God, he thought . . . the confessional chamber *is* getting smaller . . . it's closing in on me . . . "Help!" he called. "Someone! Please! *Forgive me . . .*"

CHAPTER 7

Ghost Meat

Clearfather felt a pain in his brain. Everything seemed repellent. Degenerate. Time to get back to the bus station and back on the road. An obscure little town with a name like Dustdevil, Texas, sounded like too small a place for someone not to know him if he had any connection there. And if he didn't, then he'd know the map was a dud and he'd have to form another plan.

He headed back toward the depot, trying to stay in line with the radiant Chung Center. Before he knew it, though, he found himself in a maze of derailed boxcars and shanties. Crushed car bodies stood balanced like houses of cards—colored smoke clouding between charred mannequins. Women of all ages fell back on disintegrating couches or in the trunks of cars with their legs spread. They called to him in trance-weary voices. He saw people with artificial limbs, naked men and boys sprawled over car hoods, drift nets stretched like spiderwebs, bodies wriggling—the smell of unwashed genitals like rancid lard and rotting fish. He turned to run and then he heard a scream very close by.

Behind a fluorescent graffitied Dumpster a gang of dark youths had stripped a white boy. Standing guard was a tall black man wearing a wig of fiber-optic glass nails, a codpiece that featured an LED display flashing the word SLICK—and emu-hide boots under a full-length wolverine coat. Cradled in one arm was a sawed-off Mossberg, while at his side was a genetically modified Presa Canario dog.

"What you want, Cue Ball?" the man said.

It occurred to Clearfather that he could get killed if he didn't get out of there right away. But if he did, then the boy was dead.

"This little faggot's rich," one of the kids panted. "Whatchyou think we should do?"

"Why doan you cut off one-a his arms an' fuck 'im widdit?" The black man smiled. "Violence is golden, baby."

"Stop it!" Clearfather shouted, heaving a brick against the Dumpster.

"Girl," said the black man, frowning. "What up with you, huh? Cain'tchya see ma boys got bad head shit they workin' out? Ya know, therapy?"

"Stop," Clearfather said, feeling a hot pain fill his head. "Now."

"Now? Muthafukka, did I hear you say *now* . . . to me?"

The gangstas, sensing fresh meat, eased for a moment. The white boy spluttered up a bubble of blood. Clearfather saw that it was the same kid from the Greyhound men's room. He'd lost his Madonna and Child lens.

"Leave him alone," Clearfather said. Then the pain was gone and the words of a song began to form in his mind—a song that for some reason he thought Aunt Vivian and Uncle Waldo had taught him.

"Stand back," Clearfather instructed, and one of the boys let go.

"Girl, you startin' to annoy me," the tall man spat. "You do not want to annoy Sir Slick—Dr. Double Barrel, the Wolverine Dean. Ma dick is longer, ma gun is bigger, ma dog is badder—"

"First of all," said Clearfather—and to the gangbangers' surprise he unzipped his pants.

"Shit, homes! Check it out!"

"¡Por Dios!"

"Second, that's a funny-looking gun you got."

Sir Slick raised the Mossberg but found that he wasn't holding a shotgun anymore, it was a golf club—a sand wedge to be precise.

"Fuckin' hell!" one of the kids cried.

"¡El Diablo!"

Slick flung the club away.

"And third . . ." Clearfather snapped his fingers and the 160-pound dog came over to him and sat down beside him.

The attack dog was a mass of gristle and muscle packed under a scabby coat of brindle and black hair that looked like beer and bone-meal mixed with mud. Its chest was as deep as a mandrill's but it was the head that was the biggest worry—a blunt-force trauma skull with little crusted razor-blade ears and lacerated jowls frothy with saliva. Still, behind its lockjaw ruthlessness, in the dim black sump holes of its eyes, Clearfather could see an anguish and a fear that reminded him of a child in hiding, a boy in a closet—waiting for a bad man to pass by the door. He held out his hand and the mutant lolled out an engorged wet tongue that still had the faint but distinct iron odor of blood.

"All 'ight. So y'all doan scare easy."

"I'm not sure I scare at all," Clearfather said and patted the great beast.

"Man who doan scare end up daid fast," Slick spat.

"You ever die before?" Clearfather replied, still smiling.

"¿Qué hacemos?" one of the streetfighters called.

"Well, bro," Slick whistled, shaking his glass-bristling skull, trying to regain his cool. "Y'all got some gear on ya, I gotsta admit that. And ya got a serious hocus psychosis thang happenin'. Butchyou still wrong about the gun, son. That's why we *all* have 'em!" And the other six demonstrated his point. "Now, let that little white punk go

or cut his throat quick. 'Cause I want to castrate this bald muthafukka. I'm gonna slice yer dick off an' keep it in a jar in ma crib—
whatchyou think a-that?"

"They don't make jars that big." Clearfather shrugged. "Now toss
all the guns in the Dumpster and let the boy go."

"Who are you muthafukka?" Slick cried.

"I'm not a pheasant plucker, I'm the Pheasant Plucker's son, but
I'll keep on plucking pheasants till the Pheasant Plucker comes,"
Clearfather answered, and one by one the punks lobbed their guns
into the Dumpster and let the white boy go. Half naked, cut and
bleeding, the kid staggered off between the mangled cars.

Slick was truly scared now. Nothing like this had ever happened
even when he was Hexing.

"Now," Clearfather said. "We're going to sing a song. It's an easy
song to remember. But very hard to forget."

In his mind he heard the cheerful voices of Aunt Vivian and
Uncle Waldo, as if teaching a small child a nursery rhyme.

"Just you boys now. Ready? *Here comes Peter Cotton Tail . . . hoppin' down the Bunny Trail . . . hippity, hippity, hop, hop, hop . . . hippity, hippity, hop, hop, hop . . ."*

The gangbangers' faces glassed over.

"C'mon now, everybody sing along!" Clearfather called. *"Here
comes Peter Cotton Tail . . . hoppin' down that ole Bunny Trail . . ."*

One by one the boys began to chant the words until it became a
song.

"Now put a few moves to it," Clearfather directed. "Some hopping and clapping."

And off they went . . . all singing and clapping.

Alone now, Slick was beyond fear.

"I'll let you take off your boots," Clearfather offered.

"Y-you w-want my b-boots?"

"I'm just thinking you'd run faster without them."

"P-please!" Slick whimpered, his head pouring sweat, his illuminated codpiece trembling ridiculously until it sparked.

"I believe you've pissed yourself," Clearfather remarked. "I'll give you a head start to make it sporting."

The gang leader was talking to himself in a high, crazed whisper now. He stripped off his fancy coat, his boots, and the damp, shorted-out codpiece. His wig he hurled at the Dumpster, the comlinks shattering—and with a yelp he shot off through the wasteland. Clearfather waited.

"What are you gonna do? Let the dog loose?" he heard a plaintive voice ask.

It was the white boy. He'd struggled into what was left of his dirty clothes and had wiped the blood off his face, but his lower, cosmetically thickened lip had been split.

"No," Clearfather answered. "What Slick thinks is chasing him is much scarier than this fellow . . . and a lot faster."

"How the hell did you do that stuff?"

"I don't know," Clearfather admitted. "I think God was working through me."

He tried to picture Uncle Waldo's and Aunt Vivian's faces.

"Shit," said the kid. "I guess—I should thank you. What's . . . your . . . name?"

"You can call me Mr. Clearfather. I'm going to need money and to find a hotel. They said you were rich. Is that that true?"

"Y-yeah." The boy nodded. "But I don't have any money on me. And no hotel is going to let you keep that dog. You want to stay at my house?"

"I . . . I don't know," Clearfather mumbled, suspiciously.

"You can bring the dog."

CHAPTER 8

The Life You Save

The boy seemed to know his way through the maze, which was a good thing. With the pale sun getting lower, more alarming figures began appearing: Nazis, nurses, brides, Boy Scouts.

"What's your name?"

"Wilton Brand," the boy replied. "My father's King Brand, as in Kingland Brand, former CEO of American United Steel."

The names meant nothing to Clearfather.

"You shouldn't be hanging around a place like this," he said as they passed a cage full of Asian girls.

"Don't you think I know that?" the boy quipped. "It's the Pandora. At first it was like this beautiful cloud. Everyone lusting after me—always feeling good about myself. Then the nightmare started."

Clearfather peered around at the amputees sloshing in creamed corn—the fat men squirming like salamis in their nets—and the desperate crones lashed to the wheels. The Canario growled.

"You gonna keep the dog?" the kid asked.

"I can't just abandon him. Or you."

"What are you gonna call him?"

"Warhol, I think. You . . . look like you're feeling better."

"Yeah," Wilton replied, surprised. "Sometimes when you've scored you get a little peace—but not like this."

"Maybe you can get off the drug," Clearfather suggested. "Can't you get help?"

"Where have you been?"

"I'm having memory problems."

"Shit. The drug was supposed to *be* help. That's how Nang's Disease and Increased Simplification Dependency Syndrome got started. Efram-Zev invents diseases. That's why Vitessa bought them up. They just applied their Designer Virus strategy from the cyberside to pharmaceuticals."

"How could people fall for that?" Clearfather asked as they crossed paths with a bandaged woman leading a little girl in a party dress.

"You'll see," the boy said as they stepped clear of the wrecks onto a long wet street of open grates. Halfway down was a concrete bunker where his car was parked, although the term *car* scarcely did it justice. The vehicle, branded a Nomadder, was more appropriately described as a hybrid troop carrier/Japanese all-wheel-drive mobile home.

"Fix yourself a drink or a snack," Wilton nodded, indicating the vehicle's galley kitchen and wet bar. "I'm going to grab a quick shower."

Clearfather sat down in one of the chairs shaped like a nude girl. The interior of the vehicle stank of alcohol, sweat, and old pizza. Dirty panties, tubs of lubricant, and various dildos cluttered the floor. Waves of depression washed over him. There was something about this troubled teenager that made him think of the boy in the bathroom in his vision (or was it his memory?). Guilt, fear? He didn't feel anything like sexual desire, which was an intense relief given all that he'd just seen. But there was something—poised between hope and sadness.

It occurred to him that he was old enough to be the boy's father, and he tried to feel inside himself for any recollection, any clues that might indicate whether he had children. But there was nothing. Just fuzzy hints of memories . . . Aunt Vivian and Uncle Waldo working at jigsaw and crossword puzzles . . . a porch at sunset . . . bright warm shapes whose faces were lost in the sun.

He heard a heavy bass line thumping through the insulated wall and rose to inspect the rest of the habitat. There was a small iridium box on the counter that sprang open at his touch. Inside rested a crystalline lozenge that resembled a pink argyle diamond, but had a cloying scent like marzipan—a dose of Pandora, he guessed. On the floor in the kitchen were piled Sapporo beer cans, Russian cigarette butts, condoms, and porno comic books full of zombies having sex, but around the corner he noticed a swath of blue silk like a curtain. Underneath was a bulletin board, thick with digital photograms. Some of the pictures were images from childhood . . . birthday cakes and trail rides . . . clowns, watermelons. In each of these pictures, the boy whom Clearfather presumed to be Wilton looked so small and fragile. The majority of the pictures, however, were from more recent times and focused on a willowy young girl with curly auburn hair. An older Wilton posed with her in a garden or on a riverboat. There was a wistfulness and a longing to the pictures that filled Clearfather with a deep ache. He let the soiled swath fall back into place and turned to see the boy dressed in fresh clothes.

"I'm . . . sorry," Clearfather said.

"That's Nikki. See, I'm straight really."

"I didn't mean to pry."

"It was my fault," Wilton responded, not seeming to hear.

"She's . . . pretty," Clearfather said.

"She's dead. And I'm not," Wilton replied.

"Hm. Well, not for lack of trying." Clearfather sighed.

"What do you know?" scowled the boy.

"I bet she died of the same drug that's killing you almost as fast as the guilt that's eating you up inside," the bald man answered.

The boy was about to hurl some insult but stopped in midsentence.

"Who the hell are you, mister?"

"I don't know," Clearfather admitted.

"*What* are you?" the boy sputtered.

"I'm wondering that myself."

"You wanna save me—is that it?" The boy laughed.

"I have. Once."

Wilton Brand appeared not to know how to take this remark.

"You'll be paid. My parents are rich. Not compared with Wynn Fencer—but rich enough."

"Who's Wynn Fencer?" Clearfather asked.

"Shit, you really do have a memory problem!" the boy scoffed. He picked up a moldy slice of cheese injected pizza then flipped it into the sink. "Fencer founded the Vitessa Cultporation. He's the richest man on the planet."

Clearfather tried to nod. These names from the larger world didn't interest him much. His concern was for this rich spoiled abandoned boy who spent his time and money humiliating himself with strangers and worshiping at a secret shrine, trying to regain his lost childhood and his first love, who died of the same fate that was stalking him. Clearfather noticed a bead of collagen oozing from the crack in the boy's lower lip. He wondered what he'd been like when he'd been that age. Lonely? Confused? Frightened? Whatever the answer was, it lay hidden behind a veil.

"It's time to go home now," he said.

The boy went silent and gestured toward the cab that was laid out like the cockpit of a commercial jetliner. Minutes later they were battling the hordes crossing the Allegheny. Eidolons advertising McTavish's (YEER HAGGIS IS REDDY!) and Chu's (TODAY'S SPECIAL: SALMON STOMACHS IN A TANGY PLUM SAUCE) ghosted over tanks of LPG and a village of stilt huts. Back behind them, Pittsburgh seemed to be undergoing some kind of biorobotic transformation. Mirror-bright towers and cylinders of tensuron shared the same block with older buildings that would've been called skyscrapers once, which were now imprisoned in scaffolding. In residential pockets of blight, steep tarpaper-roofed frame houses alternated with Médecins Sans Frontières trailers. Open-air flea markets pooled like oil, and heavily armored luxury hotels and apartments glared out over tent cities.

The minor bridges were all clogged with traffic, as the Fort Duquesne span now resembled an apocalyptic wagon train frozen in time. The dirty genetech bomb that Al-Waqi'a had used to attack Three Rivers Stadium during the World Series had had an unexpected effect, creating a weather-resistant botanical jungle so that all of Clemente Memorial Park was rampant with giant orchids and carnivorous plants—a fact that did not stop the homeless from seeking refuge there or hunting parties of river people exploring at their peril. Clearfather's eyes darted back and forth, trying to take it all in.

"You really don't remember who you are?" Wilton queried, blasting the horn at a wild dog pack. "Who do you think you could be?"

Clearfather figured there was no reason not to be honest. "At first I thought I'd escaped from a mental hospital—or that I was some sort of agent—drugged or conditioned to forget. What do you think? You seem to have been around."

Warhol gave Clearfather's face a bestial lick.

"Well . . . ," Wilton mused. "Apart from the born-for-porn potential, I'd say you've got the makings of a kick-ass magician. You just need a good manager."

The boy seemed so much calmer and more normal now, it was hard for the bald man not to smile. "Don't hide my light under a bushel, huh?"

"You said you thought God was working through you?"

"I didn't—don't—know—how else to put it," Clearfather said, frowning again. He didn't think it was wise to mention Aunt Vivian and Uncle Waldo. Or the vaguer form of the man at the radio station.

"I don't believe in God but I haven't felt this free of the Pandora since the first week," Wilton said. "Maybe you're some kind of healer. In any case I'm grateful for you helping me. I'll make sure you get paid well."

'Thanks," said Clearfather. "I didn't do it for the money, though."

"So . . . why . . . did you do it?"

"I don't know . . . ," Clearfather answered after a moment. "Because—I'm here."

"Some kind of savior."

Clearfather shrank at this comment, but, turning to face his young driver, he noticed that the boy's face was open and relaxed now, free of any malice or arrogance.

"I guess the question is . . . what kind?"

They drove through a crowd of demonstrating Kurds and Wilton activated the roof-mounted water cannons, which cleared a path all the way to the Access Way. They were headed northwest beside the Ohio River. Out of the left-hand windows Clearfather spotted the long grim outline of an island. Once a lush, treed home to scores of small farms, Neville Island had in its industrial prime been an inferno of steel spark/coke plant/cement manufacturing. Now all that remained of those ash-rain times was a mountain of pig iron, the boarded-up remnant of the Sunoco plasticizer facility, and row upon row of haz-chem drums that marked the boundary of the Red Cross station and Fong's Trash & Treasure.

A right-hand turn up Blackburn Road took them through Sewickley Heights and higher up the hills into the misnamed but far more exclusive, fortified seclusion of Fern Hollow. They passed through a guard station into woods of budding oak trees and scrub laurel—then through a rusted iron gate beside which two birdshit-stained granite lions brooded, and then down a long winding private drive.

Through the windows of the Nomadder, Clearfather could make out a dilapidated wrought-iron fence and a desiccated ivy wall running into an older barricade of hand-stacked fieldstones from which one might have expected a loaded musket to appear—perhaps aiming at that mythical squirrel that supposedly could have once hopped all the way to Iowa without touching the ground.

When at last in view, Wilton's "house" proved to be an immense decaying Victorian spectacle of gingerbread bowsprits and steeples, widow's walks, cupolas, towers, chimneys, and belfries. The boy drove straight toward a stable that had been converted into a high-tech garage and shut down the engine system.

"I still have both kidneys," he announced, as if this were uncommon. "That's my bargaining power with the old man."

"And how old is your father?" Clearfather inquired, scanning the grounds. Even in the fading light it was plain to see that the grand estate had seen grander days. The tennis courts were frost-heaved and all the topiary animals looked like hedgehogs, while in the once majestic animal park a lone wildebeest sheltered in a prefab kids' clubhouse.

"A hundred and twenty-five or so—but his new wife, my mom, is seventy, although he thinks she's sixty. That's why Pop's Will is so important and can be altered at any minute. Whoever's in the good books then could win the pot and be able to make life miserable for everyone else. Meanwhile Pop sits on a few boards, smokes and drinks, and is able to conduct his feud with Julian Dingler."

"Who's that?" Clearfather asked.

"Regional head of Vitessa R and D. Our nearest neighbor. Dad had him set up the house's intelligence system and now he's paranoid Dingler's spying on us."

"What was *that*?" Clearfather asked as a howl rose out of the falling dark.

"Our mastiffs. Whatever you do, don't go wandering the grounds alone."

Warhol roared back and then produced a large steaming poo on the walkway.

"Don't worry." Wilton chuckled. "It's what everyone else in the family does!"

CHAPTER 9

The Abyss Stares Back

Outside the carriage house garage, another distinctive sound reached their ears—an electronic hum and compressed-air hiss. Warhol grew tense. As the shape entered the field of light from the lantern overhead, it became clear that it was the remains of a man built into an organically sympathetic variation on a mobile gantry robot, although it was impossible to tell where the man ended and the machine began. He wore a black smartfiber jacket over a white shirt with a high collar—and where a face should've been there was a mask made of polished chrome, which acted as a convex mirror, so that observers were confronted with a fun-house distortion of their own faces. If Clearfather hadn't been distracted by the silvery light he would've warned the man about the dogshit, but as it was one of the polyurethane platform feet came down on the pile, so he thought it best not to say anything. Warhol rumbled.

"Restrain that brute or I'll taser you all," the mask echoed.

"Come here, Warhol," Clearfather called.

"How did you know I was referring to the dog? And where have you been, you little pervert—out sucking blood?"

"Good evening to you, too, Hooper," Wilton replied. "I trust you've been keeping my mother happy?"

"Who's this?" the mask demanded, pointing at Clearfather. "One of your new boyfriends? I thought you were going back to being straight."

"This man saved my life," Wilton announced with a hint of pride. "He's going to be staying with us tonight."

"Is that so?" the mask echoed. "Well, Old Smokey's having a dinner party. There's going to be an update of the Will. Ernst has wet his pants over something and is refusing to come. Improves the odds, eh? Drinks at seven sharp in the library. Be there or be square. And don't let me hear about any problems with that dog."

The man-machine hissed and clunked off with the dogshit clinging to his foot.

"It's so hard to find operational help these days." Wilton grinned.

"Who was that?" Clearfather asked.

"That's Hooper, our butler and my mom's lover. Dad owned a factory where Hooper was a foreman until he got between two robot assembly systems that were having a dispute. Dad's company couldn't meet the insurance payout so Dad got his personal reconstruction doctor, Hugh Wieviel, to do as good a rebuild as he could and invited the guy in to live with us. Now Hooper bangs my mother. See, I'm a lab job. One of her frozen eggs from ages ago and some of Dad's old sperm."

"So . . . your mother . . . she's your dad's second wife . . . ?"

"She's his fifth wife. His first wife, who died in the car accident that paralyzed my half brother Ainsley—she was cremated and is in an urn in his study."

"What happened to his second wife?"

"She was stuffed and is mounted in his study. His third wife was frozen and is in a secret vault on the property waiting to be thawed out and revived."

"What about the fourth?"

"Her heart may still beat for Dad. I suspect he recycled her organs after the 'illness' that came upon her down in Rio."

"And . . . you all live on this estate together?"

"There's more." Wilton winked. "Way back before Mom—or Ravena—married Dad, she had triplets. Three sons. They're about forty years older than me. You'll meet them all. Hooper said we're having a dinner party tonight? We have a dinner party every night, and every night there's an update to the Will."

Warhol raised a deep guttural concern, which Clearfather seconded. If it wasn't for his need of money, he'd have preferred to take his chances back along one of the riverbanks.

"And who's Old Smokey?" he asked the boy as they made their way toward the mansion, which looked like some mad dollhouse crammed with halogen flashlights.

"Dad. He's one of the last of the great chain smokers. Chain drinker, too. That's why he's trawling for a new liver. I think this is number four. But you have to remember to call him the Man of Steel. That's what people called him back when he was CEO of American United Steel."

"Are we going to meet him now?"

"No, I think we should ease into it," Wilton said. "Let's go explore the weird world of Ernst first."

"Who's that?"

"He's my other half brother. He's a hundred. His real brother Ainsley is ninety-something—and has been bedridden for around eighty years. Dad worships Ainsley. He's paid for hundreds of operations for him over the years and has set up an entire wing of the main house for him as a closed-circuit TV studio with cam units and monitors throughout the estate. Despite all the surgery, I used to have bad dreams about him, so I just interface with him on screen."

"Don't you still see his face?" Clearfather asked.

"Yeah, but . . . uh . . . it's distorted . . . like people whose identity remains secret."

Warhol made another Baskervillean grumble.

"Can Warhol come?" Clearfather asked.

"Why not?" Wilton laughed. "More fuel for the fire!"

To get to Ernst's side of the estate they had to cross the remains of the lumpy croquet ground and the marsh of the bowling green—then weave through a barren orchard and across the soggy polo field to where the observatory had burned down—then over a wobbly bridge spanning a septic-smelling pond to the former caretaker's house, which was enclosed by a fumigation tent.

"Aha," said Wilton. "They'll be in the Pleasure Prism."

At first glance Ernst Brand appeared to be a bearded, useless gentleman in his late fifties, although Clearfather realized it was possible that with the right medications and surgical procedures he could be much older. Seventy-five, perhaps—but a hundred? They found him wearing a cashmere sweater and L.L. Bean loafers with a Patek Philippe attached to his wrist, attempting to mix a martini from a portable mini bar in the foyer of a glass building that looked like a giant chandelier designed by Frank Lloyd Wright.

"This is Mr. Clearfather," Wilton said. "He saved my life."

"I'm celebrating tonight," Ernst replied. "I'm boycotting the dinner party. Thorndike is preparing predinner punch and then fresh mudcrab with an unoaked Chardonnay, and crème du chocolat silvered with ice-cold Polish vodka and glazed with Cointreau."

Clearfather could feel a twinge of pain in his head. Here was a man whose younger brother, full or half, had just returned home in the company of a stranger he said had saved his life—and the discussion focused on mudcrab?

Ernst led them deeper inside. They found huge primeval ferns and several glass structures, which were models of the larger building. The first case was an aquarium filled with amphibious salamanders of various colors.

"Axolotls," Brand said. "The Aztecs associated them with resurrection, monstrosities, and twins. I like them because they're neotenic, which means they can live their whole life in an adolescent state. They also have the handy ability of regenerating limbs."

"What's in this case?" Clearfather asked icily.

"Look closer." Brand waved. "Nature loves to hide."

"They're alive!"

"Stick insects . . . acquired outside Puerto Maldonado, a fever-ridden village on a sluggish brown tributary of the Amazon River.

"And this," he continued, tapping at a terrarium. "Doesn't it look like it came from another planet?"

"Mr. Brand," Clearfather began. "Are you aware that your little brother has a serious drug problem that will kill him if he doesn't get help?"

"It's a lungfish! Dates back to Carboniferous times. The earth was a very different planet then. Come along now—to poolside."

Warhol became interested in the lungfish.

"Starting to understand?" Wilton queried.

"What's the matter with him? Clearfather whispered.

"He has what's been diagnosed as PAID—Personal Attention Interruption Disorder. Goes back to the accident that crippled Ainsley. Dad became so fixated on Ainsley that Ernst's sense of himself became fragmented and discontinuous. It's affected how he sees and hears things. Now he has delusions that a TWIN broadcast crew comes to do profiles of his life. He's leading a tour now. His shrink says it helps make him feel like he's earned all this."

"Hasn't he?"

"Shit, no! All this is Dad's. Except for Mom, no one's earned any real money in decades. Not yet anyway. Mom was a Playpen star. Then she did that show—*And Justine for All*. Played the wisecracking judge with the huge knockers. Now she's the Fidget Woman, star of *Twitch 'n' Shout*. Got her own clothing label and a line of accessories. But you have to be careful. She's on a strict vodka-and-Ritalin diet and will fuck anything that walks."

Brand led them through a revolving door into a tiled area, where they found an exotically landscaped swimming pool. The air was heavy and moist. Great damp fiddlehead ferns rose from behind sandstone boulders and chunks of porous black volcanic rock. Clearfather glanced up and saw several peacocks roosting on top of the glass roof outside. Every once in a while one would let loose with a lonely cat-like cry.

They continued into a section of saunas and spas. Here, a woman Brand referred to as Jocelyn emerged from a flotation coffin in a one-piece floral bathing suit and began hosing herself off with a detachable shower nozzle, moaning.

"This thing of darkness. A wife—by a previous marriage," Brand explained, imagining a three-quarter camera angle. "A tragedy occurred that has affected her mind. But I've opened my heart, providing her with sanctuary. After all, they say altruism is a side effect of a large brain." He went in for a close-up.

"We were living on Cape Cod. Long ago. A bold foray into the world. She met a hotshot young surgeon with eyes like Paul Newman and a washboard stomach. Jocelyn got the good doctor to marry her the day our divorce became final. Then one day the bottom fell out. Seems the good doctor had never graduated from med school! He was a gifted amateur who looked the part—and for all intents and purposes *was* the part—until he botched an operation and the patient died. The family hired a private eye. He dug up the dirt and they blew the whistle. Unfortunately Jocelyn had become obsessed with having the doctor's baby. Odd-looking child. Reminded me of the potto, the ghost monkey of West Africa. Anyway, all was well until the doctor got sprung. Then the trauma of exposure, the anxiety about the impending civil and criminal actions, not to mention the loss of his high-powered lifestyle, drove him to despair and he strapped the child to his chest in one of those Snug-A-Bug baby carriers and jumped off the top of Boston General."

They were about to continue the tour when Jocelyn removed her bathing suit and began to finger herself.

"Where's your baby, dear?" Brand asked. "Ah, here it is." He sighed and with a flourish whipped from the tank a naked plastic doll with a vague, colorless face, as if the features had dissolved in the saline water. "Yet another one of these politically correct surrogate babies. Any features that suggest ethnicity have been detoxified—and of course it's ungendered."

Jocelyn accepted the dripping doll with a clucking sound, and they passed through another revolving door into the butterfly enclosure, a room of netting that draped down from the ceiling so that the glass appeared to be melting into a slowly collapsing spiderweb. In the middle stood a young woman. Perched on her shoulder was a blue Zalmoxis butterfly.

"Rachel, my love," Brand said, beaming. Rachel looked to be about twenty-four and wore Italian trousers with suspenders and a white oxford cloth shirt, strategically unbuttoned to reveal her impressive cleavage. She gave Wilton a wanton smile and Clearfather a frank appraisal of his groin as the butterfly flitted away.

Thorndike, the chef, rang a bell, and they adjourned to the dining area to find an enormous silver punch bowl filled with a fruity concoction that reeked of rum.

"And now a toast!" called Ernst Brand.

Clearfather reached for one of the punch cups and said, "Yes, a toast! To Wilton, who has come back from the dead. May you all support him in his rehabilitation!"

Ernst Brand's face went from smiling for the cameras to an expression of bewilderment. The TWIN broadcast team vanished. There were no celebrity interviewers. He was looking straight at a bald man he didn't recognize, holding forth in his conservatory.

"We were toasting *me!*" he thundered—his face going scarlet. "*Me!* Who in the fuck are *you?*"

"I'm not a pheasant plucker, I'm the Pheasant Plucker's son, but I'll keep on plucking pheasants till the Pheasant Plucker comes," Clearfather replied, and it occurred to him that perhaps Uncle Waldo and Aunt Vivian had taught him this, too.

Ernst peered into the punch bowl as Clearfather spoke. He couldn't take his eyes off his reflection. His beard was gone. In fact, any signs of aging were gone. His face was like that of Jocelyn's baby doll, sanitized of all features and character—deformed to the point of blankness. Ernst raised his head and uttered a strangled yelp that shook every window. The peacocks scratched across the roof. One lifted off in a blur and came crashing through a pane, smashing into one of the kerosene heaters, which exploded into the butterfly enclosure. The collision jarred one of the giant aquariums, creating a domino effect of broken glass, gushing water, and flopping fins.

Just then Jocelyn appeared, stark naked, waving the politically correct doll by its leg and sputtering, "This isn't my baby!" She pitched the doll into the punch bowl, splashing fruit rinds everywhere, and went over and found the peacock, its feathers slick with blood. She picked up the limp body and laid the long broken neck over her shoulder. "My baby's dead," she said.

CHAPTER 10

One Blessing

Wilton and Clearfather made a hasty exit following the peculiar disruption, which forced Ernst and his little clan to take refuge in the house surrounded by the fumigation tent. Warhol refused to leave the Pleasure Prism before devouring the lungfish—which he enjoyed without appreciating the creature's Carboniferous ancestry. As a consequence, Wilton convinced Clearfather that the dog would be better off in the car barn for the night, where they provided him with water and a modest snack. Clearfather, who was growing fond of his exuberant friend, bid a reluctant farewell, staring out over the Man of Steel's estate to the windows of his neighbor Julian Dingler. It was a large place, from what he could see, and seemingly empty at the moment.

The boy broke his reverie with a tap on the arm and led him to the Brands' main residence, but Clearfather took such pains wiping his feet in the mud room he missed seeing which way Wilton went and found himself suddenly alone amid brass spittoons and hollow elephant legs to hold umbrellas.

At the end of the hall he came to the Pacific Room. With the exception of a well-preserved paddlefish and Patagonian skins of guanacos and seals, the highlight was an embalmed Gilbert Islander in full battle regalia, which consisted of coconut fiber armor with a shark's teeth spear and a porcupine-like helmet made of blowfish skin.

Security cams hummed from the cornices. Then he heard another sound. Someone breathing hard—or crying?—in the next room. He checked the door, which swung open. The room was stocked with barbells and exercise machines spread out over polished Baltic pine floorboards. A woman in a unitard turned and her reflection swept across the mirrored walls, seeming to age with each panel.

"I'm sorry—" Clearfather blurted and realized that this might be the current lady of the house. Wilton's words of warning came back to haunt him . . .

"Don't be sorry," the woman commanded. "Just pass me that drink bottle."

She took a swig from a Goa water bottle, which made her scowl and spit the liquid out. "Who put pineapple juice in my Pineapple Juice?"

"I'm s-sorry?"

"I told you—don't be sorry!"

She peeled off her damp Lycra, prodigious breasts jutting forward.

"Feel these boobs. Feels like they got concrete in 'em, doesn't it? I'm gonna sue the ball off the prick who did this to me. I used to be beautiful. Now look at me!"

Clearfather wasn't sure what to say, which was just as well because she took another swig and her mood changed.

"Ya wanna fluff my muff?" she asked in a baby-doll voice. "Huh? Jes a little roll in the hay right here on the floor? C'mon. I can't take these drugs anymore. Jes a little drink mean shit. He drinks 'cause he's dyin', but me, I gotta say sober—say thin—give older women a role model. I ain't no older woman! I'm a goddamn beautiful woman! Is the plastic surgeons that screwed up!"

She picked up one of the barbells. Then she proceeded to smash the mirrored panels. When all of them were shattered, she collapsed on a rowing machine to catch her breath, and that was when Clearfather made the mistake of taking his eyes off her. She was able to lunge for his pants before he could react.

"I gotta have some!" she snargled, wrenching at his underwear. Out sprang Clearfather's penis—the sight of which seemed to stun her.

"Shit!" she screamed and fell to the floor, where she went into a spasm of pelvic bucking. He'd never seen a topless older woman with gigantic breasts squirming out of a sweaty unitard on a polished pine floor covered with pieces of broken mirror.

At the peak of the fit, she rose, sprang, and bit into Clearfather's left hand, which triggered a shiver of pain that sent his right fist flying forward. There was a *snap-crack* sound like a jaw breaking and she keeled over with a thud—as a Voice filled the room—like the ones he'd been hearing in his head.

"What's the difference between a nun and a woman sitting in a bath?" The Voice chuckled. "Hm? One's got a soul full of hope. The other's got a hole full of soap."

"What?"

"I'm like Mr. Whoopee."

"Who?" Clearfather asked, trying to locate the speaker and adjust his clothes—when he remembered. *Ainsley* . . .

"Ever heard of a pre-Millennium cartoon called *Tennessee Tuxedo?*" the Voice answered. "Smart-ass penguin. Had a sidekick named Chumly, a dumb but lovable walrus. They'd get into trouble and have to turn to Phineas J. Whoopee, the Man with All the Answers. Every episode Mr. Whoopee would pull out his Amazing Three-Dimensional Blackboard and explain a point of science that would help Tennessee and Chumly. You see—"

Hooper burst through the door and proceeded to drag the woman across the floor by her ankles.

"Pay no attention to the man behind the curtain," the Voice commanded.

"What curtain?" Clearfather asked.

"It's a joke," the Voice said. "You aren't very good with jokes, are you? Where do you find a turtle with its legs cut off?"

"I don't know," Clearfather said.

"Wherever you left him."

"Where are you anyway?"

"The dervish says, 'Wherever you turn you see God's face.'"

"Why can't I see yours?"

"Miss Piggy smashed in the monitor. Here's another one. There are ten birds sitting on a branch of a tree, and a man with a gun shoots one. How many are left?"

"Was it a shotgun . . . or a rifle?"

"It doesn't matter," the Voice said. "How many birds are left?"

"I . . . I don't know," Clearfather said. "N-nine?"

"Ten birds on a branch and a man shoots one. There are *no* birds left. They all fly away. Hooper's coming back. Go out the door and turn left. Right?"

"Turn left," Clearfather mumbled, crunching broken glass underfoot. All he could think of was, yes, of course . . . they all fly away.

Ainsley's blurred face followed him through the rooms of the mansion, appearing inside tiny monitors that began protruding from hidden panels inside the walls. Clearfather had to find Wilton to explain why he'd knocked his mother out. Then he heard the telltale hiss and clunk of Hooper's robotic frame and smelled the unmistakable odor of dogshit. He hid behind a sideboard.

The clunk moved on. Up ahead the hallway forked, leaving him with a choice of three doors. He chose the middle one and stepped into what looked like a children's playroom that had turned into a cocktail lounge. Nearest to him, a six-foot-tall bottled blonde in a pink chiffon suit stood beside a pool table. She had a bit of five o'clock shadow and a masculine demeanor—an impression that was reinforced by a brimming snifter the size of a goldfish bowl. The second figure in the room was dressed in a pastel barracuda-skin jacket with crushed-linen pants and boots made from the scales of a Gila monster. His hair was pulled back in a ponytail and he was seated in a Barcalounger with a bottle of Chivas between his legs.

By this point, Clearfather was considering that—Pink Chiffon notwithstanding—these people were Wilton's stepbrothers, a notion supported by the third occupant, who had dreadlocks and was extremely fat, dressed in jeans and a faded Grateful Dead T-shirt, puffing away at a bubbling hookah.

"Well?" said Pink Chiffon. "What claim do you have?"

"Claim?"

"Don't play dumb with us! Claim on the Will—the Will!"

"Oh, I don't care about that," Clearfather said.

"You see! He knows about the Will!"

"What is it about this 'Will' anyway?" Clearfather asked. "Can't you see this place is falling down around you?"

This appeared to be a new idea, for the three declared in unison, "It's winner take all! One Will, one way. One blessing, he'll pay!"

"You the Old Man's new bodyguard?"

"He looks like an organ seller!"

"If the Old Man gets a new liver I'm going to need a new heart!" Lizard Boots complained.

"Fuck off," gasped the hookah head. "I've ponied up a kidney."

"I see what this is," said Pink Chiffon. "Did our mother hire you?"

"Are you fucking our mother?"

"No," Clearfather stated. "I wouldn't fuck your mother."

"So you've seen our mother!"

"I came here with Wilton."

"You're fucking Wilton?"

"I'm not fucking Wilton. I'm just helping him out."

"Well, that's not very smart. It's winner take all! One Will, one way!"

"I don't care about the Will! I'm trying to help Wilton off that drug."

"Off the drug?" Lizard Boots squinted. "We just got him on the drug."

"Shut up!" Pink Chiffon snapped.

"What did you say?" Clearfather asked.

"Noth-iinngg!"

"I hope I didn't hear that right."

"Shut up."

"I hope that . . . for your sakes . . . you haven't done anything to that boy."

Pink Chiffon looked in the Roy Rogers mirror and saw that his/her skin tone was becoming hairier. "No!"

"Who are you and what do you want?" Lizard Boots asked, not understanding what Chiffon was seeing.

"To help your stepbrother. My name is Elijah Clearfather."

"Well, I'm . . . I'm Simon(e)," Pink Chiffon managed, thinking that perhaps the hallucination was due to the hormone treatments. "And on hookah tonight is Alvin. Meanwhile, representing the zany world of creepshow bizness is Theodore."

"Sit on it and rotate," Theodore replied, and then to Clearfather, "And that there's Simon(e), failed visionary behind the Fruit BBQ—tireless spokeswoman for the ecological Kanga Burger—mastermind of Salad Days, the convenient frozen salads you defrost in the microwave. Now she's changed hats yet again to become Professor Chicken! Cholesterol-free fried chicken, prepared by secret scientific formula. Lots of spicy flavor, but not a single grain of salt."

"How does he—she do that?" Clearfather asked.

"That's just what they asked him on *America This Morning*. You know what she answered? Nada."

"Shut up, Theo. There'll be a defamation suit and you'll lose."

"Fried chicken will never be healthy—that's why people like it!"

"Say another word and I'm calling my lawyer," Simon(e) threatened.

"Why? Because Professor Chicken is a big frog in a little pond?"

Simon(e) doused Theo with cognac.

"Now I'm gonna nail your ass."

"I don't understand," Clearfather said.

"Professor Chicken franchises secretly serve frogs. You've heard the old saying, 'Tastes like chicken'? Well, it's true. Trouble is, it doesn't *sell* like chicken—at least not among civilized people who can be trusted with nondigital pets."

"I'll get you, Theo," Simon(e) said. One of his/her hands shot into Theodore's pocket and with surgical precision extracted a titanium vial. Simon(e) whipped open the vial and splashed a fine mist of what looked like souchong tea. Theodore screamed and flung himself down on the carpet and began licking and snorting with groveling abandon.

"There," Simon(e) gestured. "Lick that carpet, boy! Don't miss a single precious drop! Hard to believe, but Theo was once a promising filmmaker. Then something unpleasant happened . . . didn't it, Theo?"

Clearfather felt a twinge in his head, followed by a sensation in the scarring on his back—like someone tracing over the letters with menthol.

"Theo's too modest to tell—besides he's sucking carpet—but the gist was that he was going to direct a landmark film—full-scale X-rated sex but with a real story—an honest to God fucking art film. *Priapus* it was called—and he had his male star, a fresh new talent. But Mr. Dinosaur Tool wouldn't do the friggin' gig unless his honey bunny had the female lead. The problem was dear young Theo discovered that the girl was pregnant. So Theo tried to pay the girl off—

get her to bow out gracefully. But before he could do that, the loving couple tied the knot in Vegas, which meant that Theo needed an alternative plan."

"What happened?" Clearfather asked, the menthol heat intensifying.

"Well, in simple terms, my bro flew to Vegas and arranged for the new bride to have too much access to a very questionable recreational drug."

"*Shut up!*" Theo cried.

"He *killed* her?" Clearfather asked, the freezing burn spreading across his back.

"Oh, I wouldn't give Theo credit for having the cojones to do such a thing *directly*. But yes, the girl and her baby died. The plan backfired, though. Mr. D recoiled in mourning and quit the project. Without his contribution, Theo's Yakuza backers pulled out. They wanted their money returned but Theo had already put that up his nose. They said 'No problem. We'll take your head.' Theo had to slink home with his tail between his legs and turn his cinematic skills to animal porn."

Clearfather vomited over the pool table.

"Ooh, shit, dude!" the hookah head exclaimed. "Like, make yourself at home!"

"I've never done animal porn!" Theo whimpered from the floor as Hooper burst into the room.

"Listen up," the machine-man rasped through his mask, not noticing the spew. "You will all be cleaned up and in the library within twenty-five minutes. Bald Boy, you follow me."

Clearfather wiped his mouth and glared in disgust at the brothers.

CHAPTER 11

Professor Chicken's Party

Hooper thumped down the halls like a vending machine playing hard-to-get. At last they arrived in Wilton's wing. The boy was Voyanced into an Uruguayan puppet game show, *Miniature Gaelic Football,* a Winnipeg-based panel called "Guys Who Like Babes Who Like Girls (Who Have Had Babies to Men Who Are in Prison for Killing Women)"—and the TWIN news. Upon seeing Clearfather, the boy disconned. *"Where* did you go?"

"I met some more of your family," Clearfather informed him as the nausea and anger began to subside.

"Shit. Which ones?"

"Your mother—and stepbrothers—although one of them was more like a sister."

"Simon(e). He started off male then he became a female—but he couldn't cope so he switched back—then he couldn't deal with being male so he tried going girlie again but the hormone therapy's giving him trouble. He's got plumbing problems and psychological issues up the yin-yang but he or she's a Harvard MBA and head of Professor Chicken."

"I know," Clearfather said. He couldn't decide if the faintly proud tone in Wilton's voice was honorable or sad—but he didn't have the heart to reveal the base dealings that the stepbrothers had been involved with. "What's on the news?"

Wilton touched a hologram icon and Kasai Owuzu, an African in a Savile Row suit, appeared in 3-D to tell them about the beheadings and castrations in Tehran.

"But now here's our vote for the oddest story of the day, which comes from the Pittsburgh Greyhound bus station of all places, where the eidolons of TWIN presenter Vinata Nidhu and the ChildRite Nurturing Centers' Queen Ubba Dubba and Dooley Duck caused a furor. All three eidolons broke their programming protocols, demonstrating impromptu behavior. Dooley Duck's actions were the most bizarre. The famously insecure blue duck had a cyberrevelation about his sexuality or lack thereof, which has led to a demand to be rendered with 'fully operational genitals.' And it seems that the events in Pittsburgh are not isolated. According to Sanders Lugwich, the head of Creaturetivity, the studio responsible for Ubba Dubba and Dooley Duck, the behavior of the Pittsburgh eidolons has rippled through the network, affecting the manifestations of the characters around the world.

"In an emergency ChildRite board meeting plans were made to write Dooley out of existence, but this may be fraught with more problems than ChildRite has anticipated, as shown by a group of spirited kids in Concord, Massachusetts, who this afternoon staged a nude protest to help save Dooley. Said little Ariel Sturt at the kids' press conference, 'We don't think Dooley should die just because he wants a wiener.' More pro Duck + Dick protests are planned for tomorrow in Cincinnati, Madison, and LosVegas—as well as throughout Europe and the Asia Pacific region."

"You have anything to do with that?" Wilton asked.

"I don't know," Clearfather said truthfully.

"Hm. Maybe the light's coming out from under the bushel."

"I don't know if that's a good thing or not," Clearfather replied.

"You just need a good manager," Wilton reiterated and led Clearfather to an adjoining room with an enormous four-poster bed and a very authentic-looking polar bear rug. "Hose yourself down and try on that penguin suit in the closet."

"You want me to dress up—like a penguin?" Clearfather frowned.

"A dinner jacket!" Wilton chortled and went off to get cleaned up.

Clearfather entered the bathroom. He stripped down and looked at himself in the full-length mirror, fearing for a moment that it was a screen that Ainsley could be watching. The things Simon(e) had said about Theo had revolted and horrified him. He felt like he wanted to cry but all that came out was water from the showerhead.

A scrubbed-up Wilton helped him into his tuxedo and led him down to the library, where they found the Man of Steel puttering about on a contraption that resembled a motorized surfboard on wheels, complete with independent front and rear suspension, lever-action controls, and plenty of room for his oxygen tanks, ashtrays, a mini bar, and a stand for an IV drip—which was filled with a cocktail of Prozac, Bombay gin, megavitamins, and a dash of Benzedrine. The man's face was dotted with medipatches and countercancer laser burns. His hair was thick and white, the result of surgery in which human hair follicles combined with fur from an arctic hare had been microimplanted. He wore a Cary Grant dinner suit with shoes made from the hide of a manatee. In one hand was an Egyptian oval cigarette, in the other a cigar. Around his neck was an electronic voice synthesizer collar. Clearfather noticed Ainsley's scrambled face on a monitor.

"MY SON," the Steel Man said as if he had but one. "HOOPER, OUR BUTLER, ENTERTAINS HIM IN THE EVENING. MY WIFE WILL NOT BE JOINING US. SHE SADLY RAN INTO A MIRROR."

The doorbell rang and Mr. and Mrs. Privett arrived; the latter introduced herself by saying, "My first husband was sucked up in a jet engine—just like a seagull."

The Brothers 3 stumbled in stag—Alvin and Theodore ridiculous in their tuxedos, with Simon(e) more stylish in a Coco Chanel little black dress. Clearfather recognized the next guest to arrive as the smiling Dr. Hugh Wieviel from the organ clinic in the city. He had a trace of Texas twang and a freshly applied tan, and was partnered by one of the patients he was officially sleeping with (that is, not just while she was under anesthesia)—a stacked WASP in her early thirties named Judith Beazley, who wore a boomerang-shaped brooch with light-emitting diodes and not much else.

Next came the Paddiartons. At 112, Josh was Kingland Brand's oldest living friend. Despite or perhaps because of fifty-five years of plastic surgery, the former CEO of Chemplex bore a remarkable resemblance to a Staffordshire terrier with a mouth full of roofing nails. His recently delivered Thai wife had just turned nineteen and wore a plunging kelp-green evening dress and a rope of pearls the size of a dachshund's testicles. Rounding out the table was a minor talk-show intellectual and professional dinner guest named Tina Curl, who'd been flown in from DC. Hooper didn't appear although he must've passed through earlier because there was a scent of dogshit lingering in the air. The Man of Steel was left to usher the guests into the oak-lined dining room, where he rang a tiny Waterford bell and said in his sinister metallic quack, "TONIGHT I PRESENT THE HEALTHY AND ECONOMICAL ALTERNATIVE FOR THE NOW AGE, PROFESSOR CHICKEN'S CAJUN COUNTRY SPECIAL!"

Simon(e) sat thunderstruck as a frozen-faced maid named Mrs. Stovington proceeded to fill the room with Professor Chicken cartons while Theodore made sure that the founder of the food chain enjoyed extra helpings of his famous no-fat fare.

After the main course, Chuck Privett tried to ignite interest in the subject of fume extraction while Dr. Wieviel waxed lyrical about the possibility of providing a birth-defect girl with wings. The thrill of recreational reconstructive surgery—stretching and grafting skin, reshaping bone and muscle, and then applying intensive hormonal therapy—made his blue eyes sparkle.

"Of course we could go the organatron route and roboticize her," he said, which prompted a discussion of robotics and its origins in automata.

"In 1574 a mechanical rooster was crowing atop a clock tower in Strasbourg," Tina Curl announced. "And in the eighteenth century the genius Vaucanson invented a mechanical duck that could quack and splash in water. There's even a legend about a jeweled goose that could fly, created by a secret guild of Bavarian toy makers."

Hearing about the rooster, the duck, and the goose reminded Mrs. Privett of her first husband, who was sucked up into a jet engine—just like a seagull.

Dr. Wieviel went on to discuss the convention he was going to in LosVegas devoted to the latest intelligence-enhancing drugs and the release of a new range of sex programs.

"They sent us a *free* sample." Judith Beazley grinned. "Takes a while to load but when it gets going!"

"That's right." Wieviel winked. "It's very atmospheric. You're both young teens going at it hell for leather in the velvet weed in a late-August cornfield."

"can you get me a copy?" the Man of Steel wheezed.

"You have to be careful with this new thoughtware," the doctor said. "If you haven't paid the subscription . . . there you are about to come when your partner becomes obese—or dead. Have to give them your credit number to get it going right again."

"There are some new Finnish ones that are mythologically themed . . . you know, like Zeus and Leda," Tina Curl remarked.

"Ooh," shivered Judith. "I don't think I'd want to have sex with a bull."

"A swan," Tina Curl corrected.

"How could a swan screw a woman?" Simon(e) wanted to know.

"How could anyone mistake a frog for a chicken?" Theodore croaked.

"Shut up," Simon(e) fired back.

"I didn't make up the myth," Tina Curl replied. "I'm just telling you—when Zeus knocked up Leda he took the form of a swan."

"My firsht husband was suckedup innna jetplane. Like a shea-gull," Mrs. Privett reminded them.

"AND NOW IT IS TIME FOR A TOAST," the Man of Steel announced.

Wilton nudged Clearfather and whispered, "They never learn, do they?"

Mrs. Stovington appeared with a chilled magnum of French champagne, followed by a tray of glasses, and proceeded to pop and pour.

"WE HAVE TWO THINGS TO CELEBRATE," the Man of Steel buzzed. "THE FIRST IS THAT DR. WIEVIEL HAS LOCATED A NEW LIVER FOR ME. SECOND, I'M UPDATING MY WILL TONIGHT, AND I NOTE THAT ERNST HAS ELECTED NOT TO BE HERE. MY SON AINSLEY REMAINS THE NUMBER ONE CONTENDER BUT I AM PLEASED TO ANNOUNCE THAT MY STEPSON, OR DAUGHTER, HAS MOVED INTO THE NUMBER TWO POSITION BY VIRTUE OF HIS OR HER EFFORTS WITH PROFES-SOR CHICKEN."

"Bravo the Chicken!" Mrs. Privett called and Simon(e) bowed—while Theodore and Alvin smiled poisonously.

"SO LET US TOAST—MY LIVER, AINSLEY'S LOYALTY, AND SIMON(E)'S MOD-EST ATTEMPT AT MAKING A LIVING . . ."

"And Mr. Clearfather!" Wilton added.

The Man of Steel spewed champagne over the teak-colored breasts of the new Mrs. Paddiarton. *"AND WHY SHOULD WE TOAST HIM?"*

Clearfather cleared his throat and began, "I'm not a pheasant plucker—"

"No, please," Wilton interjected. "Allow me. To you, Mr. Clear-father. May you find what you're looking for."

"Whoosh a pheasant fucker?" Mrs. Privett demanded. "My firsht hubband was shuckedup innna shetplane—such like a sheegull."

The party broke up soon after Wilton's toast. Tina Curl performed an inebriated waltz with a suit of samurai armor en route to her cab, while Dr. Hugh made the unfortunate discovery that Mrs. Privett had wet her chair. The other guests departed—Alvin, Theodore, and Simon(e) trooping off to their separate wings while the Man of Steel surfed into his elevator, which transported him up to the vastness he shared with the Fidget Woman and Ainsley's telepresence studio.

Wilton was a little sorry he'd interrupted Clearfather. A part of him was curious about what the bald man's "demonstration" would've entailed this time—but the rest of him was exhausted. For the first time in weeks he wasn't battling hallucinations or bouts of nausea or ravenous lust. He felt empty but rinsed clean.

"Here's all the cash I've got," he said when they got to his suite. "Thanks again."

"I don't want all your money," Clearfather told him.

"You deserve it," the boy replied. "You work wonders, you really do. Don't know how, but . . . you do. Besides, it means less temptation for me. I'm not going to end up a headless body they pull out of the river."

"Just stay honest with yourself, son. I'm sorry. That sounds condescending."

"Not—from you," the boy said and held out his hand. "You get a good sleep. I'll drive you to the station in the morning."

"Okay," Clearfather said, shaking the boy's hand. Then he hugged Wilton. It was an unplanned action—awkward, instinctive—and the fearful youth hugged back—the first time he'd touched anyone in months without the influence of the Pandora.

Wilton had a deep dreamless sleep that night . . . but not so the others. Certainly not the Man of Steel, who dreamed of his liver transplant—but found that the surgery had been performed on his face instead. His visage was distorted like Ainsley's—as if the cells were pixilated—continuously mutating in an agonizing blur. He woke to the sound of the heart monitor in his room and lit up a cigarette. (His sedated wife wallowed in her distant suite, her jaw having been wired shut by one of Wieviel's trainees.) Christ, he thought. I'll never get back to sleep. He winched himself onto his surfboard and motored into his private Recreation Area.

Clearfather was overwhelmed with fatigue and had fallen on top of the bed after changing back into his own clothes, but he couldn't break through the wall of dreams into the deeper dark. All night long he whirled around in a tornado of half-seen things. He saw an old radio station shack and a ghost town . . . and then he was playing with Uncle Waldo and Aunt Vivian—only he couldn't see their faces. He had the idea that his mother was dead but that his father ran a gospel radio station . . . "Please show me your face . . . ," he said. He saw the boy in the bathroom . . . and then floating up in the mirror, like the creatures in Ernst's aquariums, were three faces . . . Chinese men . . . trying to speak to him. He woke in the dark of morning to a terrible sound.

"Good Lord!" he said aloud. "Warhol!"

The beast must've gotten out of the car barn because Clearfather could hear him snarling in response to the growls of the mastiffs. I've got to find him, Clearfather realized, and leapt off the bed—only to put his foot right into the polar bear's mouth, where it became wedged tight. "Shit!" he yelped. A dogfight to the death was about to break out on the lawn and here he was kickboxing with a dead bear! He'd have to wake Wilton. But when he peered in the other room, the boy's breathing was so deep and easy he didn't have the heart to disturb him and so he began shuffling down the hallway with his foot still stuck, no idea where the front door was and all the time dreading running into the mechanical butler with the fun-house face.

The growling grew more intense and then he heard an odd noise—like a soundtrack running backward. Then silence. He reached a bay window and looked out over the grounds. In the barium-silver mist he could make out Warhol's shape. God, Clearfather thought. He's ripped the throats out of those poor mastiffs and now he's dragging one off to eat! Having seen the monster in action, he had no intention of trying to interrupt him now. He turned to head back to his room and passed what he'd thought was a mirror—but this time a giant face rippled up before him.

"All polar bears are left-handed."

"Is that you, Ainsley? You scared me. I . . . I couldn't sleep."

"All polar bears are left-handed."

"I've got a polar bear stuck on my foot!"

"All polar bears are left-handed. The more shrimp a flamingo eats, the pinker it gets."

"Are you all right?" Clearfather asked. "Your voice . . . has something happened?"

"The more worms, the more badgers," the Voice said in a fuzz of distortion.

"I'll get help," Clearfather said and swept down the hall, dragging the bear rug behind. At least he knew where the elevator was—the crippled son's studio had to be off that section of the house. Down one hall and left he noticed a glimmer of light. The smell of the Man of Steel was heavy in the air—dead skin cells, single-malt whiskey, and dark tobacco disguised by gallons of Royal Yacht Edwardian Lime aftershave. The door was ajar. He squeezed the ivory ball in his pocket and crept closer. "Ainsley?" he whispered. "Hello?"

He slipped closer, the polar bear rug still clutching his foot. The Steel Man's odor was very strong now. Clearfather crept closer. The butler's chrome mask lay on an antique table just inside the room beside the electronic voice collar. The Man of Steel, in pajamas of hand-printed Italian cotton, reclined on his surfboard, smoking two cigarettes. The floor creaked.

"So . . . you've discovered my little secret." The Man of Steel turned, and his voice no longer had the synthetic warble.

"You?" Clearfather asked, glancing back and forth between the mask and the roboframe. "But why?"

"There was a real Hooper," the Man of Steel panted, lighting up a cigar. "I was forced to accommodate him and supply him with meaningful employment as part of a lawsuit-settled insurance claim. But he didn't work. The one thing that did work was between his legs. He began balling my wife. I think the mask and the robotic apparatus excited her. One day when he was getting his fluids refreshed, I tried on the mask and fitted myself as best I could into the frame—and enjoyed her in a way she hadn't really allowed in decades."

"But didn't your wife notice . . ."

"I had help," the Man of Steel puffed, and slipped his hand into the pocket of his pajamas. There was a sound like an automatic garage door opening, and then a swelling began in his crotch—of which the ancient executive was obviously proud. Except that once risen it began to deflate. And then to rise again . . .

"Geez," said Clearfather. "That's annoying."

"You're telling me!" the Steel King fumed. "I'm afraid if she ever sobers up, she'll find out the truth. This damn unit's started malfunctioning and it's out of warranty. Wieviel harvested it out of a Saudi who died in heart surgery. Gave me a great deal on it, but it's a devil of a thing to fix."

"Couldn't you just take a drug?"

"For about fifty years or so. Then it's best to go for new equipment."

The Man of Steel's hydraulic implant kept rising and lowering.

Clearfather picked up the synthesizer. "You wear this to disguise your voice?"

"And also because I've had throat cancer."

"Oh. So—what happened to the real Hooper? Did you need a new set of lungs?"

"There's no evidence of anything illegal!" the Man of Steel snapped.

"I bet there's no evidence, period. And even your wife is happy about it, providing she's had enough vodka."

"And ether," the Man of Steel said. "Ether helps. Hooper has also given me another way of collecting information on the Inheritors."

"Who? Oh, your family! So behind that mask you spy on them?"

"Don't get holier-than-thou with me! They're a weaselly bunch."

"Not Wilton."

"He's a junkie and a pervert. I couldn't trust him as far as you could throw him!"

"That's because Theodore and Simon(e) got him addicted to Pandora."

"My point exactly! Eat the wounded, bury the aged! You have no idea what it's like to live for fifty years thinking that every day could be your last!"

Clearfather had been trying desperately to work his foot out of the bear's mouth and finally kicked the rug free with a jolt. It flew up and struck a Ming vase, knocking it to the floor, where it shattered, spilling out what looked like soot.

"That was my first wife. And a priceless vase!" the Steel King gulped. "But I don't suppose it matters now. Just go on and get the job done."

"I'm . . . sorry," Clearfather said. "W-what job?"

"Why, killing me of course. Isn't that what a hired assassin is hired for?"

CHAPTER 12

Spizzerinctum

"You can make an ass of yourself but you can't make an assassin of me," Clearfather said. "I just came in here because I thought Ainsley sounded sick. Remember Loyal Ainsley? The Number One Contender?"

"Success rates for throat-throttle attack by solitary cheetahs range from ten to forty percent," Ainsley droned.

"I'd like to meet him."

"No."

"Introduce me and I won't breathe a word about you being Hooper."

"No. Please."

"I won't leave otherwise. I swear. And everyone will know."

"Oh . . . shit," the Man of Steel groaned. He levered forward and steered the surfboard into the adjoining room. In a corner was a white-screened area like a phosphorescent cocoon. "Pull back the curtain."

"Ains . . . ley?" Clearfather began, but faltered when he saw the empty space.

"He is not there . . . he has risen." Brand sighed and burst into a fit of sobbing, which made the continued excitement of his penile implant seem even more ludicrous.

Clearfather heard the Voice say, "If beavers sense danger, they whack the surface of the water with their tails, signaling to the rest of the family to seek hiding places."

"I don't understand."

"His database includes the complete text of L. H. Morgan's classic *The American Beaver and His Works*. This," wailed the Father, "is all that's left of my Son!" He pointed to the installation of computers. "Dingler—next door—designed it. The man's a genius—a bastard but a genius. We distorted the face so the family wouldn't know."

"Ainsley's not . . . sick? He's dead?"

"His body . . . is," the Man of Steel admitted. "But his—personality —lives on in this system, and now he's dying again before my eyes. His body was damaged then—but now it's his mind!"

"A full-grown giraffe's heart is as big as a basketball," Ainsley piped up.

"Cyberdementia," sniffed the Steel Man. "Dingler injected an accelerating Asperger's Syndrome into the CPU and triggered it when I refused him membership into an elite golf club of which I am the president."

"When's the last time you played golf?"

"Twenty-two years ago. But that's not the point."

"Carefully observe the normal to detect the abnormal," Ainsley chirped.

"Can . . . can you . . ."

"Unplug him?" the Father asked. "Yes. But I'm not ready yet. What a bitter end! Look there." The Steel King pointed out the window.

Clearfather saw the doors to the car barn opening and closing madly. So that was how Warhol had gotten out.

"Dingler linked him into the home management system. I've disabled part of it, but I don't dare tamper with any more. Good thing this part is on a separate system."

"Wait a minute," said Clearfather. "I thought Ainsley was injured—"

"Eighty-eight years ago. He had spizzerinctum!" the Steel King blubbered.

"What's that? A disease?"

"*No!* It's the essential American trait. Gumption. Go-get-'em. The drive to go head-to-head and always keep your chin up. Ainsley was full of it."

"But when did he actually die?"

"Eighty-four years ago," the Man of Steel whispered.

"*What?* Do you mean to say that he's been dead—that the rest of the family has believed—that he's been this living—ghost—all this time?"

"I couldn't bear to let him go! I couldn't live without the thought of one day leaving everything to him. I know it's hard for you to understand—"

"*No,*" said Clearfather. "Your masquerade as Hooper is difficult to understand. This is on another level completely. How have you kept this secret?"

"Well," said the Steel King, trying to regain control (and about ready to rip out his implant). "Maids and nurses were paid to tell stories. And I used a mannequin in bandages. I had photos made. I even hired a ventriloquist at one point. You see, people like secrets and no one really wants to look at a monster."

"Who wasn't even there! You build up this labyrinth, so naturally everyone assumes there's someone or something in it!"

"As the technology became more sophisticated, I was able to do more."

"And Wilton thinks *I'm* a magician! Ainsley isn't just the tragic ghost of your favorite son, it's code for 24/7 internal AV surveillance."

"You need to see this from my perspective," Brand insisted. "I've worked hard to build this up. I wasn't born rich like them. When I was a boy, they used to have the streetlights on at noon!"

"Mr. Brand, you still are a boy. You've used this perverse hoax to confuse and manipulate your family for the worst part of a century. Your scheme has destroyed Ernst. And Wilton, a healthy intelligent kid with a great future, is so desperate for love and self-esteem, he's suicidal. If any of them are half as greedy as you say—you've made them that way. Bargaining organs, pitting them against each other! And the most pathetic thing is that you've been successful in boondoggling them. Not only do they believe Ainsley exists and is going to inherit everything, they believe there's something to inherit."

"How do you know there's not?" the Man of Steel pouted. "I own forty percent of Professor Chicken! And Simon(e) doesn't even know."

"That's the big prize everyone's vying for?"

"Plus the antiques!"

The Man of Steel led Clearfather through a set of doors handcarved from heartwood of Macassar ebony. In one corner was a very realistic waxwork of an aging beauty queen holding a martini glass.

"That's my second wife," the Man of Steel indicated. "Compliments of a taxidermist from Alaska."

As the decrepit former executive surfed past, one of his chemical drip bags hooked something and onto the floor fluttered a photogram. Clearfather bent hastily to retrieve it. It showed a still-old but not obscene image of the Steel Man holding a newborn baby wrapped in blue.

"Is this you and Wilton?"

"Give me that!" the Man of Steel barked, pinching the photo back and stowing it away in some hidden pocket of his robe. "Let me show you something important."

Brand pulled him into another room in front of a laser-alarm-protected glass case.

"Did you know that in South America there's a kind of catfish that grabs monkeys out of the trees when they come down to get a drink from the rivers? Theodore Roosevelt's expedition caught one. When they cut it open, they found a monkey in the belly. This is that monkey."

"*That* monkey?"

"Mummified," the Man of Steel whispered. "Signed by Teddy himself."

"Theodore Roosevelt signed that monkey?"

"Look closely . . ."

Clearfather burst out laughing.

"Stop laughing! No one laughs at Kingland Morris Brand!"

Just then the Man of Steel's artificial penis began rotating, which sent Clearfather into hysterics. He stopped laughing only when he found himself face-to-face with a Harpers Ferry flintlock.

"What do you think you're going to do with that?"

"I'm going to lock you in the basement and call Dr. Wieviel. And then instead of just a new liver—I'm going to get a new heart, lungs— who knows? It could be a real smorgasbord," the Man of Steel gloated.

A thought came to Clearfather as he watched the Steel Lord's spinning member.

"It might take more than ether to fool your wife about that."

"Shut up!"

"On the other hand—if you could *control* it—if you could decide when it went up and for how long—and if you could get a little rotary action—just the right amount at the right time—you might become very popular."

"What are you saying?"

Clearfather heard voices inside his head . . . Uncle Waldo and Aunt Vivian speaking in the singsong tone used to address children and animals . . . *Can we fix it? Yes, we can!*

"I can fix it," Clearfather said, and in his mind an image formed . . . the shadow man at the transmitter shack, some mouse-hole radio station operating from a ghost town. It was dusk and the lighted call letters KRMA came on as bright as a Mexican restaurant and the man's voice said . . . *And now a dedication going out to . . .*

The voice was lost in the wind but the song came through clear and sharp.

"I can give you back some semblance of manhood and dignity," Clearfather said. "For a lot less than what Dr. Wieviel will charge."

"Bullshit! How?"

"Do you care . . . as long as it works?"

"I can't have you hanging around here knowing what you know."

"Nothing could make me stay, knowing what I know. You give me some pocket money, then you cancel the liver replacement and agree to never have another organ transplant. Ever."

"But that'll mean—"

"Death. Eventually. Yes. But as an end of living, not as a style of life."

"But—"

"I'm not finished. You do whatever you have to do to fund Wilton's rehab program—and you stick by him through it no matter how tough it gets. Then you unplug Ainsley and have a formal memorial service that will end the farce forever."

"But—"

"I'm not finished. You ask for Ernst's forgiveness. You make Ernst and Wilton your heirs—your wife has her own money. Then you try to fix this place up so that there really is something to leave behind other than twisted memories."

"That seems a lot to ask," the Man of Steel said.

"It's a package deal," Clearfather replied.

"I'll tell you what," breathed the Steel Man. "What say we make this sporting? You win, it's as you've said. I win—and you're spare parts."

"What kind of competition?" Clearfather asked.

The Steel King slipped into Hungarian partridge shooting boots and a coat made of ribbon seal. He handed Clearfather a sheepskin jacket and a pair of deerskin moccasins, and then led him outside onto a balcony. In the still morning chill, the stale tang of Szechuan cooking mixed with barbecued pigs' feet rose from the river, the various aromas blending like the weird PVC pipe tooting of the settlers down on the floodwall. Clearfather gazed out over the estate. On the ground below was a clearing between two stands of just-budding Lombardy poplars, which was filled with rows of snowmen arranged like pieces in an enormous board game. The sun was just beginning to brighten the sky, and the figures made deep blue shadows.

"Isn't it a bit late in the season for snowmen?" Clearfather asked.

"I could never build snowmen when I was growing up."

"A learning disability?"

"No!" The Steel Man scowled. "It was because the neighborhood was too tough. The gang kids always knocked them down! So now I have them all year long. In the warmer weather they don't last very long—but they grow back like flowers. Take a closer look—you'll see they're not snow*men*."

"By God." Clearfather squinted. "That's . . . your wife . . . the Fidget Woman!"

"Yes," said the Steel King, grinning. "Ernst made a mold of her when she passed out once. I find this therapeutic."

The Man of Steel pulled a tarpaulin from one of the machines that hurled baseballs for batting practice. He awakened the ignition and proceeded to load it with tiny canisters of fluorescent paint. He sighted down the long plastic ejection tube as if manning an anti-aircraft gun, then proceeded to open fire on the frozen replicas of his wife. Washes of color poofed and splattered. One minute a snow-woman was stark white; the next it had turned the color of a cherry snow cone.

"Now," he said. "The object of the game is to get the highest number of hits—but you have to get them in every row. You take blue and yellow. I've got red and green. We each get three turns."

Clearfather stepped up to the paint gun and blasted away, turning one of the Fidget Women popsicle blue and two B-vitamin yellow—all in one row.

"Not bad," the Steel Man conceded, and then scored a head shot and a shoulder hit in the back row. Clearfather responded with two blue heart scores, but on his third shot the canister of yellow paint exploded in midair.

"Tough break," giggled the Steel King, and proceeded to nail three more virgin snowwomen on the diagonal. "Now you need a hit with every shot to stay in the game. What's that noise?"

Clearfather cocked his head. It was a growling, chewing sound. From around the other side of the house Warhol appeared, chomping at something.

"It's my dog."

"What's he eating?"

"I'm afraid it's the remains of your dogs," Clearfather said.

"What are you talking about?" the Man of Steel demanded.

"Your mastiffs. Warhol got out when the car barn doors opened. There was an altercation. Warhol won."

"But the mastiffs aren't real!" the Steel Man exclaimed. "I got rid of them years ago. A pile of mastiff shit is the size of a cow patty!"

"But . . . you mean the sounds? They're just—"

"A recording loop. You need people to *think* you've got big vicious dogs—that just makes good security sense—but to actually have them—"

"I can't believe you!" Clearfather cried, and Warhol looked up at the balcony and gave a happy bark. "But if he's not tearing up one of your dogs, what's he eating?"

"Good Lord, I hope it's not Mrs. Stovington! She's the only one who knows how to work the microwave! Where was he coming from?"

"The mastiff kennel. He took the growling as a challenge."

"Oh!" moaned the Man of Steel. "He must've found the secret vault where my third wife is—was—frozen! I installed it there because I thought no one would go near. There's a pressure plate in the paving—he must've activated it."

"Well, for what it's worth," considered Clearfather. "He's enjoying her."

"God! Reminds me of a stockholders' meeting back in the 1970s. But now it's sudden death and I'm up first . . ."

The Man of Steel fired at an ice-clear snowwoman when a man in a Lucron tracksuit jogged through. The Steel King's shot went wide, splashing off the arm of an effigy he'd already hit. "Shit!"

"Who's that?" Clearfather asked.

"That's Julian Dingler! My damn neighbor and enemy!"

The man, who looked about Clearfather's age, stopped running and stared up at the balcony, taking in the scene. Then he strutted up to one of the unstruck snowwomen and proceeded to have a vigorous piss on it. He covered the figure in bright yellow pee and when he was done he bent over and slapped his butt.

"You bastard!" the Man of Steel seethed, his temples pounding. "Get off my property!"

Julian Dingler broke off a piece of snowwoman, balled it up in his hands, and then demonstrated the kind of bazooka-like throwing arm any major-league outfielder would have been proud to own. The icy snowball hit the Man of Steel smack in the face. He fell forward onto the lever controls of the surfboard and would've launched clean through the railing if Clearfather hadn't grabbed his IV stand.

Clearfather waved to the Steel King's neighbor. Dingler seemed to wave back—the sun breaking through for a moment. Then the sun and the man were gone—and the Man of Steel's board nudged the rusted railing off the edge.

"Surf's up, old-timer," said Clearfather. "It's winner take all."

"N-no! Please" the Steel Man whinnied. "Not like this!"

"Why not? You'll shatter like that vase. Probably the same stuff inside!"

"Please!" the decayed tycoon whimpered. "I give in! You win! You fix my implant and I'll do all the things you said. I swear."

"All right," said Clearfather, and pulled the board back onto the balcony. "You show me my money. And I'll keep my part of the bargain."

They went back inside. Brand was snuffling. The bald stranger had brought everything undone. The old man motored over to his taxidermized wife, unzipped her, and began fishing out bills.

"You keep your cash in her?" Clearfather gasped.

"I couldn't trust the safes with Theodore around. I told you they're a conniving bunch. Okay, here's your bucks. Now give me my bang."

The old man laid out the money. Clearfather heard his aunt's and uncle's voices in his head again. Then the Radio Man. Then a golden stillness came and out of the stillness, the song.

"I know this will seem odd, but do you know the song 'Do Your Ears Hang Low?'"

"What?" squealed Brand.

"*Do your ears hang low? Do they wobble to and fro? Can you tie them in a knot? Can you tie them in a bow? Can you throw them o'er your shoulder like a Continental soldier? Do your ears hang low?*"

"Listen," groaned the Steel King. "You have bested me at every turn. My wife is obsessed with sleeping with you. My youngest son wants to be you. You don't need to humiliate me further!"

"I'm not kidding, Mr. Brand. Just try it," Clearfather said, and he really did feel a sudden depth of pity. Just as Wilton offered an image of the son he might've had, the boy he might've been—so did the Man of Steel suggest the father he couldn't remember or could yet become.

"How does it work? Why couldn't it be a song that isn't so . . . silly?"

"I'm sorry," Clearfather answered, shaking off his spell. "I don't know how it works, but that's the song that will do it for you. Sing it loud, sing it proud."

Much to his mortification, the crumpled old man coughed out the words, and to his surprise the implant stopped rotating and settled down.

"Try getting it up," Clearfather encouraged.

"Do your ears hang low? Do they wobble to and fro? . . ."

"You see?"

"It's working!" Brand cheered. "It's working!"

"Now it's time for you to take me to the bus station. I have either a rendezvous with destiny or just another stop on a wild goose chase."

"What do you mean by that?" Brand asked.

"I've lost my memory," Clearfather said. "I'm on a journey of discovery."

"I haven't been behind the wheel of a car in a very long time. We would both be much safer if you took a cab."

"No, Mr. Brand. It's time you got outside and saw the world again. You get yourself ready. I'm going to get my stuff and say goodbye to Wilton."

Clearfather went down in the elevator, found the front door, and whistled for Warhol. Together they peeked in on Wilton but the boy was still sleeping, even when Warhol climbed on the bed. The lines on Wilton's face had relaxed and he looked like a child again, even with the split lip. Maybe the bad dreams are all behind him, Clearfather thought, returning the kid's money. A part of him wished he could stay and watch over the boy, but he knew he had to go.

"You take good care of him, Warhol, and yourself," he whispered. "I'm counting on you."

The giant dog licked his hand. Clearfather closed the door softly and put on his own boots and coat.

The Man of Steel wasn't exaggerating. He hadn't driven anything other than his surfboard—and never farther than the end of his driveway, admittedly a long driveway—in the last forty years, so the trip from Fern Hollow into the city in his wife's Bentley had a few harrowing moments. But Clearfather remained calm.

"Listen," said the Man of Steel when they arrived downtown. "How do I know it's going to work when you're gone?"

"You have to trust me," Clearfather answered.

"But you don't even remember who you are!" the Steel Man complained.

"All you ever do is remember who you *were*," Clearfather replied. "I know something about who I am now . . . and I keep my word. But if I *ever* find out that you didn't help Wilton into rehab and that you're trying to harvest organs—"

"I get the picture," the Steel King sighed.

"You have a family that you're supposed to be heading, not cannibalizing. Oh, and take good care of Warhol."

The withered businessman was about to drive off when a strong emotion seized him. "Wait a minute," he pleaded. "Would—would you consider—staying?"

"I thought you were adamant that I leave?"

"I . . . I've changed my mind."

Clearfather squeezed the tiny ivory ball in his pocket. "No," he answered.

"Why *not*? You'd never have to worry about anything—ever again!"

"One big dinner party, hm? What about Eat the Wounded?"

"All that's going to change," the former Steel King insisted.

"It had better," said the bald man.

"Just think what you and I might accomplish—together!" Brand rhapsodized.

"You just want me to do more—magic."

"No," said the Man of Steel, and the tone of his voice and the expression on his face changed completely. "Don't you see? *You're* the son I've been looking for all these years!"

"You don't look for sons, Mr. Brand."

"Oh, yes you do!" Brand exclaimed. "If you're a leader, that's *exactly* what you do. You look for sons and daughters—and partners. That's what life's all about."

Clearfather considered the connection he felt with Wilton. Maybe the Steel Man had a point.

"I'm sorry, Mr. Brand," he said at last. "I have to go. You have a fine son in Wilton if you look for him. And I think you still have a fine man inside yourself. If you were to be the man you could be . . . you'd have no need of help from me."

"So this . . . is good . . . bye?"

"This is good luck."

The Steel Man nodded sadly and then bucked and stuttered off in the Bentley. Clearfather watched until the car was gone. For a night at least he'd almost had a family. Now he was alone again, except for the voices in his head, which had gone silent. He entered the station.

A Harijan was buffing the floor. A Laotian woman was mopping up in front of Starbucks. There was no sign of Ubba Dubba or Dooley Duck—just a hologram around the WOMEN & CHILDREN'S area that read: SPONSORED BY CHILDRITE NURTURING CENTERS . . . THE ONLY WAY TO BEGIN A LIFE . . .

When it came time he got aboard the bus and staggered to a vacant seat beside a ruddy-faced white woman with a porcupine haircut. He closed his eyes and saw the city of cyclones again. From one of the intermittent windows of the spiral a strange young girl watched him. She seemed to raise her hand—just as Julian Dingler had. When he opened his eyes he saw they were passing a group of Dooley Duck supporters. At the front of the line were the two drunks from the day before. The Greyhound welcomed those who'd boarded in Pittsburgh, and as they revved up onto the freeway he saw another of the eccentric billboards and his head seemed to explode.

"Are you all right, son?" the woman next to him asked. "Could I interest you in a nice hot cup of cocoa?"

PART 3

Ooby Dooby

The religions of the world are the
ejaculations of a few imaginative men.
—Ralph Waldo Emerson

CHAPTER I

Something Undiscovered

"Are you all right? You look like you could use some cocoa."

He looked around. "Are we in Pittsburgh yet?"

"You got *on* in Pittsburgh," the woman said.

He tried to think what he remembered. Of course. Wilton, Warhol, the Man of Steel. But why had he been in Pittsburgh? The map. He was there trying to find clues—to his past. The whole nightmare came pouring back.

"I'm Edwina Corn." The woman smiled and handed him a plastic mug of cocoa.

"Th-thanks," he said, sipping. "My . . . I'm . . . Elijah Clearfather."

"That's quite a name to be carrying around," Edwina grinned.

Clearfather flinched. Just then it seemed like quite a heavy load indeed. Outside, the bauxite-colored sky weighed down on the land as the Scenicruiser vibrated on through the clover bottoms and plains of wild rye that long ago had been replaced by steelworks and glass factories, which had in turn given way to bacteriological growths of housing . . . ashrams, refugee camps, golf courses, biolabs, prisons. He was trying to remember what the billboard had said when all the static filled his head—and was startled when Edwina Corn remarked, "The ancient Greeks and Romans used to brush their teeth with bits of cloth coated with the pulverized heads of mice and moles. They believed contact with these strong-toothed animals would make human teeth tougher. Makes you wonder, duddn't it?"

Clearfather thought that it made him sick. "How do you know *that*?"

"Because I'm a dentist . . . as I was saying. Or I used to be."

"Oh, I'm sorry . . . ," Clearfather said. "I was thinking of something else."

"That's all right." The woman smiled, patting his knee. "Cocoa all right?"

"Yes," Clearfather answered. "So . . . you're a dentist?"

"I was. Circuit dentist for a few of the Time Havens. Two New Puritan settlements and Brook Farm Two."

"What . . . is a Time Haven?"

"You sound as though you've been living in the past!" Edwina chuckled, and then glanced at him quizzically. "People live like they used to. In the past. Or they try to. But most draw the line at dental and medical inconvenience—and it's not easy to keep good doctors and dentists around, so they set up deals with people like me. But now I've had enough and I'm off on a pilgrimage to start my new life . . . following in the footsteps of Zane Grey. Just visited where he played baseball at the University of Pennsylvania."

"Who?"

"Zane Grey! The inventor of the American West! One of the biggest-selling authors of all time and the world's greatest fisherman. How many writers make the cover of *Field and Stream*?"

"Zane Grey?"

"He was a god!" Edwina pronounced, slapping her beefy thigh. "His book sales rivaled the Bible! A sailfish was named for him. I'm a bit of a fisherman myself. Been to the Kona Coast, Florida Keys.

Hooked twelve good-sized trophy fish. Not bad for a lump of mutton like me, eh?"

"N-no," Clearfather agreed, not quite sure how to answer.

"Got the biggest one in the Bay of Islands in New Zealand. Do you know anything about marlin fishing? Lots of folks think it's cruel and don't want any part of it. I felt that way, too—until I clipped myself into the fighting chair for the first time. I've been kind to animals my whole life—but I've just got this passion for big-game fishing. That's why I ride the bus. Now that I'm retired, got to save money where I can."

"How are you going to get to New Zealand on a Greyhound?"

"Zanesville, Ohio's, my next stop!" Edwina hooted. "His hometown! I'm going to see where he did his fishing as a boy, and then I'll carry on to Surprise Valley, the Zane Grey community I'm joining out in Utah."

"A Zane Grey . . . *community*?" Clearfather asked.

"People who are devoted to the life and works of ZG. There are study groups and readings—a film festival and fishing expeditions!"

"I see," Clearfather breathed.

"But in some ways it's not a new life . . . ," she whispered.

"No? Why's that?"

Edwina Corn lowered her voice further. "Because I think I *was* Zane Grey . . . in my previous life. Do you believe in past lives?"

"I—I guess . . . ," Clearfather said, feeling that his current situation somehow obligated him to.

"My ex-husband thought I had Shirley MacLaine Disease but my home diagnosticon gave me a clean bill of mental health."

They reached the West Virginia checkpoint. The bus stopped and two odd-looking white women got on the bus. The other passengers became instantly alert.

"Uh-oh," Edwina murmured.

"What?" said Clearfather. "Who are they?"

"Vitessa Inquisitors," the retired dentist whispered. "Are you in any trouble?"

"I . . . I don't know. What right do they have stopping the bus?"

"They own the roads and run the prisons, don't forget."

"What?" Clearfather whispered.

Edwina scrutinized him. "I really think you have been in a Time Warp. Vitessa bought all the roads and the prisons—that was one of the big inroads, pardon the pun, into the government. Don't you know that? Hell, they'd buy the rights to the English language if they thought they could collect the royalties."

"R-ight," Clearfather mumbled, watching as the figures moved down the aisle checking ID. The women looked like female golf pros but from the reactions of the other passengers, you'd have thought the Gestapo was aboard. They were still several seats away when they stopped at a middle-aged black woman with a motorwave haircut and bright blue glasses. Hers was the first ID they didn't scan. A hush spread through the cabin like nerve gas.

"Voleta Kincaid?" one of the Inquisitors asked. "Got a reading here. Parole violation. Is that right?"

Perspiration broke out on Voleta's face and she swatted herself and then began raking her fingernails across her skin—digging and tugging at her hair.

The scene filled Clearfather with revulsion and anger. "What are they doing to her?" he whispered to Edwina, whose ruddy face had clouded over.

"She's got a brain implant. She was in prison," the dentist shushed.

"What's going to happen to her?"

"She'll claw herself to death, if they want her to."

Clearfather couldn't stand the sight of the woman twitching and scraping herself. He wriggled in his seat and made a move to rise, but Edwina seized hold of him and hissed, "Don't! I don't think they're here for her, and if she's got an implant she may deserve what she gets, however appalling it is to watch."

"Stop," the Inquisitors said, and Voleta stopped scratching herself. "You have eight hours to check in with your PO or there'll be a total eclipse, understand? Do not leave Allegheny County again."

"B-but, my daughter gonna have a baby," Voleta sputtered—and then stopped herself. The Inquisitors looked up, examining the faces of the other passengers. They spotted Clearfather. He felt Edwina's hand squeeze his arm as they neared, no longer bothering with anyone else.

"Are you together?" the one in the pastel pink jacket asked.

Clearfather was about to say *No* to try to keep Edwina out of it when she said "Yes" and offered her hand for scanning.

The Inquisitors looked at each other but neither took Edwina's hand or said a word. They turned around and floated back down the aisle, and for a moment the whole bus was silent except for Voleta.

"Thanks," Clearfather said the moment the Inquisitors and Voleta were off the bus—but as soon as he said it he was sorry. The remark made it sound like he had something to hide. *Do I?* he wondered.

"I think that might've been a close call," Edwina said, patting his hand. "Do you?"

Now Clearfather really did fret. He'd gone from friendly, warm feelings toward his seatmate to suspicion. The Inquisitors might well have been there looking for him (although why had they just left him alone?). Maybe the net that he'd feared was going to fall in Pittsburgh had caught up with him. Either way she was probing him.

"You look shaken, son," Edwina said. "More cocoa?"

"N-no, thank you," he said as another of the Stinky Wiggler billboards appeared.

THE RESTRICTION OF THE CAGE IS PROPORTIONAL TO
YOUR HOPE.

—*Stinky Wiggler*

And then another one a mile later.

THE SAFETY OF THE CAGE IS PROPORTIONAL TO YOUR FEAR.
—*Stinky Wiggler*

Just as before, the messages dissolved, where at first they'd looked so dimensional and fixed. Again he heard voices and saw images—this time fragments of text . . . Rollo May and St. John of the Cross, Krishnamurti—philosophical ideas and religious icons . . . Zen archers, crosses . . . lotus flowers, white roses. What did he have to do with these things? Where did they come from? He tried to imagine what sort of person would call him- or herself Stinky Wiggler. Was he just imagining the billboards—or were they part of someone else's media that he'd tuned in to? He wanted to ask Edwina if she'd seen them, too, but after his rush of paranoia he couldn't.

Then came a moment of clarity. Aunt Vivian kept a grain of pearl barley in the saltshaker! She'd given him a glow-in-the-dark green skull full of bubblegum! He remembered that as clear as anything, and the images, however simple, filled him with reassurance.

"I'm sorry . . . if I did anything wrong," Edwina said. "I just had a bad feeling about those Inquisitors . . ."

"It's all . . . right," Clearfather mumbled. Uncle Waldo liked to do jigsaw puzzles—Aunt Vivian liked crossword puzzles. They lived in South Dakota. There was a porch to sit on during long summer evenings! And something else. Something important. He still couldn't bring their faces into focus but his sense of them was very real. His memory of Hermetic Canyon must've been a confusion of places. God, it was something . . . something other than the boy in the bathroom. It was family. But were they still alive?

The Scenicruiser rolled on deeper into Ohio, through fields like the one where long ago Pretty Boy Floyd was shot—past pagodas, crematoria, and a lone Burmese man plowing with a yak. When they arrived in Zanesville, Clearfather felt sad at the thought of Edwina's leaving. She'd tried to mother him and he'd become suspicious. I wonder where my real mother is, he thought.

"Thank you . . . for the cocoa."

"You're welcome, son," Edwina replied. "I know I can be nosy. But a dentist gets a good eye for people and their moods and I can see you're troubled. You know, Zane Grey said, 'In everything there is always something undiscovered. Find it.'"

"That's what I mean to do," Clearfather replied.

They said goodbye, and the automated bus churned off again. He woke up in Columbus when a seniorated white gentleman slumped down next to him. The bus pulled out among Vaqueros and Mishimas, both electric and combustion engine, along with retrodesigned models like Hennepins and LaSalles. Some flashed LED signs for Toshiba Land or the Buddhist Caves of Kentucky. One said JOHN DILLINGER IS ALIVE AND HAS BEEN CLONED in blood-red letters.

"That's where I'm from originally," the man next to him said in a phlegmy voice. "Mooresville, Indiana. Great Museum Town. I'm Wy Dove. Named for the great Wyatt Earp, Wyatt T. Dove. The Motivator."

"*The Motivator?*" Clearfather asked, regarding the man, who was dressed in a well-worn cinnamon-colored suit and pale blue tie. Did he have anything to do with the Inquisitors?

"Ah," the man squinted. "Hard to believe now, but there was a time when you'd have heard of me. I was as big as Tony Robbins once. If you'd had anything to do with sales, incentives, marketing and promotions—or customer service. Hell! You've heard of Lateral Thinking? Well, I'm the inventor of Diagonal Thinking. Wrote a book on it. Number one best seller for two days running! I had spizzerinctum! You probably don't know what that is."

"Yes, I do," said Clearfather. "It's the essential American trait. The ability to go head-to-head and keep your feet up—I mean your chin."

"That's right!" snapped the oldster with a glint in his eye. "Oh, those were the days! I'd kick off with a joke. Then! I'd hit 'em with a few quick statistics—like how it costs five, six times as much to get a new customer as it does to keep an old one—or how a satisfied customer will tell seven other people but a dissatisfied customer will tell sixteen. Then I'd tell 'em about ASPRIN."

"For headaches?"

"Aptitudes, Skills, Personality, Responsibility, Interests, Needs. Then I tell 'em about TESTICLES. Teamwork, Enthusiasm, Stamina, Tenacity, Initiative, Courage, Loyalty, Excellence, and Sense of Humor. But I'll tell you what *always* worked. The Three Bricklayers."

"Bricklayers?" Clearfather asked, wondering what bricklayers would be doing at a motivational seminar.

"You walk down a road and see three bricklayers. You go up to the first one who's slopping mortar everywhere, and ask what he's doing and he says, 'Can'tchyou see? I'm laying bricks.'

"You nod and go over to the second bricklayer who's working very carefully and ask him what he's doing and he says, 'Why, I'm makin' a wall.' Finally you go over to the third bricklayer, who seems to be the happiest of all—and you know what she says? 'I'm building a *cathedral*.' Isn't that beautiful?

"But I lost the magic," he said with a deep sigh. "I fell from grace. And then in Fort Wayne, Indiana . . . I fell from the Ladder of Loyalty."

"Is that like falling off the wagon?" Clearfather asked.

"I wish! No, you see, I'd get up and shout, 'The oldest form of marketing is yelling!' Then I'd whisper, 'The smart approach is based on *listening*. You need to target individual customers and build personal relationships with them, with plenty of added value and heaps of USPs and WIIFMs—Unique Selling Propositions and What's-In-It-For-Mes.' Then I'd trundle out a giant ladder from behind the stage. Civic centers and hotels always have big ladders and it made a great visual aid. I'd talk about what it feels like to trust someone with your business, walking them up the Ladder of Loyalty as customers. How scary it is. And sometimes I was scared. But I knew I had the power of Diagonal Thinking supporting me. Until I started banging Lindi. Met her in Little Rock," the Motivator said. "'Topless joint near the Sudanese Quarter. Made the beast with two backs then I couldn't get her out of my head. An engagement came up in Fort Wayne and that's when I fell. Splattered down on the stage, and all the king's horses and all the king's men weren't able to put me back together again."

"I'm sorry," Clearfather said, wondering if this is what had become of Uncle Waldo . . . wandering the country on a Greyhound bus, alone.

"Maybe the horses shouldn't have had first dibs," the Motivator said, trying to smile. "My wife left me. I was so busted up they thought I'd never walk again. Diagonal Thinking proved them wrong but I was washed up as a Motivator."

Dove was so shaken by these memories Clearfather had to lead him off the bus in Indianapolis, which he did before he realized what he was doing. Inside the terminal there was an anxious feeling in the air, as if something bad was about to happen.

CHAPTER 2

States of Mind

Back in Central Park, Aretha was in a state of mounting confusion, torn between his excitement about slipping away to see his son box in LosVegas and the worries and developments within Fort Thoreau.

Work on Dr. Zumwohl had progressed. THE ENTOMOLOGIST had sent scouts into the Auditorium. Fortunately the crux of the problem appeared to be confined to Dr. Henry Flipper Rickerburn, who had embedded in his diagnostic matrix a Scorpion-style disabler, which THE ENTOMOLOGIST identified as a "Vinegaroon," developed in Amsterdam by a Vitessa dirty tricks division. Aretha was pleased, but had Broadband check the Bug Man's handiwork at every turn. After the discrepancy regarding the transmission to Dingler, the drag queen couldn't be too careful, and there hadn't been time to have a private discussion with Finderz.

Of course, resolving the problems with Dr. Zumwohl didn't help Clearfather. The damage was already done. Aretha was surprised to learn that their mystery guest had left Pittsburgh so soon after arriving—bound for Texas, they assumed. Had he made contact with Dingler? It didn't seem likely. The lack of data was frustrating, especially given the outbreak of the eidolons in the bus station and the subsequent impact throughout ChildRite and Vitessa. It was almost impossible not to associate what was being called "the Dooley Duck Epiphany" with Clearfather. The question was—what other effects had he had? Spring fever had taken hold of Fort Thoreau, and people were getting friskier by the minute. It was time to beef up their intelligence-gathering capability even if it meant making the Kricket more susceptible to scanning.

There was still no word from the Corps of Discovery probe, but the military stealth insert that had targeted the hypothalamus was on the move and sending out a faint, irregular signal. What was particularly worrying was that all of the Kricket feeds into the monitor showed extreme surges in psychic energy. Finderz pulled up the schematic display of Clearfather's brain and, along with the X-rays and bodyscans, he had the anatomical images overlaying a map of America. The energy surges shimmered across the screen like magnetic storms raging over the Midwest. Dr. Quail and Lila Crashcart came in to evaluate the readings.

"What we're seeing here," said Lila, using her laser pointer, "are momentary flashes of anxiety verging on paranoia. These flickering discolorations here have the potential to become serious mental derangement."

"Are they due to the Tiresias?" Aretha asked.

"Unlikely" was Dr. Quail's opinion.

Lila agreed. "We wouldn't be expecting to see these storm systems forming as a result of the drug now—not after the Oblivion.6. And given the kinds of readings we've recorded since Clearfather left, we can be cautiously optimistic that structural damage was minimal. The stealth probe is another matter. You see this activity here? That's lust—a massive front forming. We're seeing patterns of sexual desire, fear, and anger of disturbing magnitude. The map of America that Finderz has layered in—the activity within Clearfather's mind mirrors what is happening in the country at large."

"You're saying—his brain is a microcosm of America?" Aretha asked.

"What's significant is the scale," Lila answered.

"I don't understand," said the drag queen.

"She means that the electrical output of Clearfather's brain isn't just in proportion to the country's—it's *equal* to it. Get it?" Finderz huffed, glancing down at the coils of watches on his arms.

"No," Aretha said. "I mean, yes. But I don't understand how."

"I can't explain it," the neuroresearcher sighed. "But if these readings continue, we're going to be in the same position we were in when we sent Clearfather off."

"How do you mean?"

"Look at the map. What if you had more earthquakes hitting the Now West Coast, forest fires ravaging the Mountain States, tsunamis swamping the East Coast, hurricanes blasting the South, and tornadoes running wild in the Midwest—all at the same time?"

"I'd be thinking wrath of God."

"We all know that at some point human psychology and the physical environment link. Clearfather may be a locus—like a transistor, capable of amplifying human psychic energy."

"To what end?" Aretha wondered aloud.

"Maybe he's a weapons system," Lila said. "In any case, if the turmoil within him continues to gain in intensity, he'll have a major impact not just in his local field of contact but throughout the continent. There could be chain reactions on levels we haven't even considered. And there are Jungian implications. Imagine a bomb going off in the collective unconscious."

"Psychic time bombs, cultural storms, a giant duck who wants a dick, and a ghost from the past with a mind as big as America—these aren't the sorts of issues that corporate lawyers are trained to handle," Aretha lamented. "Do we think that he has any consciousness of his powers?"

"My guess is that he's much more alert and clearheaded than when we saw him, but not tuned in to capabilities on this scale," Lila replied.

"Is it possible that he's being controlled remotely?" Aretha asked.

"He could be . . . in part. And resisting," Lila answered. "That would explain some of these readings, but not all. We know that the stealth probe is exerting an influence."

"Where is he now?"

"Indianapolis," Finderz replied, looking up from his watches. "And if he's heading for Dustdevil, he'll have to find his own transportation from Clinton or Amarillo because it's off the bus route."

"Do we have any more intelligence about what he'll find there?" Aretha asked.

"What extra Cubing I've had time for suggests there may be remnants of the love cult still hanging on, living in trailers and storm cellars," the dwarf answered. "The local reality may be more like predatory ferals. There are also a couple of celibacy sects in the area."

"Recommendations?" Aretha asked.

There was a pause, and then Finderz cleared his throat and glanced back down at his timepieces. "Locating the stealth probe is like trying to find a sniper team in the mountains of Afghanistan. But in order for it to operate it has to generate a signal—even thin and occasional. We're tracking the pulses now. If we can get a sustained fix, we may be able to target the signal and use the Mirror Field to send it back amplified."

"What would that do?"

"It'd blow the probe."

"And Clearfather's brain!"

"I'm just telling you," said the dwarf. "We've been talking damage control since he showed up."

Aretha bopped the diminutive genius on the head, and then said with lead-counsel authority, "The first thing we're going to do is to try to squeeze more grunt out of that Kricket. Then we need to reach out to the Corps of Discovery probe."

"What are you thinking?" asked Dr. Quail.

"I want better information. Plus the COD probe may give us remote navigation capability—or at least influence."

"Providing the stealth probe doesn't get it first," Finderz countered.

"What about turning the stealth unit?"

"It'll have a nova trigger."

"What if we attacked it with the Corps of Discovery?"

"Like Custard at the Little Butterhorn."

"Then that's what we'll do. There's no more risk to Clearfather than there is already, and the stealth unit may not expect such a contest. Get Broadband on it."

"There's another possible strategy," remarked Dr. Quail. "Perhaps not an alternative, more an adjunct. We send someone after him. There's no way the Kricket can rival a live witness. This is an unprecedented scientific opportunity. I'm not sure we shouldn't have done this right from the start."

"Doc, I admire your spirit," said Aretha. "But we're not going to risk you or Lila or even Finderz here on a mission like that."

"Thanks very much," coughed the dwarf.

"Well . . ." Aretha nodded, thinking about his son and the Fight for Life in LosVegas—the fact that Clearfather might be headed there, too. "I think we'll try to gather more information first. Lila, you and Doc get back to your rounds. We'll keep you up to speed on these readings. Meanwhile, if you have any other ideas, let us know."

With Quail and Lila gone, the drag queen intended to speak to Finderz about the Dingler transmission and the possibility of problems with THE ENTOMOLOGIST. Clearly the dwarf was upset, and Aretha wondered if he knew more than he was saying. There had been no words of comfort or criticism from Parousia Head. No word at all. The decision to sneak off to LosVegas was a hard one no matter what—but it would be impossible in the midst of a security crisis. And time was running out.

CHAPTER 3

Sinister Harmonies

After the Motivator shuffled off, Clearfather gripped the little white ball in his pocket and glanced around the station. There was a Harijan buffing the floor and a Haitian woman mopping up in front of Starbucks. The TWIN Voyancy Terminal was closed for "maintenance" but the liquidplex cubes showed images of pre-eidolonic news presenters—John Katz, formerly the host of *The Day Before Tomorrow*, and Bethany Quim, the onetime anchor of *Constant Entertainment*. There were no Inquisitors visible, but there was something not right about the people in the station. It wasn't the eighty-year-old man in the guava-colored leisure suit with his twelve-year-old adopted Cambodian daughter, or the black Sisters of Mercy Get Down Gospel group. And it wasn't the bearded rabbi or the quadriplegic in the automated mobile support station that concerned him. It was the men dressed up like a barbershop quartet—with neat little red bow ties and straw boaters, carrying vaudeville canes. If the people on the bus had cowered submissively at the Inquisitors, the barbershop quartet inspired something closer to terror. Especially when Clearfather realized there were five of them. Despite their different body shapes, from the husky bass to the weedy countertenor, they all had the exact same face, the same little mustache! He could feel them reaching out to him in his mind—some kind of insect magnetism.

One of them went and stood guard by his bus, which to his chagrin pulled out. Three converged inside the station, with the fifth minding the main door. The ones inside began to tap their canes and to make a sound in their throats as if they were preparing to sing. People covered their ears. Clearfather's mind was filled with feedback and fear. He didn't know what to do. Strangest of all, despite the growing panic, he felt a voracious sexual yearning come over him. I'm coming unglued, he thought. His head ached and the letters cut into his back began to burn. The rabbi ran for the restroom. The red-and-white-striped figures in the straw hats began to sing:

> *Buffalo Gals, won't you come out tonight, come out tonight*
> *Buffalo Gals, won't you come out tonight*
> *And dance by the light of the moon*

But underneath the words, Clearfather heard them say in a single locust voice:

> Speak our mind.
> You will be told when it's too late.
> Indecision is your only option.
> Doubt conquers all.

The Sisters of Mercy rose and retaliated with a bar of "Jesus Is the Answer," but the moment they'd waded into the song, the tenor pointed his cane at one of them and she let out a piercing cry as a second-degree burn began to form on her cheek. The group sat down and began comforting the injured woman, whose sobbing was now the main sound in the terminal but for the rhythmic tapping of the canes as the barbershop figures began to close in around Clearfather.

Well, he thought. Maybe I should just let them take me. Stop this searching and running. But a part of him found the idea of surrender—if not unacceptable, then very unwise. Someone had given him the map. Maybe even Uncle Waldo and Aunt Vivian. In any case, he hadn't completed his mission. He wasn't supposed to give in. If he did, he was letting someone down—maybe his family, maybe something bigger. The station went still except for the sound of the floor buffer.

"We're here for you," they said with one face, one voice.

Clearfather was about to tell them about the Pheasant Plucker when the Harijan stepped from behind a pillar with a gentle hydraulic hiss.

"U KANT," the Harijan said in a buzz-distorted voice.

The quartet stabbed their canes down together and made their harmonizing sound again. The Sisters of Mercy and the others fell back except for the quadriplegic.

The quartet made a move toward Clearfather. "We're here for you."

"GO!" the Harijan buzzed at Clearfather.

The baritone swiped his cane at the drone, but the drone was much faster and more flexible than it appeared. It snatched the cane away and slashed down on the baritone's arms and then the back of its legs. The striped figure buckled, but before the Harijan could finish it off, the others were upon it—its thin mantis frame wobbling and sparking.

"GOHHHHHH," the Harijan whined at Clearfather as a tracer dart occurred between the tenor's eyes—then a second later blew the head clean off. Clearfather looked in the direction from which the missile had come and saw the bearded rabbi braced against a pillar with a spear pistol balanced on his arm. The shot drew the attention of the others, who were about to launch into song when to Clearfather's further surprise the quadriplegic leapt from his wheelchair with what looked like an aqualung that glurped out a burst of purple-green juice. The fluid changed texture in the air, becoming a gelatinous mass that clung to the vests of the singers. Almost instantly it began smoking.

"Get out of here!" the now very mobile quadriplegic yelled and shoved Clearfather toward the door.

The crooners that had been hit with the goo were being eaten apart. The fifth member went for the rabbi but was grabbed at the ankle by the gripper-hand of the Harijan. Outside the station, the quad pushed Clearfather into the passenger seat of a taxi driven by a black man with a handlebar mustache. The rabbi leapt in through the open window and the cab shot off—but not before the fifth member of the quartet was able to fling itself on the back and scramble up on the roof.

"Damn!" howled the driver. "The countertenor!"

There was another sound—the thump of body on metal—and Clearfather saw that the bass had dragged itself onto the bumper and then up the back, the acid gnawing away the lower half of its body in a sizzling green miasma.

"Lean on it!" the quad blared. "We gotta lose these things before we get cut off!"

The cab screeched out and knocked over a rickshaw taking the turn onto Capitol Avenue on two squealing tires as the safety glass gave way in a cracked webwork of leeringly blank cyborg. The quad ripped out the panel and shoved it back at the bass, who hung on despite the impact. The countertenor's cane lasersliced the roof open like the lid of a can and worse still the two deadly units—corroding apart—began singing "Sweet Adeline . . ." Clearfather heard the words but beneath the melody he knew they were saying in blind termite voices . . . Uitessa INTEL—Maximum Response . . . No Negotiations . . . YIELD OR DIE.

The cab swerved across lanes and the biomechanoids continued to attack with the mindless fury of warrior insects. Police sirens were in pursuit now, and the countertenor had set the interior on fire with the cauterizing heat ray in the cane. The rabbi pulled out from his robes an evil-looking handcannon and let rip. The shotspray blew a hole in the countertenor's chest and tore off the rest of the jagged roof, which had the fortunate effect of flying off and decapitating the bass.

The driver feathered the brake pedal and the countertenor lost its balance—but just before it slipped all the way off to be steamrolled, it reached out its cane and hooked on, the termite voice gargling . . . DEATHFREEZEBRAINEATNOESCAPE.

The cab squealed hard left on Michigan Avenue through the Indiana–Purdue campus. Overhead, Clearfather heard the Teflon-coated rotary blades of a Black Dragonfly helicopter closing out of the south. The driver punched up a liquid crystal map readout. With savage exertion the countertenor swung up and began bashing against the shotgun-side window while the car careered over curbs. The disintegrating cybersinger droned on, but no longer with any semblance of meaning. Finally the quad scrambled through the gaping hole in the roof and pried the cane free. The countertenor uttered an indistinguishable cry and was gone. Clearfather sat lost in a whirlwind of conflicting messages and impulses. Every drive, every need and capability seemed to be firing at the same time, leaving him paralyzed as the smoking car shot on with pursuit hemming them in.

"All right," said the quad, pulling off his face. "Get them to send out the decoys."

He, or rather she, indicated Clearfather, for with the skin mask peeled away it was apparent that the quadriplegic, who'd turned out to be so agile and quick, was in fact a woman—and a redhead. The driver nodded and pressed a button on the console. Then he plucked off his mustache and pulled off what Clearfather saw was a skullcap. The rabbi lost her hat and beard. All three were women.

A giant Maori woman dressed in chain mail on a black 2000 Sergio Eliminator growled up beside them with a figure strapped on the back that resembled him. A moment later a husky blonde wearing a Viking helmet astride an exhaust-pipe-rumbling Harley appeared. She was armed with a modified Remington pump action and she, too, had a figure on the back that looked like him. Supersleek cinnabar-red Kawasaki speedbikes zipped into formation, ridden by two small figures in full Kevlar bodysuits and teardrop impact helmets. On the back of each was a dummy dressed like him.

"Lissen up," directed the redhead. "We're gonna pull off under the overpass and you're gonna be taken on one of the bikes."

"Where . . . are you going to take me?"

"You'll find out soon enough," the rabbi answered, a short woman with wary hamster eyes and hair like a toilet brush.

The convoy pulled off in the shadow of an overpass, the Dragonfly hovering out of rifle range.

"This is it," the redhead said and pointed to a big chrome Cyclone 1500 that roared up, ridden by a ham-fisted hillbilly girl in bib overalls with a Rebel flag painted on her helmet. She had a bowie knife strapped at her waist and a Ruger Blackhawk in a chiseled maduro holster. As Clearfather got out of the car, she ripped the dummy designed to look like him off the back and the rabbi and the driver stuffed it in the car and then started soaking the cab down with gasoline.

A moment later Clearfather was riding pillion behind the strapping woman and his effigy was on fire. His escort shot off in formation with five other bikes. The Dragonfly picked them up immediately but hesitated when two of the formation diverged, and then rejoined the entourage a few minutes later. Clearfather hung on as the bike raced—the formation darting and weaving, splitting up and then re-forming—straight through an automated checkpoint with alarms ringing then back through the other side to confuse them. Steel cranes shadowed the streets like giant Shanghai toys. His mind seemed to fog and then the bike bucked up over a curb and stopped. The air smelled of nasi goreng. Long strips of silver gaffer tape held the starfish of a shattered window in place.

"Here, Buck," said the big girl, who had the oversaturated scent of a hog lagoon. She leaned back and handed him a fur-lined eye mask. "Put this on—or Dixie'll get pissed."

His escort revved forward at half speed, winding around what he guessed was a network of alleyways in some derelict factory district. Finally the motorcycle stopped. He heard the rolling of a steel door. A cool garage-smelling darkness poured over him. The rider revved in over a grate. Another electronic door opened and they putted through. She shut off the bike and told him to get off. He heard the *whoosh* of a motorized vehicle. It squeaked to a halt just beside him.

Two sets of hands began searching him. He slipped the ivory ball into a fist and removed it from his pocket. The hands continued examining him, one lingering a moment on his erection. He heard the click of a metal detector and then a softer hum.

"There's a stowaway," a throaty female voice announced.

"Thought so," said another female voice. He thought it came from the vehicle in front of him. "Remove it."

Clearfather felt a prick behind his right ear as if a tiny scab had been picked.

"Did you know you had a tracking device on you?" the leaderly voice asked. "With a psychwave monitor?"

"No," Clearfather answered.

"Dusty, get one of our pigeons and secure the device to it, then let it go," the voice said—and then to Clearfather, "I'm sorry. But you'll have to strip down—we'll need to go over your clothes for any more. You've also been given a mild sedative to calm you down."

Clearfather was tempted to tell them about the Pheasant Plucker. Waves of panic came, but in between he had reassuring intuitions. Despite the awkwardness of his situation he didn't feel he was in immediate danger.

There was a hushed murmur when he'd slipped out of his underwear and stood nude. Someone made a retching sound and another woman hollered "Hooo-whee!"

"Turn around," the authoritative voice said.

He did and there was another almost symphonic silence.

"He looks like somebody," a woman whispered.

"Well," the authoritative voice said at last. "You've sure shown us yours! Take off the blind big boy and try to put that weapon down."

There were more snickerings and general exhalations as Clearfather eased off the fur-lined eye mask and blinked. He was in an old high-vaulted mechanic's garage with service pits and hydraulic jacks —a pale hint of asbestos-blue sky leaching through wire-reinforced windows behind iron bars. Mounted on the nearest wall, as if ruling over the chamber, was an ornate neon Indian in full headdress with the words KICKAPOO MOTORS beneath.

All of the figures in the room were women. Some wore feathers, some fur, others wire—with ritual scars, body piercing, and peculiar tattoos. Then there were the biosurgical modifications. A very homely white woman had hard, bony-looking growths on her head, like the beginnings of horns or antlers. Another had tusks. But what fascinated Clearfather was the Spanish woman with the tail. It was hairless and gristly but communicative, lighter in tone than the rest of her visible skin. It poked out of dark cottonex pants and curled like a question mark.

There was a logo on the back of the roller door they'd come through—a silver wheelbarrow full of pink fire. Several of the women wore navy-blue mechanic's coveralls. All of the jumpsuits had this same logo over the heart. One of those who'd been doing the inspecting—she had a bone through her nasal septum—motioned for him to put his clothes back on. He slipped the little white ball back into his pocket.

Most remarkable of all the women was the nearest—the owner of the authoritative voice. She sat in a forklift the same pink as the fire in the wheelbarrows. The vehicle had robotic arms mounted on the sides and a rotating hydraulic winch fitted on the back. She was bald but for a small patch of strawberry-blond hair the size of a golf divot on the top of her head. Her face was fleshy and profound, an effect heightened by her pince-nez. Her entire outfit consisted of a kind of metal harness. Between two small exposed breasts whose nipples were pierced with gold safety pins hung what he thought was a gourd on a gold chain, but which, as he looked closer, he realized was a shrunken human head—male. Both her legs ended just before the knee, the stumps of which were capped in anodized metal cups the same color pink as the wheelbarrow tire. From the dashboard of the forklift she fished out a cigar. A butch-pixie lit it. The abridged leader mouthed the cigar until the cherry was glowing, and then produced a series of smoke rings that wafted toward the neon Indian. "My name's Bean Blossom," she said. "I'm Big Man on Campus and this is the Kickapoo Ladies Social Club."

Clearfather could feel the relaxant starting to kick in, easing the static in his mind.

"What were those things that were chasing us?" he asked.

Bean Blossom glanced at the redhead, who was now standing next to a woman with an anteater-like profile. "They're called Disciplinarians," the redhead said.

"Organic robots," Bean Blossom explained. "Part of Vitessa Intel."

"Why were they after me?"

"We weren't told that. Our instructions were to get you off the bus and out of the station any way we could."

"Who gave the instructions?"

Bean Blossom sucked on her cigar a moment and then said, "Parousia Head, our patron and sponsor. We're a little bit more than a lesbian motorcycle club. We're a resistance unit jamming Vitessa where we can. I don't know why you're in trouble. All we know is that you have unusual gifts and that you've got memory problems—and that you're important to Parousia."

"Where is she?" Clearfather asked. "Can I meet her?"

There was a general murmur that echoed through the garage.

"She communicates when she needs to," Bean Blossom replied at last.

"Is she the one who gave me the map?"

"We don't know anything about a map," Bean Blossom said. "We were just told what you looked like and that Vitessa was on to you."

"What happens now?" Clearfather asked. "Am I . . . a prisoner?"

"No, you're not a prisoner. But our instructions are to keep you safe until we hear from Parousia. In the meantime, try to relax."

Two bottomless Asian women on Rollerblades wheeled in trolleys laden with teapots, china cups, a bowl of vivid pink tulips, and various nibblies.

"We always enjoy a proper High Tea," the crippled woman announced. "Although, mind the cucumber sandwiches!"

Several women laughed at this. Clearfather had to think calm. On top of everything else he still hadn't eaten.

Bean Blossom took an appreciative sniff of the steeping tea and then an anxious expression crossed her face, morphing into annoyance. She opened the teapots to inspect their contents. "Who made the tea today?" she demanded.

"I . . . I did, ma'am," said a young black woman in silk karate pants and red bra.

"Tourmaline," the older woman simmered. "What we have here is Spiderleg Kokeicha and Temple of Heaven Gunpowder. Those are *both* green teas. We always serve a green tea and a black tea!"

"I-I'm s-sorry, ma'am," Tourmaline sputtered.

"*Sorry?*" their leader shrieked. "*Show* me how sorry you are!"

Tourmaline dropped her karate pants and bent over the forklift. Bean Blossom cooed as she slipped her left hand into an oven mitt made of mink and with tender care began caressing the black girl's skin. With each lingering brush of the soft, almost wet-looking fur,

Tourmaline arched her bottom in supplication. As she did, Bean Blossom took her other hand and reached down for an antique military baton made of cane. This she inserted in one of the gripper-arms. Still stroking the smooth young buttocks with the mink glove, she took a couple of practice swipes. The reed made a whistling whine as it passed through the air, faster and harder than any human arm could propel it. Clearfather saw the girl's face grimace with anticipation.

"You seem both excited and horrified," Bean Blossom said to Clearfather. "You don't know whether to try to save Tourmaline or just let things take their course. It's an interesting dilemma, isn't it?"

Clearfather's head throbbed. The garage was dead still except for a creaking off in another section. He squeezed the little ball, trying to hear the voices of the old people, but nothing came through.

"Nietzsche said, 'Few are made for independence.' Are you strong enough?"

Clearfather began to perspire and tremble. Tourmaline's scent filled his nostrils. The robot arm whirred, lifting the reed like a moistened finger to gauge the wind.

"Don't push me . . . ," he gasped.

"Who are you to tell me what to do?" the stump-legged woman challenged.

There was something about this interloper that provoked her need to assert authority.

"I . . . I'm not a pheasant plucker . . . I'm the Pheasant Plucker's son . . . ," Clearfather choked. "But I'll keep on fucking pheasants . . . till the Pheasant Plucker . . . comes . . ."

The arm with the cane in the grippers surged up but froze. He could see the girl's flesh crawl. Bean Blossom tried to drive the arm down but it didn't respond. Instead the other arm activated and, with grippers clicking like castanets, seized her from her seat. The hydraulic winch at the rear of the forklift spun around into position and lifted Bean Blossom onto the hook. Hoisted from her mobile throne and rudely elevated, her mangled lump of body appeared all the more absurd in contrast with Tourmaline's. The winch swung around and the gripper-arm grasped one of her stumps, turning her upside down—teapot steam misting the lenses of her pince-nez. The arm with the cane came alive again and rose, and with the reed tickled and tinged her safety-pin nipple rings—every so often breaking away to tap on the shrunken head that dangled down into the Devonshire cream.

"What do you think of independence now?" Clearfather asked.

"I think you could dunk me like a tea bag," Bean Blossom gurgled, her voice never quite losing its authority. "But you'd have to *want* to do that. Is that what your powers are for?"

"I don't know what they're for," Clearfather admitted. "But it's not for standing by and watching someone suffer helplessly."

"What if they *want* to be punished?" Bean Blossom inquired, dragging the shrunken head back through the cream.

"Get up," he told Tourmaline. "Pull your pants up."

"She won't do it," Bean Blossom said. "She's a love slave to me. Tourmaline," she said. "Spank yourself as hard as you can."

"Stop it," he said as the winch stirred. "Or you'll end up in the lemon curd."

"You see how satisfying it is?" Bean Blossom said, bending down to touch her tongue to the desecrated cream.

Clearfather felt himself on the verge of a seizure.

"Tourmaline, I want you to satisfy him orally. Do you understand?"

"Yes, ma'am," Tourmaline said, rising up and stepping out of her pants.

"No . . ." was all Clearfather could say, but he no longer knew what he meant.

He felt quick fingers unzip his pants. Then moist warm breath.

"What are you doing?" he demanded.

"I'm demonstrating the contrary nature of submission and power. I'm hanging here like a wounded dugong and yet I'm in control."

The entire chamber was still now, which made the peculiar creaking in the distance seem that much more noticeable.

"Do you feel how satisfying submission and surrender is?" Bean Blossom hissed.

The forklift's motor awakened and the vehicle swung around, knocking a tea trolley into one of the service pits—spinning Bean Blossom from the hook. The forklift stopped, the hook snapped, and Bean Blossom flew into the crowd, her pince-nez shattering against a wall. Then the tweezers reached out and crushed the shrunken head—gunpowder tea dripping down the slick chrome of the lift—gobs of cream and curds everywhere.

CHAPTER 4

Orders from the Chief

After Clearfather blacked out, Bean Blossom and the Kickapoo Ladies had the chance to pull themselves together and clean up. Hairy Mary and the Valkyrie picked him up and carried him through the back wall of the garage into a cavernous abandoned parking facility. The redhead, whose name was Carny, went to speak to Bean Blossom. She found the abbreviated leader down in one of the service wells, smoking a cigar, bare-stumped and wearing a pair of bifocals to replace the pince-nez.

"I don't know where to start," Bean Blossom said. "When I was with the Feds, I saw examples of psi. And I've seen the stuff Vitessa has endowed their organatrons with. But I've never—"

"You had an orgasm like the rest of us," Carny finished.

"Orgasm?" Bean Blossom puffed. "I've *never* come like that in my life. It was as if the repression of his anger and his ambivalence created this storm of psychosexual energy. And he was able to project it—to impregnate each of us with it, pardon the expression! That's a helluva lot different from bending spoons or even deflecting bullets. No wonder Parousia wants him under wraps."

"How do think Kokomo will react?" Carny queried.

"Kokomo's not going to meet him! And even if she did, she's so lost in her own world, she wouldn't understand."

"One day she might just break out of that world," Carny said.

"What do you mean by that?" Bean Blossom frowned, stubbing out her cigar on one of her stump cups.

Carny noticed that the chain that had held the shrunken head had left a contusion on the older woman's wattly neck. "One day she'll wake up to where she is."

"I'm not ashamed of who I am," Bean Blossom asserted. "But it'd be best if Kokomo never knew he was here."

"What are you going to do, put her in a cage as well as that helmet?"

"Don't be snide, dear, it doesn't become you. If you had a daughter—"

"I did have a daughter. Remember?"

Sue City leaned over the edge of the service pit. "Message coming."

Bean Blossom activated the hydraulic lift, which brought them to ground level

"You want me to leave?" Carny asked.

"No. One day soon this may be yours to look after. You should get used to Parousia. It's a little unnerving at first."

Carny hopped onto the forklift and Bean Blossom wheeled beneath the neon Indian. Carny had long been teased by the suspicion that Bean Blossom was really Parousia Head—that their absent leader was a fiction to bind the tribe and lend more weight to her direction. It was certainly odd that no one had ever seen Parousia Head with their own eyes and yet she seemed to know all about them. Now facing the actual presence, it was hard not to believe in a distant but omniscient mastermind—for the air was filling with urgency and the Kickapoo chief was changing.

The intricate neon tubing with its nostalgic ice cream colors crystallized, became more complex. The colors intensified and strobed with luminous agitation until the Chief emerged out of the wall . . . and then the face came alive and the figure leapt soundlessly onto the floor. At nine feet tall with broad shoulders and a flowing warbonnet, the fluorescent eidolon appeared gigantic next to Bean Blossom and Carny. It strutted about with exaggerated male arrogance, its colors shimmering with a Geiger-counter-like static, yet when it spoke, the voice was female and sultry—the breathy promise of a lost movie starlet.

"*A passing of the torch?*"

"A sharing of the torch," Bean Blossom replied.

"*You were sloppy at the station and have drawn the attention of the Vitessa Pantheon,*" the voice said.

"I'm sorry," Bean Blossom fawned, noticing a chocolate-covered strawberry that had escaped the cleanup lying on the floor.

"*Worse still was that stunt here. He is not to be fooled with. I need to get him in for treatment.*"

The little patch of hair on Bean Blossom's scalp stood up with the static electricity emanating from the fluorescent giant.

"*When he regains consciousness, check his psych readings. Balance him with Pythagoras if you have to. In the morning he will need to be properly sedated so ensure that he gets a full dose of Hegel.*"

"Yes, ma'am." Bean Blossom trembled, averting her eyes . . . fixated by the chocolate-covered strawberry.

"*At ten o'clock tomorrow, secure him in a coffin—one of the nice old ones—and have Martha One Tribe and Fanny Anny drive him in one of the hearses to the James Whitcomb Riley Memorial in the Crown Hill Cemetery. Make sure you have a decoy. If no one is there, they are to use the public com center to contact the Crazy Horse Motel in Rapid City, South Dakota, and ask for Mr. Meadhorn in Number Six.*"

"Yes, ma'am." Bean Blossom nodded.

The Chief stopped strutting and strobing and then seemed to freeze, shattering like stained glass—only there were no shards on the floor. The great neon Indian was back in position on the wall, as if it had never left. Bean Blossom urged the forklift forward and scooped up the stray strawberry with one of the pallet loaders. The heat of the Chief had melted the chocolate.

CHAPTER 5

Big Room Inside

Clearfather had started to faint when the tornado took shape inside him. He felt the force of it possess him and then explode. Afterward there was nothing more to hold him aloft and so down he fell . . . whirling through fragments of memory or dream . . . a glow-in-the-dark green skull full of bubblegum . . . the man and the radio tower . . . the boy in the bathroom . . . jigsaw puzzles . . . women.

When he came to, he was on a cot in a shipping container in the underground parking lot of the Kickapoo Ladies Social Club. His head felt clear but ached. When not being inspected and whispered over, he'd been guarded by Rock Island Girl and Haka, the big Maori woman, both horrified and even ashamed by the satisfaction they'd experienced. But Rocky had gotten hungry and Haka had to pee, so Clearfather had been momentarily left alone. He got up from the cot. It was quiet in the enclosed parking lot. He noticed several more shipping containers. The walls, the poles, and the containers were all decorated with spray-painted images—motorcycles, animals, naked women.

He heard again the creaking that had caught his attention before.

He began to follow it. He came to a hole knocked in a brick wall. There was a hint of daylight seeping in through the barred windows and he guessed it was almost dark out. The creaking sound called him on. He entered another chamber and saw a full-sized playground swing set erected on a section of Astroturf. The sound he'd been hearing was a young woman, swinging back and forth, pumping her legs and hurling herself into space. She wore an old-fashioned camel-colored pinafore over a white crêpe shirt with brown and white saddle shoes, but it was impossible to tell her age, for her head was concealed in a spherical helmet—a thermoplastic bubble textured with airware and telecommunications links.

"I'm sorry," Clearfather announced, thinking he might have frightened her.

She kept swinging. He announced his presence several times without any change in her behavior, and it occurred to him that the helmet cut off awareness of the outside world. He'd crept up right beside her and she still pumped and soared without the slightest regard. It intrigued and annoyed him, to be ignored. He grabbed the chains of the swing as she flew back toward him. She hung in space, her body twitching like a helpless puppet. He let go of the swing.

The chains twisted, and she veered into the right leg of the set, smacking her knee. She fell out of the swing and would've been struck in the bubble by the heavy black rubber seat had he not leapt forward and caught it. He was pleased to have gotten her attention but distressed that she might have hurt herself. Lying in a heap of pinafore on the Astroturf, she appeared all helmet now, a red light blinking on the surface.

"Are you all right?" he asked. "I'm—sorry."

He knocked on her helmet. She grabbed at the air and then went still again. Then she fell into a spasm. Thinking that the helmet had shorted out, Clearfather tried to take it off. It finally released with a tiny sigh, and he caught the scent of honeysuckle.

The woman might've been twenty but had the unlined surprised look of a child who'd just pulled a sweater over her head. She was bald like him—her eyes, the vivid tropical green of monkey bananas.

"Are you real?" she asked.

Clearfather wasn't sure what to answer. "I didn't know if you could hear me. I didn't mean to hurt you."

"Stand by," the girlish figure directed and then just sat there.

"Stand by for what?" Clearfather asked. "Are you all right?"

"I can see you but I can't say you," she replied and then held both hands to her head as if in pain.

Perplexed, Clearfather peered inside the helmet. The neck and skull cushioning was made of foam-injected cyberskin, and there was a breathing filter. There were two distinct hemispheres, both upholstered with ultrafine dermatrodes like cilia. In a narrow band around the forehead there were hundreds of different-colored needles of data crystal arranged in intricate geometric patterns. He could hear faint music and voices as if there were people trapped inside, and when he looked more closely he saw honeycombs of tiny portholes, swarming and pulsing with light. He put the helmet on. There was a moment of darkness; then he felt a stinging sensation like chlorine in his eyes, and information began flooding in. Stock reports and commodity prices—obituaries, pollution levels, engineered species updates—volcano diving, dragon boat races—men in giant box kites trying to cut each other's cables. The media onslaught sloshed through his mind and everything seemed on the verge of dissolution. Then just as the bonds began to break apart, he focused a John Katz news update on Dooley Duck.

"The famous blue duck continues to develop a life of his own. Serial manifestations of Dooley throughout America and the world have seen the emergence of genitalia, which, according to a panel of animators and zoologists, are generously proportioned. Sanders Lugwich, the head of Creaturetivity, the studio responsible for creating Dooley, has claimed total ignorance as to the factors concerning the mysterious transformation of their character.

"ChildRite, a subsidiary of the Vitessa Cultporation, has initiated legal proceedings. Meanwhile, Christian Nation and the American Family Solidarity Soldiers are burning effigies of the giant duck and have taken credit for a nailbomb that exploded at a Nurturing Center in Spartanburg, South Carolina, killing four staff members and their children who were protesting on behalf of Dooley. The pro Duck + Dick movement has embraced the dead as martyrs.

"As if that's not problem enough for ChildRite, Managing Director Radinka Gruber has been sacked by Wynn Fencer himself. Given the grueling heat of the public spotlight, Gruber's shoes have proved hard to fill and no one within ChildRite has put up a hand for the job. In fact, the single volunteer from within the entire Vitessa network has been a regional R-and-D executive named Julian Dingler. When asked what would inspire an Intelligent House Services technologist to take the wheel of the largest childcare provider in the world at a moment like this, Mr. Dingler said, 'It's in times of crisis that people reveal themselves.'"

Clearfather felt the data ripped out of his mind like barbs breaking off.

"It's not calibrated for you! You fool!"

The helmet cracked open and he was back in the garage, blinking.

"See to Kokomo!" Bean Blossom commanded. "And get the psychometer."

Clearfather glanced at the bubble helmet and saw a large burned hole.

"I . . . I didn't mean to hurt her, is she all right?" he asked.

"The helmet is calibrated to Kokomo's brainwaves," Bean Blossom snapped. "It's a very expensive piece of therapy and you've damaged it."

"I'm sorry," Clearfather said. "I'll . . . pay you."

"Are you all right, Kokomo, dear?" Bean Blossom asked.

"You can't always get what you want," the girl replied.

"What's the reading?" Bean Blossom asked.

"It's okay," a woman named Fancy Nancy reported.

"Thank God." Bean Blossom sighed. She turned to Clearfather and said gruffly, "This is my adopted daughter, Kokomo. She's an idiopath. The helmet is to provide direct brain stimulus and a controlled flow so that she won't retreat further."

"I can see him but I can't say him," Kokomo chirped.

"Kokomo, come here, honey," Bean Blossom clucked. "Are you okay?"

It occurred to Clearfather that under her childish outfit the girl had a gorgeously shaped body.

"She's got a head for riddles," Bean Blossom puffed, and the bald young woman made a sound like an engine turning over—then spun around and snickered.

"What's the difference between a nun and a woman sitting in a bath?"

"One's got a soul full of hope, the other has a hole full of soap." Clearfather smiled.

Kokomo looked both petulant and delighted.

"That was rude, Koke. Give him another one," Bean Blossom challenged. She was surprised at how open and aware the girl seemed—and somewhat frightened.

"Where do you find a turtle with its legs cut off?"

"Wherever you left him," Clearfather replied, as the girl's eyes filled with wonder.

"There are ten birds on a branch and a man shoots one. How many are left?"

"None. They all fly away."

Kokomo hesitated—her mouth dropped open—then she made a motorcycle gearshift sound and sauntered over to him, thrusting her hands deep into his pockets.

Clearfather squirmed at this invasion but froze when he heard a voice inside his head that he hadn't heard before. It was a female voice and it said, *Who's the boy in the bathroom? Don't be afraid.*

Gripping his manhood, the jade-eyed vixen grinned and pumped her hips squealing, "Ooby dooby! Ooby dooby!"

Clearfather shrank from her grasp—but in doing so he felt the girl snatch the ivory ball in his pocket. With a gasp of alarm he watched as, in one fluid motion, she extracted her hand and popped the ball into her mouth! Her green eyes burned with some weird intimacy. His impulse was to shoot out his hand to close on her throat—to keep her from swallowing—but he found that before he could reach her lovely neck she was holding his hand and looking into his eyes. Her pupils reminded him of tiny tornadoes held captive in the green crystal of her irises. She turned and opened his hand and from her mouth released the white ball, warm and moist, into his palm. Then as she closed his fingers around his prize, she gave them a delicate lick.

"Well?" said Carny in Bean Blossom's ear.

"Shut up," the little woman gruffed, stubbing out her cigar.

CHAPTER 6

The Haunted Casserole

The helmet was damaged but how extensively was hard to determine. One thing was certain, it was filled with Dooley Duck, who'd become a global icon. Rampant sexuality had broken out across the entire Vitessa stable of eidolonic characters and human stars. Ratings for some programs soared while the fortunes of others plummeted toward extinction. And so the inexplicable phenomenon continued to ripple through the Vitessa Cultporation.

Carny dressed Kokomo up for dinner in genie pants, a silk shirt, and a smoky-quartz-blond wig. Bean Blossom didn't approve and sat sideways in her forklift with a pained expression on her face. The girl was suddenly coming out of her shell and now that the shell was broken, Bean Blossom wondered if Kokomo could ever fit back inside.

"Do you know about Fuzzy Wuzzy?" Clearfather asked, and the girl grinned and slapped her thigh just like Edwina Corn. "Fuzzy Wuzzy was a bear. Fuzzy Wuzzy had no hair. Fuzzy Wuzzy wasn't fuzzy . . . was he? Was he bare?"

"Oola boola, sasparoolya. You take chocolate, I'll take vanoola," she crooned in return, but as she said these words in her singsong green-eyed chatter, Clearfather heard below them, *"God does not know things because they are. They are because he knows them."*

Carny watched their visitor closely, thinking about the fate that lay ahead. Now having seen the Chief in action and Bean Blossom in submission, she could no longer maintain the theory that her stump-legged cohort was the real leader, however cunningly masked. There really was a Parousia Head—or something like her—and she had designs on Clearfather. Carny was uneasy. She hadn't felt so unsure since the death of her daughter.

Dinner was served at a long table. Tuna-fish casserole and pink lemonade. The thought that they might try to drug his food had occurred to Clearfather, but he was so hungry he'd have eaten horse dung. The flashes of pain and cross-channel blurring supported his fear that he was brain-damaged. Yet he didn't think his ability to comprehend the undermessage of the Disciplinarians or Kokomo was a symptom of this. And the concept of injury didn't explain his psychic abilities, although he didn't think of them as "his." They seemed to flow through him in moments of sexual arousal, fear, or anger. Do I have any control? he wondered. Could I move some silverware? Or a piece of bread?

Dixie leaned over to load herself another serving of casserole. But when she levered her slab of tuna crisp free, she found the piece of bread stuck to her forearm. Clearfather smiled. Kokomo's eyes flickered. He spotted Lola about to sip her lemonade.

"Don't think twice, it's all right," Kokomo chirruped.

"Shit!" Lola spluttered, her crotch soaked.

"What?" Clearfather asked, feeling relaxed and even a bit cheerful.

"I am he as you are he as you are me and we are all together."

Hairy Mary lost the grip on her glass. "Damn!"

"What's wrong?" Bean Blossom scowled. "This isn't the children's table."

"How many times can you subtract six from thirty?"

"No more riddles," Bean Blossom commanded.

"Once," said Clearfather. "Then it's no longer thirty."

He noticed Haka groping for the casserole and nudged it out of reach.

"What falls but never breaks, breaks but never falls?"

The dish lurched back and Haka put her big hand straight into the mush.

That's odd, thought Clearfather. I didn't do that.

"I said no more riddles," Bean Blossom croaked.

"Day and night," he answered.

Sadie Lady's plate was clean and empty but for her fork. He eased the fork around in a clockwise rotation.

"More party tricks?" Bean Blossom huffed.

The fork suddenly rotated counterclockwise all the way around the plate.

"Please stop this exhibition," Bean Blossom said.

A square of casserole struck her in the face.

"I didn't do that," Clearfather insisted.

"No?" Bean Blossom boiled, wiping the dribble from her cheek. "Then who did?"

Kokomo's exit green eyes flashed at him with conspiratorial delight.

My God, he thought . . . we're two of a kind.

But what kind?

CHAPTER 7

The Hope of a Traitor

When Carny went to check on Bean Blossom, she found the little titan sufficiently recovered to be instructing Martha One Tribe and Fanny Anny. Bean Blossom broke off the briefing when Carny entered.

"You all right?" the redhead asked.

"I feel the way I did when I woke up in that cannery in Hoboken and found that this is what the Tongs had done to me," BB grumbled, indicating her maimed legs. "I understand you took prompt action."

"She's resting. Psych readings show her normal level of distortion. He's been given the sedative."

"I want him gone, Carny. Martha's going to tune up the hearses. The sooner we see the back of him, the better."

"Maybe," the redhead nodded. "But what about Kokomo? You're not thinking things can just go back to what they were?"

"When he's gone, she'll return to normal."

"But for her, normal has been damaged—lost in her own mind. She can relate to him. And we've all found out something about her we never knew."

"What could you possibly be thinking?"

"I don't know." Carny sighed. "But Kokomo doesn't belong here. Not now. However painful it is to admit it."

"Painful?" cackled Bean Blossom. "Painful is having your legs inserted in a mulching machine on half speed, so wired up on gecko-starfish amphetamines you can't black out. Don't tell me about pain. And don't do anything silly or I swear, Carny—as much as I once loved you—and as much as I admire you still—I'll teach you about it. You leave Kokomo alone and execute the plan as per our orders."

Carny nodded, but she knew that there was no turning back. Neither Clearfather nor Kokomo was meant to be moved like a chess piece. That was the Vitessa way and only evil could come of it. Besides, the duo's abilities suggested just how precarious such a strategy might be. If Kokomo's powers were derived not from Clearfather but something in her that he'd awakened—how would she react the next morning to find out he was gone? Carny put a com in to her ex-husband, the message blinking back and forth through empty apartments, vehicles, and safe houses—his screening network of false premises and fake IDs. Then she went to check on Clearfather.

He was woozy—and truth be known clogged with casserole—but his eyes lightened when he saw Carny.

"Is she all right?"

"Why do I know you don't mean Bean Blossom?" Carny replied.

"You must be psychic," Clearfather answered—and the redhead grinned.

"Don't be too hard on BB. She's got Bentworth's Condition and Combat Fatigue—and Short Woman Syndrome. But Kokomo's resting peacefully. She'll be fine. She's had quite a lot of excitement today. Do you have this effect on everyone you meet?"

"Sort of," Clearfather said.

"What are your plans?" Carny whispered, pulling him behind a pillar.

"I was going to wait and see what this Parousia Head knows about me. But I want to get back on my journey, to follow my map. My next stop is in Texas."

"Who gave you the map?" Carny asked.

"I don't know," Clearfather answered. "Don't know what it's supposed to lead me to. I only have fragments of memories . . . I'm not sure it's even my past. But I have the map and I'm going to see the journey through, Parousia Head or not."

Carny smiled sadly. This odd man, who looked familiar sometimes—much older than his thirty-odd years—and at other moments childlike and fresh like Kokomo—he inspired emotions in her she thought she'd lost.

"You can't go back on the bus again, although with the tracking device gone you won't be so easy to find."

"I'll walk if I have to," Clearfather replied.

"It's not that," Carny said. "Tomorrow Parousia has ordered that you be taken."

"Where to?"

"I don't know the ultimate destination, but you're going to be smuggled out in a coffin. We run what appears to be a funeral home. Good business with the high-rise cemeteries now. It's one of several fronts we use."

"A coffin?" Clearfather groaned. "I've got to get to Texas."

"What's in Texas?" Carny asked.

"I don't know. But if I don't go, I'll never know . . . and that might be the answer."

"What about Kokomo?"

"Would she come to Texas . . . and beyond?"

"As far as I know she's never been anywhere except her own mind. But I think she'd go with you anywhere. You're connected somehow."

Clearfather thought a moment. "I think you're right. I see myself . . . somehow . . . in her."

"Would you look after her?" Carny queried. "She may have—

powers—but she still needs help. She could relapse. She could . . . who knows?"

"What do you know about her?" Clearfather asked.

"Bean Blossom was a Federal agent. Undercover job went wrong. When she was recovering, her path crossed Kokomo's and she adopted her. That's all I know."

"So you want me to—"

"I don't know what I want you to do. I just know that if that girl belongs anywhere, it's with you. You two have to work it out from there."

"I'll look after her," Clearfather said—and the way he said it convinced Carny. She led him back to his cot in the shipping container.

"Do you have any money?" she asked.

"Yes," said Clearfather.

"I've put a call in to my ex-husband," she said. "I think he'll help you."

"Why?" Clearfather asked.

"Because of me," the redhead replied.

"Why do you want to help?"

"I don't honestly know," Carny answered. "I just know it's the right thing to do."

"You see," said Clearfather. "You have a map, too—even if you don't know what it means. What does your husband—ex-husband do?"

"He's a Pentecostal preacher supposedly—but he's really a people smuggler. Makes trips to Mexico. Due for one soon. If he hasn't left yet, he's your ticket out of here. He could get you across the border."

"That's not where the map leads," Clearfather said.

"You have more to think about than just yourself now. If it came down to choosing between the map and her, which would you choose?"

"I can't answer that," Clearfather replied. "A part of me feels as though I've only been alive a couple of days. I've got to take one crossroads at a time."

Good Lord, thought Carny. What am I doing letting two such dangerous innocents loose with Vitessa closing in?

"All right," she said. "You've been given a sedative, as you've probably guessed—so you have to listen carefully. Tomorrow morning I'm going to give you a muscle relaxant so you'll really appear doped. You'll be taken out through a tunnel that leads to the funeral home and placed inside a coffin in one of our hearses. We always use decoys. I'm driving the decoy hearse, only I'm going to tell Martha and Fanny there's been a change in plans. Kokomo will have to be in the coffin already."

"What's going to happen to you? You won't be very welcome when they find out."

"No," the redhead agreed. "I'll play that by ear. I might catch a ride over the border with Jacob. Be ready for anything when you wake up."

CHAPTER 8

AWOL

The situation back at Fort Thoreau had become ec-static—flowers blooming wildly, birds nesting with manic industry, and people quite frankly fucking like rabbits—or "Doing the Dooley" as it was now being called.

Jesus, thought Aretha, is this more of Clearfather's doing? It wasn't like Pandora hysteria—all mucus and degradation until exhaustion set in. This was a mass resurrection of physical happiness. Aretha felt all the lonelier and more lustful as a result. It had been almost two years since his last dalliance—two years of media jamming, reverse neuroconditioning, and drug detox nursing. Now to be wading around in this hormonal swamp—well, it wasn't conducive to getting much work done. And there was plenty to do. The big Fight was weighing on his mind and making his heart soar all at once. What was his son thinking—feeling? He was going to face Xerxes McCallum, the Corpse Maker, alone in a boxing ring! Time was running out and Aretha still had no definite idea how he was going to get out west. In addition to all the usual risks, flying meant passing through the tight sphincter of Vitessa security. How they'd love to nail a resistance member of his standing. He'd given thought to taking the Greyhound but now with the breaking news out of Indianapolis, that didn't seem like a good idea. The word was out about their mysterious visitor and Vitessa was massing for action. Full details had not surprisingly been suppressed in the mainstream TWIN news but from everything they could gather, there'd been a chase. That an organization had tried to help Clearfather didn't surprise Aretha. There were other resistance groups scattered throughout the country and the world. They might even have been the ones responsible for Clearfather in the first place. In any case, the more Aretha thought about making it to LosVegas, the more he was forced to consider the delicate issue of approaching his wife. One of their operatives, who'd recently been murdered in Brooklyn, had done some fieldwork for the drag queen on the sly, so he knew that Eartha was still living at their old town house on 81st and Riverside Drive. He didn't know anything else about her life, but she was still there. He hadn't seen or contacted her since he'd joined the Satyagrahi and dropped out of sight. She might shoot him—and a part of him felt he deserved it. But he didn't know who else he could trust.

On top of all these problems, there was the pigeon factor. Just when they were trying to get a clearer idea of what was happening to their ejected guest, their main window of information had closed. Now their data would consist of what they could glean from any trace on the stealth probe or the Corps of Discovery, when and if it ever made contact. Geographical positioning would have to be referenced against satellite fixes—and that would mean running the gauntlet of Vitessa Intel.

Then a fragile notion began taking form again. It was just an excuse to offer the others. But it sounded good. Best of all, he hadn't been the one to think of it. Dr. Quail had put up the idea. In order to know what was going on with Clearfather, they had to have someone on the ground—right there with him. It was still possible that he was a shadow op gone wrong, but if Vitessa had known about him up-front, he never would've reached Pittsburgh. The fact that the at-tempted interception had taken a while to develop suggested that Vitessa had had to be tipped off—probably by the same mole re-sponsible for the Rickerburn fritz. One thing was certain—his power. Even now, the pigeon-borne Kricket was giving a reading that suggested the aftermath of a local psychic event of seismic propor-tions.

"That had to be Clearfather," the drag queen remarked to the dwarf.

"You're right!" Keeperz said, snapping his stubby fingers. "How could I be so stupid? We don't need the probes to track him. All we have to do is zero in on the strongest psychwave patterns—and that's likely to be him!"

"But in order to monitor him, you have to use Vitessa satellites—a big risk."

"We don't have to stay logged on," Finderz countered. "We don't need continuous positioning when we can pick him up whenever we like."

"Won't Vitessa be doing the same?"

"I don't think they understand yet what they're dealing with. I mean, *we* don't, really. Their first strategy will probably be to close in around his last known position—try to flush out what he can do. The ace they've got is that stealth probe—assuming they know about it. If it can send out a sustainable signal, they can take him out."

"Jesus!" Aretha groaned. "There's still a hope that the Corps of Discovery will make contact and take it on."

"Like I said," said the dwarf. "A massacre in the making. As I see it, the only card we're holding is the map. If he hasn't regained mem-ory function—and of course he may not have any real memories—there's nothing else for him to hold on to."

Aretha felt another pang of regret at how they'd sent him away, even if it had been out of self-preservation. And it made him think again of LosVegas. It wasn't fair that he didn't tell anyone he was leaving. It would destabilize morale and get everybody paranoid. Finderz was the logical person to tell, but the drag queen didn't have the nerve to say anything. The dwarf hadn't spoken about Aretha's son or the upcoming superbout—but he had mean private radar for those sorts of things.

Still, if Aretha left Keeperz a message explaining how he'd gone after Clearfather—he could even say the order had come from Parousia Head—that would be harder to see through. The dwarf would have to be in a little doubt. Providing Aretha got back in a few days' time, everything might be okay.

It was radical. It was foolish. But he was willing to take the risk. And if Parousia Head found out and wanted to excommunicate him—well, he was willing to risk that, too. He'd provided loyal service without question for a long time. The Satyagrahi were his adopted family but he couldn't go on living with the hole in his heart over his real family. He had karmic repair work to do. He just hoped it wasn't too late. The one issue he couldn't rationalize away was the nagging question of the infiltrator. It was time to broach the subject with Finderz, and a news replay filtering across one of the monitor walls gave him the opportunity.

"Odd thing about Dingler's promotion to the head of ChildRite," Aretha remarked.

The dwarf stilled an image of Dingler during a press conference and moved it to the workbench of his thinkstation. "It's a bit too much to see as a coincidence," he agreed.

"What's your theory about why Clearfather didn't meet him? I've been meaning to ask you, but with so much happening, there hasn't been time."

"How do we know they didn't meet?" the dwarf asked as he enhanced the image.

"Well, we don't. But Clearfather left Pittsburgh pretty quick. You'd think if Dingler was involved, more would've come of the meeting."

"Dingler's involved all right—we know that from the datafile. It's the nature of his involvement that we're in the dark about. Check this out."

While he'd been talking, the dwarf had loaded a full-frontal image of Clearfather with a layered bone scan. Beside it he placed the touched-up and screen-filtered grab of Dingler and equalized the size and image density of both.

"Pity we didn't have this image of Dingler before," said the dwarf.

"Wow," said Aretha at last. "There are serious similarities."

"You'd say they were family, yes?"

"They look about the same age. Like brothers."

"Except Clearfather's been dead his whole life, remember."

"That would make Dingler . . ."

"The missing son of Paul Sitio aka Hosanna Freed. And he would be about the same age as when the father was murdered by the Feds."

"If that's true, we ought to be able to track confirming evidence. DNA. Something."

"Don't count on it," Finderz argued. "Dingler wouldn't have gotten to where he is without learning a few tricks."

"It still doesn't explain what happened in Pittsburgh—or what didn't happen. You *did* send him that coded message alerting him to Clearfather's arrival?" Aretha asked.

"And I gave Clearfather the instructions—you saw me!"

"Just checking."

"Well, you don't need to check on me!" the dwarf whined. "I am a craftsman."

"I know," said Aretha. "What's the latest on Dr. Z?"

"We'll do a final bug run tomorrow, but we'll need a volunteer. Shall we catch one of the meat-things in the tunnels?"

"You know I hate that practice!"

"If someone's going to end up with an omelet brain we don't want it to be one of our own people!"

"I'll leave it you," Aretha sniffed. It was hard not to think that Keeperz was the better leader. Intellectually brilliant but also practical.

"What about THE ENTOMOLOGIST?"

"What about him?"

"No sign of trouble?"

"Have *you* seen any signs of trouble?" the dwarf asked.

"No, but I don't work as closely with him—It—as you do."

"Are you saying you think he's defective?"

"Well, let's not mince words: there's a saboteur among us. We've seen what he or she did to Rickerburn—what's next?"

The dwarf lowered his voice. "I think I've worked out a way to set a trap."

"A trap?" Aretha repeated, curiosity piqued.

"Don't worry, you'll be the first to know the results—but the less you know now, the more naturally you'll behave. Leave it to me."

"I don't know what we'd do without you, Finderz."

"Well, fortunately, you won't have to find out," the dwarf grinned. "I'm not running off anywhere."

Aretha tried to smile but was afraid the expression turned out more of a frown—and so slunk back to his tent and packed a small bag, and then decided he needed to bring more shoes, and of course matching accessories. Then he sat down to draft his message. He considered copying all the Strategists but then decided against it. The dwarf was his closest confidant and by common agreement the second in command. His mind was filled with anxiety—tortured by misgivings and all too aware of how fragile his situation was, how flimsy his plan—which was no plan at all really. But he couldn't turn back. Not if there was a chance of seeing his son and regaining his family. Even for just a moment. He put a delay on the hotline to the dwarf and grabbed his bag.

There was a secret route to the tunnels that his mentor Danny Geneson had showed him. He paused at the entrance. He had no idea what would happen over the next few days, and now that he was about to leave the compound, for the first time he considered the possibility of never making it back. He thought of all the desperate schemes the Satyagrahi had been involved in. This seemed the most desperate thing he'd ever done. He listened hard, wondering if anyone was watching, but all he heard was the creaking of Big Bwoy's wheels, following crazy Grody.

What seemed like days later he came up out of a manhole in Riverside Park and saw a torso hauling itself along on an old skateboard. The lights of the city—the smell of the river—the feeling of place was so familiar and yet so dream-like. On the edge of the park he stopped to refresh his makeup and apply more perfume, hoping to neutralize the stench of the tunnels. In the lighted window of a closed hair salon he spruced and primped as best he could. Yet when he caught a proper glimpse of himself in one of the gel mirrors, he was taken aback. All the time in Fort Thoreau he'd thought of himself as an exotic black beauty. Now he saw that he looked like a former linebacker on the way to a Little Richard impersonators' contest.

When he finally got up the courage to cruise by his old town house, the problem worsened. Would his wife be home now? And how was he going to get in? How could he get past the security?

He tried to hide behind the parked cars across the street to scope out the scene. There were Securitors patrolling the opposite sidewalk, but there didn't appear to be one on duty in his building. He thought there might've been, as the town house was part of a complex of similar residences all sharing a common entrance courtyard. But there was an armored entryway—a combination air lock, metal detector, and contamination monitor. Inside the booth was a vidscreen and intercom unit, along with a codeboard and iris recognition screen. The mantrap's main door would probably let him in if he mentioned his wife's name. But once inside he'd either have to speak to her there—on screen—or pray that she hadn't changed the security code. If she hadn't changed the code, he could let himself in and knock on her own door, a much more private and appropriate place for such a traumatic reunion. Doubts flooded his mind. She could be asleep. She could have a man with her. There were so many things he hadn't wanted to think about. He sucked in a breath, lifted up his bag, and crossed the street with as womanly a walk as he could achieve. He activated a motion sensor at the threshold and a composite face, ungendered and nonethnic, fractaled up on a fingernail-slim screen over the door.

"WHAT IS YOUR BUSINESS . . . ?"

"I've come . . . to see Eartha Fiske," Aretha answered, trying to summon his old legal calm in a feminine timbre.

"THERE IS NO EARTHA FISKE HERE," the Face replied and disappeared.

Aretha stood shocked. Not *there*? All his outrageous plans—or lack of plans—were unraveling. Shit! Then another thought occurred to him. He stepped up to the door and the Face re-formed.

"I meant Eartha Proud," he said. "I'm . . . her cousin."

"DID SHE GIVE YOU HER KEYCODE?"

"Y-yes," Aretha answered, praying she hadn't changed it.

"AS AN UNANNOUNCED VISITOR, NOT ON THE APPROVED LIST, I MUST INFORM YOU THAT THIS CONVERSATION IS BEING RECORDED FOR SECURITY EVALUATION. ONCE INSIDE YOU WILL HAVE TWO OPPORTUNITIES TO ENTER THE CORRECT CODE. SHOULD YOU FAIL, THE CHAMBER WILL BE AUTOMATICALLY SEALED AND A DISABLING SPRAY WILL BE RELEASED. SECURITORS WILL BE ALERTED AND YOU WILL BE CHARGED WITH CRIMINAL TRESPASS. DO YOU UNDERSTAND THESE CONDITIONS OF ENTRY?"

"Y-yes," Aretha replied. Here goes nothing, he thought as the bulletproof doors opened and with clam-like finality closed behind him. The codeboard required him to display his implant ID for scanning. Broadband had long ago tampered with his to clear him in such situations. The contact lens would pass the iris recognition cross-check for the moment, too—but his future now hung in the balance of the keycode. Would his wife have changed it, as she had her name? There was no need for her to. She'd never have to use it herself. With sweating hands he keyed in the letters G-I-V-E U-P T-H-E F-U-N-K. It was the password they'd used what seemed like a lifetime ago, when they were taking an old-time Funk Dancing class together. Aretha waited with stalled heart.

At last a beep sounded and the inner barrier retracted. He took a giant breath. But now he faced the real test—waking her up in the middle of the night and trying to explain that he wasn't dead and that he wanted her to help him get out west to watch their son get beaten to a pulp in front of a capacity crowd and two billion viewers via satellite. His heart thundered as he crept through the courtyard.

Someone was home, there was no question about that. As he got nearer the door, he heard drumming and chanting. He was impressed because the walls were virtually soundproof. The air smelled of incense, maybe marijuana. He could make out several different voices. What in God's name is going on? he thought. His curiosity grew so strong, when he rang the bell he almost forgot that he'd come out of the closet and dropped out of sight—right out of his wife's life, presumed dead. He rang the bell again. The drumming grew louder. And something else. It sounded like a chicken. He rang the bell again. What would a *chicken* be doing in our town house?

The room on the other side fell silent. He knew the vidcam was trained on him. "Eartha," he called. "It's . . . it's me." And then he found he couldn't speak.

The door at last opened and a dense haze of smoke, gin fumes, and sweat poured out over him. The figure confronting him was his wife—and wasn't his wife—at least not the senior marketing executive he'd known. She was broader and looser than he recalled—in voluminous skirts of black and lavender, with bright silk scarves wrapped around her head. Beads and shells were draped all over her body. The room—their living room—had been redecorated and now featured a centerpole painted with swirling figures. The room was filled with people dressed in bright dashikis, striped pirate pants, straw hats. On the walls were colorful sequin flags. The expensive wool carpets were gone—the wooden floor was laced with intricate filigrees of flour and cornmeal—and in the middle—a half-naked woman with blood on her face clutched the remains of a chicken.

"Eartha?" Aretha gasped.

"Den-zel?" the woman replied. "Alive!"

"And you . . ."

"I'm a Mambo."

"What?"

"A Vodou priestess. Denzel? Den-zel . . . ?"

CHAPTER 9

Out of the Coffin Endlessly Rocking

Clearfather was back inside the whirlwind but he wasn't alone. He thought the figure was the boy in the bathroom then he realized it was a girl, ancient and unborn, changing shape like the dust. Then she was Kokomo. They were together—the tornado running like a tunnel deep into the past and forward into the future. He smelled a mixture of industrial dry-cleaning solvent, pleated satin, and a hint of honeysuckle—and when he opened his eyes, his journey from the highest window of the tornado down into a body was complete. He was dressed in his old clothes and inside a coffin.

Kokomo was hidden inside the box with him, beneath him. He could feel her presence. Aunt Vivian and Uncle Waldo had given him a tiny coffin once, with a Mexican jumping bean inside so that it appeared that the body was knocking to get out—and of course it was—inside the bean in the little coffin was the larva of a moth struggling to get out. He hadn't thought of it in years. He couldn't think when he'd ever thought of it. He listened for Carny's voice but all he heard was TWIN.

"*Pittsburgh, Pennsylvania, which was the epicenter of the events two days ago concerning the sexual awakening of Dooley Duck, was rocked again this morning by an announcement of changes within the fledgling Professor Chicken empire. Kingland Morris Brand, long-retired former CEO of the struggling American United Steel Corporation and stepfather to the Professor Chicken founder and president, Simon Chupp, currently Simone, appeared in public for the first time in more than ten years at a press conference to announce that his stepson was stepping down from the organization to enjoy a well-earned rest.*

"*While refusing to comment on rumors that Simone and her/his two brothers recently suffered psychological breakdowns due to drug abuse, Kingland Brand did indicate that one of the new planks in the Professor Chicken marketing platform will be a greater commitment to the community, particularly in regard to drug treatment facilities, educational programs, and lifestyle adjustment training. Said Mr. Brand, 'We are going to set a new standard for corporate citizenship.'*

"*Mr. Brand, who has on many occasions in the last twenty years had his obituary mistakenly broadcast, also dismissed suggestions that taking the helm at PC was an act of senility or grief at the sudden death of his second son, Ainsley, a lifetime invalid who passed away last night.*

"*When asked what specific strategies Professor Chicken would adopt to become a major player in the instant-food market, Mr. Brand said, 'We're going to go straight at Chu's and McTavish's with innovative and even exotic menu items. We will be introducing bold, cosmopolitan dishes based on frogs, snails, snakes, and squirrels. We will be the first to offer not only Spicy Cajun Frog Legs but Sweet-and-Sour Lungfish. And this is just the beginning.'*"

Someone turned the news off.

Clearfather was proud of the Man of Steel. Maybe some real good had come out of his visit to Pittsburgh.

He could feel Kokomo, her mind waking out of the sedative fog. They were linked—by some powerful connection. He didn't understand it, but it was real. Carny spoke, then Haka. They addressed Martha One Tribe but the Potawatomi woman never replied. The one called Fanny Anny arrived. The voices weren't clear enough to make out every word. Maybe this is how the dead hear us, he thought. Now he felt Kokomo's consciousness rising up into his. She was scared.

The women loaded the coffin. Clearfather heard the door of the hearse slam. A moment later the engine started. Even if he bent his will, all he could do now was cause an accident. He had to wait. Minutes curved and he wondered if he'd been given more drugs than he'd first thought. Suddenly all was blank except for a raging static in his skull.

The car stopped and Rabies asked Carny something he couldn't catch. Carny said something—then Rabies yelled. Then the hearse began moving again, faster this time. Then the vehicle stopped and he heard the rear door open. He felt the force of several hands on the coffin, rolling it out on the rails and then lowering it to the ground. The lid eased open and he blinked. He was facing a dour man in a prim black suit with a pink carnation—Carny, in disguise. He swiveled his head. A similarly dressed figure slumped over in the passenger seat of an old Mercedes hearse.

"She'll be all right," Carny said, nodding. "Hurry. The others are close."

Clearfather tried to stand, staring at the landscape and the faces. One was a large black man in a robe that couldn't hide a mass of gang tattoos. Another was a Cuban-Chinese woman, hipless and peroxide blond, who despite her eye glitter looked gaunt and ill behind a gauze face mask. The two others were gay men, one toffee-colored, the other as white as codeine.

The hearse had pulled over at the perimeter of a Phoenix refinery north of Lick Creek. Smoke rose from the junk fires of a homeless camp. Cardboard boxes had been converted into wigwams, along with several sheets of corrugated iron and a cedar-shingled dog-house filled with mutant children. Beside the hearse was a battered Peterbilt. On its side in muscular gold letters . . . THE CHARISMA TRAIN—THE CELEBRATION CENTER FOR SPIRITUAL COMBAT, HUNTINGTON, WV. On the step, wearing steel-toed boots, foundry pants, and a black leather jacket, sat a black-haired man with a Roman nose.

Carny peeled out the flooring of the coffin to release a groggy Kokomo wearing a Cleopatra wig, earrings that looked like satellites, and a shiny Pacers jacket over jeans and a broadcloth shirt. The moment the girl spied Clearfather, her lichen-green eyes gleamed into life and she began making the unmistakable gestures of "Ooby Dooby."

The Roman-nosed man scowled and strode over from the truck.

"This is . . . Kokomo . . . ," Carny mumbled. "And—"

"Clearfather," Clearfather finished for her.

The man scowled harder. "Jacob," he said.

"You'll take 'em to where they wanna go to in Texas?" Carny asked.

"If we make it that far," the man answered in a clipped tone. "Sugar Bear," he said, addressing the large black man. "Get 'em on board."

The thuggish black man gestured for Clearfather and Kokomo to follow.

"Are—you coming?" Clearfather called to Carny.

"No." The wigged redhead in the dark suit shook her head. "My map goes to a different place. You take good care of her."

"I will!" Clearfather yelled, Kokomo clutching on to him, kissing him. "Thanks."

"Heaven knows what'll happen to 'em," Carny fretted once they'd vanished into the belly of the trailer.

"I'll get 'em to where they're goin'," Jacob said. "You could come."

"There's music I gotta face here."

"You'll be safe? After this?"

"You really care?"

"Wouldn't have asked otherwise."

"And you—will you be safe?"

"You really care?"

"I always have, Jake."

"I'm not coming back."

"I know."

"You sure . . . you don't . . . you can't . . . ?"

"Jacob, the only thing I'm sure of is that I was wrong to blame you for Miriam's death. You did what you believed in. All I could see was my own grief. I'm sorry."

"You're sorry!" Jacob sighed. "If I'd let her be treated—she'd be alive. We mightn't be together but she'd still be alive. I—"

"You believed God would look after her—and maybe that's what happened. Her death could've brought you and me closer but I used it, Jake. Forgive me."

"I . . . do," Jacob said, his nose sniffing at the rubbish fire. His Adam's apple bobbed but his heart felt lighter than it had in years. "Be careful," he said.

"You, too," Carny replied and stood up on tiptoe to kiss him.

The big rig snarled off in a cloud of trash and grit. A swarthy man in the early stages of Nang's Disease staggered over to the humpies with the shotgun-blasted remnants of what was either a jackrabbit or a small dog. A veiled woman crawled out to help him. Carny was just sliding back behind the wheel of the hearse as Rabies came to in the passenger seat. This time the redhead gave the short-haired woman a hypo instead of a karate elbow but the effect was the same. Once Rabies's body had gone slack, Carny loaded her in the coffin. The ferals were growing curious now so she pulled out from under the seat a shoulder-fired Dark Rain unit.

The refinery was shut down but the fractionating towers still stood threateningly against the arsenic-gray sky. Carny wondered who would be the first to arrive, Vitessa or her former friends—when up roared the Valkyrie and Taste Face on bikes. The Valkyrie had her Remington drawn. "Bad move, sweetheart," she said.

"I don't expect you to understand," Carny answered.

"You comin' quietly—or do I do you here?"

Carny thought how easy it would be to take off the Viking girl's head with the stream of metal at her fingertips. She tossed the Dark Rain rifle to Face. She knew she could've gone with Jacob—and maybe she'd have gotten away. But it wouldn't have been a new life she'd have been starting.

Her escort led her back to the funeral home via a circuitous route. Bean Blossom was waiting in the entryway with the gripper-arms extended.

"Treacherous, ungrateful bitch!"

Carny sighed, alert but not afraid.

"You should've run when you had the chance." Bean Blossom frowned.

"I'm not a sneak or traitor however much you may think I am," Carny answered.

"No?" gasped the little woman in the forklift. "You violate orders —you go against Parousia and me. You take Kokomo away!"

"She wasn't your pet to play with."

"She wasn't your pet to set free!"

"Build a bridge and get over it, Joan," Carny retorted and several of the women murmured with surprise, having never heard Bean Blossom's real name before. "I've made my peace with myself. You can't hurt me."

"We'll see," said Bean Blossom.

CHAPTER 10

The Charisma Train

Sugar Bear, the black man with the tattoos, led the way into the body of the trailer, with Kokomo fastened on to Clearfather. The peroxide-blond Cuban-Chinese summed up the girl's pelvic grinding and goo-goo chatterings with the simple observation, "That chick like you bad."

Clearfather nodded uncomfortably as the blond woman took off her mask. She had lesions on her face and the beetle shimmer of dementia in her glitter-flecked eyes.

He tried to set Kokomo down for a moment to get his bearings and come to terms with the new environment. She squealed at this and coiled into a convulsed ball. Would she be like this all the time? Half manic child, half monkey-girl in heat? How could he travel with someone like that? Yet her demeanor seemed to mirror the deeper confusion he felt and to somehow soothe it. She was drooling now and sucking on her hand, and he half thought he could feel the moist pressure on his own skin. What was it that she'd said? "I am he as you are he as you are me and we are all together."

"What's wrong with your girlfriend?" the toffee-colored man asked.

"I don't know," Clearfather answered, and it occurred to him that

Kokomo looked young enough to be his daughter. He looked around trying to take in the scene. There were rows of steel struts and plastic netting that held rigging and sections of tarpaulin. Other shelves contained flyers and a range of souvenirs like bloody crosses and bottles of holy water. What was surprising and disconcerting about the cargo was the glimmer of eyes that emerged. There were way more people than there should've been crammed into such a space. Then a sound at his foot made Clearfather look down and he realized there were more people still, hidden under the floor. Through the grates he saw that some were frightening to behold.

"It's a freedom ride," said Sugar Bear. "We pack 'em in like a slave ship. Enjoy your time out."

"Lucifer has come among us!" a woman's voice groaned from below.

"Witches!"

"No! No! It is the Holy One!"

"Hey, man! Are you like . . . the Buddha?"

These outbursts gave way to a sibilant wailing that echoed in the metal interior, followed by Hindu chanting and some mad jabbering Spanish. Then someone began intoning with great sobriety, "Ostende nobis Domine, misericordiam tuam . . . et salutare tuum da nobis . . . Domine, exuadi orationem meam . . ."

"Hold it down!" Sugar Bear bellowed and for a moment the container went silent, but Clearfather was aware of some other presence.

"What's that sound?"

"You got good ears, my man. Have a look in that other well there."

Sugar Bear didn't like the reaction these two newcomers had provoked. As a rule fugitives were superstitious and often religious to the point of psychological imbalance. Throw in some rational fear and the loss of their old lives and it was like hauling a cargo of nitro. He didn't want any trouble on this, his last run—not if he could help it.

Clearfather pried a panel up from the floor and peered inside.

The chamber was about three feet deep but extended the length of the truck. As his eyes adjusted to the dark, he made out sacks of black composite mesh hanging down at intervals, which he realized were the compartments that held the other people he'd seen. What made the sacks difficult to see was the fact that the space they hung down into was filled with snakes—pit vipers, diamondback rattlers, cottonmouths, and several more unusual varieties such as bushmasters and cobras. He slammed the panel back.

Sugar Bear grinned, his white teeth shining in the caged safety lights.

"They can't get through the mesh. If the checkpoint assholes try to do a sniffer dog search, the scent of so many snakes confuses the dogs—and of course the fear drives 'em crazy—especially if a few happen to get loose. They also confuse the vitalscans for psychwaves. Jacob worked that out. One or two snakes, no party—but hundreds of 'em and the psychometers get twitchy. It's like fire ants."

"What do you mean?" Clearfather asked, feeling the inside of his head writhe.

"A nest of fire ants gives off the same mindwave reading as schizophrenics," Sugar Bear answered. "Psychic Field Theory."

"Aren't the snakes illegal?"

"We're a registered Pentecostal Holiness Church with Signs Following. Taking up serpents is in the Bible. Christian Nation protects our rights to carry our message across state lines and that includes the reptiles."

"So why . . . ?"

"Who's going to suspect a snake-handling Pentecostal church of transporting blasphemers and degenerates? We fly the American and Vitessa flags. We're supposed to love Israel, to celebrate righteousness, to be witnesses and testifiers to the healing power of Jesus Christ Our Lord and Savior. That's why we can speak in tongues and cast out demons. That's why we have the gifts of prophecy and healing."

"You do?" Clearfather asked innocently.

"Yeah, right! Look there," smirked Sugar Bear and pointed to one of the storage lockers. Mounted on the side was a crinkled digital of a white boy in a suit, gripping a microphone. Other photograms were as greasy as playing cards and showed revival tents, abandoned coal mines, and jacked-up shacks in fields of sorghum. In and among the ghostly images was a sheaf of faded newspaper clippings and printed website postings. CHILD EVANGELIST DRAWS BIG CROWD. FREAK BOY HEALS BLIND WOMAN. MIRACLES IN ARKADELPHIA.

"That's Jacob as a young boy. His mother and stepfather raised him as a child evangelist and faith healer."

"Looks like he was good at it," Clearfather remarked, but his attention was drawn to Kokomo, who'd slipped into an almost catatonic stupor at his feet.

"He learned some tricks."

"Tricks?" Maybe it was better to let her rest.

"It was all theater. But he saw it as bunco—con. He believed his powers were real. When he found out the whole thing was stage magic and crowd hysteria he had a breakdown. I was one of the orderlies at the institution they sent him to down in Texas. I was stealing drugs to pay for my habit. He eventually got out and I eventually got clean. Worked for the cops. Years later I went undercover to infiltrate the gangs in Angola. Word got out that I was due to be shivved. Next day who should show up with a revival mission in that stinking Saint Charles Parish sun—but Jacob—all grown up. Well, the warden was a high-ranking official in Christian Nation. He couldn't refuse a Holiness mission come to save the wretched souls of prisoners. Made good media. During the revival, a fight broke out and I died my way out—or so it looked. I been with Jake ever since."

"You mean this is all a—"

"Front? You might say so. Jacob wouldn't. He's still a true believer—it's just that his theology's changed. His daughter died and he decided it was time to follow his own version of the Lord's teachings—helping people in this life and letting salvation and the world to come take care of itself."

"So you get people out of the country?"

"Everyone aboard has a sentence hanging on them. They come from all over."

Clearfather turned to the two gay men.

"Loni and Roger," the paler of the two announced. "From Ann Arbor. We were accused of cooking drugs—but it was really an antidote to Pandora."

"I was Vitessa researcher," the Cuban-Chinese woman puffed, putting her mask back on. "How old you say I am?"

"I don't know," Clearfather confessed. "Fifty?"

"Twenty-eight. Working on Milwaukee project called *Progenitor*. One my colleagues insinuate I steal data. I develop strange symptoms a week later."

"What's your story?" Sugar Bear asked. "Have I seen you before?"

"I don't know," said Clearfather. "I've lost my memory—or most of it."

"You do look familiar," Roger muttered.

"Vitessa is after me."

"Why?"

"I'm not sure. All I know is that I can move things—and make people do things."

"Psi? You mean telekinesis—and mind control?"

Clearfather glanced at the bloody crosses affixed to one of the locker panels. He tried to concentrate, to lift one free—but to his frustration it remained in place. The more he tried to concentrate, the more his mind seemed to cloud, as if he were falling away from the moment. He couldn't bring things into focus but he could feel the substance of the other reality pulling him toward it. Aunt Vivian and Uncle Waldo seemed to hover like memories or photographs on a living room wall—but the man with the radio tower was there. The ghost town—the caves. Clearfather saw Mount Rushmore and the Crazy Horse Memorial. My God, he thought, am I from South Dakota? Is that where home is? Why am I wandering America? Then he remembered that he was being chased. Someone named Parousia Head wanted him taken somewhere. Vitessa wanted him captured or dead. He wanted to go to Texas—but he didn't know why. Because of the map—something that someone else wanted him to do? Maybe the true secret of his past lay in South Dakota.

"What's the matter?" Sugar Bear asked. "Not feeling inspired?"

"N-no," Clearfather confessed.

"Fuckin' loony!"

"My Lord and Savior!"

"Shut up!"

"Maybe you should look after your girlfriend," the one named Loni suggested.

Clearfather looked down at the tangled heap of girl. "I don't know what to do."

"Do some mind control!" a voice in the dark below gloated.

"I've got a chancre that's startin' to smell—heal me!" another moaned.

"I've got Erskine's Syndrome!" a voice at the grate hissed.

Clearfather's head felt like it would explode. Kokomo lay wrapped around his ankles—the voices from the cocoons jeered at him or pleaded. He'd escaped Vitessa and the plans of Parousia Head only to end up on a cattle truck of diseased dreamers and criminals with a sleeping beauty he'd awakened from her bubble but who wouldn't stay awake and, when she did, wanted to rip his clothes off.

"Argh!" Clearfather moaned with the pressure.

"Hey!" someone below ranted. More stifled voices screamed out in Arabic.

Sugar Bear stirred from his cramped position between the struts and opened the snake well to see what the fuss was about.

"Holy shit," he whistled.

Roger was the nearest person. When he peeked into the cargo hold, he couldn't at first process what it was he saw. The snakes, the whole slithering knot of them, were no longer piled or squirming at random but neatly entwined, their bodies forming a living rope that flowed into the shape of a larger snake that took up the entire chamber, curled from mouth(s) to tail(s).

"My God!" gasped Roger when he'd comprehended matters. "That's Ouroboros!"

"What that?" the Cuban-Chinese biologist asked.

"One of the great world symbols—a snake devouring its own tail. It began as a Gnostic emblem based on a reinterpretation of the serpent in the Garden of Eden as a positive symbol of humankind's hunger for knowledge—and later became the dragon of alchemical allegory. How did you do that?"

"I don't know. Kokomo has it, too."

"The girl?" Loni asked with his nose screwed up.

Clearfather nodded.

"Shit," Sugar Bear wheezed, closing the lid. "That'd be hell to have powers like that and not be in control of them. No wonder you're afraid."

"Get 'em out of here!" someone hollered and then the ululations began again.

"Jube, Domine benedicere."

"Buddha Man!"

"They're demons!"

"I can't breathe, mon!" a woman's voice cried out.

"No, can't you see!"

"Allah be praised!"

"Sanctus! Sanctus! Sanctus!"

There were more shouts in Spanish and Urdu.

"Shut up!" Sugar Bear cracked. They'd transported dangerous, infected people and sophisticated weapons before, but nothing like this. He didn't even know if the snakes would ever unravel. When they got to St. Louis, he'd tell Jacob. In the meantime he didn't want to do anything to upset Clearfather.

"Listen," he said. "Don't worry about these people. They're just scared. When we get to St. Louis, we'll have a stretch and trade places. Till then, whyn't you and Loni and Roger shift over. There's a viewing panel—you can look outside."

Clearfather nodded. "But I'm . . . I'm scared . . . for her," he mumbled.

Sugar Bear looked down at the girl at the bald man's feet—curled in the same shape as the snakes below. In all his time on the road he'd seen unusual and perhaps even unexplainable occurrences, but he'd never come across people like this bald man and the green-eyed girl. They had an aura about them he couldn't deny.

"Has she been this way for a while?" he asked.

"I don't know," Clearfather answered. "I only met her a couple of hours ago. They had her stuck in this media bubble."

"We got a diagnosticon aboard," Sugar Bear said. "Let me do a scan. Maybe we can find out something to help—but don't get your hopes up."

Sugar Bear gestured for the Cuban-Chinese woman to help him with Kokomo while Loni and Roger moved to keep Clearfather occupied, a task Roger decided was best addressed by playing the old "Who Am I?" game, where each person is assigned a famous identity and players have to ask questions and guess who they are.

Loni guessed he was Wynn Fencer while Roger was one question behind in identifying himself as the hypermodel Trinidad Slade. Then it was Clearfather's turn.

Just at that moment the truck passed another of the curious billboards.

IF A CHAMELEON SEES ITSELF IN A MIRROR,
IT CHANGES COLOR.

—*Stinky Wiggler*

It sparked off explosions of imagery again in Clearfather's mind.

"Am I . . . *Stinky Wiggler*?" he asked, feeling an icy tingle of intuition.

"How did you guess that so quick?" Roger shouted.

Clearfather shook his head. "Who *is* Stinky Wiggler?" he asked.

"You don't know who you are but you guessed who you were?" Loni puzzled.

"Everybody's heard of Stinky Wiggler," a woman below insisted.

"He's called himself different names over the years," Roger remarked. "His real name is—or was—Ronwell Seward. Child prodigy. Made a heap of money in cybertech with Fencer. But he was way smarter. Went to med school when he was nine. Then MIT. Then— so the story goes—he wrote and recorded a symphony called *Disjecta Membra* and the triple-platinum *Preaching to the Perverted*—having never played a note of music before. After that he started taking massive quantities of drugs and making his own drugs—doing music hypnosis experiments—designing organic computers."

"He was responsible for the first sophisticated organatron," added Loni. "All by himself. A black blues guitar player called Blind Lemon Jackson Jefferson Johnson Jones. For a while he was hitched up with Felatia, the porn star. They did that movie *American Eden* together. After it bombed, she accused him of molesting her adopted mutant African children."

That rings a bell, Clearfather thought, but he couldn't be sure.

"Felatia went nuts. Set the kids on fire and hanged herself. Wiggler disappeared. People say he's cloned his own religious cult and lives on an island or is cryogenically frozen in 20th CenturyLand."

"Then who's doing the billboards?" Clearfather asked.

"What billboards?" Roger frowned.

CHAPTER 11

Marriage Counseling

"Would you like a cup of cocoa?" Eartha asked, examining the bump on the back of Aretha's head from where he'd hit the floor.

"I would . . . love . . . a cup of cocoa," the linebacker-sized drag queen confessed—an admission that seemed to come from the depths of his being.

"Okay," his wife said with a firm gentleness. She handed him a cool compress and rose toward the kitchen.

Aretha stared around. He was back inside his old town house except that everything was different. His marathon-running marketing executive spouse had stacked on a bit of nicely distributed weight and to his utter astonishment had become the priestess of a Vodou church. All around the once plush living room were paintings and ceremonial figurines—not to mention the odd alligator skull. Where there used to be crystal vases and brandy decanters, there were now gin bottles stuffed with plastic flowers and bowls of fried pork rinds.

When Eartha returned with a steaming mug for him, she recounted how she'd taken a Comparative Religion course at the Columbia extension program. Later she'd visited Benin and had been initiated in Haiti. It was a development that he'd never considered—and listening to her prattle on about Papa Legba and Baron Samedi, he thought he had to be experiencing a pre-law-school drug flash-back or some creeping new delusional disease. Was it possible? She even had a tattoo of Danbala the Great Snake! How could his wife have a tattoo of a snake? And on her bosom! Holy moly, he thought —I'm checking out my wife's titties.

She smelled sweaty and narcotic. It was the middle of the night—he hadn't seen her in years—he hadn't been alone with a woman in years—he didn't know how to explain where he'd been and what he'd been doing since going underground—he didn't understand all that had happened to her—and he was afraid of everything that lay ahead—and before he could think to stop himself he was kissing her—and she was kissing him. Then they went at it in every position that the loas of physics allowed until they fell apart exhausted on one of the banana-skin mats.

"You prick!" Eartha gasped.

"What about me?" Denzel groaned. "I thought I was going to have a heart attack! I'm out of practice with this stuff."

"Bullshit!" His wife laughed. "I haven't been porked like that since Benny."

"Who's Benny?"

"Benny Hoo."

"That's what I wanna know!" Denzel snapped, smacking her butt.

"Benny Hoo—the guy who delivers Chinese. Remember him?"

"*Him?*"

"He knows ninja sex secrets. Besides, I was on the rebound from Monroe."

"Who in the hell's Monroe?" Denzel huffed—and to his surprise he felt his rod begin to stiffen again.

"Wide receiver for the Newark Neutrons."

"What are you saying? You're doing younger men now?"

"Only Monroe—and Lucas Trayne. Oh, and Murray, the super's son."

"Little Murray?" Denzel gagged.

"Ain't nothin' little about Murray." Eartha winked, squeezing his shaft.

"Wait a sec—have you turned into a ho?"

"A ho? I'll ho-ho-ho you!"

They wrestled for a moment—and then they were at it again. Holy shit, thought Aretha—I've got to stop fucking my wife!

Twice more they collapsed into panting heaps of bewildered pleasure, trying to work out what was happening to them.

I've got to ask her about Minson, Aretha—Denzel thought. We've got to stop this crazy screwing and get down to business.

"Are you going . . . ?" he asked. "To LosVegas?"

"Of *course*," she answered. "You didn't think I was going to miss an event like this? That's why we had the service—to ask for help from the spirits."

"You approve . . . of Minson boxing?"

"Hell no. But I'm gonna be there for him. I'd a been there for you. Shit, I *was* there for you. All those years of you drinking."

"I know." Denzel sighed, remembering.

"I'm worried he's gonna get his head caved in, but he says he's gonna win."

"Really?" Aretha breathed. "You've spoken with him?"

Eartha looked at him with surprise and sadness.

"We meet on the phone every week and he comes up to visit often. I been down to see him, too. You could've been doing the same. If you—"

"I know." Aretha sighed.

"All this time . . . I was so damn mad at you . . . so hurt when you came out. Not because you wanted to sleep with men or dress up like a woman. But because you'd lied for so long. Lied to Minson. Couldn't accept him as he was."

"That's because I couldn't accept myself," Aretha answered.

"But I could," Eartha replied. "I could be angry about it. I could be hurt by it. But I could live with it. It was the untruthfulness I can't abide by. Now all these years—"

"Does he ever talk about me?"

"You stupid motherfucker! 'Course he does! You may have dropped out of sight but you haven't been out of mind! He thinks you're dead. The rumor was suicide."

"I thought that would happen."

"It was after the law review dinner."

"Yeah." Denzel winced. "I was drunk."

"Drunk? You showed up in a peek-a-boo evening gown and stiletto heels. Justice Fulton thought you were one of the hookers he'd ordered! After that everyone believed you'd done yourself in, but I convinced Minson that one of your old cases had come back—wanting revenge. But me—I never thought you were really dead."

"What did you think?" Aretha wondered.

His wife looked away. "That you were in prison—for the money shit."

"What money shit?"

"Your CEO came to me after—produced evidence that you'd been taking bribes and secret commissions on settlements."

"They slimed me," Aretha moaned. "No surprise . . . but shit . . ."

"You're not gonna lie about it, are you?"

Aretha thought for moment. It would be difficult to explain how he'd been recruited by the Satyagrahi—and how Fort Thoreau was surrounded by a top-secret counterperception barrier—and although he was nominally in charge of the forces bivouacked there, the real guidance came from a woman named Parousia Head, a master saboteur whom no one had ever met. How could he convince his wife that

Beulah Schwartzchild and the McDonald's board members were doing penance among the psychically damaged and HIV-infected? What would she think when he told her that his associates included a vinegary dwarf with a massive IQ who'd been charged with treason, an encryptionist without ears, and a child-primitive lesbian who drove a lab-animal dogsled team through the tunnels under the city?

"I'm not going to lie," he said to her. "Not after everything that's happened. I didn't take any secret commissions—I never engaged in any criminal activity as a lawyer. But I did end up in a kind of prison. A mental institution. After I slipped up, they had me committed in return for the severance pay and the stock options. You did get those?"

"The severance pay but not the options."

"Those lame-ass motherfuckers!"

"Why didn't you contact me?"

"At first I was too screwed up and—too ashamed. I had to work through things on my own. Then when I tried—I found out I couldn't. They had me sealed off. A private sanatorium in Connecticut. I thought I could leave whenever I was ready. I found out differently. I vowed to get away but that wasn't so easily done."

"You escaped? Are they after you now?"

"Probably. I sure can't go back to being Denzel Fiske, corporate lawyer."

His wife didn't speak for a minute. "For real? What are you gonna do?"

"I don't know. I know I want to see the Fight. I want to be there for Minson, whatever happens. After that I can't say."

"That's why you came back here?" Eartha asked. "For my help . . . getting to LosVegas. Only you can't just hop on a plane . . . even if I paid?"

"N-no," Aretha admitted.

"Would you tell Minson the truth?"

"Not before the Fight. He's got enough to worry about. But later."

"All right," Eartha said. "Here's the deal. Monroe is flying me out tonight in his private jet. I've done him some Vodou help. We got a suite at the Sun Kingdom."

"I thought you said you broke up!"

"I did. We have. But you know how it is when you gots the good butt. Anyway, you could put your makeup and wardrobe skills to use and come as my ugly-ass cousin." Eartha grinned. "You get a free flight on a very private jet—and get to stay in a luxury suite in the same hotel where the Fight is. Nobody'll get hip to the truth unless you blow it. You still on the booze?"

"I've been sober since I saw you last."

"Good. One less thing to worry about."

"So I've got to go along, pretending to be your cousin—"

"My *ugly-ass* cousin. My dumb, ignorant ugly-ass cousin from Alabama—who has just arrived in New York!"

"And then—I have to sit back and watch you doing the hootchy-kootchy with young Monroe the jillionaire?"

"You just may."

"All right. Whatever you say."

"Say that again," Eartha whispered. "I like the sound of it."

CHAPTER 12

Black Surprise

A few blocks away Finderz Keeperz was calling the other leaders to IQ-HQ for a briefing on the latest crisis to rock Fort Thoreau. Everyone was a bit discombobulated—it had been a busy last few days. Exhausted in body, they seemed refreshed in spirit. The air was saturated with the scents of ozone and pollen. Honeybees were on the move and birds flocked. Not just robins and the usual sparrows and pigeons, but cardinals and scarlet tanagers, orioles, doves. Rainbow lorikeets swooped over the psych ward. A toucan was sighted on the roof of the HIV Lounge—and a bald eagle perched on top of the Information Station. No one knew what it meant but everyone was sure it had something to do with Clearfather.

So it was an already woozy team of Strategists that Finderz summoned that morning to hear a startling announcement. The Data-Master had been mulling it over ever since he'd received the hotline from the drag queen—examining the options and the implications until he was sure he was ready to make his play. This development was almost too good to be true and he had to make the absolute most of it.

"As you all know, we have had a traitor in our midst," the dwarf began. "As terrible as it sounds, someone in a position of authority and respect . . . has turned on us. Now I'm deeply shocked and sorry to say I've found out that Aretha has gone over to the other side."

All of the faces suddenly sagged or wrinkled. They were all ears now (except Heimdall).

"Aretha?" Natassia cried. "No fucking way!"

"Way," the dwarf replied. "I know it's hard to accept—but late last night there was an attempt on the main datafile. Fortunately I'd laid a trap."

Finderz rotated a thinkstation around for them to view.

"I traced the data tunnel back to Aretha's terminal. I think you'd agree that it's unlikely anyone else had access. The attempt failed— the alarm was triggered—good thing I'd been anticipating such a move."

"Wait a minute," Broadband interjected. "Didn't she"—he always referred to Aretha as *she*—"advise you to set that trap? She was the one who called our attention to the breach of security in the first place."

"A classic disintelligence ploy," Keeperz retorted. "We were all fooled."

"Where's Aretha now?" asked Lila. "Let's see what he's got to say."

"That's just the thing," Finderz said. "Our esteemed leader is gone. Vanished in the night. No forwarding address."

"I don't believe it!" scoffed Natassia.

"No." Dr. Quail winced. "I went by his tent early this morning. No sign."

"That doesn't mean anything!"

"No?" said Finderz. "But with the attempted raid, we know there's trouble."

"This is a serious accusation," Lila pointed out.

"We've had a break," Finderz answered. "The man's made his move and now we've got to do the same."

"So you're calling the shots now?" Natassia glowered.

The dwarf didn't return fire. "I'm quite happy for there to be a new vote," he said.

"What do you propose?" Heimdall growled.

"Shut down all operations. No telling how deep the infection runs."

"We can't do that! There are people who need treatment. Plus there are campaigns under way. We've got three raids in progress and a major jam plus the stuff we're coordinating with the Sophrosyne in Europe. The slightest hesitation undoes months of dangerous work!"

"There has to be a reasonable explanation why Aretha would leave," asserted Natassia. "And I wager it has something to do with Clearfather."

"That's right," Lila agreed. "How do we know he's not on a secret mission like Parousia Head? Maybe he was sent off by her."

"Finderz is about to tell us that Parousia's in on the plot," Natassia said, grimacing.

"Listen, my friends," the dwarf announced. "This is a very black surprise. No one is sorrier or more distressed than I am. I, too, would like to think there's an innocent explanation for Aretha's departure—but even if there were—which we aren't aware of—we're left with the telling attempt on the main file. I'm afraid it's the combination of these two factors that makes the accusation so regrettably compelling."

"What proof do we have that Aretha made that run?" Natassia demanded. "You say the link is to his terminal. So what? Couldn't anyone smart enough to get in here have set it up to look like Aretha?"

"If Aretha wasn't behind the run, then the culprit would have to be someone who knew that Aretha was leaving—or they wouldn't have been able to access his terminal. Now, what mission, however important, could've called him away at such a delicate time? Even if deadly secret, you'd think he would've alerted at least one of us. He certainly didn't tell me."

"How do we know Aretha hasn't come to harm?" Dr. Quail posed.

"I thought about that," Finderz returned. "And it's an awful thought. But practically, it would be hard to hide a body his size for long around here. And then consider it in military/espionage terms. Why ice Aretha if your real target is the data? And if assassination were the objective—and if someone could get this close—why not take out the whole compound? No, I think if we take a cold hard look, we see that my interpretation is the scenario that most economically explains the sabotage of Dr. Zumwohl, the failed attack on the master file, *and* the disappearance of Aretha."

"I just can't believe it," grumbled Natassia.

"This hinges on your word about the run on the master," Heimdall pointed out.

The dwarf kept his composure, although a close look at the right angle would've revealed an aberrant spark in his eyes.

"You're right," he acknowledged. "But the technical evidence on that score is here for you to evaluate. Meanwhile, our esteemed leader is not. If the body turns up, I'll gladly—sadly—revise my opinion, although the last thing I think we should do is get the camp into a panic searching for a corpse."

"What do you propose then?" Lila wanted to know.

"I vote we press the PAUSE button on all activities until we've had time to check that nothing else is going to blow up in our faces."

"Might as well throw in the towel." Natassia shrugged.

"It's called 'a strategic retreat,'" the dwarf answered. "And sometimes—like facing up to unpleasant truths—it's necessary."

"Isn't this just what Vitessa would want?" Heimdall complained.

Finderz narrowed his eyes.

"If Vitessa had their way, this camp and everyone in it would be either vaporized or plugged into their theology. I think we should count ourselves lucky that we've had such a high level of infiltration and have sustained as little damage as we have."

"He's right," lamented Quail. "I don't see that we have any choice."

"A drag queen!" Broadband grimaced. "A wolf in sheep's clothing."

"Enough!" shouted Natassia. "There's work to be done—undoing everything."

"Don't be so dramatic," the dwarf grunted. "Besides, I'm not sure much work's been done around here lately. From what I can see it's been marathon humping."

Dr. Quail had just slipped his hand between Lila's legs without even realizing it. The remark from the dwarf brought them all back to the immediacy of their problem. Even Natassia, with her fiery lips and tireless hips. "All right," she conceded.

They trooped out into the spring sunshine that seemed wintry again now. The dwarf filed out last, heading back to IS. From behind a tree stepped Hermes. The DataMaster froze before a collision—but he was forced to confront again the annoying fact that the boy was a couple of inches taller. The albino's cold stare reminded him of what an enormous risk he'd taken—how the sudden opportunity Clearfather had presented had forced him to move much faster than he would've liked. Indeed, he'd violated one of his basic operating principles—he had no backup plan. He glanced down the ladder of wristwatches on his arms. At least not yet.

CHAPTER 13

Dust of the Road

Rolling out of Joplin, the Charisma Train was behind schedule, Jacob popping Grand Prixes like there was no tomorrow. Alongside the thruway, giant Choctaw eidolons advertising gambling resorts battled Baptist ministers forty feet high for attention, along with unmanned solar farms, strip malls, bunker-style condominiums—and off in the distance, dead towns of windswept Chinese elms and hubcap-covered husks of barns. Several communities advertised themselves as DRY or showed couples wearing full-body suits with messages like NO SEX IS SAFE SEX and KEEP IT CELIBATE. Others described the punishments that would be applied within their jurisdictions, from excommunication to chemical castration—or public maiming for homosexual encounters.

There was no trouble in Claremore or Tulsa, but west of Oklahoma City, Jacob noticed a formation of black maxicopters trailing close and a freight train hauling bright orange unmarked containers. The maxicopters never swept in to intercept; the freighter never varied its speed. Though the homing system may have been disposed of

in Indiana, it was plain that Vitessa was still able to track Clearfather—or had anticipated his arrival. The question was, when
would the ambush come?

The Clinton checkpoint was closed but there were state police
vehicles everywhere—and an air force Firedragon at a local airfield.
The maxicopters had fallen back but heading east was an entourage
of sleek dark cars—and still the freight train with its seamless unmarked orange containers paralleled them west.

"Get them up," Jacob instructed Sugar Bear at a sign for Sham-
rock.

The big man dipped his shoulders through the hatch door into
the body of the truck where the other passengers dozed fitfully.
Down in the silk sling Clearfather was dreaming of the city of cyclones again. He saw the young girl inside. Then the three Chinese
men. They were trying to talk to him but he couldn't hear their
voices over the wind. Then he woke up.

"C'mon," Sugar Bear urged. "We're almost there."

Minutes later the truck slowed and stopped. The interstate was
no longer visible. Jacob opened the truck's main back doors. There
was a graveyard of sun-crusted cars, two trailers, and a bungalow
made from a converted boxcar, along with a couple of yurts—all
seemingly empty. A convenience store with a Phoenix fuel pump
looked vacant but was alive with weather vanes—hundreds of them
covering the roof like shoots of hair. The embellishment on the arrows took all kinds of forms—proud eagles, Indian chiefs, silhouettes of locomotives with great cabbagehead smokestacks, Gabriel
blowing a golden horn. A ways off Clearfather spotted a small wind
farm, the white- and silver-bladed turbines looming against the sky.

"C'mon," said Jacob, helping them down out of the truck. "We
gotta hurry."

"I want to thank you," said Clearfather, noticing a little stone
monument that rose out of the scrub grass.

"I don't know if you'll thank me later. They knew you were coming. Good luck."

Clearfather nodded. Then Jacob and Sugar Bear and the truck were gone, and he and Kokomo were left in the dust and the wind.

An S-113 strike cruiser banked out of a cloud. Clearfather didn't see that the silver-blue arrowhead released a much smaller craft, perhaps a tenth the size. It drifted down out of the sky in absolute silence, tracking Jacob's truck.

An explosive blast lit up the horizon. Out beyond the windmills a dustdevil rose like a child's hand.

PART 4

Dark Harvest

And so I ask, with shaking head,
How many of my selves are dead?
—James Whitcomb Riley

CHAPTER I

Bend Times

Voyants were unplugging and reconnecting with the lives of their bodies and their local communities. Total media immersion was down around the globe, as was neurochemical consumption. The only sustained point of involvement was the sexing of Dooley Duck and the romance between the giant blue eidolon and his busty orangutan cohort. As more and more people sought the immediate physical experience of Dooley and Ubba, dependence on TWIN weakened. "Doing the Dooley" became a phenomenon of epidemic joy. Mass celebrations of intimacy broke out in otherwise bland, grim cities like Davenport, Iowa, and Wichita, Kansas—and overseas, from Antwerp to Auckland . . . Kraków to Kyoto. Even the Muslim countries and the Mormon enclaves were feeling the influence. And the nature of the celebrations just made the Dooley movement that much more miraculous. Sensible hygiene was discreetly practiced—and effective birth control. For couples who'd long struggled with infertility or who'd been driven broke by Vitessa's deathgrip on IVF technology, there was at last fire in the hole and satisfaction in the action. Rapes were down by 90 percent, and wherever there was Dooleyizing, Pandora fever began to cool.

The Pantheon, Vitessa's shadowy board of directors, was in a tizz. TWIN's fortunes were falling but ChildRite, under the leadership of Julian Dingler, had turned the emergency into a public relations triumph by rebuking the Christian Nation and their allies—suggesting that the fleshing and erecting of Dooley might not be the work of hackers trying to humiliate Vitessa but the work of a Higher Power reminding us of our divine and inescapable animality. In a move that sent shock waves through the Vitessalith, Dingler announced that a free, frank, and fun approach to sexuality would become an important new element in the ChildRite philosophy. Overnight ChildRite had become the darling of the empire and Dingler was being hailed as a Savior.

It was a very different story elsewhere within Vitessa. Bitter rivalries and manic finger pointing broke out as technical faults and product contaminations were reported throughout Europe and Asia—while in Toronto, a resistance organization calling themselves The Church Invisible discovered that Efram-Zev was about to release a suite of psychoactive drugs under the guise of diet pills (and then later their punitively expensive antidotes), which triggered specific phobias such as arachibutyrophobia, the irrational fear of peanut butter sticking to the roof of the mouth. There were further indications that this insidious science of cultivated disability had reached unimagined depths with research into an agent intended to heighten the resentment and distrust of both Muslims and Orthodox Jews (as well as those few remaining lumberjacks) by instigating pogonphobia—the fear of bearded men.

No wonder Vitessa was worried. But in addition to these tactical dramas, there was Clearfather. Dependent entirely on intelligence oozed to them via a previously unknown agent, the Pantheon struggled to come to terms with who and what he actually was. That he had indeed come to Texas, as their Mystery Informant had predicted, only marginally increased their confidence. This traveler, whose code name was FLEEING ANGEL, had already shown himself to be a dangerous nuisance. What was he capable of and who had sent him? Their data were crude—the information channel unproven. Worse still was their faceless snitch's insinuation that Julian Dingler was somehow involved. Dingler was the moment's Golden Boy. To investigate him now would only generate more instability. The irony of this wasn't lost on the great creators and distributors of uncertainty. They who had pioneered such post-democratic stress disorders as Tuttle's Syndrome—the obsessive-compulsive checking if one's fly is zipped—knew very well what rich and strange shapes uncertainty could take. They didn't know about the stealth mind probe that might be detonated if the signal could be pinpointed, as Finderz had kept such information to himself. And they didn't know about Kokomo. So their proposed response was an unsubtle blend of massive assault and infectious disease control. Military roadblocks went up across Texas. Disciplinarians sealed off the quadrant. As Finderz Keeperz sat back in Fort Thoreau wondering what steps Vitessa was going to take, forces he had no knowledge of prepared to close in on Dustdevil.

CHAPTER 2

Skull & Crossroads

Clearfather held Kokomo close as the weather vanes whined on the roof of the dirty-windowed store. The reek of the explosion had already blown away on the breeze but the aftershock seemed to keep hitting him. He hadn't actually seen the truck hit but he knew what had happened, and it sickened him. He knew he was the cause. Vitessa or whoever it was after him had a deadly business in mind. Only his fear for Kokomo's safety kept his mind clear. He looked around at this patch of Texas nowhere. What had he expected? What did he remember? The attack on the Charisma Train blurred his mind as the dust stung his eyes.

He tried to listen for voices but no words or instructions came. He'd followed the map. He'd kept his appointment but there was no one to meet him, at least no one visible—just a bony dishwater grey-hound nosing between the wrecked cars.

Kokomo's eyes were as green as kiwi fruit, but her face was stiff and vacant. He didn't know if she was suffering withdrawal from the media helmet or if the trauma of leaving Bean Blossom and the Kick-apoo Ladies had crashed her mind—but he was afraid. She was all that he had to hold on to except for his dubious map. A part of him longed to yield and be done with whatever it was he was doing. I bring trouble with me wherever I go, he thought. Jacob and Sugar Bear and the others are gone. Soon we may be, too. And yet he couldn't escape the fact that despite Kokomo's incoherence, he felt comforted by her presence. Even in this lonely waste she brought him strength and reinforced the stubbornness inside him, the will to go on. To find the truth. Because it wasn't just his truth. This wasn't just his journey. It was hers, the lost Charismatics'—and Carny's, too.

He stepped over toward the little monument that peeked up through the starburst thistles—a smooth curve about four inches thick and a foot high. He couldn't tell what kind of stone it was made out of but it was free of lichen or scratches. Looked at from the right angle it seemed to shine with brilliant flecks of yellow like the peridot crystals found in meteorites. Etched beneath the smooth flat surface was a tiny spiral that suggested a lock of a girl's hair and the words:

THE HIDDEN MAY BE SEEKING
AND THE MISSING MAY RETURN

Is this *it*? he thought. Am I the missing who has returned? He clutched the miniature ivory ball in his pocket and turned around. The earth trembled. He tried to regain his balance—but his next step fell away underneath him. He shot a glance at Kokomo . . . his fingers straining at the air . . . falling . . .

When he stopped he was lying down, his right leg hurt, and there was a heavy smell of grave earth and iron. Gradually his eyes became adjusted to the faint light. He faced a steel screen anchored in concrete. Above him he saw a patch of light but not sky. Frantically he yelled out to Kokomo. A muffled voice chuckled. He struggled up. A shrewd repugnant face pressed close to the screen, a spot-welded claw clutching a polycarbonate and rubber-ringed baton. Clear-father caught the fumes of rutabaga-derived alcohol.

"Way-elll," grinned the face, which was like an opossum's but lab-oratory-soft and hairless, with red-rimmed eyes like bloody eggs.

Clearfather felt hornetfire and thudded into the back wall of rail-road steel.

"Thas jes a taste, fren. Yoo moove mifout n I say so El fry yer balls off! Unnerstend?"

Clearfather nodded and clawed himself into an upright position despite the pain. He didn't know how long he'd been lying in the steel-walled chamber. Minutes? Or hours? The disgusting creature gave him another dose of the baton.

"Wee got yer pootykin," it wheezed—and then belched—a wretched reflux smell that Clearfather found almost more debilitat-ing than the taser.

"Syut up!" another voice snarled.

The mesh wall slid back and a sawed-off Savage side-by-side pointed up out of a hand and an arm and, indeed, a body unlike any he'd seen before.

"Doan worry bough Chemo," the peculiar figure announced. "His breath's worse annahis bite. Come outtadair buh keep yer arms up."

With the screen slid back, more light filled the space. A yellowish glare emanated from a freestanding grain oil lantern. Sections of earthen walls were reinforced with heavy steel retainers, the ceiling supported by a mix of concrete pillars and coal-tarred railroad ties. It was cool and damp but the man with the sawed-off gun barrel was sweating and naked except for faded floral board shorts. He was cabled with muscle but his hands were misshapen as if he suffered from rheumatoid arthritis and his face was dominated by a nose that could best be described as a snout—one that didn't provoke any confidence that it was either original equipment or even human. Two beady nocturnal eyes shone on either side of the proboscis.

With a prod of the gun the snoutish man drove Opossum Face scurrying down the passage. Clearfather followed, surprised to find that any pain or damage he'd sustained in the fall had passed. They entered a much larger concrete chamber, illuminated by a battery-driven light rod and a colza oil lantern. Opossum Face was nowhere to be seen, but there were other figures present.

One was a wrinkled codger without visible arms or legs, his torso nerved into a Taiwanese version of the robotic exoskeleton that the Man of Steel had used to impersonate Hooper. Above the man's terrapin head was a safety roll bar. Mounted on it were three bedpans. Clearfather noticed the other denizens directed their attention to the bedpans rather than to the shriveled face below. Two of the other occupants were women. The one with a blue-vinyl beehive and swollen collagen lips, which made her look like a platypus, reclined on a chaise lounge. The other woman looked considerably more normal facially, and much younger—but she was a Sirenomelus, her legs were fused together like a mermaid's. Clearfather got one quick look at her before she hopped to a walking frame with the brand name Tractioneer™ and wiggled into it with relief.

The next individual was a very individual presence indeed. Of unknown age, and even race, he had skin with a raw, peeled quality as if he'd been turned inside out. He sat within a transparent shelter composed of some advanced polymer. The surface fogged in time with his respiration. When Clearfather peered in, the man leaned forward in his bedchair.

"Who the hell's this?"

He spoke these words into a wireless microphone tuned to a speaker that was lodged in the mouth of a peccary mounted on the wall. The others turned their attention to the wild swine head in the same way they consulted the bedpans when the old man tried to communicate. Only the snout man addressed everyone directly.

"Syut up, Davin!" he grunted and waved the barrel of the Savage at an E-Z Boy recliner—then fished out an air dart and injected it into his right butt cheek. "Haah's bedda," he snored, sucking a swollen knuckle as the anti-inflammatory kicked in.

The room they were in was like a large basement. A steel vault door stood open just wide enough to suggest a passageway leading to still more chambers—as if a series of storm cellars or fallout shelters had been connected with tunnels. Clearfather sat gingerly in the E-Z Boy, fingering the white ball in his pocket, hoping Aunt Vivian and Uncle Waldo would give him direction. The terrible headaches he'd experienced and the bursts of lust and revulsion had abated, at least for the moment, as had the pain in his leg following the fall. It made him wonder if he'd been drugged again. He had to be careful now. These folk weren't Vitessa. But he knew that whatever this troglodytic clan's agenda was, it wasn't good. The man called Davin kept misting inside his enclosure. No one spoke.

"Where's my friend?" Clearfather demanded.

He tried to feel her presence but all there was darkness and static.

He felt a sharp twinge in his head again and heard a quizzical sound. Everyone gazed over at the control board facing the peccary. It was a thinkstation with a datascreen and sensor lights intermixed with chains laden with different sizes of bells. A row of the bulbs had begun winking, and now the smaller bells shivered.

"Wind's up," the relic on the chaise lounge remarked. Next to her the old roboman's bedpans swiveled like parabolic radar dishes.

Clearfather spied swirling masses of meteorological images and streams of changing numbers on the screen.

"What's this all about?" he asked. "What do you want with me?"

The Mermaid made an indescribable sound and then the peccary, or rather the man called Davin, piped up.

"What do you want with *us*? That's the better question. We weren't sneaking around where you live. Why are you here?"

Clearfather realized that nothing he could say would make sense. He didn't know where he lived. He wasn't sure why he was there. That's why he'd come.

"Ah'm Van Brocklin," the Snout said, resting the shotgun in his lap and rubbing together his fingers, which made a crackling sound as if crystals of gristle were breaking up in the synovial fluid.

"He's the Odd Vark!" the witch with the big lips guffawed.

The Odd Vark nickname got them all sniggering and hooting.

"*Syut up!*" Van Brocklin boomed and pointed the shotgun at the peccary head, which he blasted off the wall.

The noise was deafening. The shot disfigured the trophy head, which ended up on the floor—but the speaker, a golf-ball-sized Manila dinger, landed in one of the bedpans. Van Brocklin tore the bedpan off the roll bar and hung it back on the same hook the peccary's plywood shield had occupied a moment before.

Davin tried to say something—but the tinny echo his voice made whining out of the bedpan discouraged him, and he went back to misting and gurgling. Van Brocklin sucked his lubricating knuckles. The bells gave another shimmer.

"I don't know who you think I am, but I don't mean any harm," Clearfather said.

"He's a scout!" the Mermaid shouted.

"Who would I be a scout for?"

"The Celibaters of course—and them others—the Nightcrawlers."

The bells tinkled again, louder this time, more urgent. Van Brocklin left the chamber, still carrying the shotgun. He was gone for several minutes and in that time no one spoke although they all stole peeks at Clearfather, which he found very disconcerting. When Van Brocklin returned, he'd mopped the sweat from his body and put on a faded T-shirt that read STINKY WIGGLER—PETRIFIED AMERICA TOUR. Clearfather jolted at the name. Van Brocklin leaned the shotgun against Bedpan Man's robotic frame and held up a smooth silver box with rounded corners. Inside was a set of teeth made of acrylic resin. He examined the dentures with pride and then inserted them into his gash of mouth.

"Can't have plastic teef in da sawna," he said. The bells tinkled again.

"Is someone coming?" Clearfather asked. "Vitessa?"

He glanced back to the datascreen and saw luminous blue and green spirals and little icons, which he recognized as the weather vanes on top of the Phoenix station. The constant appearance of these icons made him wonder about the items he'd seen covering the roof above. What if the seemingly dilapidated convenience store was really a weather station? Were these people capable of that?

"Now," said Van Brocklin. "Da Nourisher wants to see ya."

"Who's the Nourisher?" Clearfather asked. "And where's my friend?"

Why couldn't he feel Kokomo?

The alarm bells rang again.

CHAPTER 3

The Nourisher

The rheumatoid muscleman led him forward. The adjacent space was an air shaft designed to incorporate a skylight and a drainage system supporting a series of tiered gardens. Again, Clearfather doubted if the individuals he'd met so far were capable of such things.

Van Brocklin pushed open a rubber-rimmed door that led to the next chamber. Inside, Clearfather was surprised to see Kokomo. She was lying on the floor as if her leg was hurt, surrounded by girls, fifteen or so, all under the age of ten. They were sprawled on a square of dirty Berber carpet cuddling what he assumed were pets—and then animatronic dolls—but when he looked closer he realized were living babies. Some of the infants were the size of squirrels. Some might well have been squirrels, for they had claw-like hands. Others had oblong heads with bodies like large tapeworms bandaged in diapers.

The other occupants of the chamber were boys about the same age, naked, inside spheres made of Vistex with breathing holes perforating the surfaces. A couple of the thermoplastic balls rolled around the room or slammed into walls. A few boys had mastered their directional skills and, by contorting themselves, were able to steer through a slalom course of high chairs and Porta-Potties into a concrete area that was set up like a pinball game. Here they had to navigate between various barriers made of nets and rope, roofing steel, or bales of fetid hay. A sweeping gate arm bumped the spheres around while two pressure pads embedded in the walls sent the balls careering whenever they were struck. There were also shallow pits to get stuck in. One was directly beneath a robot shovelmouth, which would rapidly descend and engulf any waylaid balls and then retract to full ceiling height before releasing them.

Clearfather was startled by these goings-on and even more curious about Kokomo's affinity for the young girls and their unexpected offspring—but she at least wasn't imprisoned as he'd feared, so he let Van Brocklin lead him on.

They reached a cul-de-sac where across the passage a black scrim of microlatticed wormsilk hung. Van Brocklin snuffled loudly.

"Come," a breathy female voice said.

Clearfather reached his hand forward, parting the fabric. The hairs on his arms stirred with static electricity as he stepped into a cross between a large vivarium and a hospital room, dimly lit by an organic cell panel. He noticed the sickly-sweet scent of lactic acid and, beneath that, the greasy personal odors of Vaseline and sweat.

"Here," said the voice, and he heard a weight shifting.

The amber light from the hexagons shone in his face. He thought back to the luminous cocoon that supposedly housed the invalid Ainsley in Pittsburgh.

"Come," said the wheezy voice again. "I've been waiting for you. Oh . . ."

Another light came on. The woman—if that was the right word—was enormous, distended. Her bulk hung from a hydraulic chain hoist. Around her neck dangled a container that seemed both transparent and metallic depending on how the light struck it. Clothed partially in gauze, most of her skin was exposed. Immense stretch marks, glistening cold sores, and cracked, scaled patches revealed themselves. The longer he dared look, the more she appeared not to have breasts but to *be* breasts—rows of teats. He couldn't stay focused because he was too busy trying to cope with the people that were suckling. They all lay tangled beneath her, butting and wriggling like newborn puppies.

The woman shook herself like a sea elephant, adipose tissue jelly ing so hard it ruptured tiny blood vessels. The braided steel wires supporting her sang with the stress. With yelps, grunts, and more than a few curses, all the sucklers rolled away and made their way out of the chamber. The woman applied a power winch to rotate her back. Clearfather tried to look her in the eyes. Her face might've been pretty in another lifetime. Now it was a mask of flesh, stretched and wrinkled.

"Is that . . . why they call you the Nourisher?" he asked.

"Yes," she answered. "I am a source of sustenance and an addiction—which is why they both adore and abhor me."

The great female's voice had the emphatic desperation of a last whiff of oxygen bled out of a tank.

"I—don't understand," said Clearfather. "Aren't you . . . too old . . . aren't they . . . ?"

"LifeForce, a division of Efram-Zev, did this to me—or began the process—long ago. My milk contains a special enzyme that stimulates the production of antibodies. I'm the source of what little health they have—or so they believe. We all survive on belief, don't we? Until my milk runs dry, they need me."

"Where do these people come from?"

"Doreen and Judd and their adopted daughter Lanette—the one with the fused legs—were here when I returned. She'd been convicted of Security Crimes and sentenced to surgery. They were squatting in one of the trailers here till Van Brocklin brought them below

—like Davin, the man in the tent. He found out how to work the Phoenix station."

"You didn't set that up?"

"No," the Nourisher replied. "The building looked old and run-down, but it wasn't."

Camouflaged, Clearfather thought. But why?

"What about Van Brocklin?"

"I'm not sure how he got here. He never tells the truth. But he and Cubby keep the Celibaters and the other parasites away."

"Who's Cubby?"

"You don't want to meet Cubby."

"And the kids . . ."

"It's the hormones and chemicals in the feed. The boys are all autistic or have Tasmanian Devil Syndrome. You have to stop them from hurting themselves or others. The obstacle course is called the Randomizer. It keeps them occupied."

"Are they . . . yours?"

"No," she answered. "They're outcasts from the Celibaters and the research labs. Van Brocklin saved them."

Lord, thought Clearfather. "What's the deal about the wind?"

"They worship it," the Nourisher replied. "Tornadoes. They hope for more Gifts. Sacred things the tornadoes bring."

"What things?" asked Clearfather.

"Would you like to view them, my love?"

"What?"

"I'll call Gog and Magog. They were brought here by tornado, too."

CHAPTER 4

The Sacred Gifts

The Nourisher summoned Gog and Magog by speaking into a palm-sized mike. They were both microcephalics, or what were once called "pinheads"—both without the slightest hint of body hair. Their visible skin had the glistening osmotic texture of newts. They stood or rather leaned about five feet tall, with the girth and sturdiness of Sumo wrestlers. Unfortunately, any such activity would've been quite beyond them, for someone with a formidable grasp of orthopedics, microsurgery, and immunology had reversed their arms like bendable action figures. They each had one human hand and one bear paw—and one leg much shorter than the other. As a result they tended to move together, trying to coordinate their four legs as a unit. Both wore dirty T-shirts that read BLACK HILLS PASSION PLAY—SPEARFISH, SD, and old Bermuda shorts.

They each had one gaping tarsier eye and another that made Clearfather think of a puma. Their ears were long and fleshy like those of basset hounds, but moist and sensitive like the rest of their skin. Their mouths were offset by dewlaps or throat fans, like the colorful sacs sported by tropical male tree lizards, which inflated in explosive orange display as a means of communication. The moment they saw Clearfather they made bubblish exclamations and a gesture that reminded him of the Harijan in the bus depot in Pittsburgh.

"He wants to see the Gifts," she said. "Show him. Then bring him back here."

The creatures inflated their throat fans in unison. The one nearest to him reached out a bear claw, and Clearfather resisted the urge to withdraw his hand. They escorted him through the scrim in the opposite direction from the way he'd come, past a glass-walled ant farm of impressive dimensions. At several junctions within the labyrinth there glowed clumps of what he took to be the ants' chemical secretions. He recalled what Sugar Bear had said about the psychic field created by fire ants.

The so-called Gifts were set out on a stainless-steel table beneath a fluoro light in a small tiled room. Judging from the throat fan action, Gog and Magog felt either fear or awe in their presence, leaving Clearfather alone. He started with the miscellaneous pieces: a vintage Colt .45 revolver with the words U.S. 7TH CAVALRY engraved on the barrel—and a silver spoon commemorating the Pan-American Exposition in Buffalo in 1901, exactly like the one he'd seen in his mind.

When he recovered from his shock, he examined the first container, an old steamer trunk. Emblazoned on the top but scraped and worn was the wheelbarrow-of-fire insignia he'd seen in Indianapolis, and the Latin inscription NITIMUR IN VETITUM.

Opening the lid, he found a clutter of objects seemingly bound for a yard sale: an Egyptian papyrus, a Stradivarius violin, a First Folio Shakespeare, and a brass sextant with a plate that said H.M.S. ENDEAVOUR. Next to the trunk was a strongbox. Inside, bound in calf's leather, was an ink-smeared holograph of *The Confidence Man* by Herman Melville and a first edition of *The Varieties of Religious Experience* by William James—signed with a flourish by the author, out of which tumbled three sepia postcards. One showed a baroque-looking steam-powered roller coaster; another, ladies with parasols strolling between the legs of a giant Uncle Sam—and the third, a masked carnival figure dressed like the Pied Piper, opening his shirt to reveal a nest of gear wheels. Beneath this were yellowing telegrams of congratulations from Percival Fawcett, Arthur Conan Doyle, Aleister Crowley, and Sarah Bernhardt. These were joined by a sheaf of technical schemata depicting the singer Janis Joplin, complete with computer printouts of her DNA and toxicity profile at the time of her death in October 1970. Completing this bizarre assortment was a box made of an undetermined kind of metal, with a hologram of the wheelbarrow of fire again. Inside was a pair of green crystal goggles, very lightweight.

"Try 'em on," a voice out of the dark said.

Clearfather twisted around, expecting to face Van Brocklin's accusative snout. But there was no one there—just the voice. "I got a camera and mike set up," it said—and this time he recognized the wheezy inflection of Davin.

"I got a few links around the place. Borger set 'em up for me before he died. Don't tell the others."

"All right," Clearfather answered.

He set down the box and picked up the glasses. The second he put them on he felt a menthol green fire in his eyes and realized he was staring straight into Gog or Magog's tarsier eye, even though they were still on the other side of the wall. As his eyes became adjusted, he was able to see through the other wall into a warren of rodents—and a small-scale meatworks where a man and woman with hairnets were slaughtering and skinning the little mammals.

"What are those things?" he asked.

"What do you see? The prairie dogs? We raise 'em. Taste like rabbit."

Clearfather glanced at one of his hands, but the sight was disconcerting. He whipped off the glasses and set them down.

"Now feel over to your right," replied Davin.

Clearfather swept his hand through the empty space but clasped something. Looking at it in the light he saw that it was almost invisible, as clear as Vistex but soft and pliant, about the size of a cigar.

"Move it," said Davin. "But keep your eyes on where you put it."

Clearfather put the curious object inside the strongbox and closed the lid.

"Now find it again," Davin said.

Clearfather opened the lid and felt around. The object wasn't there. He examined the interior of the box carefully. The tent man chuckled.

"Go back to the table. The exact place you found it."

Clearfather did as directed. "Hm."

"Good trick, huh? Wherever you put it, it always ends up back in the exact same spot. What do you make of that?"

"I don't know," Clearfather admitted. "What's it made of?"

"A special kind of energy."

Clearfather shook his head. "All this stuff came from a tornado?"

"Six different twisters. Very small—like a revolving door opening."

"To where?"

"I was kinda thinkin' you might know something about that."

"I don't," Clearfather said.

"You know *something*," Davin stated. "I see that you recognized some things."

"That's true," Clearfather acknowledged. "I had a memory about a spoon like this—or maybe it was a dream. And I've seen that symbol, the wheelbarrow with the flames, before—but how these things got here and where they're from—I've no idea."

The admissions seemed to convince Davin, who after a silence made an admission of his own. "Not *all* these things were blown here. The old trunk was already here. It's like these things wanted to be together—they sought each other out. Gog and Magog? They didn't come together. Gog, or so we call him, showed up first. Terrified. Two days later Magog comes tumbling in. You shoulda seen them when they were reunited. Their little throat things were ballooning like mad."

Clearfather turned this over in his mind. "I wish I could see one of the twisters in action," he said.

"You may just get your wish. There's a system forming. Highly localized."

"Any signs of anything else?"

"Yeah, as a matter of fact. There's a freight train stopped two miles away. Fifty unmarked containers under heavy droid guard. You know about that?"

"It sounds like you don't think I'm a spy anymore."

"I don't know who you are—but the Nourisher's pretty sure she does."

"Who does she think I am?"

"You ask. Her temper's worse'n Cubby's."

"Who's Cubby?" Clearfather asked.

"You don't wanna meet Cubby. Now you better get back before she gets upset."

CHAPTER 5

The Past Comes Back to Taunt You

"So who do you think I am?" Clearfather began the moment Gog and Magog had led him back to the Nourisher's chamber.

"My . . . husband," the woman answered, shifting her bulk. "My savior! My saint!"

Clearfather felt bile rising in his throat.

"You're disgusted by what I've become . . . and you hate me for what I did. I don't blame you! But this is my punishment! And I've repented! I've remained loyal—that's why I came back—to the scene of such love—then such terrible sadness."

"I don't know what you're talking about," he said emphatically.

"I suffered. I prayed. I waited. I believed!"

"What did you believe?"

"That you'd . . . come back!"

"Where do you think—I've come back from?"

"The dead, my love!"

"The dead?" he repeated—but even as he said the words, a sickening uncertainty washed through him.

"Tell me . . . ," he told her. "*Everything*. From the beginning."

The woman wiped her eyes with her hammy flippers. "Is this—my test? Oh, I'm ready! I'm ready! It was . . . thirty years ago. I wasn't as beautiful as the other wives but I wasn't anything like this. You looked the same—except your lovely hair was long. That's what confused me when I saw you. You see, Chemo has rigged up cameras for me throughout the tunnels so I know what's going on. But even with your hair gone—I knew instantly."

"I had more than one wife?" Clearfather asked.

"You had thirteen wives—but all the women shared your bed. We were your followers. We built a complex here—The Kingdom of Joy!"

"I was a . . . cult leader? And you're saying I—*we* built these tunnels?"

"That's one of the mysteries," the Nourisher gushed. "We dug storm cellars in case of tornadoes. That's when we discovered that there were older tunnels here. It was as if you'd been expecting to find them."

"What's my name?" Clearfather asked.

"You called yourself Hosanna. Hosanna Freed. But I know that your real first name was Paul. Something abominable had happened in your past—and you'd sold Amway—but you'd found your hope again."

"And what was—is your name?"

The Nourisher looked distant for a moment. "My name is Alice . . . Alice Kruchinski. But you . . . *you* called me Lily. I was eighteen. I'd escaped from the Nelsonites."

"Who are they?"

"I'm from DeKalb, Texas. Where Ricky Nelson's plane crashed."

"Who?"

"Ricky Nelson. Like in *Ozzie and Harriet*. And singing. 'Poor Little Fool.' And movies . . . *Rio Bravo* with John Wayne . . . *The Wackiest Ship in the Army* with Jack Lemmon. He was a big star. He fell in our town. Nineteen eighty-five. The pilots got away but Ricky and his band burned to death. Eleazar Drinkwater was there when it happened. He was the Founding Finder. He started the tradition. Set up a plywood-and-chicken-wire airplane—then lit it on fire while everybody sang Ricky's greatest hits."

"He set a miniature airplane on fire?"

"No miniature. Full-sized. That was the way it was every year—until Eleazar choked to death on a cruller. Then Dufresne McCormick started the sacrifices."

"Sacrifices?"

"Started burning people in the plane. Drew the name by lottery. I had to get out because my number came up. I was heading to Taos when I passed through Amarillo. Met you and some of the gals at the Dairy Queen."

"What sort of cult leader goes to Dairy Queen?"

"They made great frozen chocolate-covered bananas. And you were there with these pretty women, and you said if you could put Jesus and the Buddha and Dionysus together, you'd really have something. You all looked so happy and alive. You invited me back for tacos. That was the first night we made love."

"We . . . did?" Clearfather hiccupped.

"Well, along with about twenty other people. I don't know how you kept going. Everyone loved you . . . worshiped you."

"So what happened?"

The Nourisher's face clouded over and hot tears leaked down her cheeks. "I betrayed you," she whispered. "There were stories in the media of orgies and rites. Christian Nation hated you. The Muslims were angered. The Mormons were envious and worried. Women First resented the devotion you engendered. Efram-Zev and the pharmaceutical industry were afraid of your message about enjoying sex without drugs and implants. The outsiders began to band together. And that was when I met with a Federal agent in Amarillo to plot your overthrow."

The Nourisher was sobbing now, gagging on her emotion.

"Why?" Clearfather asked.

"I was young and silly! I was the thirteenth wife. I grew jealous! So I gave the Feds information on how best to raid The Kingdom of Joy. There were wonderful buildings then—and gardens. We raised chickens and sheep—there was even a big tom turkey called David Letterman."

"But you wanted to end—"

"I wanted to punish you! I thought they'd come and arrest you. They gave me their word—no violence! Hah. They came to slaughter with military weapons!"

"And I died?" Clearfather said softly.

"Along with many others—including all twelve wives and the babies they were carrying."

"Babies? They . . . killed babies?"

"The bullets started flying like rain. The choppers came to fire-bomb the buildings. Once they had you hemmed in around the Obelisk in the center of the farm—they struck in force. I wanted to die with you—I was so ashamed. But I couldn't bring myself to lose my baby . . . your baby . . . our son!"

"Did you say a baby? A son?"

"Yes!" the woman cried and held up the peculiar vessel she wore around her neck. "This was a part of the punishment—you see?"

Clearfather felt the pain in his head return, a dark rage rising within him. This couldn't be. None of this could be true!

Staring closer at the cylinder, he saw that it was a small museum jar. Inside was a stillborn fetus, more tadpole than human, freeze-dried.

"You see, they wouldn't let me die! I had no friends—my family wouldn't help. For months I was held in a hangar at Altus Air Force Base. I was never charged—never tried—never convicted—but I was sentenced to a LifeForce research complex in northern Mississippi. They induced my baby's stillbirth . . . and turned me into this!"

Surgery after surgery. Gene treatments. Hormone therapy. Year after year. I was only released when they thought I was going to die. I lived on the shriveled charity of relatives until I joined a sex lodge servicing Christian Nation heavies. But I needed too many drugs to stay normal. I turned back into this and then it came to me in a dream— as clear as I see you now . . . *I would see you again.* My punishment would have an end! I was to come back to Dustdevil—back to the ruins of The Kingdom of Joy—and one day you would return. You would see that I'd been faithful. You would forgive me. We would live as husband and wife again. So I at last came back. I came back! I found Van Brocklin and the others. And there were Signs. Someone had been here since The Kingdom of Joy had been destroyed. The tunnels had been rebuilt—and the Phoenix station was here— and the tornadoes started—and the Gifts came. And now you've come. You've come back to find me! Come my love . . . forgive me! Let us begin our new lives!"

Clearfather thought he might faint. At last he found his voice. *"Shut up!"* he roared.

"You're still angry—you have every reason. But see how I've suffered—"

"I have not come back from the dead! I came from Pittsburgh. I don't know who you think you're waiting for. *But I am not the one!*"

The Nourisher's face flared with anger for a moment—then deep hurt. Then a knowing splinter began to gleam in her eyes.

"Take off your clothes," she said.

"What?" Clearfather coughed.

She shifted in the hammock to spread the huge rolls of cellulite that were her legs.

"My suffering has not been in vain! I've believed. I've endured. I *know* you've come back to me. You are my Nourisher!"

With two of her meaty fingers, she squeezed a nipple and squirted a jet of milk at him. "Reveal yourself to me."

"No!" he said, and the steel wires twanged and the bulk of the Nourisher slammed to the floor. But he could do no more. The horror was crawling toward him.

"Yes!" she whispered. "Don't you see how I have waited—and suffered? You are my dream, my hope, my love!"

She bit into Clearfather's left hand, which triggered a shiver of pain that sent his right fist shooting forward. There was a *snap-crack* sound and she fell back with a thud—as a voice filled the room—like the ones he'd been hoping to hear in his head.

"Quick!" it gurgled, and Clearfather recognized the voice as Davin's. "You gotta get out of here, Chemo . . . he's taken an interest in your little friend."

"Can you tell me how to get up top?"

"All right," Davin breathed. "But you gotta hurry!"

"Nah sa fast!" Clearfather heard Van Brocklin whistle through his long lump of nose, followed by a click of a shotgun. "Ah'll syow 'im da way."

CHAPTER 6

Cubby

Clearfather's head pounded. The letters in his back burned. He didn't know what to do. He was afraid for Kokomo. He had to find her—they had to get out.

"Dis is Cubby's room." Van Brocklin smiled and wagged his snout.

Clearfather braced himself to confront a steroid-cranked gladiator. But the shadow that filled this other, larger-domed ceiling room was more intimidating in its own way. It belonged to a plump white, freckle-faced boy with hair the color of hay. He was dressed in baggy improvised cargo shorts and a T-shirt made of bed linen—and was barefoot. He was only about seven or eight years old but he stood twelve feet high and must've weighed eight hundred pounds.

"How . . . how did he get so big?" Clearfather marveled.

"Hexperiments. At Genetica. Ah 'elped 'im get away. But 'e's got behaverural problems. Da growth 'ormones an' shid fucked 'im up. Turrible temper Cubby hass." Van Brocklin grinned malevolently. "Now you're gonna keep 'im ennertained."

Van Brocklin shoved him forward, slamming the steel door shut behind. Shit, Clearfather thought. He heard the storm bells ringing down the tunnel. The wind was rising and Kokomo was with Opossum Face—with Vitessa waiting to pounce! He tried to reach out his mind to her but all he could feel was a seething black pain. He didn't know about the psych implants inside—he only knew that his allies, the voices, were lost in a rage of pink-and-white noise—and that he was confronted with a giant Special Child.

Pieces of machinery and the heads of animals lay scattered. There were no bones visible, but Clearfather thought it possible the young ogre ate them. The boy's bed was a slab of insulation from a refrigeration car, his roommates a family of punching bags with crude faces drawn on them. The single point of interest was a model train set laid out on a table of two-by-fours. Most of the cars had been hurled against a wall or broken in half but a few remained intact, stopped midbridge on their journey around the miniature town, where cars were parked on the roofs and the few remaining citizens seemed to be worshiping a Chewbacca the Wookiee PEZ dispenser.

Cubby grunted. Clearfather moved behind a pile of rotten phone books.

"Cubby wanna play!" the kid announced and charged toward him.

Clearfather leapt over a pipe well and heard the voice of the Nourisher. Was she in his head, too? No, it came from the ceiling, he realized—a hidden speaker.

"I can save you, my love!" she wheezed. "Just as I betrayed you in your earlier life—I can save you now. And I will save you! I begged for your forgiveness—now all you have to do is ask for mine! Let me forgive your unkindness!"

"No!" Clearfather called.

At that exact moment the Corps of Discovery mind probe crossed paths with the stealth unit, drawing the attention of the combat probe away from its mission. The result was a surge of confidence and the emergence of a song in his mind—a variation on a song he remembered singing with Aunt Vivian and Uncle Waldo.

"Ah'm gonna wring yer neck!" Cubby grinned, groping out for him.

"No, you're not, Tubby," Clearfather replied, sidestepping him.

"Cubby!"

"You're a big bully, Chubby."

"*Cubby!*" the overgrown knee-skinner bleated.

"And I'm going to teach you a lesson. But first, I'm going to teach you a song. *Someone's singing, Lord . . . Kum-baya . . .*"

"Argh!" Cubby groaned, clubbing his big dirty ears with his hands.

"*Someone's singing, Lord . . . Kum-baya . . .*"

"SYUT UP!"

"*Someone's whining, Lord . . . Kum-baya . . .*"

Cubby swung at Clearfather, who hurtled to one side as the galumphing boy's fist connected with the steel door.

"Arggggggggh!" Cubby yowled, sucking his hand, as Clearfather dashed around and yanked the boy's shorts down to his ankles.

"*Someone's pants are down, Lord, Kum-baya . . .*"

Cubby stabbed his damaged fingers out, but Clearfather rolled underneath and drove an overhand right into the youngster's testicles, where it sunk as if into uncooked dough. Cubby's eyes crossed —he cupped his hands to his crotch and crumpled. The gargantuan brat staggered forward but forgot about his shorts. Tottering—he beat his arms to maintain balance, but it was too late—he fell with full force facedown upon the village, impaling his right eye on the church steeple. Clearfather grabbed the PEZ dispenser.

"Cubby!" a voice wailed as the door burst open and Van Brocklin's fleshy snout swung in. "Ya've killed Cubby!"

Clearfather shot past and slammed the door behind him before the Odd Vark had a chance to use his shotgun.

"That was good work," he heard Davin say. "Now find Guinefort, the greyhound—he'll lead you. But look out for Van Brocklin. Turn left."

"Bravo, my love—you Monster Slayer! But you can't escape that easily," he heard the Nourisher thrum. "You are my dream, my hope, my God!"

Damn it, thought Clearfather—both Davin and the Nourisher had the tunnels mined with cameras and microphones. He'd reached the ant farm when he saw the Bedpan Man in his robotic frame and the Mermaid in her Tractioneer™, clutching a Charter Arms Bulldog.

"Doan you make me shoot you now," she quavered, the barrel of the oily .44 making circles in the air.

Clearfather pitched the PEZ dispenser as hard as he could at one of the bedpans on Judd's roll bar and hit the deck. The noise so startled Lanette, she pulled the trigger, missing Clearfather by a good four feet. The first two-hundred-grain handload blew a clean hole in the ant farm. Her second shot, aimed low, inflicted a fracture in the surface and the transparent wall exploded, flooding the hallway with dirt, ruptured glass, and a cascade of pissed-off insects.

By the time he was close enough for her to hit, he had the gun in his hands and had shot out the motor in the Tractioneer™. The sharp corrosive scent of formic acid filled the corridor. "Hurry!" Davin called, and off Clearfather ran—just catching a gargle of consternation as the ants reached Judd—followed by the frantic sound of Lanette hopping for her life. Seconds later he heard a sequence of shotgun blasts echoing down the tunnels. He arrived back at the room where the boys in the bubbles rolled and the girls sat silently with their babies. They were all just as he'd left them. He ran through the air-shaft gardens to check on Davin and saw that someone had slit open the membrane of his envirotent, which had collapsed around him like soft wet glass. The man sat microphone in hand with a suffocated, shrink-wrapped expression on his face. Beside him was the platypus woman, Doreen. She raised a prairie dog boning knife. Clearfather raised the .44. With a squawk of terror she fled. He ran back into the children's area—and there was Van Brocklin, reloaded and covered in ants. "Ya killed Cubby!"

Clearfather raced between the high chairs into the Randomizer. The rheumatoid madman blasted a hay bale apart. Then a bubble spun toward Clearfather and he kicked it at one of the pressure pads—which whooshed the boy into Van Brocklin, who tripped into the pit beneath the robotic shovelmouth. The open jaws plunged down and shot back to the ceiling, jerking the muscleman in half. When the jaws relaxed, the torso thumped to the concrete.

Clearfather spotted the greyhound between the bubbles. He followed the dog back to the air shaft and saw Kokomo, trussed up in one of the garden terraces. Between the terraces was a narrow flight of stairs leading up to the light. The greyhound barked. He untied the green-eyed girl and, cradling her, began clambering up the earthen stairs.

CHAPTER 7

The Harrowing

At the top of the garden stairs Clearfather kicked through a door. The skylight had been camouflaged from ground level and he noticed a tripwire, which he was careful to avoid. The greyhound was nowhere to be seen. It was late afternoon but from the look of the sky and the way the clouds were moving, time might have started running backward. Lightning pulsed, and the wind was heavy with ozone and nitrogen oxides. He set Kokomo down and glanced around, imagining windmills and oil pumps stampeding like frightened animals—fleeing something giant but invisible.

In fact what was closing in was about to become very visible. From the cardinal points of the compass rumbled four triceratops tanks the size of barns. Called Grim Reapers, they were modeled on giant combine harvesters but armored and equipped with terrain-leveling suspension tracks and Dark Rain cannons capable of replacing the air with jacketed steel for up to an hour without pause. Churning forward at a constant crawlspeed, the vehicles powderized pheasants and abandoned cars alike, obliterating everything in their paths.

Outside this perimeter, the winter wheat had been blanketed with Jack O'Lanterns, beach-ball-sized land mines with evil faces painted on them, marching on spidery legs wherever their heat-seeking sensors directed them. Then there was the ominous orange freight train. Vitessa felt confident they had nothing to fear.

The whirring of the weather vanes grew louder, and somewhere Clearfather heard a terrible clanging of irrigation pipes. Kokomo limped into the wind farm, spreading her arms between the towers of conical steel. Her right leg, the same one he thought he'd hurt when he fell in Chemo's trap, looked damaged, but other than that she appeared uninjured—her eyes shining tornado green. He ran to her. The weather vanes began spinning like tornadoes themselves. The great blades hummed, the rotors swimming hard to keep the turbines yawed against the wind. Clearfather wavered. How could he deny the signs the Nourisher had referred to? There was the silver spoon from his vision, the dreams he'd had of the women bleeding around the pillar—and the telltale emblem of the wheelbarrow of fire. He couldn't dismiss all these resonances no matter how little clarity they provided. Maybe I *have* come back from the dead, he thought. Is this why Vitessa hounds me? He heard Kokomo begin to sing and held her in his arms. Hope surged through him. If he'd released powers within her, now he felt her releasing powers within him. They would stand together against Vitessa. Their minds would join. Let the others come, he thought. Let them bring their chemicals and weapons. Kokomo and I will unleash the wind! We will empty the pits and burrows. We will open a tunnel in the sky and send all these creatures to the stars. Together, we are One.

Still the Reapers ruthlessly advanced, the hinged track belts clanking like pile drivers striking bedrock, digging deep into softer earth, spewing out shotsprays of soil that looked like cottage cheese mixed with blood. At last they reached the containment point past which they would be in each other's crossfire. They paused. At the edge of their range all that was left was a small circle of the immediate ruins of Dustdevil. The weather vanes were shrieking in their sleeves now—violet flames rippling over the husks of the cars. Clearfather looked up and saw the death machines surrounding them. And at that moment the Reapers ceased fire and there was movement within the orange train two miles away. The side panels of the boxcars slid back and released their cargo. Clouds of tiny wings rose up with a high-pitched whine to blacken what light was left. They swarmed over the dead oil fields and arid farmland like a haze of poisonous gas.

My God, he thought as they drew closer—they're *locusts*. Then the first of the legion reached him and he crushed one in his hand— and saw that they were actually miniature winged robots, part organic, part titanium. Whatever they landed on they consumed, releasing a ravenous molecular solvent. Kokomo sang louder, and he found the words struck a memory chord within him. "Dust in the wind. All we are is dust in the wind. Dust in the wind. Everything is dust in the wind."

Below these words he heard another message . . . rising like the tempest . . . words he remembered as if from a dream . . .

"Then the earth shook and trembled; the foundations also of the hills moved and were shaken, because he was wroth. There went up a smoke out of his nostrils, and fire out of his mouth devoured: coals were kindled by it. He bowed the heavens also, and came down: and darkness was under his feet. And he rode upon a cherub, and did fly: yea, he did fly upon the wings of the wind. . . . Yea, he sent out his arrows and scattered them; and he shot out lightnings."

At first the mini combat craft were navigable. Clearfather could hear them humming—but as he began singing along with Kokomo, the gusts began to drive the microfighters into turmoil. Louder and stronger their voices lifted as St. Elmo's fire glowed from the hoods of the abandoned vehicles and the weather vanes blurred. Clearfather felt the wind double and shift so that it appeared the windmills were no longer being driven by the force but creating it. The locusts hesitated in the air or tried to land to steady themselves. But the windmills were too strong, sucking the winged terrors into their whizzing circles; the black clouds of miniature robots vaporized on impact.

Then the four windmill towers crashed into the dust, raising a cloud, and out of each cloud whirled a distinct, individual tornado pluming a magnetic field of sparks. When fully formed, they began to move in a chaos of partridge wings and aluminum cans, heading in the direction of the Reapers, gaining speed and size by the second.

The air stank of steer manure and stressed metal. Vitessa Remote Command reawakened the Dark Rain cannons but the whirlwinds were revolving too fast for the steel projectiles—and what could bullets hit or hurt anyway, confronting giants without true form—only energy endlessly changing shape and yet maintaining force?

In high-resolution machine vision Vitessa Intel watched as each of the Reapers was stalked by a separate hyperventilating tornado. One by one the spiral soldiers engaged the death harvesters, engulfing them. The armadillo-like tractors trembled on the edge of the twisters, their epicyclic knifedrives gouging at the ground, tank tracks bouncing, trying to hold their position—then one after another they merged and were absorbed, rattling apart and disintegrating into the air. Onward each of the tornadoes marched, dredging up the detonating Jack O'Lantern mines and inhaling the spent Dark Rain cartridges. When all the land around had been cleared of the explosives, the whooshing tornadoes converged on the old store. The doors and punctured window screens had all been swept away but the building still stood, boards clacking. The four tornadoes joined to form a single funnel in a howling boom of urgent air, like a backburn hitting an accelerant. The roof of the general store ripped off, shooting weather vanes from their perches like arrows. The weather station exploded—the Phoenix pump sailing away. The unraveling shape of the unified tornado bore down into the soil—radiant tongues of light licking the car bodies that one by one snuffed into the coil like cigarettes. Then up out of the ground groaned the elevator that had serviced the tunnels below—and Clearfather saw the Nourisher wrapped in torn gauze, flushed red with the strain of movement—nose broken—eyes wild. She'd been able to make the journey hanging on to Judd's robotic walking frame, which still contained the ant-attacked remains of the old man. She staggered the skeleton off the cast-iron platform as the structure wrenched free from the shaft—cables splitting—pulleys flying—hovering for a moment in midair, rusted and huge, before it spun up the spiral stairs of the wind.

With the elevator torn loose, the buried farm poured forth. Bedpans and prairie dogs—deaf girls with their deformed babies and the Randomized boys. Van Brocklin's corpse and Chemo's spastic form blew by—canned goods—ammunition—ant dirt and the flailing figure of Doreen followed by the desecrated pig's head. All of the Sacred Gifts would go, too—along with Gog and Magog—but Clearfather was no longer watching, for the Nourisher was waddling toward him, Judd's corroded exoskeleton barely able to propel her.

She was almost to him when Clearfather felt something pierce him like a spear of ice. It was one of the weather vanes—the angel Gabriel blowing a tin horn. The Nourisher reached out for the end. He winced at the pain in his chest. He thought she was trying to ram the barb into his heart. She pulled the arrow free as he yanked the cylinder around her neck—the seal bursting—the tadpole made of golden sand whisked away. He saw the Nourisher ascend into the chaos gripping the silhouette angel. "Forgive me!" she cried and then was gone—and with her the tornado, which receded into the sky like a ladder pulled up behind the last climber.

CHAPTER 8

A Party on Ronald Reagan Boulevard

LosVegas, Nevadafornia, had been described as the Emerald City on crystal meth, with generous portions of Osaka and São Paulo thrown in. But whatever the subjective impressions, the disaster-born megacity was undeniably the home of the World's Largest Burrito and the World's Largest Buddha. Aretha had been west only once since Bigfoot had bitten off the most populous sections of California, leaving Mount Whitney towering over the Pacific. Quick to seize opportunity from misfortune, IMAGINE-NATION, the theme-park and entertainment division of Wynn Fencer's Vitessa Cultporation, bought up the land from the Panamint Ranges down to the Mexican border, creating a series of waterways and lagoons—and not so much theme parks as complete recreational worlds enclosed in giant domes. Seemingly overnight the city of Las Vegas was renamed and boundaries redrawn to form the "Now Frontier" state of Nevadafornia.

The robotronic skyline, which continuously changed, had changed considerably since his earlier visit. As Monroe Hicks's personal pilot overflew the megalopolis, only the humble old Stratosphere Tower seemed familiar, poking up in the shadows of the Hasami Totem, the Sony Cone, and the West Coast Vitessalith.

They landed at Hillary Rodham Clinton Interdenominational Airport as the sun set. Aretha was glad to be back on the ground. Storms had plagued the Midwest on the flight out, and TWIN had reported a possible "environmental emergency" in conjunction with the tornado havoc in Texas. A so-called Black Corridor of air security had been established, and several air force Raptors had been seen in the sky. Aretha was certain the incident had to do with Clear-father—and not knowing about the betrayal of Finderz Keeperz hoped the testy dwarf had found a way to debilitate the stealth probe.

There was nothing the drag queen could do about either of them now, plus he had his own problems. For starters, his wife had introduced him to Monroe Hicks as her cousin "Ernestine" from Alabama. Eartha enjoyed seeing him in such an awkward situation and, much to the drag queen's discomfort, he found himself torn between being attracted to the sports star and extremely jealous.

They cleared the airport checkpoint without hassle, and a limo ferried them to the hotel—with the former corporate lawyer unable to stop blinking at the sights of the city from the Tom Cruiseway. Even though it was early, Merlin could be seen leading a laser "War of the Wizards" at Camelot. The Valhalla had a flamethrower and dry-ice showdown between Frost Giants—and the forty-story Genie from *The Arabian Nights* continued to disappear and re-form by virtue of several cubic miles of mist pumped in and then vacuumed out of the micromesh spidersilk, lit from within by the largest collection of fireflies in the world. From the cerebral palsy beggars on Billy Crystal Way to the holograms advertising the Komodo dragon fights at the Jennifer Lopez Memorial Auditorium, there was a spectacle at every turn. And the eidolons! Every religious organization and instant-food franchise was represented: I-HOP, Pizza Shed, Curry Favor. Professor Chicken was a very small frog in this pond—up against Chu's with their kung fu fighters or McTavish's with the Highland Zingers and the Sassy Lassies, along with the Flying Haggis Fleet, a squadron of tartan blimps customized to look like the famous culinary delicacy.

Monroe's entourage checked in at the Sun Kingdom, the multibillion-dollar marvel of temples, lily-littered lakes, luxuriant jungles, and mosaicked pathways. Within minutes Monroe's assistant PA was on the screen to room service ordering a chilled bottle of Dom and flaming Korean dog tongue while the superstar's personal chef took over the suite's kitchen and began preparing Malaysian hairy crabs served with Ca Cuong, the rarest condiment in the world: a secretion recovered in minute amounts from beetles in northern Vietnam.

Aretha took the opportunity to slip out and recon the bizarre bazaar, and the moment he was past the Harijan doorkeepers the propositions started. Care for a sex change? What about a hit of Trimurti?

"What's Trimurti?" he asked the woman who was wrapped like a mummy to protect her genetically modified skin.

"It's one of the shape-changing drugs named for the three forms the godhead takes in Hindu mythology."

"No thanks," Aretha said and pulled away.

Next door at The Parthenon—with its millions of tons of white marble, pristine fountains, and reflecting pools lined with statuary, which were living men and women coated with latex—a temperature-controlled wind stirred the oracular oak leaves, and the Now Millennium's Alternative Mind Congress and Spiritual Expo was winding down after a busy opening day. The foyer buzzed with Andean nose flutes while female monks in pale blue taffeta tunics with tellurium headbands demonstrated an ancient martial art that had recently been developed in Denmark.

The other big convention in town was the biotech and cognitive sciences extravaganza held at The Time Machine at the gateway to 20th CenturyLand. Among medical folk from around the world, Dr. Hugh Wievicl of Pittsburgh was there and was at that very moment scheming a way to steer a big-breasted neurologist from Philly into a psychoactive bubble bath.

Earlier that afternoon in a double ceremony at the Babylonian, the local manifestations of Dooley Duck and Ubba Dubba had been married, while Chipster, a rhyme-slanging boxing kangaroo, led a choir of emperor penguins in a hip-hop version of "Chapel of Love." As if all this weren't enough, there was the Fight for Life. Still twenty-four hours from the first punch and the fantasy empire was strutting its stuff down Tom Hanks Avenue.

The Trumpanile sent an army of Donald Trump lookalikes. The Amazonia offered a tribe of headhunters and panther women, while the Celestial City sent robotic terra-cotta soldiers. From the Jungfrau marched busty milkmaids and men in lederhosen and feathered caps blowing a spirited ranz des vaches on giant alpenhorns. From Dreamland came southern belles with pink parasols walking tapirs on leashes—and from the El Dorado, a parade of gilded men accompanied by naked virgins. Next, the fakirs and white elephants of the Taj Mahal and the Knights of Camelot on chamfron-bedecked thoroughbreds, with a troop of hunchbacks leading Irish wolfhounds and an elastofoam dragon breathing fire. Bringing up the rear was a contingent of gay men from around the world, who'd come to rally behind Minson.

Aretha flowed on with the crowd. You could bet on how long a convicted CFO could last in a tankful of barracudas or which couple would triumph in a tug o'war to win an adopted child. But the most popular and the largest-scale entertainment offered players the chance to control giant robotic battling action figures that took the form of crusty old showbiz legends: a fire-breathing Tom Jones going up against an acid-spitting Wayne Newton—a guitar-swinging Elvis against a cigar-shooting Colonel Parker—or a Black Hat Garth Brooks taking on a White Hat Garth (Garth Wars). The female characters were even more popular, whether contemporary stars like Mekong Delta and Sinergy or golden oldies like Sandra Bullock catfighting Julia Roberts. The biggest star of all was Oprah Winfrey. So popular was the giant Oprah, IMAGINE-NATION had developed two models, one known as Skinny Oprah, the other Big Oprah. The lines for the martial robots were long, and in the two-hundred-acre maintenance hangar on the shores of Lake Mead, the repair teams worked around the clock.

On the corner of Cher and Spielberg, Aretha paused to catch a TWINplex update on the odds for the Fight. The Corpse Maker was favored one-hundred-to-one to win. The question was whether or not Minson Fiske would die. How encouraging, the drag queen thought. Then the Fight news was swamped with the latest Dooley Duck demonstrations—including highlights of the wedding that had been sponsored and officially blessed by Julian Dingler, the new CEO of ChildRite. Rippling time-release ceremonies were now in progress around the globe.

Aretha crossed through a maze of arcades to Ronald Reagan Boulevard, and that was when it happened—his own epiphany—the sudden manifestation of the big blue duck and his giant orangutan bride—right there in front of the drag queen and a gathering crowd!

"Listen carefully," said Dooley, and gave his famous neck roll. "Ubba and I have a message and we want you to hear it clearly. It's time for all of us Americans to raise our voices together—so that the rest of the world will understand. From Bhutan to Botswana, it's time for us to pray to the downtrodden of the world for forgiveness."

"It is?" people gasped, surging around the giant bright animals.

"Forgive us our insatiable need for stimulation and abundance. Forgive us our impossibly high opinion of our supposed generosity and our merciless disregard for anything but our own prosperity. Forgive us for seeing you—the war-torn, weary, diseased, and deserted people of the world in your billions—as simply billions—indistinguishable cartoons of despair. Forgive us for turning the promise of America into a commercial virus that threatens to destroy the other cultures and indeed the whole environment of the earth."

"Shit," people in the throng said. "That's pretty heavy."

"Imagine how I feel," Dooley replied. "I'm a big blue duck. You think you've got problems? I'm an icon of all that is trivial and tragic in our civilization. I'm what the last and greatest of all human dreams has degenerated into. But I've had a revelation and a rebirth—and so can you. Today Ubba and I launch a new political but a very old philosophical party—the *Surprise Party*. We've all had too much to eat and drink. We need more to think. Wherever two or three are gathered in our name, let's Party!"

Aretha couldn't be sure if he actually had sex with everyone who'd stopped there on the corner—but he had an amazing sense of connection and communion—as if they'd all joined to form a larger and more powerful creature. Everyone was naked, transparent, and seemed to be glowing—not like eidolons, but as he'd imagined angels would look back when he was a boy growing up in Fort Greene. He returned to the Sun Kingdom feeling younger and healthier than he had in years. But back in the suite, sitting in one of the carved chairs holding a champagne flute filled with grapefruit juice, was none other than Minson Fiske, the son he hadn't seen in years!

"Minson," said Eartha. "This is my cousin . . . from Alabama. I haven't spoken of her much . . . but I hope you'll welcome her into our family."

"Hey," said Minson. "Pleased to meet you. I'll have to do you proud tomorrow night, won't I?"

"You already have, son," Ernestine answered. "You already have."

CHAPTER 9

Wrangling Dangler

An eerie quiet fell over the land after the whirlwind. The sky turned a dead purple and there was no sign of military or police forces. The orange freight train had vanished. The great attack planes with their bellies full of weaponry had been scrambled back to Oklahoma or Nebraska. Vitessa's Intel network was festering with the implications of psychic and meteorological warfare. Best to make a strategic retreat and consider an alternative ambush site when they'd collected more data.

Kokomo's leg didn't seem to be bothering her as much as before. Clearfather wanted to get them moving. The greyhound that had led them up out of the subterranean passage wandered off toward the highway as if showing them the way. "C'mon," he said, picking her up. "We can't stay here."

The ground was dry and lifeless after the cyclonic winds, but the air smelled heavy with rain. They followed the dog. After the sun was gone they saw shimmers of sheet lightning. At any minute he feared Vitessa would strike again—or the sky would open and spill out all the bodies and the bullets. They came to the railroad tracks and then a county road. No sign of any cars but they could hear roadtrains beginning on the interstate, which suggested that Vitessa had lifted the blockades. Soon he suspected they would send in a ground team to incinerate the area.

To the north were sporadic gunshots, and he recalled what the crew at Dustdevil had said about the Nightcrawlers. The tremblings of heat lightning turned into barbs—black licorice ozone storm smell. He still couldn't believe what had happened. The forces released— the look on the Nourisher's face as she rose. The way his wound had healed before his eyes. At last they came to the outline of a building. It was a cowboy bar, a honky-tonk shot to hell and long abandoned. Clearfather stuck his head in and listened. He couldn't see or hear the dog. Then the sky ruptured and the rain ran over the steel roof like the rats scurrying across the dance floor. He pulled Kokomo inside. A blue bolt stabbed down near the parking lot, irradiating the air. He caught afterimages of a towering headless cowboy and tried to pick out any details inside. Kokomo let go of his grasp. The rain bucketed down. He tried to listen for any inhabitants—any danger. Then another flash of lightning struck. He saw an animal! The greyhound snarled—or perhaps it was Kokomo. Shit, he thought—it's a giant mutant rat! He was dashing across the dance floor, sending the other rodents flying—when he saw that Kokomo was on top of the beast— riding it. He seized the monster and realized that it wasn't alive. It was only the knife-hacked remnant of an old mechanical bull! He gave out a long deep laugh that rolled like thunder through the honky-tonk.

"I . . . I thought it was a giant rat!" he chortled, and they fell together on the turd-stained floorboards, laughing. Kissing. Sucking. The rain slowed—and they rolled. He tasted her mouth—her eyes like the lightning—the deep smell of her skin. Ooby Dooby, Ooby Dooby.

He peeled back her stained satin jacket and pressed his tongue against her neck. The letters in his back burned but not as before.

She kissed his mouth—her tongue snaking inside him in the dark—entering him—her hands pulling at his clothes. She pressed her hand against where the weather vane had pierced him—then she held his right hand beneath her firm breast and for a second he experienced the penetrative shock again. Her skin was slightly beaded, as was his there. The rain fell like silver spoons and skeleton keys on the leaking roof, rat eyes shining. Ooby Dooby...

In another specter of lightning he saw a pale hooded shadow above the bandstand. Fear gripped him—but when the lightning came again, he calmed, glimpsing a hint of wingline. He expected it to be a barn owl—a white face the shape of an apple cut in half. But in the next pulse he saw that perched on the empty light rod above the bandstand was a bald eagle. The creature unfurled with primal authority—its claws shiny enough to reflect the lightning. What it was doing there, he had no idea, but it closed its wings like hands in prayer. From its hook-beaked mouth drooped the tail of a rat. Then the lightning stalked off and the deserted nightclub was crowded with darkness again. He leaned into Kokomo.

"I am he as you are he as you are me and we are all together," she whispered. Then she kissed him. Everywhere.

That night he had a deep, peaceful dream. He was back on the summer porch in South Dakota, Uncle Waldo and Aunt Vivian's house. He was snuggled down listening to the gentle, regular breathing . . . of a dog . . . his dog! His dog—Lucky! Uncle Waldo and Aunt Vivian had given him a dog named Lucky. He remembered!

They woke after sunrise. The eagle was gone and there was no sign of the greyhound. He flashed back to his dream—the warm, doggy smell. It was so vivid—but they had to get moving. We've got to get to the nearest town, he thought. Maybe charter a plane. Even though the map had lied so far—or worse—he couldn't abandon it. In fact, the attack seemed to make it all the more important that he complete his mission, whatever it was. Vitessa must know about the map, he realized; otherwise they wouldn't have been lying in wait. They'd set a trap in LosVegas. But knowing that there would be trouble had to give him an advantage. He felt the little ivory ball in his pocket. It felt warm and a little moist, as it had when it had been in Kokomo's tender mouth.

He whistled for the dog but got no response. The rain had cleared and the sky was brightening. Alongside the headless cowboy in the parking lot, the stripped letters curling like a rope trick said THE D NGLING RAN LE R. A haz-chem suit fluttered from a Cyclone fence. Five hundred yards across a muddy field they reached a road, and a mile down that a bigger road. Kokomo was walking fine again. He wished he knew where the dog had gone.

A few minutes later they heard a car. The terrain undulated and they had to wait for it to clear the rise. Clearfather had half a mind to get them running, but there wasn't much cover. He listened for help from the voices but all he heard was the approaching vehicle. Then the car crested. By God, he thought, and had to smile—it's a big hot dog on wheels!

The driver rolled down his window. "You look like you could use a lift," he said with a friendly but tweedy voice.

He was apparently alone—afflicted with that boyish fifty-something tidiness that Clearfather was beginning to think was an epidemic among white males of means. He was dressed in a light-weight burgundy cardigan and microfiber slacks, sporting a Palm Desert cosmetic tan, an artificially full head of hair, and a premium Voyancy connection.

"Big Dick Driving!" Kokomo squeaked and then proceeded to do something that looked like a rain dance.

The driver was at first taken aback by these antics, but then with plummy calm announced, "This is an authentic 1990s Wienermobile, one of those marvelously absurd promotional vehicles pioneered by the Oscar Mayer wiener company."

Clearfather was concerned that Kokomo might try to mount the roof. He'd hoped for help and guidance. Maybe this was it. Then again, maybe it was a trap. But what choice did they have?

"Where are you going?"

"LosVegas," the man smiled. "With a brief detour in Nuevo Albuquerque to pick up me dear ol' Dad."

"We're heading to LosVegas, too," Clearfather said before he could stop himself.

"Well, then," said the man with a wave. "It must be meant to be."

Clearfather noted that the fellow's face was severely expressive, as if his whole skull were a puppet mask manipulated from inside by a restless hand.

"Aren't you going to ask us why we're out here walking, looking like this?" he asked at last.

"I suspect you'll tell me in your own time," the man replied. "I, myself, have always depended on the kindness of strange people. Come. You can both recline back in the Wiener Lounge . . . or one of you can ride up with me."

Clearfather accepted the passenger seat, with a jab of remorse about the greyhound.

"Why don't you let your—uh—friend—listen to this."

"What is it?" Clearfather asked, on his guard again.

"A bootleg of Stinky Wiggler live in Omaha, called *Suffering Succotash*. Go on!" The man gestured to Kokomo. "We must put pedal to the metal because Dad is picky about punctuality and I'm running behind schedule after the tornadoes. And that Vitessa roadblock. Biowarfare danger, my eye! They spoiled my pilgrimage!"

"To where?" Clearfather asked, ears pricked.

"The little hamlet of Dustdevil. A very mysterious place."

CHAPTER 10

Where There's a Wiener

Clearfather never wanted to hear the name Dustdevil again. But the man didn't seem to notice his concern, and Kokomo was already wiggling into the Wiener Lounge. He slipped into the front seat, and the long hot dog took off.

"You look . . . familiar," said the man as the car got up to speed.

"I have one of those faces. My name's Elijah Clearfather. My friend is Kokomo."

"Distinctive names," the man replied. "Well, you've probably recognized me. I'm Thaddeus Meese—Dr. Tadd, famous for *Complexity Made Easy*, *The Value of the Meaningless*, *The Ancient History of the Future*, and, my biggest commercial success, *Everything You Didn't Realize You Wanted to Know About Almost Anything You Can Think Of*. As Don Quixote said, in my profession it is necessary to know everything."

"Oh," Clearfather said. "You're like Mr. Whoopee."

"Ahhh!" cried Dr. Tadd, effervescing. "What a compliment indeed —and in kind! Phineas J. Whoopee! You prove my point beautifully. *Tennessee Tuxedo*! My favorite was the sea lion sidekick, Chumly."

"Walrus," Clearfather said. "Chumly was a walrus."

"Are you sure?" snapped Dr. Tadd. "Getting Chumly wrong would be like thinking Uncle Waldo was a weasel and not a fox."

"Who—who did you say?"

"Uncle Waldo. Waldo J. Wigglesworth in *Hoppity Hooper*."

"I have—or I had an Uncle Waldo," Clearfather muttered. "At least . . . I think I did."

"Well, there you are," said Dr. Tadd. "You *think* you had an Uncle Waldo. You see? There are so many points that one can never be certain of. That's why it's vital to resolve these sea-lion-versus-walrus debates. Of course, the other side is that if all such questions could be answered—if nothing were ever forgotten or lost—we might also paradoxically be able to say that nothing could be found. As T. S. Eliot remarked, 'All our knowledge brings us nearer to our ignorance.' In any case, I still say Chumly was a sea lion."

Dr. Tadd continued nattering on but Clearfather found it hard to concentrate, although he liked the sound of the man's chatter. It reminded him of what Ainsley might've been like if he hadn't died as a child—if he'd been able to grow up as a man and not a ghost. The Wienermobile wheeled by shuttered motels and blossom-blown mimosa trees and then got on the interstate, clearing the droid-monitored checkpoint without question. This made him paranoid again.

Dr. Tadd explained that he'd added a powerful alt-fuel engine that had cost him his entire consulting fee to IMAGINE-NATION for work on 20th CenturyLand. He felt it was worth it because it allowed him to hum along at an impressive but environmentally sensitive speed. And hum they did, past fields of winter wheat, bright red all-season safflowers, a game reserve, and a Buddhist monastery. Then they were in Amarillo—and again no questions at the checkpoint. Clearfather felt powerful surges of unease and vague longing.

"I can see you're curious about the lack of official attention paid to us," said Dr. Tadd. "I hadn't intended it, but the Wienermobile seems to fall below the drone threshold of concern. I only get stopped by human Securitors and police. Maybe it's the vehicle's humor and extraneous design."

Clearfather considered this a reassuring but depressing thought as they drove by a Chu's (TODAY'S SPECIAL: SUCKLING PIG TROTTERS IN BIRD'S NEST SOUP). On the deck of a pontoon camper moored in a sediment pond beside a helium plant, a Kashmiri man scaled a giant carp with a potato peeler. Monster pickups and armored jeeptors shared the drag with Solars and expressionless Chinese on bicycles or wealthy Triads in mirror black limousines, some pulled by Mexicans.

Dr. Tadd obviously knew his way around because he made passing reference to features of the town—like The Big Brim, a revolving restaurant in the shape of a cowboy hat overlooking pens of genetically enhanced cattle. They ended up at a primitive Pullman car diner in a grove of pecan trees. The place was called The Patty Melt and was run by a woman who spoke with a barbed-wire twang. The three of them each devoured a plate of buttermilk hotcakes and smokehouse sausage, a chicken-fried steak with iron-skillet gravy, and two eggs sunny-side up. Kokomo's mouth was always full and open. Clearfather had doubts about leaving her alone with Tadd but he had no choice because he had to go to the restroom. When he got back to the table Dr. Tadd and Kokomo were wolfing down apple Danish and seemed like they'd known each other for years.

"Weef been harving a marvelous dishcussion—Somnia a Deo missa," Dr. Tadd announced. "Dreams sent by God. Absolutely fascinating."

"You . . . have?" Clearfather was puzzled.

Dr. Tadd excused himself to visit the restroom. Kokomo was still hungry, and by pointing at the menu and chattering like a chimp she was able to order a bowl of chili with onion rings and a slice of loganberry pie. Dr. Tadd returned. "There are only two other places like this left in America," he asserted. "One's in Chicago, near my home. They still make sauerkraut soup. The other that I know of is in Rapid City, South Dakota. Must go back."

"South Dakota?" Clearfather repeated.

But the topic got lost in Kokomo's chomping and the radio. Spurning a TWIN link, and not popular with Voyants, The Patty Melt was a proud supporter of American Pirate Radio. The big stories were about Dooley Duck and Ubba Dubba, the odds on the prizefight coming up at the Sun Kingdom, and the miraculous occurrences that had happened in the wake of the Texas tornadoes.

In the museum town of Dodge City it had rained prairie dogs (the first ever such recorded incident), while in Tenkiller Lake a Baptist minister, who was fishing, was knocked out of his boat by a first edition of *The Varieties of Religious Experience*. Meanwhile, an unexploded Jack O'Lantern blew up a controversial Planned Parenthood center in Fayetteville, Arkansas. The Right to Strife protesters who had gathered to celebrate were annihilated in a hail of children—some inside Vistex spheres that resembled hailstones. Dr. Tadd, who was a connoisseur of such phenomena, was exhilarated despite the personal inconvenience and felt that a whole career could arise from the analysis of that one day.

Kokomo finished scarfing down her chow and Clearfather picked up the tab. He sat up front again.

"You mentioned you're from Chicago," he tried as his food began to settle.

"City of the Big Shoulders born and bred," Dr. Tadd confirmed. "Used to be on the faculty at the university—but I had to resign for health reasons. Fortunately my royalties have funded my freedom."

"What was wrong with your health?"

"Mental health," sighed Tadd. "I had an acute religious phase, which they diagnosed as nonspecific Saint Anthony's Syndrome. I'd been studying the Venerable Bede, the eighth-century scholar who set out to record the market penetration of Christianity in England. That got me interested in Iceland, where Christianity was officially adopted wholesale in AD 1000. I wanted to know how they'd handled it, at the sod hut level, so to speak. I came upon an account from AD 1008 about a monk who went to visit a family on an isolated farm to see how their practice of Christianity was progressing. They invited him into their humble house for dinner. They said grace, which he was pleased about, and then they passed around a blackened mandrake-looking thing that he realized was a mummified horse pizzle. They said a blessing over this as well—and that's when I had my revelation!

"What was the leathery, black horse phallus but a talisman of vigor and life passed down through the generations—just as a part of Christ is Tammuz, the vegetation god who's reborn each year with the new harvest? I saw that this little tribe, who could worship Christ and an ancient fertility symbol concurrently, would be right in step today, because this is a culture where it's never been a question of the Crucifix or the Horse Cock, but of the Crucifix *and* the Horse Cock. Trouble was, soon after that insight I started hallucinating these little Chinese men."

"You did?" Clearfather perked up. "I—I've seen them, too!"

"Yes." Dr. Tadd nodded. "I've since discovered many people have. My theory is that they're an archetypal form speaking to us through the collective unconscious."

"Do you still . . . see them?"

"Not since the Bigfoot earthquake. I was doing a seminar at the Esalen Institute in Big Sur and they appeared and told me that I should return to Chicago at once. If not for them, I could've been in the hot tub when Bigfoot struck."

Clearfather felt better about this. "How . . . how did you recover? You have . . . recovered . . . haven't you?"

"I take a regular dose of a synthetic called Pythagoras. But what brought me back from the brink was Stinky Wiggler's music, especially *Psychopomp*."

"Hm. Do you think Stinky Wiggler's still alive?" Clearfather asked.

"I certainly hope so," Dr. Tadd replied. "He's alive for me."

They arrived in Tucumcari, which was in part a Route 66 theme park with new old motor court cabins and tepee trading posts and the Giant Tumbleweed: THE LARGEST FREESTANDING CARBON FIBER STRUCTURE WEST OF THE MISSISSIPPI. Dr. Tadd filled up at a Phoenix station.

"So what brings you to LosVegas?" Dr. Tadd asked when they pulled off again.

Clearfather thought a moment, as if it were one of Kokomo's riddles. "You."

Dr. Tadd grinned and tooted the horn at a tangle of brown children, startling the cave bats out of a Blockbuster store.

"Seriously," Clearfather continued. "We're going to meet some people . . . I think. And start a new life—I hope. And you, where did you say you'd been—Dustdevil?"

Dr. Tadd shifted in his seat. They passed a haunted Kmart.

"Well," he began. "My special province is the theme park and the obsessional private theme parks that America is so rich in. This trip I wanted to return to the Garden of Eden, which I hadn't visited in a while."

"The Garden of Eden?"

"Built by Samuel P. Dinsmoor in Lucas, Kansas. Wonderful character. Married his first wife on horseback in 1870. Then at the ripe young age of eighty-one married a girl of twenty. He built an allegorical sculpture garden devoted to biblical imagery and a critique of modern civilization. That was my first exposure to the art form years ago and it still holds up. But anyway," said Dr. Tadd, lowering his voice. "My next project is about Lloyd Meadhorn Sitturd, the great neglected genius."

"I've never heard of him," Clearfather said.

"That's because he's neglected," replied Dr. Tadd.

The geological intensity of New Mexico opened before them,

stratified ramparts soaring into the sand-painting-blue sky, a few smoke signal clouds as white as desert chicory—and over the Pecos River a giant hologram announcing the distance to Wal-Mart World.

"What . . . does he have to do with Dustdevil?" Clearfather asked.

"Sitturd's father, Hephaestus, was a blacksmith-*cum*-failed-inventor," Tadd replied. "Always dreaming of new inventions he never finished. Married a mulatto conjure woman named Rapture Meadhorn in Ohio. Sitturd was born in 1838. A twin sister died at birth. Swamped with debts, Hephaestus inherited a patch of dirt in Dustdevil, Texas, and later moved the family there, where young Lloyd built a monument for his dead sister on the property . . . and one day while he was tending it . . . he was taken up in a tornado . . . and brought back twenty minutes later. To the *exact* same spot."

"Really?" gawked Clearfather.

"Well, that's the legend." Dr. Tadd shrugged. "What we know for sure is that his skills began to accelerate in unexplainable ways. He became a pioneer in cinematography and went on to invent many of the special-effects techniques used by filmmakers from the Lumières to D. W. Griffith. He was the first person to formulate the scientific principles of camouflage and emphasized that camouflage must not merely obscure real targets, it must create the perception of targets where none exist.

"He experimented with cryptography to convey subliminal messages. He even developed the prototype of what he called the Translinguisticon, an invention intended to communicate with the dead. But he pissed a lot of people off. He had a monstrous sexual appetite and was always going broke trying to run his private kingdom, Labyrinthia, in South Dakota."

"South Dakota? How did he make his money?" Clearfather asked as the Wienermobile shooshed by a bombed-out mosque and a Piggly Wiggly Supersite.

"Ah," warmed the driver. "Many people were eager to harness his talents. For instance, a rubber baron named Faro down in South America hired him to reorient the continent's river system. Faro was married to a beautiful Indian girl from the headwaters of the Amazon. Alone in the palatial house with infested harpsichords and rotting Caravaggios peeling off the walls, Sitturd was there about two days before he was balling the wife. The rubber king's skeleton was later found in the wake of an army ant invasion that Sitturd and the Indian girl survived. They lived together in the decaying house—and in that time the girl bore Sitturd a son. But the child died. You see, in South America, there's a kind of catfish that grabs monkeys out of the trees when they come down to drink from the rivers. One snapped up Sitturd's son when the mother was giving the boy a bath. The girl believed the river god was angry with her and drowned herself. Overcome with grief, Sitturd left the mansion to crumble back into the jungle, which is, coincidentally, the same fate that met Labyrinthia. In the time he'd been gone his caretakers had looted the place, tramps and moonshiners had set fires, and the wildcats and hoot owls had taken over. Not even a chimney remained."

Clearfather was filled with a sense of sympathetic sadness at this story and turned his mind out the window to a Costco the size of a small town. But Dr. Tadd was not one to be diverted in midlecture and a moment later remarked, "Sitturd arrived back in America with a royal blue macaw and a case of malaria.

"At first he did nothing but drink absinthe with prostitutes. Salvation came in the form of a commission from a consortium of the great industrialists of Pittsburgh. They wanted him to design an amusement park called Macropotamia, which was one of the titles for the new western states dreamed up by Thomas Jefferson—located near where Three Rivers Stadium used to be. Sitturd developed the largest assemblage of miniature automata the world had ever seen. There were ice sculptures, firewalkers, beer gardens, oyster bars, and great tents where whole steers were barbecued. But one of the most interesting features was the midway—which instead of freak-show attractions offered a range of lectures by university professors and theologians, as well as the services of astrologers, prestidigitators, clairvoyants, mesmerists, and oneirokritai."

"What are they?" Clearfather asked.

"Professional dream interpreters. But where Sitturd crossed the line was with the world's first true roller coaster. It was inspired by his experience with the whirlwind and was first called Lodemania, in honor of his sister—and then The Rapture. People were knocked out by the thing. Bret Harte wet his pants on it and Edison, who loathed Sitturd, got a hernia. But what many others experienced was something like a religious vision. Well, you can imagine what the church elders of Pittsburgh and the country at large thought about that! Take an amusement-park ride and see God! Then one summer afternoon three schoolgirls went on it. And went into labor. When the doctors made their examinations, they found all three hymens intact. There were no signs of intercourse! Virgin births! In Pittsburgh!"

"Wow."

"Wow is right! Nothing went right after that. Sitturd had a falling-out with his backers. A mysterious fire destroyed Macropotamia, which many people insinuated that he set himself. He went into seclusion—perhaps in Australia. But he eventually returned to Dustdevil to found a spiritual community."

"He became a cult leader?" Clearfather choked.

"No, no. He was never a *leader*. He was a sponsor of possible behaviors—a catalyst. But he fell afoul of the women's reform movements as well as the captains of industry. The church demonized him. His fellow scientists were threatened, and artists thought he was too successful at bringing his art to life."

"So what happened? Was he killed?"

"He disappeared," replied Dr. Tadd, dodging a squashed armadillo on the road. "That's why I wanted to visit Dustdevil. His last home and now there's probably nothing left. Macropotamia is gone and no one knows where Labyrinthia actually was in South Dakota. The trail goes cold on the most Diagonal Thinker of all time."

"Maybe that's the way he wanted it." Clearfather sighed. He longed to fall in a nice soft bed somewhere for a hundred years.

"Perhaps," agreed Tadd. "But there are intriguing loose ends. For instance, Ronwell Seward—Stinky Wiggler's real name—bears singular resemblances to Sitturd, and no one really knows much about Seward. The other point is that Dustdevil was also the scene of a siege massacre between the Feds and a pagan sex cult thirty years ago. Another reason to go to LosVegas."

"Why is that?" Clearfather said, coming alert.

"The Feds and later Vitessa have suppressed the details quite effectively, but there's a man I met when consulting to IMAGINE-NATION who claims to have some artifacts."

"Who?" Clearfather asked, trying to mask his curiosity.

"Olly Podrida. Runs the Hall of Notorious Americans on Brando Street. Anyway, it's just unfortunate that Vitessa decided to close down that entire part of Texas. I'd have taken my chances with the weather. Did you see anything of the Big Blow?"

"We got out just in time," Clearfather replied. "There were guards—and robotic things. We were more worried about our own people than the twisters."

"I know that feeling," Dr. Tadd concurred, pointing out the Masai tribesmen herding miniature cattle.

"Well, we certainly appreciate getting a ride all the way to Albuquerque."

"New Albu," Dr. Tadd corrected. "Eight out of ten citizens were having trouble with the spelling so they bagged it—plus that biochem stuff during the war. But I hope you don't think you're going to be turned loose upon arrival. Dad would love to meet you. He has more than enough room for you to sleep comfortably, and we're leaving for LV early tomorrow. Why not come with us?"

"That's a nice offer," Clearfather hemmed. "But we wouldn't want to intrude."

"Come and meet the old chap and see how you feel. You can at least have dinner."

Clearfather felt a rush of gratitude. After the headaches and uncontrollable urges, a moment of peace and kindness seemed delicious. Delicious but suspicious.

CHAPTER 11

Root for the Home Team

Between the Somalis, the Beijing Opera antics, and the mujahideen wanted poster holograms, there was a lot to process upon arrival at the New Albu checkpoint, not to mention all the ultralights flittering over Samsung City. Dr. Tadd's father lived in a Pueblo-style Sustainment Village between the surgery resorts and one of the city's more popular sunset parlors. They were greeted at the gate by an armed human guard with a name badge that said FEDOTOV and waved straight through. Dr. Tadd gunned the engine but then immediately pulled over in a landscaped area full of fishhook cacti.

"Never seen 'em so bright," he remarked—and then looked his passenger in the eye. "Do you know the expressions, 'Don't throw out the baby with the bath,' or 'The child is father to the man'? Well, please don't mention them around Dad."

"Why?" Clearfather asked, surprised.

"Dad went through an aging crisis a few years back. Got involved with that Dr. Wieviel character back in Pittsburgh."

"I've heard of Dr. Wieviel!"

"Everyone's heard of Evil Wieviel! Man's a backstreet butcher!

Anyway, he started this Vita-Repair business based on suspect and totally unapproved anti-aging drugs. And Dad fell for it."

"The drugs didn't work?"

"Oh, they worked—in one sense. Dad's body underwent a reversion."

"He got younger?"

"He got smaller. He's now the size of a baby. But the shock and stress to his body have been severe. His bones have been partially gelatinized so that he has to live suspended in special fluid . . . in a tank."

"A tank?" Clearfather said. "Like an aquarium?"

"A *small* aquarium—but don't say that—he's very sensitive. He may look like a baby, but he's really a grumpy old man."

"And he lives in the tank . . . all the time?"

"Mrs. Mendoza takes him out for physio- and vitamin therapy . . . and changes his fluid. She's his nurse and carer, but they've been in love for years."

"She's in love with him?"

"Together—well, they've developed this religious thing. It's harmless. Has to do with baseball. I think in its own way it's healthy."

"Wait a minute," said Clearfather. "How can you take him to LosVegas if he lives in an aquarium?"

"A *small* aquarium," Dr. Tadd corrected. "It's not easy. But it makes him feel better. He's got the world at his fingertips in a virtual sense, but it's not the same as me taking him on an actual trip. This time he wants to go on a roller coaster!"

"I see," said Clearfather, even more confused. But he had to admire the doctor's devotion. "I promise I won't say anything. But I can't guarantee anything about Kokomo. She speaks her mind whatever it says."

"And a fine mind, too," Tadd declared. "I had no idea that Saint Anselm's ontological proof of God had been denied by Thomas Aquinas, reaffirmed by Descartes, modified by Leibniz, refuted by Kant, and revamped by Hegel."

Clearfather shook his head in puzzlement. "Neither did I. At least . . . I don't think I knew that." He'd barely heard Kokomo speak at all, in the usual sense.

The "old man" turned out to be exactly what Dr. Tadd had described. Somehow Clearfather was expecting it to be a joke. But Dr. Tadd's father did in fact inhabit an aquarium tank, the weight of his fragile body buoyed by an unctuous blue liquid. His frame was the size of a young toddler but his skin was stretched and spotted, and his face had the substance and emotional weight of an old man. His apparel was a pair of tight bikini briefs. From the middle of an otherwise smooth chest, one stubborn tuft of gray hair undulated like kelp.

"Dad, I've brought people to visit. They had trouble on the road. I'm hoping to persuade them to stay the night and catch a ride to LV mañana."

"Good Christ!" gruffed the baby. "Whose house is this? Do you know you're late? You could've called. Why didn't you call?"

"Basta, muchacho," came a firm but affectionate female voice. "Buenas tardes, Thaddeus, y buenas noches."

"Chaps, this is the beautiful and long-suffering Señora Mendoza."

The woman was a bosomy middle-aged Latina with lustrous black hair and the softest hazelnut skin Clearfather could imagine—but he didn't have a chance to say hello because Kokomo charged the tank and proceeded to smush her face against the glass like a fish.

It was several minutes before Clearfather and Dr. Tadd could get things calmed down, and in the end it was Mrs. Mendoza who wisely escorted Kokomo off to a bathroom to have a much-needed wash.

"I'm sorry," said Clearfather. "My friend doesn't know her own enthusiasm."

"Holy shit!" grumped Mr. Meese. "Thought she was going to jump in with me!"

"Fascinating word, *enthusiasm*," pondered Dr. Tadd. "En theos. To have God within."

"Shut up, Tadpole."

"Father, you know I detest that nickname."

"'At's why I use it!"

"Well, anyway I'm sorry," Clearfather professed. "I hope you're all right."

"What do you think I am, a big baby?" demanded Mr. Meese. "Don't be sorry. It's pathetic. At least she's got spirit!"

"If I haven't already, may I introduce my father, Nathaniel Meese. Dad—Elijah Clearfather."

"What sort of name is that?"

"You'll have to excuse my father's crustiness. He needs to soak longer."

"Come in here and say that, squirt."

"Dad was once the director of the Phoenix Energy Company's Corporate Image Department," Dr. Tadd pipped. "Just don't ask him about the strategic planning retreat in Hawaii," he whispered. "That's the other thing we don't talk about."

"What about the strategic planning retreat in Hawaii?" Clearfather asked.

"Hawaii?" Nat splashed. "Don't mention that pineapple plantation to me! That's where you go when *doom* is at hand!"

"There's no stopping him now," sighed Dr. Tadd. "This is the incident that triggered the whole anti-aging debacle."

"For years I'd worked on positioning the Petroleum Business as Morally Responsible, Financially Sensible, and Environmentally Sustainable for another hundred-plus years. Do you know how hard that was? Then wham! The company forged a new vision," Nat boiled. "First, there was a Category shift, from 'old rust belt energy' to 'new sunrise energy.' Hah! Secondly, an Ideology shift from an Industrial Age exploitation culture to a Knowledge Age solutions culture. Hah! Then there was a Branding shift, which precipitated an Image shift. This led to an Icon shift. Tanya Claymore, the new CEO, got up at the podium in that five-star hotel and told us, 'New Phoenix Energy shows the New Way in the Now Millennium!' After that we had a luau with male hula dancers and pigs on spits. Then she took me behind the miniature volcano and offered me poi and told me I'd been pink-slipped."

"I'm . . . sorry to hear that," Clearfather said.

"I will not eat humble poi!" he yelled, almost capsizing himself. "I sued those bastards the next day—and got raped again."

"Oh, you did not!" scoffed Dr. Tadd. "You've got this splendid residence and a very healthy portfolio. You definitely made them feel your pain."

"I did?" Mr. Meese smiled as the fluid level calmed. "Well, anyway, let's talk about happier things. Like Bob Gibson striking out seventeen Tigers in the World Series."

"Too right," said Tadd. "Why don't you let Señora M show him the System? I'll vouch for his honesty."

"You will? He won't try to steal it?"

"I doubt that anyone but you two could understand it," Tadd replied.

Mrs. Mendoza reappeared and led Clearfather deeper into the residence, which was appointed with Navajo rugs and blankets, Spanish leather couches, and even an original watercolor by D. H. Lawrence. Everything tasteful and southwestern, however, was eclipsed by the pervasive theme of BASEBALL. Mythical American icons loomed out of the walls. The Babe, Musial, Maris, Mantle, Sosa, and Bonds. There was a huge glass case filled with signed game balls including the last ball pitched in Don Drysdale's record-breaking sixth consecutive shutout game on June 4, 1968. One entire wall was covered with broken bats, each with a nameplate underneath. But clearly the pride of Mr. Meese's and Mrs. Mendoza's life began on the wall in the kitchen. It was like a snaking, genealogical tree. It wandered out of the room and into the hall and into the bedroom and back, covering the ceiling down to the floor, erupting every few inches in a baseball card, so that patterns were formed, resembling an endlessly mutating version of the Sephirotic Tree of the Kabbalah.

"It's taken years to perfect—and we're still learning," Nat confided, floating on his back. "You see, baseball is an immensely intricate game that holds America together. This is the secret system that lies *behind* baseball."

Clearfather took a breath and contemplated this remark. He had to admire what Nat and his carer had accomplished. It's not everyone who can invent a secret religious system to keep a nation in balance.

Mrs. Mendoza showed them to the guest room. Clearfather's anger and revulsion at what had happened in Texas softened. The stuff Dr. Tadd had told him about Sitturd explained some of the things about Dustdevil, but not all. Maybe the man who ran the museum in LosVegas had the answers.

He had a bath while Kokomo washed and dried her wig and then joined him. Seeing her naked in the light was a whole new experience. She was small, but perfectly formed, with high breasts and a hot round ass that stuck out behind her like the curve of a question mark. She had not one hair. Not a wrinkle. Not a mole. The only mark on her body exactly matched his, where the weather vane had pierced his chest, and even that you had to look closely to see. He had so many questions. And so did she.

"What's the beginning of eternity, the end of time and space, the beginning of every end, and the end of every place?"

Later he realized the answer was the letter *E,* but in the moment he was too busy—their two bodies melting in the water, waves chopping at the tiles, rising to the brim and over.

Mrs. Mendoza provided them with some of Mr. Meese's old clothes, soft tracksuits and baseball jerseys—and they joined the family for cocktails. Mr. Meese, who'd donned a sheer blue bodysuit for dinner, enjoyed his through a very long straw. They ate while Dr.

Tadd outlined his plans for LosVegas, including his scheme to get his father on the famous Sidewinder roller coaster, which so worried Mrs. Mendoza, it looked for a moment as if Mr. Meese was in real hot water.

"Is there a conspiracy against me having fun?" he whined.

"Dad sees conspiracies behind every cactus," announced Dr. Tadd.

"Look who's talking. You once said if you can't find a conspiracy, you're not paying attention! Still beatin' the dead McKinley horse?"

"Which horse?" asked Clearfather.

"Dad's referring to my interest in President McKinley. Assassinated at the Pan-American Exposition in Buffalo in 1901," said Dr. Tadd.

"You think there was a conspiracy behind that?"

"Depending on your definition, there's a conspiracy behind everything. It's just a question of how big and how well organized," Dr. Tadd replied. "Take the plane crash that killed Buddy Holly, the Big Bopper, and Ritchie Valens. My theory is that the plane was sabotaged by government operatives acting in concert with the Christian Right to try to control the spreading popularity of rock and roll among white teenagers. The op backfired and Buddy Holly became a saint."

Kokomo farted.

"It's a good thing we didn't have frijoles," said Mrs. Mendoza.

"Don't you worry, lil girl," said Mr. Meese. "No harm in a bit of a bubble."

Clearfather felt like he'd known these people for years. Behind was horror and darkness. Maybe there was some hope ahead.

After dinner, while the world hung on every second of the Fight for Life (which ended up being just a matter of seconds), Clearfather and Kokomo were treated to what was obviously a ceremonial family entertainment of great significance.

"What we're about to watch . . . ," Dr. Tadd prefaced, "is something that Dad has been working on for several years. It's an ongoing analysis of the 1968 World Series won by the Detroit Tigers. Dad and Mrs. Mendoza are of the view that 1968 was a watershed in American history, and that baseball holds clues concerning what was really going on—and what ended up happening later. Right, Dad?"

"Right!" avowed Mr. Meese, rotating like a baby porpoise. "That was the year that Denny McLain won thirty-one games, a tremendous feat! And yet, in the Series, it was Mickey Lolich, who'd pitched in McLain's shadow all year, who proved the real hero and MVP. Later, as you may know, McLain got busted for gambling, racketeering, robbery, and fraud. It's a great American Tragedy. We think the effects rippled out in time."

Clearfather was impressed by the seriousness of this submission. While one of the biggest moments in sports and contemporary culture was taking place live in the very megalopolis that they were headed to the next day—they were watching recorded highlights of an event that had happened well more than half a century before. Only afterward did they learn of the unthinkable outcome in LosVegas—a stunning third-round KO of the Corpse Maker by Minson Fiske, now the first gay Heavyweight Champion of the Earth. Champagne, blood, and personal lubricants were flowing freely in the streets.

"Just as well we're not there tonight," Dr. Tadd said as they were heading to bed. "Sounds like chaos has been loosed."

Clearfather and Kokomo slipped off into the guest bed. As tired as they both were they made love—and the more gently they moved, the more intense the waves of ecstasy were, until he couldn't tell where he ended and she began.

Out in the D. H. Lawrence darkness, he heard a swish in Mr. Meese's tank, as if their eroticism had fevered the little amphibian's dreams—or maybe Mrs. Mendoza was with him doing whatever it was they did. Love takes so many forms, Clearfather thought as he drifted off to sleep with the rich scent of Kokomo filling his dreams and the peaceful, regular sound of her breathing as reassuring as his dog Lucky's had been back on the summer porch in South Dakota, long ago.

CHAPTER 12

Every Day Is Today

Love was taking very strange forms indeed in other parts of the country. In LosVegas, where Fiske Frenzy had taken hold, Aretha Nightingale, aka Denzel Fiske—and as far as Monroe Hicks was concerned, Ernestine—found him- or herself in a very complicated position. Following the third-round knockout and a celebration featuring marbled Matsuzaka beef, farm-fresh Maine lobster, and cases of Bollinger's—the drag queen, officially in disguise, ended up hugging and then dancing with his victorious son and then very publicly tongue-kissing his equally emotional wife. Surprised by this behavior, Monroe, who'd secretly bet against Minson, set his mind on a threesome, thinking that Eartha and Ernestine were kissin' cousins. Imagine his disappointment, a little later, to find Eartha in bed with Ernestine—and not engaging in Sapphic pleasures. Not by a long hard shot. If only he hadn't been naked himself, because when he stomped out of the guest boudoir in shock and anger at the trick that had been played on him, he stepped into the Jacuzzi room to find a gaggle of young white Minson Fiske fans who were snorting Fairy Princess and dousing each other in vintage bubbly without the slightest idea of where they were. The sudden sight of Monroe in the nude brought the hot tub thrashing to life.

Meanwhile back in the Mirror Technology–hidden heart of Fort Thoreau, Finderz Keeperz was in a state of cold panic. After the stupendous defeat of the forces at Dustdevil, he was forced into the agonizing reappraisal that he would have to take the Clearfather problem into his own hands or run out of time and risk exposure.

During the skirmish between the Corps of Discovery and the combat probe in Clearfather's brain, the sum total of energy produced a distinctive enough signal to lock on to. It struck the dwarf that he'd underestimated the resilience of the Corps, which might still play to his advantage. Now he cranked his profound knowledge of system vulnerability up to full heat. Master of backdoor trojans, worms, weevils, and insidiously propagating viruses, he was also a firewall cracker extraordinaire and one of an elite guild capable of navigating the maximum-secret precincts of the Vitessa Central Nervous System. It was here that he delved now with increasing desperation, searching, seeking, sneaking peeks at his many wristwatches. Against a host of cyberpredators, guardians, and trapdoors, he maneuvered with adrenaline-focused concentration, for he could not afford to fail. Not now. Deeper and wider into the multitudinous infosystem he delved, becoming ever more desperate—until—he found it. Yes! A huge grin of relief wrinkled across his face. Just the right weapon. Powerful enough, but incidental enough not to be well guarded. Just the thing. Just the perfect thing.

He'd discovered a satellite used to monitor brain-implanted prisoners, code-named *Azazel*. The satellite was shaped like a black stealth angel, in synchronous orbit over the middle of the United States. At any time during its orbital period it could send an electromagnetic pulse to any of the implants in its directory. A hot white explosion would occur, like an extremely clear and final idea.

Aretha could soon be returning. The dwarf had to move fast. He'd seen that Vitessa could not be trusted to handle the Clearfather situation expeditiously. But if he could strike Clearfather down himself—if he could bring the brain of the Messiah Weapon to Vitessa on a silver platter, having used their own metaphorical bolt of lightning—he would have his criminal record expunged and no longer have to live in a filthy tent surrounded by inferior minds with egalitarian visions. He might well be given a Region to head. Hah!

He hacked into *Azazel* and entered the transponder code based on the frequency of the combined signals from the earlier confrontation between the probes. The moment they engaged again, *Azazel* would be alerted. And if they didn't, still all was not lost, for he would leave the line open, allowing Vitessa to trace the hack. Once their position was triangulated, the Mirror Field would eventually be deduced and Fort Thoreau would be under permanent siege. And as for Clearfather, even if he survived *Azazel,* sooner or later the invasive brain insert would accomplish its deadly mission. That would have to be worth some consideration. As long as Keeperz could escape Fort Thoreau.

Out in New Albu, Mrs. Mendoza let the troops sleep in before shifting into high gear. Dr. Tadd, Clearfather, and Kokomo were treated to a late breakfast of huevos rancheros; Mr. Meese was left to enjoy pumpkin-colored goo. Señora M had arranged for the Village laundry service to mole-clean their clothes. Then came the delicate task of moving Mr. Meese's tank and installing it in the Wienermobile, along with his many supplies and support equipment, including catheters, unguents, drips, drops, and fluid treatment tablets.

Clearfather saw that there might have been more to the choice of vehicle than Dr. Tadd's sense of humor and relish for Americana. The passenger section had just the right amount of added ceiling height and total length to allow suspension of his father's tank by carbon cord from two anchor points, thus minimizing vibrations and allowing the old man the best view, both through the retractable UV-guarded Wiener Bun sunroof and the normal tinted windows.

Mrs. Mendoza packed them a generous lunch, fired several hundred instructions at Dr. Tadd, many in Spanish—and a stern warning about the Sidewinder. She nodded politely to Clearfather, gave Kokomo a hug, and then became very restrained and proper saying goodbye to Mr. Meese (although Clearfather later noted the steamy heart-shaped impression of her lips on the tank). The sky was huge and cornflower blue, and the Wienermobile went like an environmentally sensitive rocket past enormous eidolons of Geronimo and Billy the Kid.

Kokomo wanted to sit up with Tadd so Clearfather sat in the back with Mr. Meese, which was a little awkward because the tank took up so much room, and very awkward because he didn't know what to say. Then he discovered that Mr. Meese was tuned in to an ancient baseball game and didn't appear to be very interested in conversing anyway, so he checked out the Stinky Wiggler music that Kokomo had been listening to earlier. Dr. Tadd had the whole catalog—*Preaching to the Perverted, Sealed for Your Protection, Open Slather.* Clearfather activated one disc called *Conditions Apply* and slipped on the headphones. He listened. But he didn't hear anything. He checked the player selection and the volume. There was complete silence. At first he thought it was a joke. But the more he listened, the completer the silence seemed, as if the disc absorbed all peripheral noise. Time seemed to drift. The sense of calm was hypnotic.

Another disc was titled *Manifest Disney.* He put it on. Again, he heard nothing at first—then there were faint suggestions of sounds —horses' hooves, river rapids, gunfire, machines. It wasn't like any music he'd ever imagined. He closed his eyes and a series of powerful eidetic images emerged. The first was a railroad track at night, running between tall pines. Out of the dark there appeared a steam train with a piercing lantern and a gaping smokestack. The locomotive was enormous and black, except for the driving rods and the cowcatcher, which were made of solid gold. As the train approached, the cross-ties it passed over came alive, like sleepers rising—and he saw that they were Chinese men and women. The train grew nearer and he could make out the engineer and the fireman, their faces and hands burning with flames, the same red as the firebox, which they fed with little cigar-store Indians carved of sequoia and oak. The train reached a river and across the canyon was a trestle, which in the light of the lantern he saw was made of the horns and antlers of animals. Then the music—or the silence—changed, and he was on a modern commuter train coming down from Westchester into Manhattan. In the Bronx a large black bear got on and ambled down the aisle, but no one noticed. The commuters were all Voyancing or reading. A herd of deer grazed in the middle of Fifth Avenue and the cabs kept driving. No one commented on the giant beaver dam outside Radio City Music Hall or that Rockefeller Center was teeming with muskrats. Then he was riding on a train full of raccoons and red-winged blackbirds all the way to Coney Island—and out on a desolate pier he saw Henry Hudson wrapped in a Bowery overcoat swigging Thunderbird Wine beside a saltwater taffy stand covered in placas. The wretched explorer huddled, watching the gulls and a couple of old Jewish men cutting open a beached whale. They'd found a bottle in the mammal's gut and inside the bottle was a message . . .

Clearfather suddenly looked up and saw the fantasy parks rising from the yucca—and out of the sky there appeared to leap an enormous astronaut, who landed in a cloud of eidolonic glitter and said, *"That's one small step for a man . . . and the second step's a doozy! Welcome to LosVegas! Where every day is Today!"*

CHAPTER 13

The Notorious Frontier

Aretha and Eartha slept late. Figuring that the damage was done as far as Monroe was concerned, they had an extended lovemaking session. When they emerged from the sprawling opulence of the guest quarters into the smeared decadence of the main suite, they found it was oddly quiet. Monroe's chef was passed out beneath a mountain of hairy crab shells. The master bedroom was a shambles of silk underwear, drugs, bottles, and the occasional sliver of dog tongue. In the spa room the mirror walls were covered in dried bubble bath, K-Y jelly, and Matsuzaka beef. There was no sign of Monroe.

A Harijan and two Bolivian women came to clean up while Aretha and Eartha went out for brunch (and a little shopping). When they returned the suite was spotless except for the print of someone's butt cheeks on a wall in the spa room—but there was still no sign of Monroe. They made plans to have a quiet dinner with a very hungover Minson at the Reef and Beef on the corner of Eddie Murphy and Cameron Diaz. As the suite was paid for for another night, there was no point in not enjoying it. If Monroe doesn't show up by tomorrow morning, Eartha thought, I'll call the police. If Monroe does show up, there'll be trouble, Aretha thought. But he didn't care. For the first time in years all he could think of was the moment.

"Just look at those cars!" Dr. Tadd marveled in the speakerphone as the Wienermobile cruised down Ronald Reagan Boulevard. On the corner of Goldie Hawn there was an eighteen-wheel papaya-green Le Roi and a Prussian blue bobsled powered by a Rocketdyne liquid oxygen and kerosene engine called a Hegira. "The main nerve of the Now Frontier! More murders, millionaires, mental institutions, and resources consumed each day than anywhere else on the planet," purred Tadd.

"Slow down!" Mr. Meese called from the tank's intercom. "I wanna check out the honeys—did you see the hooters on that one!"

Clearfather had never imagined so many aloha shirts, all-terrain vehicles, and automatic weapons—and that was just in one store, which took up all of George Clooney Drive. And the people! Sikhs, Yogis, and the Dead Girl gangs of Little Phnom Penh. The sunlight flared off the octagonal panels of the envirodomes as the Wienermobile passed topless tapas bars, pet counselors, and clinics that specialized in genital resculpturing. POWDERPUFF WHUPS BULLY the buildings flashed as the giant laser ghosts flickered and danced. FRUIT BEATS MEAT!

Dr. Tadd cruised Seismic to Colorado River Way, into the dense tangle of avenues named for lost stars of yesteryear. The air was thick with camel shit, Acapulco Gold, and food. You could buy guinea pig enchiladas or sea slugs in hoisin sauce, or wander among the eel and snake restaurants of Michael Douglas Mall—or the specialty shops offering giant Chinese salamanders in Nicole Kidman.

Dr. Tadd and Mr. Meese were staying at the Amazonia, the largest thatched structure in the world, surrounded by jungles of rain forest hardwood and pools and fountains turning into miniature rivers, complete with thundering waterfalls (which locals regularly threw themselves into when their drug, gambling, or psychiatric debts over-whelmed them). Mr. Meese liked the sound of running water and was welcomed by the loinclothed doormen; Dr. Tadd was a big tipper wherever his father was concerned.

"If you have any doubts where to meet someone," said Dr. Tadd, doffing a Panama hat, "go to Lucas Square. Sooner or later all the action passes through. Rather like the lower bowel. Meanwhile, if you need anything, we'll be here three nights. Then on to MormonLand. Dad's never seen it."

"Thanks for everything," said Clearfather wistfully. "Maybe we'll stop by when we're settled."

"I hope so."

"I hope so, too," Clearfather said, thinking that here was another fatherly figure that had appeared to help him. "By the way—that museum—the owner you said has the Dustdevil artifacts? I'd like to meet him."

"Olly? It's the Museum of Notorious Americans on Brando Street."

"How do we get there? Can we walk?"

"Oh my, no," said Dr. Tadd. "It's on the other side of the Streisand Canal. You'll want the Synapse Train. You see the Encephalon ride . . . the big pink brain? Go between that and the Bill Cosby Center and you'll see the lake. You get off at the Ono station, I think—but ask the train. Just don't go through the botanical gardens after dark. The place is crawling with satanists."

"Thanks," Clearfather smiled—grateful and sad at the same time.

They were standing on a bamboo bridge when a monkey leaned over to pull off Dr. Tadd's brim. The branch it was balanced on sagged and the creature dipped to water level, where a large catfish breached and swallowed it whole.

"Tough town," said Dr. Tadd. "Stay alert."

Standing alone with Kokomo again, Clearfather felt as exposed as they had been back in Texas. Vitessa was probably watching them at that very moment, and he knew he should've been scared but he wasn't. (He didn't know that the Corps of Discovery had triggered an endorphin release inside his brain; he thought it was the excitement of arrival and his gratitude for Dr. Tadd's assistance.)

Clearfather could see the elevated ribbon of the Synapse Train firing along. We can hop on that anytime, he reasoned. Best to stretch a bit and get the lay of the land. This time he was certain there was someone waiting for them.

Kokomo had a funny expression on her face. She held on tight to him as they navigated the bustling causeways below the billowing American and Vitessa Cultporation flags, catching sight between the minarets and adrenaline rides of eidolons of Kuan Ti, patron god of the Triads, and on Mount Meditation, the breathtaking gold Buddha, which stood as tall as the Tower of Bagels.

They cut through Nuevo Tokyo, past the pavilions where the Go masters sat deep in thought over hologram games with giant tortoises for playing stones. They boarded the train in the Pacino District. The crystalline gel-steel domes of 20th CenturyLand, HolyLand, Musica-Land, the other IMAGINE-NATION parks lit up the dusk, revealing the black outlines of hundreds of fruit bats or flying foxes making their way back to the trees in the botanical gardens.

Brando Street started off bright and sleazy like Patphong Road in Bangkok and then darkened into what seemed like a garage sale for the Mayo Clinic, with discounted offers for all sorts of surgical procedures, although it was hard to understand the hawkers and barkers because they yacked in different languages and many wore oxygen masks.

The couple finally located the Museum of Notorious Americans between a boarded-up digital pet repair shop and a gender bender bar called Thingmakers. The building if not the enterprise as a whole appeared torn between being a Macao gambling den and Grant's

Tomb, with a strong hint of Redondo Beach Elks Club circa 1974. Admission was ludicrously expensive, but Clearfather was in no mood to quibble. Once inside, they found Olly Podrida, a tense and sweaty gentleman in a Hong Kong suit, deep in consultation with his principal tech head, trying to work out a problem with J. Robert Oppenheimer.

"You look familiar," the museumeer gruffed. "Meesy called and said you were on the way over. Want a cream soda?"

"No . . . thanks. We've—I'm just after information."

Life-sized eidolons began to appear as if at a cocktail party in a dream. Clearfather was surprised that the outcast Detroit Tiger Denny McLain was among them.

"El Doctoro says you're interested in something from the private collection?"

"He said you have artifacts from The Kingdom of Joy, the love cult in Texas," Clearfather answered.

Olly Podrida sprayed cream soda.

"Something wrong?"

Olly set down his drink and motioned for Clearfather to follow him through a mirrored door in the wall. Kokomo wandered over to check out Denny McLain. The hallway behind the mirror was cluttered with laser componentry. In a workshop Brigham Young and Mae West wavered in and out like divorcés on a blind date.

Olly ushered him to a back room crowded with props.

"We were gonna include Hosanna Freed but we had trouble with the face," Olly said. "Almost no reference. Vitessa put the whammy on it. Besides, the big thing with him was his unit. We're not licensed for genital nudity—but I had another idea. A year ago I met up with an old hombre I knew in Texas. He was fencing stuff this lab chick had boosted from a Vitessa facility in Dallas. He showed me this."

The museumeer pulled out a long veranium cylinder with the diameter of a tea saucer. Olly opened an invisible seam down the length to reveal a nesting of moist umber foam that appeared to be alive. An empty space stared back like an open grave.

"There was a preserved human penis in here," Olly said. "Huge but human. I'm certain it was severed from Freed's body after the massacre thirty years ago."

"It's gone!" Clearfather whistled.

"Stolen," answered Olly. "Two months ago, this cat who claimed to be the personal procurer for Wynn Fencer came to me. Very odd. Like he didn't have bones. He'd heard I had the organ—I'd gotten drunk with Meese and shot my mouth off at a party in 20th Century-Land. He asked if I'd sell. I'm like no, I have plans for it. He said Fencer had gotten into black magic—I could name my price. I naturally got suspicious. Told him no. Couple weeks later another character shows up. An old black dude pretending to be blind. He says he runs a big mojo store and mail-order business in South Chicago. Sells gris-gris bags—goofer dust. Makes me an offer, too. I start thinking there's more to the penis than meets the eye—so I lock it up in my floor safe. Couple days later I see Edgar Allan Poe wandering around back here and I think . . . how can the eidolons leave a projection area? Well, it wasn't Ed. Knocked me cold and skedaddled with the dick. Brought his own container, too. Weird, huh?"

"Yeah," Clearfather agreed, trying to figure out what it meant.

"I'm convinced the penis was Hosanna Freed's. Don't know whether those dudes worked for Fencer—I doubt it. But they cleaned out everything I had on Freed."

"Do you know anything about the woman who stole the penis from Vitessa?"

"My buddy just said she was a lab rat."

"So it had been in Vitessa's possession all those years?"

"Looks like it."

"What makes you think it belonged to Hosanna Freed?"

"The size! Plus the way it was stored. And that it was found in

Texas—a lab that Vitessa bought up when they coalesced. What's your interest in all this?"

"Doing research."

"You sure do look familiar. You any relation to Freed?"

"Maybe," Clearfather answered coyly. "That's why I'm doing research."

"Well, be careful what you find. And who you tell."

Clearfather thanked the museumeer and went to retrieve Kokomo, who now looked very pale—and ill. He was so intrigued by what Olly had told him and so concerned about Kokomo's change in appearance he didn't notice that the apparent eidolon of Senator Joseph McCarthy left immediately after them, following them down Brando Street.

The panhandlers were becoming more deformed and insistent. (There's nothing worse than having someone in your face who doesn't have a face.) Clearfather hustled Kokomo along. Not wanting to cross through the gardens, they headed into a maze of markets that reeked of shashlik and fajitas. You could buy an Ecuadorian cretin or barter DNA. They settled for Hokkein noodles. Big Joe kept close.

Back behind them the robotic structures conducted their stylized Noh theater transformations—the giant rides like the Wyziwyg and Zero G blinking—monolithic Easter Island heads announcing PRIME RIB SPECIALS. They came to a burgeoning campground full of cargo cultists and Ghost Dancers. Out beyond the perimeter, Clearfather saw an intricate reticulum of ponds and trenches full of organic-smelling sludge. Huge robotronic bulldozers were at work, pushing hulks of cars and rubbish into the ponds. Underneath all the other noises he could hear a low bubbling sound.

To drive the LosVegas engines of entertainment and illusion required extreme energy resources that tapped the ingenuity of the species. Tidal, solar, hydro, wind, and orgo-molecular generation combined to keep the juices flowing—creating a heat island like the Great Red Spot of Jupiter. It was just fortunate that a bioexploration division of Vitessa had discovered, deep in the remains of Burundi, a form of algae that could ingest refuse metal and plastics. This life-form, on the threshold between the plant and the animal, literally ate the excretions of American consumer society and produced oxygen—and still more money for Vitessa. People called them the Goblins and the name stuck.

The couple found their way back to the Synapse line. Two long stops away they spotted a vandalized statue of Lionel Richie. Clear-father hailed a rickshaw pulled by a young white guy—an English major. He recommended a place called Noah's Park. "It's not the cleanest or sanest in town—but the owners have their hearts in the right place," the rickshawer said.

The owners turned out to be Bob, who ran the motel side of the operation, while his wife, Kayleen, looked after the animals—per-forming animals that had once been stars downtown. A sourpuss cougar wallowed in a hammock between two kumquat trees, ignor-ing a disgruntled pair of snow leopards that lay on recliners—while the pool was dominated by a pygmy hippo named Bernadette and an obstreperous family of trained seals called the Osmonds. This wasn't the kind of accommodation I was thinking of, Clearfather thought to himself. But it was cheap and, like the rickshaw kid had said, it had a good vibe. Kokomo went straight to the heart-shaped bed in the clean but simple Room 6 and lay holding her head. Clearfather grew more anxious about her. Her distress or discomfort was his. He tried offering her a cool damp cloth but she didn't acknowledge him. The red light on the old phone by the bed lit up.

"Someone's at reception for you," Bob said. "Should I send her along?"

Reverse Theology

When Konrad Kriegsspiel, the Now West Coast director of Vitessa Intel, had a particularly difficult assign-
ment, he turned to Cyrilla Lundquist. It was she who'd scoped on
Clearfather and Kokomo at the Amazonia and tracked them to the
museum, where she'd changed her disguise to follow them as Big Joe.
When she'd established their location at Noah's Park, she morphed
out of the Hallucinarmor.

Her mission was to gain Clearfather's confidence or, failing that,
to inspire uncertainty—to buy time. After the humiliating events in
Texas, a great trembling had shaken the Vitessalith. Here was a new
weapon, materializing out of nowhere, without a clear suggestion of
who was behind him or to what purpose he'd been deployed. At the
same time, Dooley Duck and Ubba Dubba had torn loose from their
technological moorings and were leading other creations astray. Cy-
bersimulated characters were appearing everywhere—having sex
and preaching anti-commercial rebellion. Carefully cultivated and
coordinated micro-mental-illnesses were destabilizing or disappear-
ing. To top it off, Vitessa's secret informant had gone quiet. Now the

awful Dustdevil affair, instead of being a tip-off they could trust, was beginning to look very much like a setup. And what a slaughter! Millions of dollars in technology lost and no clue what they were up against.

All their attention now was focused on Room 6 in Noah's Park, and yet somewhere in the labyrinths upon labyrinths that formed the liquidata molecular intelligence network of the Vitessa Central Nervous System, an alarm was ringing, like a tiny bell deep underground warning of a big wind. There was a monitoring system monitoring this system—and a monitoring system to monitor that—on up a chain. But the message was lost in the network's own immensity. Someone had commandeered a satellite. Their secret informant was making his own play—a long-range sniper shot. And just as Keeperz was feeling so close to the fulfillment of his scheme, his new masters were cursing him for the doubt he'd created, doubt that now undermined them like an uploaded Scorpion.

Clearfather heard the rowdy splashing of the Osmonds, which made him think of Mr. Meese. If only the quest could be behind him, all the secrets revealed and the magic ended. He just wanted to live as normal a life as he could with Kokomo. There were footsteps approaching. He pulled a thin blanket over his love and stepped outside.

"Good evening," the woman said.

Clearfather's eyes vacuumed in details. A svelte Krav Maga disciplined figure, shoulder-length topaz-tinted hair, and synthetic eyes that had the disorienting luster and density of Broome pearls. She wore a palladium-colored all-weather bodysuit seductively unseamed to reveal fine full cleavage precisely tanned to complement the metallic sheen of her outfit. On her feet were black chrome stilettos.

"Hold your fire," she said, and ran her tongue along her lower lip.

"What?" he said, hearing Kokomo tossing on the bed. "Come out here."

Warily, he led the woman out to the patio. The Osmonds slid off their tiered platforms as if defending their territory. The woman picked up one of the colored balls and lobbed it into the pool. The biggest of the Osmonds gave her a flipper-smack of water.

"I don't think they play ball," Clearfather said.

"How annoying. What good's a trained seal if it doesn't play ball?"

The giraffe agreed, which prompted a chorus of grunting from the seals and some sustained splashing. Apparently, while the Osmonds were reluctant to cooperate, they still possessed the synchronized comic timing that betrayed a lifetime in show business.

"I'm Cyrilla Lundquist of Vitessa Intel," the woman with the artificial eyes announced as she dabbed the projected moisture from her pert left breast. "Relax. No one's going to harm you."

"Is that because you're not going to try again or because you can't?"

The woman smiled and bit her lip—full and sensual, the color of a fine Bordeaux.

"Can we sit and talk? In peace?"

"You first," Clearfather said, indicating two lawn chairs.

"I'm here to help you. I know you don't believe that, but hear me out. You're having memory problems. You don't know who you are or what you're doing. Right?"

Clearfather noticed that the Osmonds were harassing Bernadette the pygmy hippo.

"What you don't realize," Cyrilla Lundquist continued, "is that you work for us. You're with Vitessa Intel."

"What?" Clearfather asked and the zebra spun in its sling.

"You're a secret Vitessa project that's malfunctioned. I've been sent to bring you in for treatment and debriefing. I know this is difficult to understand. But you're having technical problems. The military maneuver in Texas was a field test to find out how serious the problem is."

"Did I pass?"

"Yes! But if the goal was to foreclose, you wouldn't be here now.

I'm here to bring you in safely. I don't know all the details. I just know the Pantheon wants to protect their investment—and that if you don't come peacefully, they'll be forced to trigger the fail-safe self-destruct implant you have."

The cougar gave a grumpy growl.

"Let me get this straight," said Clearfather. "I come with you and I get treatment and reprogramming—"

"Debriefing."

"—or someone flicks the switch and the lights go out. What would you do?"

The Osmonds began barking and splashing boisterously.

The Nourisher told him he'd come back from the dead. Now this smooth-talking woman was saying that he was a "secret project."

The Osmonds waddled up the steps of the slide and whooshed down. Bernadette submerged. Cyrilla Lundquist remained unruffled despite the occasional spray.

"You have to make up your own mind," she shrugged. "If we try to force you, the self-destruct device will activate. But I can promise you, you'll soon have a breakdown. You wouldn't want to end up hurting your girlfriend, would you?"

Clearfather flinched at this possibility—but then it occurred to him that the way she said *girlfriend* indicated they didn't know about Kokomo's powers. If he was really part of Vitessa Intel, they'd know about her—wouldn't they?

"I can see you need convincing." Cyrilla smiled. "I would, too, in your shoes. What can I do to show you that what I'm saying is the truth?"

"You could start by telling me who I am—what I'm supposed to be doing."

"Okay," Cyrilla said and moistened her lips. She pulled from her breast pocket a quartz crystal and pointed it out in front of her. A hologrammatic image began forming, as if made of grains of light. A giant amusement kingdom in miniature.

"This is 20th CenturyLand," she said as the miniature protective dome vanished to reveal a configuration of uranium silver spheres that trembled as if made of water. Tiny figures of people entered or merged with the spheres, which then projected a series of images: three-dimensional scenes that shifted from a bunker on Iwo Jima to the streets of Berkeley—to Saddam Hussein. One of the spheres she appeared to levitate with the crystal. It melted open to reveal leafy streets and a bucktoothed boy on a Sting-Ray bike in the midst of a paper route.

"This is FamilyVille," the sultry agent said. "It gives single people, older people, and childless couples the chance to hire children or parents of their own and delight in the fun of a more innocent era. There's a hedge maze and a mohair ranch, and the Happy Hen Fun Farm. We tailor situations to people's specifications. Like attending a beloved grandmother's funeral or watching an ideal daughter giving the valedictory address. This proved so popular it led to our Real Reality program in towns and cities like Moscow, Idaho. Seattle. Tucson."

"Those are . . . theme parks?"

"They're strategically designed and maintained recosystems aligned to fit specific cultural values and security parameters," Cyrilla said and waved the miniature amusement empire away with the crystal.

"So you control . . . and all these places are . . . fake?"

"None of them is 'fake.' They're as real as Youngstown, Pennsylvania. And we don't 'control'—we manage and guide. Our environments are dynamic. They evolve and change. Things even go wrong. Take the community of Shaker Heights. Under the apparent affluence, drugs and divorce are rife—sexual dysfunction through the roof. They even have crime. You can't have high belief indices in authority structures without micro-instabilities. Which brings me to our most secret project. Code-named Green Pastures."

Bernadette resurfaced with a snorky sound. It reminded Clearfather of Kokomo. He hoped she was all right.

"Green Pastures is on the surface that mythical small town that once lay at the heart of America's dream of itself," Cyrilla explained. "Got a shopping mall and a Lions Club picnic area. There's even an eccentric woman who carves the busts of famous people out of cheese."

"What's so secret about it?" Clearfather asked.

"Because it's really a psychiatric prison," Cyrilla replied. "Almost everyone is a high-level criminal. There are hackers, jammers, and sandstormers—cops, politicians, and civic leaders—a whole townful of people who, like your seal friends here, wouldn't play ball."

The Osmonds began barking again, which woke up the two snow leopards.

"Not one of them knows they're there. Or, they know they're there. They just don't know *why* they're there—or more importantly who they are. All of them have been given a personality implant that overrides their true sense of identity. The beautiful thing is that this still allows us to tap into their minds—without their knowing. We monitor their subconscious. We track their dreams. We've been able to derive quite a bit of valuable counterintelligence this way. And in several important cases we are now ready to reinsert these people back into their old lives with more or less complete command guidance capability."

"So where do I fit in?" Clearfather asked.

"Do you remember the name Parousia Head?"

"W-why?" He almost said yes.

"She's the most wanted criminal in the world. There are no records of her—no ID data. No one's ever seen her that we can be sure of."

"Then how do you know there is such a person?"

"We wouldn't have so many suspicions otherwise," Cyrilla answered. "But even if the woman I'm going to tell you about isn't Parousia Head—she's very worrisome. Calls herself Lodema Honeyflute. Has a questionably thin, clean file. Now she's taken up a rather influential residency."

"She's moved to Green Pastures? How did she get in?"

"Anyone can get in and leave when they want. There aren't any walls or bars except in people's minds. The inmates think they live there. The personality implants give them only a few contacts outside, all managed by us. The rest of the residents we monitor. Sometimes there are problems, but not like this. Parousia Head or Lodema Honeyflute has become the leader of a religious cult."

"A cult?"

"Calls her followers The Real People. Has a lot of witty slogans, like 'The shortest distance between two points of view is the truth.' Preaches in the Lions Club picnic area by the coin-operated barbecues. Her prophecy is based on the notion that the apparent reality of Green Pastures is an illusion and that behind the scenes lies a hidden reality. I think you can see how disruptive such a suggestion seems to us."

"Yes." Clearfather nodded.

"In what has been called 'the Barbecue Sermon,' she's promised the arrival of a Messiah who will disclose to them the real reason why they're there. She's begun primitive deconditioning rituals to get people to remember who they really are."

"What does this have to do with me?" asked Clearfather.

"You were developed to be the Messiah she's been predicting. We couldn't send in a neutralizer without the risk that she would become a martyr. That might give the cult the crucial ingredient to evolve into something beyond our guidance."

"So you want me to go to Green Pastures or whatever. Then what happens?"

"You fulfill her prophecy but subvert her authority. She becomes obsolete and we maintain guidance. Maybe the religious vulnerability is a side effect of the implants—we need more data. In any case, as Pascal observed, we couldn't have invented so many false religions unless there was a true one. We have to ensure that ours is the true one."

"And you want me to come now?"

"Have a nice night with your girlfriend. You could even bring her along. Command said they could write her in. Or another woman— if you prefer."

This last comment was made with a salacious glint in her eye, which would've been much more effective if the Osmonds hadn't given her such a dousing.

"You've got till tomorrow morning," Cyrilla huffed and klocked off on her stiletto heels to find a towel and a change of clothes.

Clearfather went back to the room. He knew the woman was lying but he didn't know what to believe instead. He found Kokomo crying on the bed. All he wanted to do was love her and live what was left of whatever life he had now with her. Even if they couldn't communicate very well, there was something they exchanged that was more important. He took her in his arms. They were two of the same kind. They were One. However she'd done it, she'd eased his pain before, and now it was his turn to help her.

I am he as you are he as you are me and we are all together," he whispered.

If only he'd known the truth or been able to believe what he suspected. Her pain *was* his pain. Deep inside his brain a firefight was under way, and the energy released was ringing a bell to attract the attention of an angel of death floating over America. He kissed her. Her rainwater and estuarine sex smell filled him with desire and assurance. Then he stripped up her shirt and saw the horror.

On her perfectly smooth young back, which had previously not had a single mark, were now the same malignant letters that he had cut and burned into his. He could see the agony and disruption in her eyes. "There are no llamas in the Bahamas," she tried bravely through green tears—but he heard the words *Om mani padme hum*. He didn't understand what they meant.

"No," he said in answer, smiling, "but there are llamas here. Want to see them?"

She didn't look like she understood. He took her hands in his and kissed them. She was running a high fever now—and then she began quivering with chills. He took off his clothes and helped her out of hers, cuddling her as the shaking became more intense. He didn't know what else to do. What doctor could help them? What was happening to her? He feared any move would draw the fire of Vitessa, and he couldn't face a struggle with her sick. He kissed her and clenched her, feeling her sweating body vibrate into him, not knowing it was the other way around.

Paranoia overcame him and he pressed himself deep into her, her heart beating like a bird. Then he was inside her. He wanted nothing between them now but love, not even skin. She became apoplectic. He thought at first it was an orgasm. But it was an horrendous metamorphosis. Her flesh became rubbery—then plastic. In his panic he thrust himself deeper inside her, holding on for dear life, the accursed writing that had appeared in her back glinting with a hot brass leer. Then she morphed—the breasts retreating into pectoral muscle. Her gorgeous ass condensed to angular meat—and then he knew. He saw! The nightmare was not upon him—he was inside it— expelled by the mutating flesh. Kokomo was transforming into him. They were indeed One. And just in time—for *Azazel* was targeting the signal in his brain. So close they nuzzled—then the realization of the form she'd taken—he cringed away—the surge of heart sickness lit up his brain and therefore hers. A shudder racked her body . . . the green of her eyes blurring . . . and in a single instant the transformation was complete. She was him and she was hit. A piece of lightning. An angel's bullet.

Clearfather died in his own arms and was saved.

The second he felt the body go slack, the letters in his back burst alight and he heaved himself to the carpet to extinguish the flames. He tried to stand but couldn't, clawing out for Kokomo, who lay on the heart-shaped bed—and then he did stand and felt flesh—but not hers. Not hers! He stared down at her body and saw that he had not been wrong. On the scalp, just as with her stim helmet, was a crater of crusted skin and black bruising, as if something inside had exploded, breaking through the atmosphere of the skull. He leapt upon the inert lump—the lingering scent of honeysuckle a vicious joke—for the body he held to his chest was a miserable replica of his own, down to the exact torture words embedded in his back and the mulish organ, detumescing as he watched. The terror and wonder of it filled him as the flopping weight could not and he sobbed—for he knew that she had saved him. She had taken his pain inside herself. Just as he'd entered her sweet darkness, she'd been inside his mind and had sacrificed herself. This was Vitessa's ambush. Not out in the open—but in his own dark.

The quest was doomed from the beginning, he realized. I was carrying some kind of bomb inside me. Kokomo gave her life to save me. How she did it, I don't know—but she did. One flesh. One flesh!

"God!" he yelled through scalding tears. "I followed the map but it was all a lie—it was just a trap. All I found was the hurt and horror of the past. For whatever I was, why did Kokomo have to pay? She was all that I had! I loved her. I loved her! And—I hate *you*!" he ranted, beating at the body—the pathetic clone—and then a wave of desperate yearning overwhelmed him—and he realized that the body he was attacking was what she'd become to save him. It was her—transformed—for him. The meat he hated was his own. He smashed his head into the mirror and it refreshed him like cold water. He battered his hand against the wall and felt the warm reassurance of broken bones. He stabbed his legs with the ice tongs and writhed off the bed, pounding himself, tearing at his flesh. He longed to destroy himself. But the wounds healed almost as fast as he could inflict them. He was a mass of silver nerve fire—the ice-burn of accelerated self-repair. "I have powers!" he laughed sickeningly. "But not enough! There is nothing left!" And he looked down at the jigsaw pieces of shattered mirror—and the shining wreckage of reflections mocked him. I'm like Cubby and Van Brocklin, he thought. A freak. A mutant. Like the Nourisher.

He dove among the shards of bloody glass, raking the ragged edges against his skin—weeping for Kokomo—weeping for death. He contorted his body like the boys in the spheres, jackknifing—becoming fetal—until he could take his own penis into his mouth—deep into his gagging throat—and he bit down as hard as his jaws could crush. He meant to strangle on it, his mouth filled with blood—and then his body convulsed and disgorged the organ. It lay before him—an intermediate life-form. The pain was unthinkable. Slick with gore, he cradled his severed penis to his breast. He thought of the deaf girls beneath the ground in Dustdevil with their deformed offspring—and Ernst Brand's ex-wife with the limp-necked peacock. Already the blood was clotting, crusting away like paint. His desecrated loins had sealed over. The ripped tubes and flapping skin were turning into a stump of angry scar tissue. Tenderly he wrapped the organ in Kokomo's jacket, no longer weeping. Beyond tears. He looked back at the body prostrate on the bed. The light had left. All that remained was plastic flesh, stiffening with absence.

My quest is over, he thought. I have been baptized in my own blood. I have given birth to a new monster of myself. Now it's time to bury the dead child of my past. In honor of my lost love I will give the gifts of vengeance and destruction. I summon the violence, I call forth the fears, I command the dreams. My kingdom gone, my will be done. *As it is in my mind, so will it be in the outer night.*

Painting the Town Red

It began with trouble with the giant Russell Crowe. It was first believed that the robot went rogue due to a programming error that confused its field response system, leading to an attack on the control blimp, which was forced to make an emergency landing on Harrison Ford Parade, killing a group of Golden-agers from Madison, Minnesota, the Lutefisk Capital of America. Crowe then went on to pick a fight with the Hasami Totem but the building's defense system torched him in his tracks. Case closed—or so Vitessa thought. But almost as soon as the ambulance and fire crews had finished cleaning up, Combatron Control noticed that the giant Liberace was kicking the crap out of Elton John. The problem was, neither machine was in use—they'd simply come alive. Within minutes emergency alarms were ringing as one by one the giant battle robots animated and left the hangar on the shore of Lake Mead or disengaged from their duels and began marching en masse for the city.

Fire-breathing Tom Jones got Wayne Newton in a headlock and flung him into the MusicaLand dome. He then went on a spree, stomping stretch limos and sushi bars, boiling a couple of white elephants in the reflecting pool of the Taj Mahal before breaking off at the knees. The giant Dean Martin and Jerry Lewis hissy-fitted into the spinning lights of the Chunder Wheel. Giant Frankenstein and Dracula caved in the bubble of FairytaleWorld, and Big Michael Jackson, with huge glinting dark glasses, and Big Woody Allen, with huge glinting normal glasses, chased hysterical children into the Grand Canal as terror gripped the megalopolis.

Giant Arnold Schwarzenegger strangled Sylvester Stallone as Charlie Chaplin had his derby crushed and cane broken by an enormous Shirley Temple wielding a lollipop. Big Elvis tore the head off Colonel Parker and began pulling apart planes at Hillary Rodham Clinton Interdenominational Airport. Then he headed for downtown. Raptors and maxicopters began filling the sky—as did furry clouds of spooked fruit bats, which smashed through cockpits and windscreens on the Tom Cruiseway.

Vitessa sent platoons of drones to try to wrest control of the streets but nothing could stop the giant celebrity machines. Big Elvis reached the center of the city. Repelled by the defensive shields of both the Hasami Totem and the Vitessalith, he took on the Sony Cone and began to climb the outside, strike planes drilling him with Dark Rain projectiles. He made it to the top as Predation rockets shot wide—inciting a chain reaction of interbuilding defensive lasering.

Frat boys at the Camelot ravaged the hunchbacks and the wenches (in that order)—then stole the Holy Grail, which was later found in a mud bath at the Stardust Bunny Run in Boulder City. Women began plundering the boutiques like schools of Winona Ryders. Gamblers started behaving like corporate CEOs, stuffing their pockets with cash. The carcasses of the buffet tables were picked clean, and Donald Trump impersonators were running wild. Meanwhile, every one of the eidolons in the Museum of Notorious Americans walked off the job, blending into the mayhem.

In HolyLand all hell broke loose as Mel Gibson and Charlton

Heston pushed the Wall of Jericho over onto a group of Camp Fire Girls from Oshkosh, Wisconsin. There were exploding beasts and angels—loaves and fishes everywhere. The Snake in the Garden roller coaster catapulted off its track and slammed into Mount Sinai, sending all the passengers to Heaven—but not being designed to hold so many all at once, the flooring gave way, making the occupants plummet into the lion dens, which triggered a riot that left a crucified Jesus alone to face a giant Britney Spears, who plucked out the cross and thumped off to use it as a stake to plant in the heart of Big Madonna—only to run headlong into Skinny Oprah, who stabbed her in the back with it then dragged the blonde to the Goblin ponds and threw her into the digesting algae.

Waterspouts on Lake Fonda flung houseboats as far as the Lucille Ball Civic Center. The Leno Bridge snapped apart like LEGO blocks as tons of basalt and extruded websteel hurtled through the panels of VictorianLand, showering St. Paul's and the Old Bailey, burying wigged barristers and tourists from Manchester, England. Gas jets and carbide lamps ignited as the dome imploded. The flames jumped, catching Icarus, whose hang glider flared and then plunged into the Natalie Wood Lagoon as MythologyLand and FairytaleWorld went up in cyclones of unraveling circuitry—fusing into a mushroom cloud over the Grand Canyon. Later a photogrammer clicked an award-winning picture of a tortured Little Red Riding Hood fleeing down Hualapai Street like a napalmed villager during the Vietnam War.

Through the tumult of roving jaguars and squashed conquistadores, Clearfather came—telcom lines crackling in his wake. Thousands of people lay tangled and suffocating in revolving doors or trapped in cooking elevators. Tapirs stampeded, dancing stallions drowned in singing fountains, and spider monkeys screeched across abandoned cars.

Aretha (dressed again as Ernestine) and Eartha had been on their way to meet Minson for dinner when the turmoil began. At first Aretha thought it was just a local malfunction—but he suspected Clearfather's involvement—and then he saw Clearfather on the corner of Jerry Seinfeld and Robin Williams, naked and on fire. My God! he thought. Clearfather's a doomsday weapon sent into the heart of IMAGINE-NATION!

"We've got to find cover!" his wife shouted as giant Bruce Lee and Jackie Chan began kicking the shit out of each other over their heads.

"No!" hollered Aretha, tugging off his wig. "We've got to find Minson. I'm going to tell him the truth!"

"What about Monroe?" Eartha called.

"He's on his own!" Aretha cried—as they heard the triple-action telescoping gas-filled shock absorbers in the mammoth knees.

He pulled Eartha out from under the giant feet and both of them flipped away their high heels for a dash to the Reef and Beef as colonnades crashed and hobbits and Daleks collided.

Just at that moment Monroe Hicks, wide receiver for the Newark Neutrons, felt very much on his own. Following the encounter in the Jacuzzi room, he'd broken training with several mango daiquiris and a line of uncut Dr. Phil—and then found himself not just participating, but *starring* in a gay orgy at the Delphi. After that things became a little blurry—until he woke up naked in the yin-and-yang-shaped sandtrap of the seventeenth hole of the Silverado Golf Club with giant Oprah bearing down. Calling on that 9.7 hundred-meter speed that had made him a Pro Bowl starter three years running, he headed south for Needles and was never seen again.

Sirens howled and smoke billowed as spotlights and tracer fire rent the night sky. Clearfather finally reached the Amazonia, wanting to protect Dr. Tadd and Mr. Meese—but the building had armored itself and begun retreating underground after Julia Roberts had put a fist through the atrium, which an overzealous designer had stocked with killer bees. Clearfather stepped onto the bamboo bridge and released his penis from Kokomo's jacket. It fell into the water as one of the resident catfish rose to engulf it. He laid the satin coat over the face of a bee sting victim and noticed that he still had in his hand the little white ball he'd found in his pocket. He gripped it tight. It was all he had left, all that he wanted to take with him into the final dark. Everywhere he turned horns honked, guns blazed— and odd intersections of characters kept occurring.

Dr. Tadd, as horrified and afraid as he was, couldn't help feeling perversely grateful. To actually see J. Edgar Hoover and Walt Disney mingle for a moment! This is a psychotic episode that has penetrated our collective unconscious, he said to himself. Thank God I'm here to witness it!

Dr. Tadd and Mr. Meese would've been at the Amazonia to face the combined assault of giant Julia Roberts and the killer bees had it not been for Tadd's obsession with getting his father on the Sidewinder. Of course the drone attendants insisted that all passengers had to be 42 inches tall—which caused a furor in the tank. So they weren't aboard when the roller coaster shut down at the top of the S-bend, leaving the frenzied passengers at the mercy of Big Jim Carrey, who whipped the chain of cars off the rails—snapping the spires of Dreamland and bashing in the Bank of New Delhi.

But they were still almost compressed into mush because there was no one around to help Dr. Tadd lift the tank back into the Wienermobile, everyone thundering by like Gadarene swine. Even the Good Samaritan from HolyLand raced past. Thank God, Harry Potter and Princess Diana stopped, and together they got Mr. Meese inside as the swarm of killer bees stormed through, stinging the McTavish's Bagpipers, creating an impenetrable knot. Then they heard a terrible sound. *Dum, dum, dum.*

Clearfather picked out the highest nearby point still standing— the Holy Roller.

Dum, dum, dum. The threatening sound grew louder as Dr. Tadd urged the Wienermobile through the debris—Harry and Di crammed in the back with the tank.

"Dad," he called into the speakerphone. "I know I don't say it very often . . . but I love you."

"I know you do, son," Mr. Meese splashed over the tank's intercom. "We'll get through this."

Dum, dum, dum. It was the Goblin-chewed remains of Britney Spears creeping along on hands and knees! The devouring algae were doing their dreadful work but she dragged on, driving a frantic herd before her down Nicholson. Of all the last visions, Dr. Tadd thought —the Three Wise Men and the Three Little Pigs running from a giant decomposing Britney Spears with the cross embedded in her back like a windup key!

Big Britney stretched out to capture the Wienermobile but the eidolon of a baseball player distracted her.

"Holy shit!" bubbled Mr. Meese. "It's—Denny McLain!"

At that exact same moment—Dr. Hugh Wieviel, in town for the convention on intelligence-enhancing drugs, stepped through the smoke and stopped cold. The entrepreneurial medical man had been with the big-breasted neurologist from Philly. They'd been trying out new fantasyware based on an Adam and Eve scenario and were amazed to find that all was not right in the outer world. In fact, he was so amazed he left his playmate in the middle of Dick Clark Avenue—intent on carjacking his way to the airport if need be. Now he was looking up the barrel of Big Britney.

The eidolon of Denny McLain caught her one functioning eye just as she was about to scrunch the Wienermobile. Then the specter of the disgraced pitcher vanished as Dr. Wieviel suddenly fell in the shadow of giant Janet Jackson, her famous pierced right breast bared. The sight proved too much for the disintegrating Britney robot, who lost her alga-eaten face panel and toppled into the street—but not before she'd managed to yank the embedded cross from her back and walloped the gothic-looking Ms. Jackson. The blow struck the exposed enormous boob with its sunburst steel nipple piercing—which had once been a chandelier at the Rainbow Chicken Ranch in Henderson—and the breast malfunctioned, springing forward with a foam-injected flop onto the pavement, where it struck and suffocated Dr. Wieviel, whose last thought was that he'd always been a tit man.

"Did you see that?" splashed Mr. Meese. "Did you?"

Dr. Tadd was fazed, knowing that something of mystical importance had transpired—but alert enough to hit the accelerator before giant Janet could grope after them. The Wienermobile peeled out, swerving through the rabble and the rubble of Poitier Lane with Mr. Meese sloshing in the tank. They reached the remains of the Katharine Hepburn Hotel's ballroom and drove inside, joining a zoo of shelter seekers.

Eidolons of Japanese Zeros from Pearl Harbor buzzed Big Elvis, now the tallest structure in the world atop the Sony Cone, making him flail with rage—and then an escaped Flying Haggis, one of the tartan blimps promoting McTavish's, bumped into him and he lost his balance falling just as Cubby had, with the needle of the Stratosphere Tower punching through his left eye, triggering a massive head attack, the body busting apart on impact and raining into downtown.

Clearfather arrived at the impaired but still intact Holy Roller and began scaling the scaffolding to reach the tracks. Big Oprah bludgeoned Janet Jackson with the World's Largest Burrito, tromped the Olsen Twins, and then twisted Julia Roberts's neck around so she could see her ass as she stumbled into the Elizabeth Taylor Memorial Rehabilitation Center. Then she trashed old Las Vegas from Circus Circus to the Mandalay Bay, actually eating the pirate ship at the tattered Treasure Island casino, crossbones and all.

Most of the male-themed robots self-destructed. Their heads blew up or they clutched their chests and toppled. The rest, Big Oprah throttled. One by one she piled the corpses of the miswired celebrities on top of the remains of 20th CenturyLand. ("So this is the way the world ends," Dr. Tadd would later write. "Not with a bang, but a Winfrey.") Then she fixed her eyes on the great golden Buddha atop Mount Meditation. Big Oprah grabbed hold of the gleaming statue and began rocking it until it broke free—then she raised it up overhead and heaved it at the Vitessalith.

The Buddha struck the force field of the grand tower that stood like the last data crystal of the civilization. There came a rumbling not heard since Bigfoot. All around the proud technosentient spike, veins of green lightning ran, encasing it in a throbbing net of emergency overload. The edifice began to waver—and then a roaring came from below its sub-basement, where the master controls were housed in steel-reinforced bunkers. The tower trembled like a rocket on the launch pad and then dematerialized—condensing into a cloud-shaped spire filled with multicolored fire. Slowly it whirled, turning a vivid blue until the unmistakable profile of Dooley Duck emerged. Big Oprah stumbled, killer bees and fruit bats plastered against her, limbs twitching, servomotors smoking. In a chest wound inflicted by Big Jerry Springer, a stranded spider monkey clung. At last she came to the Holy Roller, where Clearfather stood on top of the Loop of Faith. The fur-singed monkey in the gouge in her chest leapt across onto his naked shoulder. He gripped the ivory sphere in his fist. Big Oprah keeled over the roller coaster and burst into flames. Then Clearfather felt a soft blue wind engulf him and down into the graveyard of IMAGINE-NATION he fell.

PART 5

The Mind That Time Forgot

The ego is a too much thing.
—CHARLES MANSON

CHAPTER I

Necropolis Now

Clearfather crashed back into himself and felt a voice prodding him. He opened his eyes to see a ferociously ugly black man in a tank top and satin gym shorts, with a stitched eyelid and a swollen jaw the color of eggplant.

"Who . . . are you?" Clearfather asked, becoming aware of his body again. His groin was a dull agony. He was dressed in a white waffle-weave robe and terry-cloth slippers—lying on top of a clean made bed.

"Xerxes McCallum, man—who you think I am? Former Heavy-weight Champion of the Planet—an' also the Solar System."

"And . . . where . . . am I—are we?"

"Man, this is the Patrick Swayze Center for Serious Depression."

"I . . . I don't remember . . ."

"They say you bit yo own dick off. Shit, I thought I was depressed. You a muthafukka!"

"Is this LosVegas?"

"Whass lefta it. Look outta window, you see some serious-ass deestruckshun."

"How long—have I been here?" Clearfather asked, painful flashes of wreckage and faces coming back to him.

"Since yestiday."

"When did everything go crazy?"

"Two nights ago. Hitler helpin' Osama bin Laden. Then Big Oprah shovin' Siegfried up Roy! I never seen shit like that."

"It must've been scary," Clearfather said, too scared to touch his groin.

"I am Spiro Stavros and I want to play Ping-Pong!" an accented voice replied from behind a curtain.

"Who's that?" Clearfather asked.

"Doan know, but he's a muthafukka at Ping-Pong. But I tell you what—watchin' robot Sammy Davis Junior kick Frank Sinatra's ass —an' then those jets flyin' over rainin' fire—next day the streets covered with burned birds an' pieces of them big-ass machines—like one of Wayne Newton's hands, man, crawling down the Strip. Shit."

"I'm . . . sore," Clearfather said, feeling like he might pass out.

"Muthafukka, who wouldn't be? How could you do it?"

"It was very large . . . and I'm pretty flexible."

"No! I doan mean how'd you do it! How *could* you do it?"

"I don't know," Clearfather said—and when he saw Kokomo's face in his mind he thought he'd cry.

"I am Spiro Stavros and I want to play Ping-Pong!"

"Well, I heard 'em say you gotta pretty good stump, an' that may see you through. After all, you a white dude."

Despite the man's appearance, Clearfather could hear in his tone a genuine attempt to help. "What are you here for?" he asked.

"Was about to jump off the Ellison Tower."

"Isn't trying to kill yourself worse than cutting off your dick?"

"No way! Well . . . in one way . . . but man . . ."

"I am Spiro Stavros and I want to play Ping-Pong!"

"Shut the fuck up, man. We'll play soon—an' this time I'll beat yer ass."

"Why did you want to kill yourself?"

"Where you been? I got whupped by a pansy-ass social worker!"

"How did that happen?" Clearfather asked. Talking about someone else's problems helped take his mind off his own.

"Damned if I know! Muthafukka moved like a mamba. I got a
standin' eight-count in the first twenty seconds. My last five fights
haven't even gone twenty seconds! Haven't been hit for real in two
years—only the droids'll spar wiff me. Muthafukka! That gay boy hit
me so hard in the second round I started to cry—with billions of
people watchin'. Doan 'member the third round."

"So . . . you lost?"

"Fuck yeah I lost! My title, my pride. I got whupped by a faggot! I
jes thank God he wuddn't no white faggot—then I wudda jumped."

"Well, he must've been a good fighter," Clearfather said.

"Muthafukka!" Xerxes yelled and began jumping up and down on
his bed. "I am a *great* fighter! I am the Corpse Maker! This fuckin'
sissy knocked me out!"

"Well," Clearfather said. "Either he's not a sissy, or being a sissy
isn't what you thought it was. Anyway, what kept you from jumping?"

Xerxes McCallum peeked around as if someone might be listening and whispered confidentially, "I had a vision, man—standin' up
there on that observation deck overlookin' the hockey rink anna
Fishbowl Lounge—I felt like my life was over. So I broke down the
steel door an' got out on the service ledge, lookin' out over all them
parks an' the lights way out on the beach between the lagoon anna
Colorado River . . . an' I saw them giant robots dukin' it out—bein'
controlled by little people in them fancy blimps—an' I realized that's
what I was. Jes some robot. I thought I was in charge—but I wasn't
really. An' I went to jump, thinkin' I'd end up either on the Zamboni
machine or in a big ol' bowl-a shrimp cocktail. Then I saw Dooley
Duck, man. He was bigger than all those robots. Way bigger. An'
Ubba Dubba came up out of the river. An' then—this is the really
weird shit, man—they had a baby with them. It wasn't like anything

you've ever seen, part duck, part orangutan—an' part human, too. An' lookin' out over all the lights an' shit, I saw that this baby, whatever it was—it was the Future, man. An' I said to myself, I wanna see that Future—I wanna be part of it. I doan wanna fall in no shrimp cocktail—an' I doan wanna be no rock 'em sock 'em robot no more."

"I am Spiro Stavros and I want to play Ping-Pong!"

Clearfather looked around and saw that they were in the Alec Baldwin Ward, and from the sounds of things down the hall, the facility was operating at peak capacity. He went to the armorguard window and peered through the curtain. It was dark but the sky was full of blood—powerful Naked Moon searchbeams on the maxicopters probing through the fog like the lights of the battle tractors and cranes sifting through the powdered remains.

He was speechless. Where before a glittering Kuala Lumpur–*cum*–Magical Kingdom had risen arrogantly above the Martian canals that linked the desert to the ocean, now what greeted his eyes was more like an endless fuming Kabul or worse. A Nagasaki. The illuminated theme-park domes had all been ruptured or squashed, the great hotels flattened or torched. The casbahs and pleasure dungeons were buried under what looked like a million Taco Bells, and even through the military-specified windows he could smell the stench of burned fuel and flesh, contaminated water and fear—blind mob fear. What have I done? he thought. What in God's name have I done? But the sickness inside was too intense for him to consider the answer. This was not God's work. He shuddered with grief as wave upon wave of remorseful realization racked his heart and flooded his being. I had no right to do this, he said to himself silently. No matter what my pain or sadness. For this, I should die. For this, I should die and stay dead.

"Hey man!" Xerxes whistled. "Stop freakin' out. Iss time to get back in the game."

"What?" Clearfather asked, as if in a dream.

"Ain't you heer-a Diyagonole Thinkin'? Get back in the ring! You still alive!"

The words seemed to echo in the room. Clearfather tried to shake off his daze. The Swayze Center wasn't an imposing structure, but as one of the few buildings still intact on the southeast side of the city, it dominated the flea market/flea circus that LosVegas had become. In the distance he could make out the charred brontosauric skeleton of a roller coaster. All below was a mess of splintered rickshaws, over-turned cabs, and crumpled buses. Most of the surviving colony of bats had taken refuge inside Big Ozzy Osbourne, who'd fallen on a bunch of leprechauns from The 4 Leaf Clover. The satanists were in Heaven with all the dead bodies—their enthusiasm tempered slightly by the hunting dogs and members of the Sacred Aryan Posse who'd taken cover during the siege but who were now fully loaded on bourbon and Benzedrine and keen to lynch any so-called terrorists.

Vitessa had dispatched robot locusts to contain the killer bees, along with squadrons of drone Securitors to support the LosVegas riot police. The Triads and other gangs had their own enforcers out to defend what remained of their interests, but it was clear that the official strategy was every man for herself and Devil take the hind-most.

When Big Oprah had hurled the Big Buddha at the Vitessalith, wherever the offices of the Vitessa Cultporation were located, from Mumbai to Stockholm, the Vitessaliths in those cities had all felt the impact. The lights dimmed, the foundations shook—while at the home office in Minneapolis, the most poignant blow to the empire was struck when Wynn Fencer, in the midst of a crisis meeting of the Pantheon, collapsed in a coma on the world's biggest boardroom table and was rushed to an exclusive medical facility with an aneurysm in the brain. Small wonder that the Pantheon had eliminated all men-tion of the catastrophe on TWIN—a policy that was about to be re-versed by Julian Dingler, who in that same crisis meeting had been named by Fencer as his surprise successor.

But if TWIN was trying to put a lid on the disaster, American Pirate Radio was broadcasting loud and hard throughout the wards

—filled with reports of how Dooley Duck and Ubba Dubba had thwarted total destruction of the city, bashing the Oprahs and protecting the bookstores, universities, and thousands of innocent people in hospitals, psychiatric wards, and brothels. Clearfather took a deep breath and stepped back from the window. He remembered the map, the meeting with Cyrilla Lundquist—Kokomo—the attack inside his mind and how she'd saved him. On top of the Loop of Faith, he'd wanted to take as much of the world with him as he could . . . but then the giant blue cloud had come. The cloud had cooled his hatred and despair. But I fell, he thought—off the tallest roller coaster in the world—with a traumatized spider monkey hanging on. Now I'm here. Alone. With so much blood and cement dust on my hands. There's no more map to follow. There's only one more place to go to find any answers . . .

"Man, you gotta snap outta this shit. I jes lost the Manhood Champion of the World. Whatever happened—you gotta be thinkin' comeback."

"I am Spiro Stavros and I want to play Ping-Pong!"

"That's the kine a-spirit I'm talkin' about."

"I wonder how I got here?" Clearfather said aloud.

"The dude in the baffroom—he brought you. Now he stuck here."

"Who?"

"Cowboy muthafukka. Say he found you unner a rolla coasta. Cat's been climbin' the walls, man. An' those other people comin' to check you out. Freaky."

"What other people?" Clearfather asked.

"Two white wimmen. Looked like golf pros."

Shit, thought Clearfather flashing back to the Greyhound bus. If Vitessa had found Kokomo's body . . . thinking it was me . . .

The sound of the toilet flushing brought his attention to the bathroom door. A tall older man decked out like Wild Bill Hickok emerged.

"You're up," he remarked. "Good."

"I understand I have you to thank . . . ," Clearfather began—but given that he'd wanted to die, he wasn't sure what to be thankful for.

"Dooley Duck saved you," the man replied. "I just brought you here. Now I'm not so sure it was such a good idea. You tell him about the clown?"

"Jes those wimmen and the priest. That muthafukka was not right."

"What priest? What clown?" Clearfather asked.

"Swiggle. The Psychiatric Clown. Supposed to stroll around cheering people up. He's been in here checking on you."

"Sounds like a lot of people been doing that."

"Which is why I'm not so sure I did the right thing."

"Man, you ass me—that priest waddn't no priest."

"You in trouble?" the old wildcat inquired. "Vitessawise?"

"I don't know," Clearfather answered. "I'm having trouble remembering." Which wasn't a complete lie.

"Well, if you are, I'm sorry . . . I didn't mean any harm. You look like you're doing a good enough job of that yourself."

"You brought me here?"

"All the hospitals were full, so I came here. They got a look and took you straightaway. Trouble is they took me, too. Building's under lockdown. They say your wound's already healed. Don't know how. But if you're in trouble with Vitessa it won't be long before they make their move," the buckskinner said. "The good news is that I found a way out of here and I'm a-going to git. You want to come? I feel sort of responsible for you—seeing I got you in here."

Clearfather glanced through the curtain again at the mountains of steel and glass. He felt responsible for everything.

"Shit, man! Trouble comin' right now!" Xerxes exclaimed.

Clearfather peeped down the hall and saw four candy stripers. Their hair was blond and shining, their caps and shoes white. Their steps were springy and full of community spirit, but they all had the same face, with eyes the translucent gelatin color of termites.

"Now or never, youngster! There's an air duct in the bathroom that leads to the laundry chute. We can at least get to the basement."

Clearfather stood rigid. Then he thought about Kokomo and he knew that she would want him to get away. "I don't have any clothes," he said.

"No time for that," the old-timer called—standing on the toilet and releasing the grate he'd pried off before. It was a very tight fit inside the duct, but the old man moved nimbly.

"You coming?" Clearfather asked McCallum.

"Naw, man. I'll hold 'em off. You try to keep what's lefta yer dick—you hear?"

The candy stripers were almost to the door. Clearfather hoisted himself up and in. The moment they entered the bathroom they'd see what had happened, but they didn't get the chance because Xerxes unleashed that pile-driver right hand—then the Left of Death. Then he got serious.

"Hey, Spiro, man! These ladies say you can't play no more Ping-Pong!"

By that time Clearfather was sliding down the chute into the laundry room, where the Harijans were loading and unloading the mole-tanks. They made the same gesture toward Clearfather as the Harijans had earlier in the bus stations.

"We need to get out of here," he said to them. "Can you show us the way?"

The machine-creatures buzzed in their mantis language then pointed with their long articulated limbs at a refuse wagon filled with mole-damaged laundry. Once they were hidden under the stiff white piles, one of the Harijans wheeled the cart into the next room. Through the fabric, Clearfather could see a human Securitor.

"Where are you going with that?" the human said and then waved his stun cannon.

"Damaged. Below standard. No room."

"No doors open. Lockdown. Comprende?"

"Damaged. Below standard. No room."

"You stupid-ass bugs. Fuckin' hurry—or I'll leave you out there."

Secure-seals whooshed, the ram-proof door opened, and the Harijans trundled them into an alley. Copter blades thudded and the torso of John Wayne sparked in a grove of American flags. The Harijans had moved to unload the substandard laundry into one of the building's molecular incinerators when they tipped the cart over.

"Run," one of them said, and Clearfather and the old man did just that—out into the Baghdad-smelling ruins.

CHAPTER 2

The Curse of the Brubakers

They cut through an alley strewn with cat skulls and empty cans of Olde English 800. Even in boots the old bastard was quick—and he knew where he was going, which was a good thing because it would've been easy to get lost with fire crews and riot squads running everywhere and the stilt-legged drones called Storkers picking their way through the mess.

Clearfather felt ill with shame and woozy from the physical pain but there was no time for self-pity. Building façades were still falling down as they ran past fountains full of suitcases and dead birds. Out in front of the blasted Johnny Cash Country Grill, gulls quarreled over the remains of a frat boy who'd been mauled by an Irish wolfhound protecting one of the hunchbacks from Camelot. Waves of disgust and horror threatened to swamp Clearfather's resolve as they limped past roulette wheels and rotting dolphins—he imagined Bob's wife, Kayleen, combing the streets trying to save what animals she could.

The old man finally led him down a narrow section of what was left of Little Saigon. At the end of a lane they came to a cheval-defrise of razor wire and Pokémon dolls. The old man found a piece of fishing line and pulled. It drew aside a section of the knife-edged metal and he wormed his way through the barricade. Clearfather followed bare-kneed and, once through, saw the silhouette of the surviving section of the Holy Roller looming like a carbonized sea horse in the searchbeams. There was a smell of water and he realized the old man was pulling at another line, dragging a paddleboat toward them.

"This is the back of FunForAll, the park with the Holy Roller and the Wyziwyg," the old cowpoke said in a low voice. "C'mon."

Clearfather climbed into the walrus paddleboat, and the old man shoved off. Cars had fallen in the water—and a crashed Dragonfly copter. They pedaled as quietly as they could for a small island under one of the hardest-banking turns.

"It's not much," the old-timer announced when they arrived.

Clearfather didn't know what to say. This man had saved his life twice in as many days and if he lived on a dirty little hummock of saw grass under the world's biggest roller coaster, at least he wasn't Vitessa.

The searchlights and spotfires lit up the sky. Above their heads, supported by long tiki torch poles, was a fine mesh of camouflage netting that blended in with the saw grass. The old man led him to a wigwam of scrounged timber atop a dredging platform. Pieces of roller-coaster track and signs that said REMAIN SEATED and KEEP YOUR ARMS INSIDE THE CAR were visible. Inside, Clearfather found a bunk made of offcuts, a small fuel bead oven flued with harvested metal, and a very expensive Japanese field kitchen that he suspected was stolen. The walls were insulated with life preservers, which he presumed had been filched from the paddleboats. Covering them was a collection of historical TV Western memorabilia. It reminded him of Mr. Meese's baseball shrine, and he felt a stab of deep remorse. Were Dr. Tadd and his father safe?

"Not bad on a budget, eh?" the old man chuffed and clicked on a battery lantern.

Clearfather tried to nod, noticing a smattering of pictures of a young boy and a girl among the faded cowboys.

"My name's Winchester Brubaker," the man announced. "Named for the legendary Winchester Rifle."

"I'm . . . Elijah Clearfather."

"But I want you to call me Marshal—as in Marshal Stack Dixon."

"You're a marshal?" Clearfather asked, glancing at the cowboy nostalgia.

"I was. Why don't you try to find some clothes in that trunk. I'm going to have a swim in the lagoon and freshen up. Then we'll have some grub."

The clothes he found were theme-park castoffs. He pulled together an ensemble that made him look like something between a Pony Express rider and a buccaneer. Outside he heard the swimming strokes of the man and thought again of Mr. Meese in his tank—and the devoted Dr. Tadd—praying that they'd survived his wrath. *Oh, Kokomo*, he felt his heart cry . . . suddenly he was dizzy with longing for her . . . and for Wilton . . . even the Man of Steel.

The Marshal returned, wrapped in a Yosemite Sam beach towel. He went to a cupboard, brought out a bottle of Yukon Jack, and took a swig. "That's better," he said and held up the bottle.

"No thanks." Clearfather sniffled. "I've been on a lot of medication."

"I'm hip," said the Marshal and threw down another splash.

From another trunk he produced underwear, a white western shirt, dark pegged trousers, and a Lee J. Cobb black string tie. Neatly dressed, he turned on another lantern and proceeded to open cans of food while singing softly in a rich baritone . . .

Boot Hill, Boot Hill
How lonely you've made me

You've taken all my friends
Their voices still I hear in the whisper
In the sigh of the cold, cold wind . . .

As he sang, Clearfather tried to distract himself by inspecting the memorabilia-lined walls with the help of the extra light. Many of the pictures showed a man who looked like the Marshal but huskier, posed with Hollywood legends like Glenn Ford and James Arness. Others showed a man Clearfather took to be a young Marshal, on the boardwalk streets of a frontier town.

His host and rescuer heated up cans of chili con carne and poured the contents over steaming rice. They ate in silence, listening to the sirens and the rumbling of the loaders echoing over the lagoon.

"Well," said Clearfather as the Marshal sterilized drinking water. "I guess you want to know why."

"Son, I think there are things we're just not supposed to know about. Maybe you're one of 'em. But that doesn't mean I'm not going to help you."

Clearfather smiled. Outside a flamingo landed with a *shwoosh*. "So . . . you . . . live here?" he said. "Must've been loud."

"You'd think so, wouldn't you?" the Marshal replied. "But the rides were so constant, it was like the sound of the ocean. I think the noise has helped keep me young. That and the mischief."

"Mischief?"

"Stealing stuff from under their noses," the Marshal chuckled. "I'm kind of an urban myth among the security staff."

"Why do you call yourself Marshal? Were you some kind of star?"

"A star's something you never stop being," the man replied, wiping his mouth. "Not in the old sense. There was a time when stars had class and dignity. They set an example. They were heroes."

"You mean actors . . . who played heroes," Clearfather said.

"You know what Jack London said about inspiration?"

"Who?"

"He said, 'Light out after it with a club—and if you don't get it, you will nonetheless get something that looks remarkably like it.'"

"I don't understand."

"Most people don't. The point is, you are who you think you are—who you believe yourself into being. If you can't think who you are, then you can only be what somebody else thinks you are. And who can you trust to think you right?"

"I see what you mean," said Clearfather. "So . . . who . . . are you?"

"Well," said the Marshal, rolling a joint. "Let's go out and sit by the water. I haven't had so much silence or male company in five years."

In the distance M-20 fire mingled with a Beach Boys song. They dragged two worn director's chairs through the saw grass and sat under the severed spine of the roller coaster that stood like a new mathematical symbol. In the fanning beams, when fish rose, the slow circles wrinkling the water made it seem as if the stranded machines were coming to life.

"I am, as I said, Winchester Brubaker," the Marshal began, which struck Clearfather as a name only slightly less unlikely than his own. "But I'm still Marshal Stack Dixon. Just like my daddy was Tristan Brubaker and Marshal Jim Badge."

"I'm sorry," Clearfather said. "I've never heard of any of those people."

"That's the Brubaker Curse," the Marshal sighed, blowing smoke rings to rival Bean Blossom. "Daddy was cast as Jim Badge in *Frontier Lawman,* bringing Truth, Justice, and Fairplay to Abilene, Kansas, the wild and woolly end of the Chisholm Trail. *Frontier Lawman* was set to be the biggest new show of the 1962–63 season."

He scrambled back to the hut and returned a few moments later with the Yukon Jack and an old kid's lunch box with a thermos inside.

"The old man was on a lunch box. He was ready to round up desperadoes and open shopping markets. He'd bought my mom a house in the Hollywood Hills."

"What happened?"

"A young whippersnapper of a network executive canceled the show at the last minute. Said there was too much competition. Said the tide was turning on the Western—they wanted to cut their losses."

"What did your father do?"

"He rode his horse into the little prick's office and lassoed him. Hauled him around the old Universal lot kicking and screaming and finally dumped him on the lawn of the *Leave It to Beaver* house. Then he rode back to the *Frontier Lawman* set and dug in for a standoff with studio security. He was stoked with live ammo so they called in the LAPD SWAT team, who shot his beloved palomino and then tear-gassed him. Dad spent the next two years in a mental institution in the San Fernando Valley. When he got out, his agent got him a gig at Knott's Berry Farm, working with a rodeo clown who'd been kicked in the head. Second day on the job, Dad drove down La Cienega and put a can of Dr Pepper on his agent's head and told him he was going to shoot it off if he didn't find real work for a real marshal."

"What did the agent do?" Clearfather asked.

"Soiled his pants. Next day he got a restraining order. Dad disappeared after that. That's why I set my sights on becoming a marshal, too. And I made my dream come true thirty-five years to the day after my dad went missing. I got the role of Marshal Stack Dixon in *Star City,* an attempt to resuscitate the Western with a science fiction theme. The premise was aliens land during Wild West days and begin taking over the townspeople's bodies. But some—like the heart-of-gold gal who runs the brothel, and me—are immune. The only person who knows the truth is a wandering gunslinger named Spark Riles, who's wanted for murdering my brother—which resulted in my marriage to my brother's old sweetheart, although her body's now been taken over by an alien and I'm in love with Katie, who runs the cathouse and saloon."

"That sounds a bit complicated," Clearfather said.

"That's just what a little weasel of a producer named Purkiss said!" the Marshal snapped and whipped out a Heckler & Koch P9 and took aim at a fruit bat that he'd spotted hanging from the underside of the roller coaster. A bullet barked and the flying fox tumbled out of the manga-colored air into the water, sending furrows out among the junk.

"That's the Curse of the Brubakers. Canceled on the edge of stardom. Then I forgot that I was a marshal—a hero. Thought I was an alcoholic. Convinced everyone else, too, including my wife and two children, Quanah, named for the half-breed Comanche chief Quanah Parker—and my beautiful Pilot. My wife died years ago of breast cancer. Pilot died in an anthrax attack in the Holy War. My son Quanah, he designed the Holy Roller right here."

"Really? Does he . . . know . . . about you living here?"

"I wouldn't want my son to know I was living on an island under his world famous-roller coaster!"

"But wouldn't he want to know you're alive—and all right?"

"Never be too sure what folks want to know about their past," the Marshal said and plugged another bat. "And now we better be hittin' the hay. I think my stay on the island is about over. They'll start cleaning out the lagoon soon, and I sure as hell don't want to be here then."

Clearfather thought a minute. His money was gone—he'd left it back at Noah's Park. He had nothing but borrowed theme-park clothes and faint memories—memories of dreams and horror and sorrow and more blood on his hands than any lagoon could ever wash clean. And still he was determined.

"You don't happen to have a car?" he asked.

"You wouldn't think so, would you?" the Marshal cackled. "In fact, I do have vehicular capability—if a building hasn't fallen on it. Why do you ask?"

"I need—a ride. Bad. And I don't have any money."

"Where to?"

"South Dakota."

"South Dakota! Shit. Sacred heart of the Sioux Nation."

The Marshal was about to pop off another bat when a searchlight lit up the remaining curve of the Loop of Faith. Clinging to the rail was a bald eagle—the first one the old man had seen in fifty years. "Did you see that?"

"What?" Clearfather asked.

"Damnedest thing." The Marshal sighed, but when the light sliced back the bird was gone. "You know—I think I just got a Message."

"I get those." Clearfather nodded. "What did it say?"

"I think it said . . . to help you get to South Dakota."

"You sure?"

"No. Yeah. Well, hell. I don't know. But I got a good ear for the high white sound. C'mon. You can have the bunk. South Dakota's a long way."

They carried their chairs back to the hut. As the Marshal was rummaging around, setting up a bedroll, he slapped his head and went to find his buckskin costume.

"Here," he said. "You had this in your hand when I found you. What is it?"

"I don't know," Clearfather said, pocketing the little white ball. "But thanks."

CHAPTER 3

Area 51

For a while Clearfather lay awake, listening to the old man snoring. It was a peaceful, human counterpoint to the loaders piling and unpiling rubble, feeding the Goblins with pretzeled steel. Gradually everything went hazy and broke apart, and he slipped off into a soft cyclone of honeysuckle-smelling wind. He found himself curled up on a cot back on the summer porch at Aunt Vivian and Uncle Waldo's house with his dog Lucky. It was a gentle, fulfilling dream . . . like a dose of forgiveness. He woke slowly, reluctantly, refreshed but yearning to be back in time. The only thing that puzzled him was that he couldn't remember what kind of dog Lucky was.

The Marshal was up before dawn muttering about what to salvage. It was clear he had no intention of returning to the island. In the end he decided on the *Frontier Lawman* lunch box, photos of his wife and children, the silver marshal's badge from *Star City,* a small pack of clothes, a box of freeze-dried food, a canteen of sterilized water, and his weapons, which along with the P9 included a Harrington & Richardson break-action 12-gauge and the Winchester

.30/.30 lever-action carbine for which he'd been named. Clearfather had just the ivory ball and the clothes on his back.

The Marshal said a silent but emotional goodbye to his jerry-built home and then doused everything with oil and turned on the stove. He didn't want his son to find out who'd been squatting on the island. His "vehicular capability" proved to be a 1953 Indian motorcycle, an eighty-cubic-inch Blackhawk Chief with telescopic front forks and a Princess sidecar painted an immaculate American red.

"This was the first thing I bought when I signed the *Star City* contract," he said with fondness. "And I hung on to it when I'd lost everything else."

The bike had been languishing in the back of a warehouse, which the Marshal was unnerved to find a Vietnamese wholesaler had started using as distribution center for his heroin network. The building was still standing but was filled with bodies, as the attack of the monster celebrities had occurred during a divvy. Blue Metal cartridges and trampled shrimp wafers littered the floor—along with plenty of dead presidents and spilled China White.

Clearfather didn't know which surprised him more, that the bike started right up or that the Marshal seemed serious about riding it all the way to South Dakota. But he didn't have any better ideas and even if the old man was a bit loony, under the hobo-hermit despair he could tell that there was a soul filled with honor and spizzerinctum. If anyone could get him to South Dakota, he figured it was the Marshal.

From the bag of clothes the old man produced a woman's wig, which had blown off the Holy Roller, and a milkmaid's outfit from the Jungfrau. "I think you should wear these," he said, trying not to smile. "At least until we get out of the city. You'll be less noticeable from the air. In case anyone's looking for you."

Securitors were out in force now but there was still so much wreckage, it was impossible to police all the arteries. A motorcycle, even an overloaded one with a sidecar, was a good way to navigate the urban wasteland. The Marshal stowed the rifle and shotgun in a leather scabbard mounted off the handlebars while Clearfather, in wig and milkmaid bodice, sat holding the P9 with an extra box of jacketed hollow-point cartridges.

A smear of gray-brown haze dulled the sun along with ghastly holograms of Condoleezza Rice. Dark Rain exchanges erupted along Zellweger—diableros hacking up camels or trying to rob trapped guests. The datacom buildings of Midshore and New Tel Aviv had all been leveled, and De Niro and Tarantino were still on fire. Half an hour later Clearfather spotted another of the mysterious old billboards peeking out of the looted pawnshops at the corner of Sean Penn and Pamela Anderson.

THERE'S NOTHING SO QUAINT AS A FUTURE BEYOND YOUR WILDEST IMAGINATION.

—*Stinky Wiggler*

Instantly the billboard vanished—but he saw images of a frontier town like the one on the Marshal's wall. It was covered in bunting and he heard a marching band. He didn't know what the images meant, but they encouraged him. And he needed that. It was a long way to go and he didn't know if the Marshal had any money. Maybe they'd have to rob their way to South Dakota.

They hit a snag in Nellis. Following Bigfoot, the air force had consolidated their secret activities deeper in the old nuclear testing site to the north, or moved operations to atolls in Micronesia, turning Nellis Air Force Base and the infamous Area 51, like many of the notorious twentieth-century facilities such as Dulce, New Mexico, into Vitessa theme parks. Unfortunately, none of these parks had done well commercially. Once the official barricades had come down no one believed that what they were seeing was real, which of course it wasn't. The military removed the intrigue along with the classified equipment. The result was that Nellis had become a slum district.

They circled a ghetto of defunct satellite dishes stitched together with laundry and rope ladders and covered in Spanish and Arabic graffiti. Vitessa had reopened the checkpoint but it was still possible to cut through the park, and that's what the Marshal had in mind. Amid rattlesnake weed barracks and quivering Cyclone fences, the gel-suited bodies of dead aliens lay, costumes so cheaply made they looked like big condoms. A row of F-111s planted nose-down outlined Majestic Avenue, which wound them to a worn g-force ride clanking in the breeze. An Apache jumping spider basked on the hood of a dead Corvette.

They could see shrouded nomads vanishing between corrugated Quonset huts. Back behind them, maxicopters and Raptors surveyed the smoldering megaplex in greater numbers, but their emphasis was on what remained of the luxurious mountainside estates and waterfront high-rises, leaving the riffraff to slug it out to the northeast. Automatic weapon fire flashed in the greasewood.

"Feels like cold turkey in Tijuana on the Day of the Dead." The Marshal grinned. "But don't you worry . . . we'll get through."

Clearfather was glad of his company. Particularly when the dune buggies roared up over the rise. One was painted to look like a tarantula and mounted with a Gatlinger. Another was armored with spikes like a horned lizard and equipped with a harpoon gun, while the third was dressed up in the colors of a king snake and armed with a flamethrower. The Indian lugged up an asphalt service road with the Marshal prepared to turn and open fire, but when they cleared the crest they saw a series of mounds stretching out over a dry lake. Out in the middle leaned one of the giant celebrity robot's heads.

"That's John Travolta!" the Marshal hollered.

"Who?"

"It doesn't matter—what's that other thing? Shit—it's a Flying Haggis!"

With the dune buggies closing, the Marshal had no choice but to race for the lopped-off head of John Travolta, which appeared to have one of the Flying Haggis Fleet of small promotional blimps floating above it. The rig with the Gatlinger edged up closer, teasing them with bullet bursts. Clearfather turned to aim the H&K when his wig blew off. It hit the harpooner in the face and sent his cannon-launched spear through the chest of the tarantula buggy driver, who rolled and took out the flamethrower-mounted vehicle in a fireball of cage and torsion bar.

"Nice work!" yelled the Marshall.

They reached John Travolta's head, jolting to a halt between the mounds. From the ear of the colossus ran an anchor line up to the Haggis. A shot rang out from the mangled pile of dune buggies.

"We're not going to get out of this without a fight!" whispered the Marshal. "I'm going to go around and try to get behind them. You stay here. The shotgun will keep 'em honest if they try to rush you."

"Hey there!" a female voice called. "Doan shooot!"

"What was that?" hissed Clearfather.

"It came from up there!" The Marshal pointed. "Somebody's on the Haggis."

"I wonder if it would still fly?" Clearfather asked.

"I'm beginnin' to hope so, son. Look!"

More dune buggies were coming up over the hill now, ATCs with warpainted riders and a big green Hummer covered in cattle skulls and space alien masks—waving a Mickey Mouse flag.

"We've got to board the Haggis!" cried the Marshal. "They're flying the Mickey!"

"What does that mean?"

"They're cannibals—they'll eat our brains!"

The Marshal scrambled back to the Indian and wrenched out of the saddlebags what he thought they could carry. Then he flipped a toggle switch under the seat and directed Clearfather to start climbing the rope.

"Hey there—whatjew doin'?" the female voice called again.

Clearfather ripped off the milkmaid costume. A bullet whistled past as he jerked himself up the braided nylon. Out of the Hummer came an enormous goonda in a Kevlar body diaper, a SpongeBob SquarePants T-shirt, and a welder's helmet, carrying a bazooka. He was followed by a towering blond transsexual in a fur bikini with a harlequin Great Dane. Clearfather threw himself over the deck of the Haggis as the giant blonde produced a bullhorn.

"This is our turf, darlings!"

"We're just passing through!" yelled the Marshal as a bullet smoked the mound between him and the Hummer.

"The only thing you're going to pass through is my digestive system!" the blonde exclaimed, and the savages howled with laughter. Some wore only jockstraps or G-strings and combat boots—their skin covered in melanomas and tattoos. Others were fully robed or decked out in theme-park castoffs. Atop their pickup trucks and armored cars were the rotted mascot heads of *South Park* characters and the Powerpuff Girls confined by S&M masks.

Clearfather tried to quiet his mind, listening for the voices. He and the Marshal needed help. Desperately.

"Whooo're yoo?" he heard a frightened voice in the cockpit call.

"I'm not a pheasant plucker, I'm the Pheasant Plucker's son—but I'll keep on plucking pheasants till the Pheasant Plucker comes," he answered. And suddenly he grasped a new meaning in those words. What if the Pheasant Plucker never came? There were still pheasants that needed plucking. He'd have to do—he'd have to make do. That was what spizzerinctum and Diagonal Thinking were all about.

"I ain't no pheasant," the girl snapped.

She was a big-haired white chick, eighteen or nineteen, dressed as a Sassy Lassy and crazed with fear. On the floor of the cockpit was the pilot, stone dead—and on the small passenger deck lay another lass in a pool of blood beside the corpse of a large Highland Zinger.

"Listen," said Clearfather. "I don't mean you any harm, but the people below sure do. Are there any weapons aboard?"

"Noa!" sniffled the girl. "Jest haggises—promotional precooked giveaways."

"What's that for?" Clearfather asked, pointing to the sound system. The underbelly of the Haggis, which consisted of an aluminum shell on a welded steel tube frame, was laden with heavy-duty concert speakers.

"I can't take noa moa bagpipe music!" the girl groaned. "Thass what made Big Elvis go postal."

A cry went up below as the big blonde called for the Martha Stewart portable barbecue.

Clearfather hit the PLAY switch and cranked up the volume. When in doubt, try to create confusion. A swelling bagpipe tension poured down over the mounds like an airborne psychosis—and then squelched into a mind-jarring burr . . .

> *Fair fa' your honest, sonsie face,*
> *Great chieftain o' the puddin-race!*
> *Aboon them a' ye tak your place,*
> *Painch, tripe, or thairm:*
> *Weel are ye wordy of a grace*
> *As lang's my arm.*

My God, thought the Marshal, pinned down in the mini blimp's shadow. That's Sean Connery! Reciting Robert Burns's "Address to a Haggis."

The savages swatted their hands to their ears, dropping their weapons, while Clearfather began raining down FREE promotional haggises, each with the fiery leer of Mr. McTavish promising in red tartan letters YEER HAGGIS IS REDDY!

The ferals swarmed on the haggises—or were hit in the head with them. The Marshal saw his opportunity and scurried up John Travolta's neck, loosened the catch-hook, and hung on. The Haggis instantly rose but not enough—and the Marshal could see he was going to get raked across the dry lake if he didn't ascend. But he couldn't hang on to everything he was carrying and the rope—he had to let go of his father's lunch box. The release was dizzying—and therapeutic, too. It hit the Kevlar brute with the bazooka and, even with the helmet, momentarily knocked him out.

"I'll blow you out of the air!" the blonde screamed—but she couldn't hear herself because of Sean . . .

> *The groaning trencher there ye fill,*
> *Your hurdies like a distant hill,*
> *Your pin wad help to mend a mill*
> *In time o' need,*
> *While thro' your pores the dews distil*
> *Like amber bead.*

The transsexual picked up the goonda's bazooka and took aim. Fortunately there was enough sunlight to make the surface of the Marshal's badge from *Star City* a blinding mirror. With his left hand squeezing itself white on the line, the Marshal took his right and twisted the star, focusing the reflection into the blonde's eyes. She wailed as if a laser had hit her, sending the rocket into one of her own armored cars.

Clearfather was torn between trying to get moving and getting the Marshal up the rope. Figuring that if they couldn't get away, the savages would start skeet shooting, he ran to the cockpit. "Do you know how to fly this thing?" he yelled. But the girl couldn't hear.

His knife see rustic Labour dight,
An' cut you up wi' ready sleight,
Trenching your gushing entrails bright
Like onie ditch;
And then, O what a glorious sight,
Warm-reekin, rich!

Clearfather needed a tornado. He pressed the starter button to awaken the turboprop engines and got a sandstorm instead. Shots whizzed past but only one connected, embedding itself in one of the support battens, which were designed to withstand the impact of a flock of geese. Steering the vessel wasn't so easy, especially with the Marshal fluttering below.

The vertical fins were rudders—the horizontal fins elevators. Fore and aft ballonets balanced the helium pressure and stabilized the trim. Air in through the valves, out through the scoops. Okay, he thought.

Ye Pow'rs wha mak mankind your care,
And dish them out their bill o'fare,
Auld Scotland wants nae skinking ware
That jaups in luggies;
But, if ye wish her gratefu' prayer,
Gie her a Haggis!

"Pull him up!" Clearfather yelled—but the girl wasn't strong enough.

"Take the controls!" he called while he yanked at the rope.

The Great Dane, driven insane by the amplified Scottish accent and having consumed its haggis, ran barking across the sand waste. Fearing a collision with the approaching ridge and not knowing how to gain altitude, the girl was forced to bank hard. The Marshal hung on but the grappling hook drooped down low enough to pick up the giant dog by its spiked collar, and the cannibals found themselves suddenly faced with a very surprised harlequin Great Dane swinging at them like a wrecking ball. They scattered, giving Clearfather time to haul up the Marshal, although the added weight of the dog almost broke his arms.

"Somebody hep me—we gotta git higher!"

They were headed back toward the ghetto of satellite dishes. Clearfather made one mighty heave and the Marshal collapsed gratefully onto the deck. Clearfather ran to the cockpit and steered the Haggis back around but he couldn't turn tight enough to clear the cannibals, who now had an open and nearing target. But they were afraid to fire for fear of hitting the blonde's huge dog. The Marshal took advantage of their hesitation, taking aim with the Winchester. He picked off one shooter on the roof of an old UPS truck while Clearfather tried to master the ballonets and fins.

The bikinied blonde was on the roof of the Hummer now, pointing a sniper rifle with a laser scope. Her first shot fouled the barrel of the Winchester and drove the Marshal to the floor of the passenger deck. She braced for a second and final shot, intending to turn the floating Haggis into a flaming ball of helium, when the Sassy Lassy lowered the boom and a shadow dropped out of the sky. The transsexual glanced up—too surprised to shoot or leap—as two hundred pounds of harlequin Great Dane landed on her like a giant haggis, caving in the roof of the Hummer. Instantly the dirigible gained altitude. A moment later an explosion shook the ground, flinging a figure into the ear of John Travolta. The Marshal cheered.

"That big bastard with the welder's helmet tried to ride my bike. I had it booby-trapped. Rest in pieces, old friend! May your spirit always be whole!"

CHAPTER 4

Once Upon a Haggis

Clearfather sent the dirigible into a steep ascent and then leveled off when he was sure they'd clear the next ridgeline. The Sassy Lassy looked less pale but even more confused.

"I'm Elijah Clearfather," he said. "And this is my friend the Marshal."

The girl twisted her hair. "I'm . . . Maggie. Maggie Kane. I guess . . . I should thank yoo."

Clearfather wasn't sure what to say. The blimp, which the Marshall discovered bore the name the *Billy Connolly,* sailed over the windblown airfields and once secret testing facilities, heading toward the Valley of Fire and the northern tip of Lake Mead.

"We're on a mission," explained the Marshal.

"What kine a-mission?" Maggie asked. "Yoo dope smugglers?"

"No!" Clearfather shooed. "We're going to South Dakota."

"Sheet. Why?"

"I think—I have—family there," Clearfather explained. "See . . . I've lost my memory."

"And that's not all," the Marshal mumbled—then clapped his hand to his mouth.

"Whass hee mean?"

"He means I've lost my penis."

"Say whot?" The girl frowned.

"I've lost my penis . . . my dick. Or a lot of it."

"I shure as hell knowa whotta peenis is—doan yoo worry 'bout that."

"Bet you know what to do with one, too!" the Marshal remarked.

"Hush yer mouth, Gramps. I'm jest sayin' it ain't the kine a-thin' yoo loooze."

"No," Clearfather agreed. "I bit my mine off."

"Say whot?"

"Seriously."

The craft was equipped with a GPS Omni navigation system. Clearfather searched for the coordinates for Rapid City and locked them in. The 525-horsepower turboprop engines delivered a cruising speed of eighty miles an hour. The question was, did they have enough fuel?

"Mister, I doan knowa whot game yoo playin'," Maggie said and looked out over the platform. Below were scattered RVs and convoys, Clydesdales pulling stripped-down Isuzus like medicine-show wagons.

Maggie Kane had been through the worst forty-eight hours of her life—and that was saying something. Trapped aboard the Haggis—the pilot had died of anaphylactic shock after being stung by killer bees, sending the craft careering with bagpipe music playing at merciless volume—straight into Big Elvis, who was swatting attack planes atop the Sony Cone—a collision that claimed the life of her friend and fellow Sassy Lassy Astrid, leaving her alone with Angus McLaren, one of the Highland Zingers. Figuring that it was his last night alive, he decided to go out with a bang and proceeded to mount Maggie, a notion she objected to strongly enough to stab him through the throat with one of the com-links. Out of control, with bagpipe music still playing, the *Billy Connolly* eventually swerved over Nellis when Maggie, in sheer desperation, heaved out the anchor line, which dragged across barbed-wire fences and corroded car bodies before latching on to the ear of John Travolta's decapitated head, which provided enough resistance to trigger the Haggis's emergency shutdown mechanism, ending the flight of terror but leaving her stranded in Area 51 with three dead bodies and a lot of promotional precooked haggises.

Being alone on board with those same three dead bodies plus now a lecherous old cowboy and a bald man who claimed to have bitten off his own penis wasn't necessarily an improvement.

"Don't jump," advised the Marshal, reading her mind. "Please. Without a parachute, you'd be like a bug on a windshield. I promise you nothing dishonorable will happen."

"That's right," said Clearfather.

Maggie tried to relax. She'd survived killer bees, Big Elvis, and Angus McLaren, and she hadn't jumped overboard yet.

Raptors and Dragonflies were present but they paid the Haggis no mind. To the south lay the eroded red masterpiece of the Grand Canyon, the Colorado River snaking green and brown. To the north, the condominium and high-rise sprawl of St. George smeared into the sandstone labyrinth of Zion National Park. The whir of the turboprops was steady and now without the booming Burns there was peace. For a moment Clearfather could almost forget the terror he'd released. Just then he looked down over where old I-15 turned into the elevated Robert Redford Environmentally Sensitive Expressway and saw . . . the Wienermobile.

Dr. Tadd and Mr. Meese had survived! They were on their way to MormonLand! It had to be them, he thought. It had to be. Thank God! Thank . . . God.

The joy of seeing the ludicrous vehicle safely on the road and well out in front of the refugees was interrupted by the Marshal raising the practical question of how they were going to dispose of the bodies. The old man consulted the map screen and concluded that the most discreet and respectful place would be Zion National Park. They chose the lava field side of the peak known as North Guardian Angel.

They all felt better when the grim cargo had been jettisoned. Maggie particularly. She knew that she'd been justified in defending herself against Angus, but the authorities might not be so easy to convince. At least her new companions knew what questions not to ask. She felt relieved—just as long as they didn't try any funny business. She'd had enough of that. Along with haggis. When the Marshal microwaved sloppy joes for lunch she almost wet her pants and ended up sufficiently relaxed to recount her short unhappy life, which had arisen out of the once famous case of the "Demon Cheerleaders of Tacoma."

Nineteen years before, the so-called Fearleaders had been charged with dismembering their varsity football team, including the head coach Hunch Torbach, in revenge for the death of Blair Kane, the former head cheerleader, who'd become pregnant to quarterback Dow Cleary.

Abandoned by Dow and suffering from postnatal depression, Blair turned to food for succor, gaining 275 pounds. Classmates testified to witnessing her devour twenty-nine Sara Lee frozen cheesecakes in less than three minutes. McDonald's was still in existence, and one outlet went so far as to seek an injunction against the teen mother because her behavior disgusted other customers. Blair vowed to eat the outlet out of business and in one day consumed more than 317 Happy Meals. By nightfall she was dead—a tragedy that prompted a controversial and ultimately unsuccessful lawsuit and new legislation regarding the legal liabilities of restaurants in "Responsible Retailing of Food" as well as a wave of training seminars for staff on "Sensitively Serving the Compulsive Eater."

The pitiful metamorphosis of Blair Kane was the inciting factor in the butchering of Hunch Torbach and the varsity team—but the jury not so much hung as tangled, the judge had no choice but to declare an anti-climax and the girls were free. Disallowed from selling their stories to the media, they faded into obscurity, anorexia, and/or the fashion industry.

Things weren't so simple for Blair's baby, Magdalena. It wasn't easy being raised in a rain-soaked shipyard suburb by stiff-necked Lutheran grandparents who'd become paranoid about the slightest morsel of junk food or after-school snack. She was teased about her "pig" of a mother from the moment she could remember that her mother wasn't there to read her stories—and all the stories she ever heard seemed to have a moral about gluttony and the dangers of sex. By age fourteen her idea of a good time was three longshoremen, four Demerols, a fifth of Jack Daniel's, six pepperoni pizzas, and a good spew. Eventually she made her way to the Now Frontier and started turning tricks.

"I met this black dude. Hee hepped git me clean—an' I deecided it was time to git seerius 'bout my career. Thass whot led to this Sassy Lassy gig. My firss onnus job an' look whot happens!"

CHAPTER 5

Must Be 42 Inches Tall to Ride

After seeing Clearfather in the crowd, Aretha Nightingale and Eartha tried to make their way to the restaurant where they were planning to meet Minson, but at the first sign of trouble Minson's bodyguard Walpole had whisked him back to the Will Smith Hotel. But not even halfway there it became clear that the city was coming unglued, and Walpole urged them to head for the airport. Minson couldn't bear the thought of leaving his mother to the monster robots and refused. Walpole insisted. Minson knocked him out and took the wheel of the limo himself, driving to the Sun Kingdom, where he hoped to catch his mother and Cousin Ernestine. He never made it. One of the huge stainless-steel treble clefs in the sculpture on the corner of Diana Ross and Paul McCartney fell down, forcing him to crash through the Gardens of Gucci to Steve Wynn Drive, where he had a four-car pileup and had to get out and run—only to find himself charging headlong into a throng of hungover but still rabid fans. And so he sprinted off searching for refuge.

Which is exactly what his parents had done when they reached the Reef and Beef and found that he wasn't there. Faced with giant fighting machines, rioters, exploding gas mains, and stampeding animals, they took shelter in one of the abandoned Chinese salamander restaurants on Nicole Kidman. And it was there—in a flopping mass of the amphibians and the clutter of an interrupted game of Pai Gow—that they forgave each other for the past—and then on top of a lazy Susan, Ernestine took Eartha—or so it appeared to their son, Minson, who couldn't decide if he was more afraid of his own fans or Big Oprah and had rushed inside—and in his shock at seeing an obscure female relative wielding a woody and Doing the Dooley with his mother while the city fell down around them—slipped on a giant salamander, hitting his head on a table.

Meanwhile, back in New York, Finderz Keeperz was giddy with success. The moment the dwarf had zeroed in on the combined signal of the Corps of Discovery and the stealth probe *Azazel*, the satellite used to monitor implant prisoners and terminate them, if necessary, had launched its pulse weapon. The accuracy was deadly—but the system wasn't designed to anticipate something as sophisticated as the empathy of Kokomo, who became one with the target, absorbing the fatal energy, protecting Clearfather from everything except his own grief and rage. To Keeperz, it was a direct hit. The Messiah Weapon, if that's what Clearfather was, had been taken out. No more being on the losing team. Now it was his turn to kick booty.

It was this burst of confidence, his arrogant glee, that made him vulnerable. Ordinarily he'd have been bristling with suspicion if Natassia sauntered into the Information Station scantily clad and oozing friendliness. But he needed a way to celebrate and the bloodlust was upon him. And so he let himself be seduced, thinking that Nasty had finally seen the light. He was so engaged in his own fantasy he forgot how gifted the raunchy brunette was. She didn't know what had happened to the drag queen and feared that maybe the twisted story Finderz had told was true—but the little Napoleon had moved too soon with too much enjoyment. He needed to be taken down a peg before he outgrew his britches—and that meant getting him out of his britches.

No one in Fort Thoreau ever found out all that she had to do to get him into position. They only knew that across the night came the swelling sound of amplified voices. At first people feared it was a Vitessa breach. Gradually the voices became recognizable and people emerged from their tents and listened, grinning. Soon the whole fit population of Fort Thoreau was gathered around the speakers, doubled over. For they could see in their minds that Finderz Keeperz was listening to his "Mommy" give a rude and suggestive reading of *The Little Engine That Could*.

The stifled hysterics were more than some could take. Framegrabber and Ten Pigeons had to seek shelter in the recreation train. Dr. Quail slipped a disc—and the normally restrained Heimdall broke wind when Finderz started chanting, "I think I can! I think I can!" with Nasty encouraging him heartily, "Come on, little engine!"

But the little engine that could—couldn't. Or more precisely he could and did but failed to convince Natassia, who at last got to deliver the line she'd always wanted to . . . "For God's sake, stick it in!"

"It *is* in, you bitch!"

"It can't be—I can't feel you! I need more! Your arm. Your head!"

"My *head*?"

The crowd erupted in one simultaneous orgasmic belly laugh. The next minute a hideously red-faced Finderz blasted out of Natassia's tent wearing fuzzy baby-blue children's sleepers. He stamped past the contorted community. He was going to contact Vitessa immediately, take claim for dispatching Clearfather, and summon the assault troops to surround Central Park. He would see his "colleagues" taken away in chains. But when he got back to IS, he found a note taped to the DataCube, which infuriated him further—and yet also frightened him. It said . . .

MUST BE 42 INCHES TALL TO RIDE.

He ripped off the paper and was so discomposed he hurtled up into the harness without changing out of the sleepers and slid forward into the normally reassuring blue cyberscape, ready to ride the whitewater all the way to the surround-wall screens of the Pantheon's boardroom—when a familiar face filled his field of view.

"Hello, my friend. Off on another fishhhing trip perhapss?"

"Get out of here! Before I nullify you."

"You can't do that. And you can't get through without the passsword."

"What password? Get out of my Cube!"

The veins in the dwarf's huge forehead throbbed, and he shook the harness from side to side.

"Can't you guess the passsword. Suchh a ssmart little man like you!"

"Give me the password—you!" the dwarf screamed.

THE ENTOMOLOGIST chuckled, the round hint of the metal-rimmed glasses glinting. *"Rumplestiltskin.* Don't you think that'ss amuussing?"

"I'm going to personally cancel you!" Keeperz vowed. "File by file."

But even as he threatened, he entered the password, so eager to shoot the rapids and reveal himself to the Pantheon. A loyal new ally!

He submitted the last of the code letters and entered. There was a *whish* like a leaf breaking free of rocks, flowing downstream, and then a fiendish *zang* that wrenched him back in the harness and neither THE ENTOMOLOGIST nor the cyberblue estuary that led to the deeper system could be seen. Instead he saw a field of stars. Gleaming dots against an infinite black background.

"It'ss sso hard to sstep in the ssame datastream twicce," THE ENTOMOLOGIST hissed. "But thiss looks more like . . . a *pit.*"

"Shit! Those—are *eyes*."

"Yess. And they're moving. Toward *you*."

"What . . . are you doing? What's going on?"

"I think the password has triggered a trap."

"You can't trap me!" the dwarf menaced. "You're nothing I can't unplug."

"Are you so sure?" the voice asked—and it was no longer the wheedling voice of the Bug Man—it was a woman's voice, calm and authoritative.

Keeperz was frozen in the harness now, sweat beading on his massive brow. The eyes were moving, the darkness taking the shape of a pit, with him at the bottom.

"Do you see what the eyes belong to now?"

"Y-es," the dwarf stammered, seeing the bodies—just barely distinguishable from the black walls of the pit.

"You've heard of the black widow and the brown recluse—deadly spiders—but solitary and shy by nature. In the East Kalimantan jungle of Borneo is a different kind of spider. The native name means 'Crawling Star.' You can see they're not as large or fierce looking as tarantulas—and yet there is something terribly frightening about them, isn't there?"

"Y-ess," whimpered the dwarf.

"Perhaps it's because there are so many."

"P-please . . . ," mumbled Finderz.

"The Klingtang people were masters of poisons, and they worshiped this spider. Its venom is a powerful neurotoxin that stimulates the release of adrenaline while simultaneously cramping all muscles. The victim cannot even twitch, and yet is filled with a nauseous electric fear. The time it takes you to die is a matter of how long your heart can endure a self-manufactured and extremely pure form of terror."

Keeperz screeched, "Please! I'll do anything!"

"I see that now. I see you clearly."

The creeping spider dark was gone and the face of THE ENTO-MOLOGIST again filled the Cube.

"You betrayed us, Finderz. And yourself. I put my faith in you."

"I had no choice!" the little schemer wept, sweat thickening around his wristwatches. "We can't win!"

"Oh," said the voice. "An ideological decision. No question of personal gain. Well, this has been your test, and you have failed your new masters as completely as you have failed us. Look at this . . . this is what's happening in LosVegas. You think your assassination plot was successful? Judge for yourself!"

Keeperz had been so busy congratulating himself and then succumbing to Natassia, he hadn't been monitoring the news out of the West. Where the images were coming from he couldn't say—but the devastation was unbelievable—airplanes and sky towers smashed like toys—canals burning.

"Not quite what you planned, is it? Imagine how grateful Vitessa will be when they learn of your involvement."

"Oh, my God!" Finderz gasped, trembling in the harness so that it squeaked.

"Better the verdict of the spiders, hm?"

"N-no! You can't! You can't do this to me. Who . . . are you . . . really?"

"Haven't you guessed?"

The veil fell away from THE ENTOMOLOGIST's helmet. The round metal-rimmed glasses came off.

"My God! You? You're—"

"Appearances can be perceptive, yesss? Time to board the Crawling Star. Must be 42 inches tall."

"NO!" the dwarf screamed as the face faded into the field of stars, which turned again into the eyes of the spiders.

The dwarf's cry was heard all the way to the HIV Lounge but

everyone was still having such a good time imitating the Stomp of Shame, it was a few moments before anyone thought to be worried. By then Heimdall had started picking up Pirate Radio reports about the madness in LosVegas.

Lila Crashcart made the hard visit the next morning—and found Keeperz—fingernails squeezed through his fists, jaws locked —the clenching force having driven several teeth through his lips. A sharp aluminum odor of fear and piss filled the Cube. The three-dimensional screen was blank.

Broadband was of the opinion that Finderz, in his anger at Natassia's prank, had overreached his Cubing ability and had tried to negotiate a mammoth wave of oblique data. But Dr. Quail, who arranged for an autopsy, took the view that something much odder had befallen the dwarf, noting that all his Canal Street wristwatches had stopped. The remains of the stunted body were disposed of according to Fort Thoreau custom, and a crab apple tree was planted —which was soon covered in mistletoe. The Strategists agreed that decisions would be made according to majority vote until Parousia Head appointed a new leader.

CHAPTER 6

Over the Rainbow

Clearfather adjusted the cruising speed to seventy-two miles per hour as the *Billy Connolly* sailed over the Promised Land of the Mormons, home of the Great Salt Lake and thousands of acres of chemical weapons stockpiles. For a while he was able to tune in a Pirate Radio broadcast. Dooley Duck and Ubba Dubba had been crowned the homecoming king and queen in what was being called the Soul Carnival, a world celebration that was even more ecstatic than the earlier outbreaks of "Doing the Dooley." Prominent Voyants were ordering their chips removed and their portals sealed. The giant metro monitors, access terminals, and private Mind Theaters were boycotted. Robotic factories started dismantling themselves. Millions of doses of psychoactive medication were burned in bonfires while hundreds of psychologists and neurological researchers were publicly experimented with.

The only other news that Clearfather could pick up concerned Professor Chicken. The company had just appointed Wyatt T. Dove, the once famous business author and inventor of Diagonal Thinking, as head of customer relations and creative product development. According to a press release from Brand's office, "The Professor

Chicken family takes pride in reinstating an American innovator. We have acquired a very special ally in Mr. Dove, and his expertise and vision are already having an influence."

The news cheered Clearfather. Professor Chicken was turning the tables on Chu's and McTavish's—and Dooley Duck's Surprise Party was taking the battle to Vitessa around the world. Back aboard the Haggis, Maggie continued to relax. With the disposal of the bodies and the sky clearing as they got farther away from LosVegas, the trauma of the giant celebrity tantrums began to fade. Clearfather was grateful. To think that such anger and annihilation could've arisen from inside him. If there was an explanation or a resolution, he felt it lay in South Dakota—the only place he seemed to have any connection with that he hadn't visited. Even if there was tragic news waiting for him there . . . secrets . . . or worse. He had to go. He had to find an answer to the mystery, whatever it was.

When he'd found himself on the bus to Pittsburgh, he thought that he'd lost his memory. Now he had to face the possibility that he really had come back from the dead—and not only that he'd come back—that he'd been *brought* back. There was an agency behind his return and therefore a purpose—a meaning—if only he could discover what it was.

He had but pieces of the puzzle. Stinky Wiggler. A stolen penis and a frightful scar. A place in Texas where at two different points in history communities that practiced open sexual communion had been attacked and disbanded—and then fragments of memories— as of crimes he'd committed—contrasted with happy morsels of childhood. Holding these elements together was the shadow of Vitessa, the recurring image of a tornado, and the ghost of Lloyd Meadhorn Sitturd. He recalled what the Marshal had said about lighting out after inspiration with a club—how, even if you failed, you would find something very much like it. But what if you set out for South Dakota in a Flying Haggis—what would you find then?

"He's a deep thinker, our expedition leader," he heard the Marshal say, and he broke from his reverie to see puffs of clouds.

The Marshal and Maggie were becoming quite chummy. The old man matched her accounts of unusual anatomical features and special requests of sex clients with his thoughts on mental institutions, the roller coaster as metaphor for the journey of the soul—and a steady intermixing of facts about the Old and the Imaginary West. (Clearfather wondered if Dr. Tadd knew that Jesse James's wife was named Zerelda Mimms or that Britt Reid, the Green Hornet, was the Lone Ranger's grandnephew.)

So the daylight drifted like the *Billy Connolly*. As they neared the Colorado border, with the Yampa Plateau and Dinosaur National Monument to the north, Clearfather noticed the fortifications of a Time Haven. The peculiar thing was that there was a small school of fishing boats mounted on hydraulic platforms, and several people aboard were involved in some sort of simulated fishing activity.

"Hand me those binos," Clearfather asked the Marshal. Hadn't Edwina Corn said her Zane Grey community was on the Utah–Colorado border? By God, he thought, there she is—on the *Lassiter*—practicing marlin fishing!

Clearfather smiled and picked up the cockpit's microphone and flipped on the speakers. "Ahoy the *Lassiter*!" he proclaimed in a screech of feedback. "In everything there is something undiscovered. Find it!"

"Geez. That'll sure get 'em wondering," said the Marshal.

"Probbbubbly make 'em poo thair pants," Maggie suggested, noting the consternation that had resulted on the boats.

"Maybe that's what we should do! Just float across America in this craft making cryptic pronouncements," the Marshal mused. "People everywhere would hope to see us—wondering what we were going to say next."

"Not mee," Maggie insisted. "Wanna git back on the ground an' shower. Iss only 'cause yoo two stink that yoo doan notice."

"I resent that," said the Marshal. "I bathed just last night."

"'Sides," Maggie mumbled, "wee ain't got enuff fyool."

"Shit," said Clearfather, remembering the fuel gauge. The tank had been less than half full when they'd started and there was no manual or help function to indicate what the craft's cruising distance was. The flight computer calculated 872 air miles between their point of departure and the Rapid City Regional Airport. He had no idea of where they were going in the area—and there were no coordinates for Hermetic Canyon—if that in fact was where they were headed. He eased back on the speed.

Below flowed the Vermillion and Little Snake rivers, while to the east the peaks of the Rockies thrust up into the red of late afternoon. The Marshal rummaged around in the pilot's locker, found a bottle of Laphroiag, chipped ice out of the freezer, and passed around drinks at sunset. Maggie grew more sociable and even a little bit flirtatious, which made Clearfather think longingly of Kokomo. It was hard for him to imagine he'd only been with her a couple of days. His whole life had been a series of moments.

"What I want to know," the imaginary lawman began, "is what we're looking for supposing we do get to South Dakota?"

Clearfather figured he owed the Marshal as much of the truth as he knew.

"I don't know what we'll find in South Dakota or where exactly we're going—but I'm hoping to find out the secret of my life. Who I am. Why I'm here."

"Christ!" laughed Maggie. "If I had a dollar fer evertime I herd that!"

"You don't have any idea who we're trying to hook up with?"

"I have one idea," Clearfather admitted. "But I think whoever it is knows I'm coming. I think we'll get a Sign."

"I want more whiskey if I gotta bee ridin' with loonies," Maggie called.

The Marshal whipped up a Middle Eastern Lamb 'n' A Can®

meal as the shreds of pink clouds turned to purple, then mauve, then white and as wispy as his hair. Between mouthfuls he recited for them (complete with camera angles) the script for the pilot episode of *Star City*. Maggie became absorbed, identifying with the character of Katie, the cathouse madam. An hour or so later the moon rose full and round over the Medicine Bow Mountains as the Haggis edged into Wyoming. The props stuttered for the first time. Despite the Marshal's assurances, Clearfather was worried. Without power they were at the mercy of the wind. The old man passed around the bottle again and regaled them with tales of Jim Badge's Abilene, which reminded Clearfather of Edwina Corn's obsession with Zane Grey. Over Douglas, Wyoming, the motors died.

Down below, the highway to Cheyenne spilled like gunpowder in the moonlight. Maggie nodded out, and the Marshal laid a McTavish's tartan blanket over her. The air was cool and the stars were the brightest that Clearfather had ever seen.

"I have to say, I find this invigorating," the Marshal announced. "Chased by cannibals and now adrift over the Rockies. Whatever happens, I want you to know I'm grateful, son. I'm sorry, that sounds condescending."

"Not from you it doesn't," Clearfather replied.

"Good. Anyway, I thought I was rescuing you, but I think it's the other way around."

"I hope you can say that in the morning." Clearfather smiled, pulling up his blanket, his eyes fluttering with fatigue and whiskey.

He didn't remember dropping off—but he must've because he saw the three Chinese men again, floating alongside the *Billy Connolly*. It was in the cold blue moments before dawn. They were telling him something about his past but he couldn't hear because the air was filled with music. *I want to take you higher . . . boom lacka lacka boom lacka lacka . . .*

At first he thought a maxicopter had overtaken them. But there was nothing visible. He rose to check the sound system. The Marshal and Maggie were curled up together like dogs. The whole console was shut off and still the music played. *Boom lacka lacka boom lacka lacka.* Then it stopped. The Chinese men were gone, too.

"*Immaculate Reception,*" he heard a voice say. "*This is Stinky Wiggler, coming to you live from KRMA in Hermetic Canyon, Self Dakota . . .*"

The Marshal stirred at his feet and the music faded away. Their speed had dropped to twelve miles an hour and the compass bearing had shifted east—but he wasn't worried now. They were headed in the right direction. They had to be. He slumped in the cockpit, dreaming of his dog Lucky . . . wondering what had happened to him and how long ago it was they'd snuggled together on the porch . . .

When he opened his eyes, the machinery of the sky was on fire and in the distance he could see the Black Hills studded with dark ponderosa pines and to the east the suggestion of the spires and buttes of the Badlands. The Marshal was up and fumbling with instant coffee. Maggie was still asleep. The lines on her face had relaxed, and she looked like a child again.

"You look like you got a Message," the Marshal observed, and Clearfather nodded.

"Me, too," the old man said and pointed off the port side. A large bald eagle soared alongside them. Clearfather thought back to the Dangling Rangler.

Maggie stirred when she smelled the coffee but got sick and spent a long time in the little cubicle of the bathroom.

Down below they saw miles of motels and bright plastic restaurants, trout farms, petting zoos, campgrounds, buffalo burger bars, and venison steak houses.

"I suspect Crazy Horse would be mighty unhappy about all these go-kart tracks," the Marshal remarked. "But it makes me nostalgic. Mom brought me here on vacation ages ago. Let me eat corn dogs and ice cream. Trying to make us a family."

"Did it work?" asked Clearfather, thinking of his own flashes of memory.

"Naw. But that wasn't her fault. A lot of other people had the same idea. Looks like they still do. If I didn't know better, I'd say we've flown back in time."

Maggie emerged from the bathroom in time to see the herds of bison on the rolling hills of Custer State Park. The Black Hills swelled up out of a sea of prairie, Harney Peak spiking highest, in its shadow the Crazy Horse Memorial . . . and to the east the famous sixty-foot-high visages carved by Gutzon Borglum and his son.

"Hm," the Marshal said, staring through the binoculars. "I might've spoken too soon about things not changing. Mount Rushmore seems to be behaving oddly. Look at the four presidents—they've turned into the Marx Brothers. No wait—it's the Beatles! Say—the Beatles weren't American!"

"I think you're overlooking the fact that Mount Rushmore isn't supposed to change at all," Clearfather replied, taking the field glasses.

But when he peered at the great granite heads he saw Sitting Bull and Martin Luther King, Dooley Duck and Ubba Dubba. That's not possible, he thought—but he didn't have a chance to take another look.

"Holy shit!" gasped the Marshal. "What in the Sam Hill is *that*?"

The eagle had been joined by a giant bird with orange metallic feathers and a peacockish tail. Its head was that of a dog—like Warhol—and its claws reminded Clearfather of Gog and Magog.

"I've got no idea . . . but I'd say it's a definite Sign."

"Yeah! To keep the hell away!" Maggie wailed.

"One thing's certain," the Marshal observed. "That bird's not native to South Dakota."

The *Billy Connolly* drifted over the fluorescent carpeted acres of Big Sky Mini Golf and the Homer Simpson Inflatable Family Fun

Park—when the giant bird veered closer and tore at the skin of the Haggis, releasing a whistling jet of helium.

"Weer goin' dowwn!" Maggie bawled.

"Hold her steady!" the Marshal cried.

Clearfather fiddled with the fins and ballonets as best he could, trying to retard the rate of fall. The wind pushed them harder toward the Badlands. The fading dark pine peaks and crags of the Black Hills seemed cushy and inviting compared with the jagged towers and foreboding canyons they were approaching. On and on the wind drove them as they slowly lost altitude. At last the eagle tracked down into the shadows of weather-eaten rock—and the monstrous bird flew up, grasping the netting around one of the battens just as the hole in the skin blew clear and the craft started to seriously dive. Down into a canyon the Haggis was lowered, the bird's enormous wings almost brushing the sandstone crust of the walls.

CHAPTER 7

The Eagle Has Landed

The canyon was deeper than it appeared from the air, the steep walls riddled with caves and crevices that formed ancient faces in the rocks. The shadow of the great bird's wings and the depth of the fissure took them out of the morning sunlight—and yet it wasn't dark. They passed through a belt of spray, but as they descended, Clearfather saw that it was actually a mist of shimmering transparent leaves. Each of the leaves was a face. The mist illuminated the canyon walls like a dense cloud, so that it was impossible to tell what time of day it was. Maggie stood frozen. The Marshal gripped the rifle. Out of the color-banded mudstone below, a group of derelict buildings emerged, resembling an old western ghost town. The *Billy Connolly* collapsed softly down on the roof of the livery stable, and the balloon finished deflating. The mutant bird let go and flapped up a flurry of gypsum dust as it rose to the mouth of one of the caves and disappeared.

"I knew I shudda stayed trickin'," Maggie said.

The Marshal retained the damaged Winchester but handed the 12-gauge to her. To Clearfather he offered the H&K.

"I don't think we'll need those," Clearfather said.

The Marshal shook his head. "I see a bird the size of a house with the head of a dog and lion claws, I bring the guns. May not do any good—but I feel better."

The old man sprang over the deck and across the roof to the fire escape of the broken-windowed Red Cloud Hotel. Clearfather followed, noticing a flag atop the courthouse that showed a striped skunk with the words LOCO FOCO— MAKE A STINK. Refusing to be left alone, Maggie straggled after them. Through the luminous mist above they could just make out the lip of the gorge.

"Must be an old mining town," the Marshal said, pointing to the ruins of an ore-crushing mill. Still visible were the remains of the crusher, the furnace stamps, and the steam engines. "Reminds me of *Star City*."

It reminded Clearfather of Cubby's model train town. Around the perimeter ran a miniature railroad line.

"Whot was that?" Maggie shushed. "Yoo hear that?"

Clearfather stared back down the main street. He'd heard something, too—but he was distracted by the peeling red schoolhouse. He could've sworn it was one room—but now it was clearly two, and hanging across the dirt street between the saloon and the funeral parlor was a banner that read WELCOME HOME.

"That's promising," the Marshal remarked, but Clearfather wondered how it had come to be there so suddenly. And what did that word mean . . . HOME? This place? Was this what he'd been seeing in his visions?

"Look!" The Marshal gestured. The eagle was perched on the roof of the train station, which was adorned with a weather vane featuring a wheelbarrow with flames rising. As they neared, a steam whistle tooted, and from around the other side of the town there clicked a scaled-down locomotive with a big smokestack. On the platform was a faded wooden sign of a cartoon owl dressed as a train conductor with a message that said . . . MUST BE 42 INCHES TALL TO RIDE. KEEP YOUR ARMS INSIDE THE CARS AT ALL TIMES. AND PLEASE—DON'T LITTER!

The engine stopped. Behind were three open cars.

"All aboard?" asked the Marshal.

"Wee have a choice?" Maggie grunted—and Clearfather felt a twinge of fear. He swung into the last seat. His companions took the other two, and the whistle hooted. He thought he saw a shadow in the newspaper office, *The Clamon,* but he couldn't be sure because the locomotive chugged off. The schoolhouse now had a library.

The train clacked through a moonscape of cones and culverts, occasionally passing more battered signs—a weathered raccoon dressed as a cavalry scout or a splintery old hound dog panning for gold. Clearfather had the disconcerting feeling that they were being watched but he couldn't say from where or with what attitude.

The tracks skirted a quarry filled with iridescent green water and rusted cranes—huge fossils embedded in the cliff walls. Thirty feet ahead the rails had been broken apart and the train slowed to a halt.

"Looks like the end of the line," the Marshal surmised as they clambered out. A moment later the engine began backing up the way it came.

They were beside two hangars. The first had once been a mixture of clean room and laboratory, with a series of operating theaters and stainless-steel refrigeration units. On the floor lay prosthetic devices—actionatronic limbs and articulation joints. The interior of the next hangar contained thousands of religious images . . . crucifixes, oil paintings of Annunciations and Last Suppers . . . the Three Magi and the raising of Lazarus . . . Madonnas, Nativity scenes, Stars of David . . . murals showing Marduk creating the world out of Tiamat's body . . . Buddhas, Hindu gods, Islamic mosaics . . . Kwakiutl totem poles, Pennsylvania Dutch hex signs, bark paintings, Mayan and Egyptian hieroglyphs . . . fragments of machine language code.

Bewildered, the three kept exploring, weapons at the ready. Gradually they became aware of a rough, haunting music.

"Over there." The Marshal pointed.

The song was "Love in Vain" by Robert Johnson. The mournful blues reverberated off the rocks, drawing them through a maze of smashed slot machines. They came to a shack with the letters KRMA and a spear of transmission tower rising from the roof.

"I've seen this in my dreams!" Clearfather cried.

"Ain't that a reeleef," Maggie commented.

Inside there was a rocking chair. No equipment, no music, and no person. Just shed rattlesnake skins and an old ladderback rocker. Clearfather's heart fluttered—he'd been braced for a meeting. Still the blues drifted on . . . a black voice . . . the guitar talking back . . . like spit on a griddle . . . then sliding off into morphine sadness. "If I Had Possession Over Judgment Day."

They rounded a crusted spire and saw a man in the company of two Harijans kneeling beside an extremely large set of paw prints.

"Ah!" the man whirled. "Terribly sorry to have missed you at the station. Bit of a prickly situation here—hah. So glad you made it! Welcome to the Canyon! Yes!"

The Harijans made the same gesture of greeting and respect that Clearfather had seen before—then set out fast in the other direction, both armed with stun rifles.

The man not only was bald, but gave the impression that he'd never had any hair. He wasn't young but his skin was clear and unlined, the color of maple syrup. He was of average height and weight but there was something about his movements that gave the impression his body was cartilaginous like a shark's. He wore a white sarong, a T-shirt advertising the BIG THUNDER GOLDMINE, deerskin moccasins, and little round shades of methylene blue. But when he turned, Clearfather caught a sparkle of emerald green behind the lenses.

"Questions, questions—I can see you have so many questions!"

he bubbled. "You, my dear, are wondering about the bird—oh, and I see about your mother, too. A glimmer of hope—that you'll one day meet her—yes, very sad—who knows? Of course. My, well . . . anyway the bird is called a Simurgh—a mythological Persian bird that has lived so long, it's seen the world destroyed three times. I'm sorry if you thought it a bit extreme. Sometimes my enthusiasm runs away with me! And you, Marshal, are curious about the mist. Well, it's complicated to explain. Think of it as a hazing system—a reflective energy field that counters perception. I'm something of a stickler for privacy—and your father—yes, well that's very sad, too—and you," he said, wheeling back to Clearfather. "We'll get to your questions, too, of course. Perhaps sooner rather than later, eh? Oh, my!"

"Are you . . . who . . . I think you are?" Clearfather gasped.

"Moi? I, sir, am the Pleasure Principal—Lord of Misrule, Abbot of Unreason—King of the Weird Frontier. But as to whether or not I am who you think I am . . . that would all depend on who you thought I was," the man smiled.

"'There's nothing so quaint . . . as a f-future . . . beyond your wildest imagination,'" Clearfather stammered.

"Emerson said 'I hate quotations. Tell me what you know.'"

"S-stinky . . . Wiggler?"

"Here am I!" the man bowed.

"Whot?" said Maggie. "Stinky Wiggler?"

"I've worn many faces and names over the years," the man answered with a flicker of annoyance.

"But—but what are you doing here?" the Marshal inquired.

"Well, actually I *am* here."

"Duh!" Maggie said.

"No, I mean—yes. Well . . . we may need to warm up to that notion. Let's just say for now that I like being nestled among seventy-five million years of geology. Plus it never pays to live too far away from the National Museum of Woodcarving."

Maggie looked at the Marshal, but the old man just shrugged.

Wiggler stepped toward them, and a blind black man cradling a guitar appeared from behind a water tank like a patch of shade come to life. The man was old but spry—with a bent back and long supple limbs. He wore sunglasses, a damp white shirt, suspenders, shiny black pin-striped pants, and a pearl-gray Stetson Whippet perched on his head, which had a dusting of white hair.

"Blind Lemon Jackson Jefferson Johnson Jones!" Clearfather exclaimed.

"Blind Lemon Five," Wiggler replied. "There have been upgrades."

The Marshal's mouth dropped. This was no droid—this was a living man. Surely.

"You mean he plays better?" Clearfather asked.

"Allas learnin' to play better," the black man replied, looking directly at Clearfather's face. Then he sniffed in Maggie's direction and began moaning and strumming, *"You can squeeze my lemon till the juice runs down my leg."* Clearfather noticed that Maggie's finger seemed to be itching on the trigger of the shotgun. Fortunately the Marshal was engrossed in the guitar work.

"He's got six fingers! On each hand!"

"Yes," Wiggler replied. "I told you there'd been improvements. They're longer and stronger and more flexible than normal, and linked to a very edgy micromedia effector unit. He's also got an audiographic memory and perfect pitch. At first I thought it was cheating—but then I thought what the hell."

"But his skin!" the Marshal marveled.

"You wouldn't get the right acoustics otherwise. You need the heartache and the thousand natural shocks that flesh is heir to."

"You mean he's *real?*" the Marshal gawked.

"What are those words of Pindar's? 'A dream about a shadow is man.' He's as real as you are—physically and philosophically. In fact, much of the nervous system was designed by an AI that I humbly believe is more sophisticated than you are, called Savoir Faire."

"Savoir Faire?"

"You probably don't remember *Klondike Cat*," Wiggler squinted. "Klondike Cat was a Canadian Mountie. His nemesis was a sneaky little Canuck mouse named Savoir Faire. Perverse as I am, I always took the side of the villain. At the end of every episode Klondike would insist, 'I always get my mouse,' although in fact SF would always escape. Whistling on the wind, we'd hear his catchcry, *Savoir Faire ees everywhair!*

"My Savoir Faire did the intricate nerve mapping for this Lemon. I cannibalized some of the humor from BL Two—and kicked in a fully organic Epiphany processor and a Mnemosyne backup. Then for the fine cellcraft, which I find tedious, I used EVE—a biodesign system I invented that's demonstrated excellent evolution of its own. Throughout new creature development it operates as an incubatory consultant. In earlier models I'd grown the eyes and then blinded them, or set in place a targeted malfunction with a time delay. The new EVE suggested eliminating the eyes right from the start. But I also beefed up the olfactory and auditory facilities and added a couple more input channels and an onboard magnetic navigation system incorporating ultrasonic air transducers for proximity sensing and obstacle avoidance—"

"Mister!" Maggie screamed and fired the shotgun into the air.

"Huh? Oh. So sorry," Wiggler fidgeted. "Forgive me."

Clearfather glanced up as the blast echoed between the walls—and saw a couple of sleepy saber-toothed tigers emerge from a cavern. He heard that other sound, too. He was certain now that hidden eyes were watching them.

A mariachi band ran past, pursued by a naked woman on a horse.

"What was *that*?" the Marshal asked.

"Just a stray thought," Wiggler shrugged. "Milton said the mind is its own place. So make it a fun place! But the beasts are yet to come. Come, you can have showers and then we'll have a nice morning—tea!"

He clapped his hands and the earth began to tremble—and from around a bend of volcanic ash there appeared two enormous creatures with the leathery gray hides of rhinos and the extended necks of giraffes. They stood more than fifteen feet at the shoulder and must've weighed many tons. Each was saddled with a miniature pavilion. In unison the giants knelt and Wiggler assisted Blind Lemon, gesturing for Clearfather to join him, while the Marshal and Maggie mounted the second beast.

"Are these—dine-o-sores?" Maggie was at last able to inquire—with an expression on her face that helped distract the Marshal from his own alarm.

"They're indricotheres," Wiggler replied. "From the Oligocene period. I've always found dinosaurs clichéd unless they're miniaturized. I'm more of a giant mammal man."

The sheer bulk of the animals was awesome, the plodding movement hypnotic. The procession arrived at a fork and had to go single file as they wound through a separate canyon. Beside them in places, either pools of rain and river remained or springs had flooded eroded indentations. The deeper bodies teemed with life—enormous wading birds and bizarre hippopotamus-like animals with elephantine trunks. Above, Clearfather caught a glimpse of the Harijans, negotiating a rope bridge. Their movements and alertness made him think of hunters.

"Basic atavism," Wiggler waved, indicating a high-walled enclosure. In one section was a gigantic carnivorous terror bird from the Eocene, looking sullen and bored. In another, two glyptodonts—massive armadillos with spiked tails—engaged in ponderous combat. "I much prefer chimeralogy."

"What's that?" Clearfather asked.

"Making up my own creatures—or executing difficult composite forms. The physiology and of course the psychology is far more fulfilling."

Clearfather surveyed the tunneled walls and again felt the presence of unseen eyes. None of this was what he'd imagined he'd find in South Dakota. He couldn't think where he'd expect to find it—except in someone else's dreams.

They came to a compound of Cyclone fencing and concertina wire, inside which they observed a tribe of rhesus monkeys lying among discarded circuit boards and DC motors. Many of the animals had open sores as if they'd been exposed to an aggressive defoliant. Four scruffy chimps—one without an eye, and another with a partially amputated arm—jabbered over a game played with ESP cards and a collection of trinkets—Cracker Jack prizes, Secret Squadron decoder rings, and what looked like little glow-in-the-dark green skulls. Leaning against a salt dome, like the headman of a village, sat a large proboscis monkey swathed in dirty bandages. On his head he wore a stained golf hat from the Bob Hope Desert Classic. He was seated astride a cracked porcelain toilet, wearing an oxygen mask linked by a rubber hose to a large cylinder of gas. Every few moments the withered fingers would open the valve and the creature would get a blast.

"Whot's wrong with 'em all?" Maggie gawked.

"Various experiments in accelerated learning and transitional development."

Stone-still lorrises stared down from a jungle gym like electroshock patients.

"Look at that!" the Marshal gasped, pointing to emaciated macaques shooting each other with tranquilizer darts.

"Why don't you put them out of their misery?" Clearfather asked.

"How in-Hanuman, eh?" Wiggler answered. "Well, you could—if you were being very narrow-minded—say that what I'm interested in *is* their misery—what forms it takes. The experiment is ongoing. New data is always being gleaned. Just remember that. We exist to create new data—a provisional meaning of life."

The indricotheres lumbered on across a stream, which flowed into a nest of caves inhabited by things better left unsaid.

They came in sight of a building constructed in a Tinkertoy shape. Wiggler made a clicking sound that caused the beasts to kneel. "Come," he said, dismounting. "Nothing here will harm you—at least not while I'm along."

Inside, they found a larger laboratory than the one they'd seen before, where there appeared to be several autopsies in progress. A library of data crystals bore titles of scientific studies ranging from *The Initiation of Mating Following Removal of the Frontal Lobes* to *Microelectrical Bionics.* Across the room in a full-sized aquarium tank they saw a sockeye salmon as big as a dolphin.

"What are those things growing there?" the Marshal asked.

"Pineal glands. According to Descartes, the pineal gland is the point of contact between the body and the soul," their unusual guide remarked.

"Yoo musta had a royally fucked-up childhood," Maggie proclaimed.

"On the contrary, my dear, I'm continuing to enjoy it."

"Howa yoo'd git doin' all this?"

"I'm primarily self-taught," answered Wiggler. "Although I've had many accidental instructors. Actually, you know, you look like a younger, prettier version of one of the few teachers whose advice has stuck with me over the years."

"Choose something like a star?" the Marshal suggested caustically.

"N-no," Wiggler snipped. "We were making puppets for the Christmas pageant, and she said, 'Try to make your puppets' voices fit their characters and don't think that just because they're puppets, they must all speak in squeaky voices.' The subtlety of that remark is still sinking in."

He pointed to a series of tall curtained cylinders. The curtains opened and the cylinders were illuminated to reveal a naked body of uncertain sexuality in each.

"Shee-it!" Maggie sighed, peering closely.

"This . . . is . . . sick!" cringed the Marshal.

"Oh, don't be so uptight!" Wiggler chided. "You're bringing vertebrate/mammalian prejudices to bear. Our mollusk and annelid friends know all about the values of hermaphroditism, as do fish. Heretofore, humans have been obsessed with sexual preferences and appearances—a crude nip and tuck or the odd intramuscular injection of progesterone. What we're looking at here is the possibility of changing one's sexual *options*. Creative endocrinology."

"But why would anyone do that?" asked the Marshal, shifting the dented Winchester from hand to hand.

"Variety . . . curiosity," Wiggler answered. "You've heard the admonition to men to bring out their feminine side? Are we not women? Hah! Men actually discover the clitoris when they have one themselves, believe me."

"That's awful!" the Marshal barked.

"A pot that complains of having handles," scoffed Wiggler. "I've simply moved or added some handles. But I should've waited until after you've been refreshed. I'm sorry. You'll find showers and fresh clothes in there—" He pointed to another curtain. "—then we'll start celebrating. Everyone's dying to meet you!"

"I hope that's not literally true," the Marshall whistled.

Wiggler gave him a wilting smile and then glanced at Maggie, who was staring out the window, her face hardened into a mask of near-terminal distress.

"Wittgenstein!" Wiggler bellowed. "There you are!"

CHAPTER 8

A Badlands Tea Party

Wittgenstein would've been a more or less ordinary porcupine had he not been the size of a shuttle bus. Long after the drones had sedated and transported the creature—a feat that required the collaboration of the indricotheres and a mobile gantry robot—Maggie was still experiencing what Wiggler referred to as her "Wild Surmise." It took all the Marshal's concentration and persistence to get her through the formalities of showering and dressing—and it was only when she realized that the "old grubber" had seen her naked (and scrubbed her, too) that she finally broke out of her trance and began complaining normally again.

Clearfather, meanwhile, felt as though he'd circled around to where the riddles began, not ended. This sentiment was reinforced when, after showering, and dressed in simple white Nehru suits, they returned to the ghost town to find the buildings neatly repaired and freshly painted; the Red Cloud Hotel couldn't have looked more opulent or inviting. A long table was laid out in the street beneath the WELCOME HOME banner, covered in silver teapots and dishes of sweets and savories. Joining the banner strung across the street were two chains of bright piñatas. Beside the table a stage had been set up, draped in red, white, and blue bunting, with enough seats for a large band, plus a grand piano. Maggie's place was marked with a live dimetrodon and a stegosaurus that could fit on her tea saucer (although neither had any intention of remaining there—the vegetarian stegosaurus attacking the cheese logs, the sail-finned carnivore opting for the pigs-in-a-blanket). Marking the Marshal's seat was a stagecoach the size of the sugar bowl. Clearfather's place was empty—until he discovered a long almost transparent object like the one he'd found among the Gifts in Dustdevil. His teaspoon commemorated the Pan-American Exposition in Buffalo in 1901.

Wiggler offered them tea and snacks but seemed too wound up to partake of anything himself—and, as the visitors were so filled with questions and disbelief, the miniature dinosaurs had a field day with the macaroons.

As he sat, trying to formulate which question to ask first, Clearfather noticed that they'd been joined by an immense and frightful bear-like creature dressed in a little girl's party dress, with its own table with separate cups and saucers.

"Uh, this is CJ . . . as in Jane . . . as in Calamity Jane."

"W-w-*whot* . . . is she?" Maggie gulped.

"She's a bit shy," Wiggler answered.

"Noa . . . I mean . . ."

"She's a megatherium—a giant ground sloth. Downsized of course. Do you know how difficult it is to housebreak a sloth?"

"What's she doing?" Clearfather asked after watching her awhile.

"She's having her own tea party," Wiggler said. "An imaginary tea party."

"I had them," Maggie said. "Bee-fore I started boozin'."

"You're welcome to join her. She'd love a playmate!"

Maggie choked. "Mister, I ain't sittin' with noa hairy-ass freak!"

Calamity Jane let out a squeal of dismay and batted her tea set to smithereens.

"Ms. Kane," Wiggler replied with simmering calm. "I appreciate that the consciousness-raising experience you're undergoing is un-settling—but see what you've done. A moment ago CJ was playing happily—sharing in our presence and enjoying her own fantasy at the same time, which is no mean feat. You've hurt her feelings, Ms. Kane. You've been cruel—not to further an end or identify a bound-ary—but out of pure thoughtlessness."

"I'm . . . sorry," Maggie sniffed, chastened by the moping animal as much as she was frightened by the commanding tone of Wiggler's voice.

"So cruelty's all right if it's part of an experiment?" the Marshal gibed.

"Knowledge never comes without a price," Wiggler countered. "The squalor you witnessed earlier has made other kinds of progress possible. That's what progress is—squalor striving—grace stumbling."

"Can't make an omelet without breakin' some eggs, eh?"

"I'm not going to bandy truisms, Marshal. There's nothing easier than making assumptions. When you're willing to examine yours, I'll gladly debate with you."

"Doo yoo think—shee'd still like—to play with mee?" Maggie whimpered.

"She'd love to," Wiggler said. "I confess she's a bit spoiled but she never holds a grudge—and she is a lot of fun. But if you play hop-scotch, give her plenty of room, and I'd recommend letting her win. If you play dolls, don't let her pull the heads off. She eats them and they clog her up. Oh, and she loves Nancy Drew mysteries. Maybe you could read to her. But don't be too long! The entertainment starts soon!"

Maggie got up and followed the sloth, which was still almost twice her size. The Marshal sat looking pensive.

"You said earlier . . . you know . . . about my father?" the old actor said at last.

"I know about your sadness and your curiosity about what hap-pened to him."

"How do you know that?"

"The simple answer is that you broadcast it. How I'm able to receive the transmission requires a dense technical explanation."

"Is it that obvious? Even after all these years?"

"We most quickly reveal that which we try to conceal—especially from ourselves. You can't outgrow a ghost, Marshal."

"So—*do* you know—what happened to him?"

"He's in hiding."

"For God's sake, where?"

"On an island . . . in the shadow of a roller coaster. Inside you."

"Shit!" groaned the Marshal. "I've left that island!"

"Yes, and you've willed it to your son," Wiggler replied.

"Goddamn it, I have not! My son doesn't need me—he's very successful!"

"As you wish."

"Christ. What do you know? You're just playing mind games with me!"

"Well, then, it's time to play a new game. Cigar?"

"I only smoke marijuana," the Marshal grumbled.

"And what about you?" Wiggler asked Clearfather—producing one of the mysterious transparent lengths like the one at his setting.

Clearfather picked his up. "Is that what this is?"

"You know what they say about guys who smoke big cigars," the Marshal snubbed.

Wiggler's became visible and lit at the same time, and he sat back blowing smoke rings. "Sometimes a cigar is just a metaphor. But what could be more potent, eh?"

"What?" said Clearfather, picking up his, which also became visible and lit.

"This—is a metaphorical cigar," Wiggler said. "When I finish smoking it, it's there to be smoked again. Wherever I put it I can always find it."

"You're saying—the cigar is an *idea*?"

"You say that with condescension," Wiggler replied. "What were you expecting—advanced physics? An exotic new form of energy perhaps?"

"Well . . . yes," Clearfather answered. "I was."

"Ideas *are* energy. And *very* exotic forms at that. The whole science of physics is a case in point."

Clearfather tossed his cigar away—and found it again, semitransparent and back on the table.

The Harijans reappeared dressed in crisp white linen, carrying buckets of chilled champagne, followed by another kind of drone wearing a tuxedo and a gussied-up Blind Lemon in a red suit and snap-brimmed hat. Wiggler addressed the Harijans in the mantis language—although Clearfather caught the name Walt Whitman. He noted that Wiggler used another type of language with the drone in the tuxedo, made up of nonsense words that reminded him of Kokomo. With Calamity Jane, he supplemented speech with a private sign language—and with Blind Lemon he seemed frequently to be communicating telepathically. All happened seamlessly, and Clearfather had the suspicion that Wiggler interacted continuously and invisibly with many other presences.

A few minutes later Calamity Jane returned hand in claw with Maggie. Wiggler stood and tinged a fork against an empty champagne flute. Simultaneously the bell in the church steeple chimed.

"Thank you all for bearing with us in the matter of Wittgenstein. Wittgenstein and Walt Whitman are ever our guides when it comes to the individual and the improvisational!"

So saying, a skunk the size of the locomotive emerged from behind the depot.

"Sheeit!" Maggie squirmed. "Talk about a stink bomb!"

The giant skunk sidled up to Wiggler, who gave it an affectionate fondle and directed it to lie down beside him, which it did (and began snorting up tartlets and clam puffs). Their host then produced a cane baton, exactly like the one Bean Blossom had threatened to use on Tourmaline's rear end.

"Now, in honor of the occasion," Wiggler announced, "the Canyoneers would like to perform for you. I do hope you'll enjoy it!"

Wiggler sat down as the drone in the tux climbed the stage, extending its four articulated appendages, with the cane baton delicately pinched in a gripper. The drone tapped the cane on the podium—then through the street came a remarkable marching band. Some of the members were droids and drones of various designs—others were surgical and genetic improvisations like centaurs. The bass drum player was a silverback gorilla—but the largest visually cohesive unit was composed of a group of stocky, heavy-limbed people with large foreheads and serious expressions, all of whom looked out of place in their white collegiate uniforms with the wheelbarrow-of-fire insignia emblazoned on the chests.

"Who are those—people?" whispered the Marshal. The music was raucous.

"For-git the people . . . what about them other . . . things!" Maggie replied.

"They're Neanderthals!" Wiggler answered over the din. "This song is called 'Tusk'—originally done by Fleetwood Mac with the USC Trojans Marching Band!"

Once assembled on stage, the ensemble battled their way through "Greensleeves," featuring an intent but tortuous euphonium solo by a technically proficient but not very inspired grizzly bear and a genuinely lyrical bassoon contribution by a drone with a chem-cultured face. This was followed by a discordant, robotically smooth/mammalian high-energy version of the theme to the movie *Rocky*. Then the grim-browed Neanderthals powered the band home with a primal rendition of "Seventy-Six Trombones" (which had a visible geological effect on the Canyon walls).

"Bravo!" Wiggler crowed. "Bravo! Yes! Oh, bravo!"

The three pilgrim fugitives sat openmouthed, not knowing what to think, let alone say. At last Clearfather managed a clap. It was more a pat than true applause but it echoed in the stillness through the caves and across the pools—and the looks on the faces of the band were touching. The Neanderthals beamed. Electrostatic auras bloomed around the drones. The satyrs primped—primates raised their instruments—even the pedantic bear on the euphonium—all glowed with pride. Then the church bell rang again and from the far end of town there appeared an elegant black carriage with the wheelbarrow-of-fire emblem on the side. It was pulled by a single white horse and driven by a Harijan in a black suit with a white boutonnière.

Wiggler got up from the table and took the stage, seating himself at the grand piano. The carriage stopped. The Harijan driver hopped down and opened the door, and from the vehicle there stepped a huge-chested male baboon with rainbow colorations in his face. He was dressed in a sumptuous black suit of Italian-tailored silk, with a white ruffled shirt and a blazing red carnation that matched the color of the wheelbarrow fire, and he carried a cello and a bow. The band all pulled back their seats so that the baboon's chair became the center of attention on stage. No one made a sound—not even the Neanderthals. Wiggler nodded to the baboon, who sat down gravely and checked that the cello was in tune.

"Yo-Yo and I are going to perform the "Allegro, ma non tanto" from Beethoven's Sonata in A Major, opus sixty-nine," Wiggler announced.

An exquisite, muscular music commenced. All of the faces—whether gel-mold, veranium, or furry—went under a spell. Even the Marshal was moved.

When the piece was finished, all three of the visitors applauded. Wiggler rose and bowed to Yo-Yo. Then he held up his hands for quiet.

"Thank you! Thank you. What a pleasure to play with such a magnificent artist as Yo-Yo! But with respect to my talented colleague—and to my own humble abilities—there are many who are capable of Beethoven. There are few who can really play the blues. And no one is its master. Except our own Blind Lemon. Come on up, Mr. Jones, and do it to us!"

The old black biomechanoid rose, his Foster Grant wraparounds shining. With a stooped, hemorrhoidal shuffle, he was helped to the stage by the Neanderthal who played the triangle and the piccolo-playing drone (who looked like an enlarged version of its instrument). The old man first picked up the cheap wooden guitar he'd been carrying earlier and played Robert Johnson's "Me and the Devil Blues"—singing in a moaning growl that struck Clearfather as what Walt Whitman would've sounded like if he had a voice. Then, with the help of a Neanderthal woman, he exchanged the acoustic for a Stratocaster that didn't appear to be plugged into anything but was nevertheless amplified—and a steel slide—and Wiggler joined him in a blues that oscillated between the clean, note-by-note picking of T-Bone Walker and the gritty South Chicago slidework of Muddy Waters.

> Seen my shadow in the river,
> My reflection in the rain,
> Climbed the mountain in the darkness,
> Survived the fire's pain.
>
> I went up in the whirlwind
> And it was there that I did learn,
> The hidden may be seeking
> And the missing may return.

The hairs on the Marshal's neck were agitated, like filings around a magnet. Maggie's watery blue eyes dilated. Wiggler drummed the ivories as Blind Lemon worked the slide. At last the music seemed to move on like a windstorm of leaves. A polymer drone with a crystalline face led the old man down off the stage. Wiggler followed, shining with perspiration.

The Harijan waiters began utilizing their auxiliary limbs in the pouring and passing of the flutes of champagne to all assembled, including Walt Whitman, who—like Mr. Meese—was provided with a long straw.

"Fellow Canyonians!" cried Wiggler when everyone had a glass. "A toast! To the return of my son Elroy! And to his two brave friends! May they always be with us!"

"Hear! Hear!" the Neanderthals bellowed, swilling and foaming.

But Clearfather didn't hear them for he'd fainted—his face falling into the lemon curd.

CHAPTER 9

Drunk as a Skunk

"Shit!" cried the Marshal. "Are you really his—? He's your—"

"Hee soo doan look good," Maggie said.

"Damn it!" Wiggler groaned. "He's in free fall! Come on, we'll take him up to the hotel. I don't want to bring him to the lab if I can help it. Can you hear me?" he called to Clearfather, wiping the lemon curd from his face.

"ᴛʜᴇ ᴍᴏʀᴇ ꜰɪꜱʜ ᴀ ꜰʟᴀᴍɪɴɢᴏ ᴇᴀᴛꜱ, ᴛʜᴇ ᴘɪɴᴋᴇʀ ɪᴛ ɢᴇᴛꜱ," Clearfather struggled to say. He saw Kokomo's face . . . and the three Chinese men . . . then the whirlwind took him away.

"What did you hear, Marshal?" Wiggler asked, sliding his arms under Clearfather's shoulders.

"Yama, King of the Dead—something about the mirror he uses to read your life."

"I dint hear that."

"Tutti Frutti!" Wiggler called to the congregation on stage. "Aw rootie."

Instantly the festive mood died and the assembled multitude

began exiting the stage in single file with Walt Whitman waddling along in the rear. Blind Lemon sat tight at the table while the two Harijans took charge of Calamity Jane.

"You're his . . . father?" the Marshal said, still gasping. "He thought he had family here. You shouldn't have just blurted it out like that. Your timing—"

"Who are you to tell me how to welcome my son? I was excited, all right? I was just going to have a toast and then I got carried away. You don't realize how *important* he is!"

"You were showing off! That's what it was!" the Marshal chided as they staggered across the street, supporting Clearfather between them, Maggie following.

"At least I'm not hiding from my son on an island!"

"You're hiding from everyone in a canyon! With a whole zoo of weird pets!"

"I'm not hiding—and they're not pets. They're family! I care for them all!"

"Well, look what your caring's done," the Marshal grumped as they hauled Clearfather up the stairs of the Red Cloud Hotel, which was now plush with Oriental carpets, brass fixtures, and polished oak.

"This place smelled like batshit and all the windows were broken. How did you clean it up so fast?"

"It's complicated," Wiggler answered.

"I LOVE TO GO SWIMMEN WITH BOWLEGGED WIMMEN . . . ," Clearfather lolled.

"What did you hear then?" Wiggler asked.

"A Latin thing . . . Kwem colorem habit . . ."

"Quem colorem habet sapientia. That's Saint Augustine."

"Whot's wrong with 'im?" Maggie asked, squeezing past to open the door that Wiggler pointed to.

"He's had a system crash."

"Sheet. That happins to me all tha time."

"I don't think that's what Mr. Big means," the Marshal said. "What's really going on, Wiggler? I don't want you hurting our friend. He's been through enough."

"I couldn't agree more, Marshal." Wiggler sighed as they laid Clearfather into a feather bed in the Lodema Room. "And I know too well what he's been through. He's my greatest creation."

"Creation? You mean . . . he's an . . . experiment?"

"As are we all, Marshal, as are we all."

"He's a creetchur—or a machine?"

"A Creature-Machine is an apt description for many organisms—but what you mean by a creature and a machine and what I mean by them—"

"Oh, get off it!" snapped the Marshal. "We know you're real smart. We got that. But you called him your son. Children aren't science projects. What's the story?"

"Krishna says, 'Strong men know not despair, Arjuna, for this wins neither heaven nor earth,'" Wiggler shouted, pummeling Clearfather. "Pull yourself together!"

The Marshal whipped out the Heckler & Koch and pointed it at their host. "Leave him alone. You've done enough damage."

"Unless I miss my guest, Marshal, you could no more harm me than I could harm him," Wiggler said coolly.

"You have harmed him."

"Then shoot. Or is that just a metaphorical gun?"

"Lissen up!" Maggie yelled. "Yoo two wanna have a pissin' contest, yoo doo it right. Meenwile, hee's sick big time, an' all yer ceegars an' guns ain't helpin'!"

"Well said, Ms. Kane." Wiggler grimaced. "He needs Blind Lemon."

"That old black man? Who's not a man?"

"Never underestimate the power of the blues, Marshal."

"But . . . didn't you make him . . . too?"

"I initiated him. But he is his own creation."

"How can that be if you invented him?"

"We have all been 'invented.' But what he knows can't be taught."

"Hee's coming nowa!" Maggie called, looking out the window. "That big skunk's leadin' 'im! Yoo ain't gonna let that stink bomb in heer?"

"Walt has the run of the Canyon. Wittgenstein's another matter. Would you please go help Lemon up the stairs, Ms. Kane?"

Maggie surprisingly did as she was asked without comment—although by the time she returned, leading Blind Lemon, who had his acoustic guitar slung over his shoulder, she was fired up.

"This ol' thing gooosed mee! Grabbed mee right up my crack!"

"Anna fine crack, too!" Blind Lemon cackled. "Heee-heee."

"Yoo bline ol' wrinkly robot!"

"Booty in the hand of the beholder, lil girl. Heee-heee."

"Come," said Wiggler. "We'll leave Lemon to his work."

Their bald host led them out the door and down the stairs. The French glass doors were open to accommodate Walt Whitman, who took up most of the lobby, his bushy tail flowing into the parlor—which the Marshal noticed had deteriorated since their arrival. The paint was worn and cracked in places, and the floral wallpaper had started to peel. Upstairs, they could hear Lemon's guitar, harsh and gentle—his voice simultaneously tired and young. The Marshal looked more befuddled than before.

"Blind Lemon's just going to *sing* to him?"

"Yes. But there's no 'just' about that."

"With all your technology and medicines—and God knows what else?"

"There are more things in heaven and earth than can be accounted for by your idea of science, Marshal."

They returned to the long table in the now desolate main street, Walt Whitman shuffling after them. Yo-Yo's red carnation lay trampled on the stage. Shards of CJ's tea set glinted in the dust and the WELCOME HOME banner fluttered sadly in the breeze. The dimetrodon, having consumed all the cocktail frankfurters, decided to eat the stegosaurus and was gnawing on its leg when Walt Whitman ate them both. Wiggler collapsed dejectedly in a chair, lit up a metaphorical cigar, and wrenched a bottle of champagne out of an ice bucket. Maggie accepted one, too.

"Soa whass yer boy El-roy sup-posed to bee?"

"A paraclete." Wiggler sighed, blowing smoke rings of little winged creatures.

"Sheet. Noa wondur hee's fucked up! Yoo got big skunks and lil sloths—whatchyoo want with a big parakeet."

"A paraclete! A spiritual guide. A holy spirit."

"You're not serious!" the Marshal choked. "You mean . . . like an angel?"

"More powerful."

"Damn!" said Maggie. "Yoo try to make some Jesus? Hee died on the cross!"

"A cross is just a plus sign that's been stretched," Wiggler replied. "The Upanishads say, 'Who knows God becomes God.'"

"But that doesn't mean you can *make* a God," the Marshal lamented. "You'd have to be God . . . or at least *a* god."

Wiggler blew a large smoke ring halo that to the Marshal's frustration drifted over his head and remained for several minutes, rotating like a hula hoop.

"Even John von Neumann long ago recognized that it's possible for a machine to make another machine more elaborate than itself once it breaks through the complexity barrier. This is the story of life . . . the emergence of Something from Nothing."

"Whatchyoo got in them cee-gars?" Maggie smirked.

"The problem," said Wiggler, refusing to be baited, "is that you think of *making* as in manufacturing. I think of it as creating dynamic relationships—partnerships. If you set out to make something greater than yourself, you become greater, even if you fail for lack of skill. If you set out to make something less than yourself—because of a lack of courage or vision—you diminish."

"So, what is Clearfather . . . or Elroy? A robot? Don't you think he's got a right to know?"

"He's a psychepoid . . . a rekindled soul . . . in a body that's almost fully organic." Wiggler sighed. "But sustaining, regenerative. I'll tell you more when he recovers. It's not right for you to be told first."

"How could you name a messianic figure Elroy?"

"I was going to name him Ganesh, the much-loved elephant-headed Hindu god—the son whom Shiva murdered in a rage of temper and could only bring back to life by giving him the head of the first thing he saw."

"What made you change your mind?"

"You probably don't remember that old Hanna-Barbera cartoon *The Jetsons* . . . but George Jetson's son was named Elroy. 'His boy El-roy.' You probably would've chosen something biblical—like Elohim."

"Something that isn't silly anyway," the Marshal retorted.

"E-lie-ja . . . El-o-heem . . . El-roy—whass the diff? Hee bit his own dick off an' now hee's sick. Whatever yoo had in mind—it ain't good enuff."

"You speak the truth, Ms. Kane. The raw, guttural, unmistakable Truth."

"Yoo can't jest say somethin' nice—or simple—can yoo?"

Wiggler reached for another bottle of champagne and popped the cork. Except for becoming more disconsolate, he showed no visible effects of the three bottles of champagne he ended up consuming, although the Marshal noticed that the architecture of the town underwent many subtle and not-so-subtle transformations, including the appearance of a couple of new buildings and the disappearance or collapse of others. Wiggler paid no mind to these changes and offered no explanation. Walt Whitman, who'd been sucking on his own bottle through a straw, curled up beside his master and started snoring, occasionally twitching as if in a dream. Eventually the drone conductor reappeared, having exchanged his tuxedo for a white robe with the wheelbarrow-of-fire logo.

"Doo lang doo lang doo lang," Wiggler said—and the device made its way to the hotel, returning with an exhausted-looking Blind Lemon shuffling along behind.

"Well done," Wiggler said gratefully—then to the drone—"Shoo bop shoo bop."

The drone crossed to the saloon and returned with a bottle of whiskey and a glass and poured the bluesman a snort.

"He drinks whiskey?" the Marshal asked.

"Ain't nothin' wrong with a nip," Lemon wheezed.

"Nip my ass!" Maggie yawned. "Probbly drinks like a fish!"

"Actually, freshwater fish hardly drink at all," Wiggler remarked. "It's the marine bony fishes—"

"Mister—yoo jest can't leave it alone, can yoo? Noa wondur yoo down heer in this can-yen makin' yer own playmates!"

Wiggler's face flushed with anger for a moment and the Marshal braced himself—but instead the bald man laughed and said, "Ms. Kane, you really do have a gift—a rare refreshing gift. Go along to your rooms and rest now—they're laid out in the hotel. Your friend is sleeping. We'll talk more at dinner."

The Marshal escorted Maggie back to the hotel, leaving Wiggler blowing smoke rings with Blind Lemon and Walt Whitman. Maggie nodded off to her bed, too drowsy to fuss. The Marshal looked in on Clearfather, who was, as Wiggler had said, asleep in his room. The lines on his face had relaxed, and he looked like a child again. Maybe the bad dreams are behind him, the Marshal thought—but he couldn't bring himself to believe it. He went into his own room and pulled off his boots.

It occurred to him that he'd never actually slept in an old western hotel room before. He was meant to in *Star City*. In fact, there was going to be a big episode when he leaves the wife he no longer loves (not knowing she's really an alien) and moves into the hotel. He lay back on the big four-poster bed and closed his eyes, thinking of the episodes that might've been. But he bolted awake and almost fell off the bed because he suddenly remembered what Wiggler had said in his toast. "May they *always* be with us!"

As in *forever*.

CHAPTER 10

Wheels Within Wheels

Clearfather awoke to hear the church bell echoing. He was on the bed in the white and airy Lodema Room of the Red Cloud Hotel, and yet he could see that the room wasn't made of bricks and lumber. The apparent solidity was due to the sustained intersection of countless whirlwinds of light. His own body shared the radiance. Then he realized that he hadn't woken up because of the bell. The bell had awakened because of him.

Maybe I am Home, he thought, as the plaster and pressed metal stabilized. All the faces and images came deluging back, curiously normal in his mind . . . mutant but mundane. But how can Wiggler be my *father*? What about my mother? What about Uncle Waldo and Aunt Vivian? What did this have to do with Hosanna Freed? And how can my name be Elroy? Surely I would've remembered *that,* he thought.

He recalled Wiggler's toast and the beaming Neanderthals—the lemon curd. What had happened after that he couldn't say. It was embarrassing, after so wanting to be welcomed and celebrated—to faint. Now he needed to find out how much time had passed and what had happened to his friends.

He thought of what Dr. Tadd had said about the possible connection between Lloyd Meadhorn Sitturd and Ronwell Seward/Stinky Wiggler. What if Seward's true identity was Lloyd Meadhorn Sitturd? Was that what Dr. Tadd had been hinting at? He'd be well over two hundred years old—though for someone of such legendary inventiveness—who knew what was possible? But why would he be rooting about in a forgotten canyon in an obscure state like South Dakota? And how did Parousia Head fit in? Is she my mother? Clearfather wondered. Is she in hiding, waiting for the right moment to reveal herself? And Kokomo? Perhaps no force could bring her back—but to know . to understand . . .

One thing seemed clear. If I *am* home, he thought . . . and I'm *welcome* . . . then I'm welcome to roam around.

He felt for the little white ball in his pocket. He'd been careful to transfer it from his IMAGINE-NATION togs to the Nehru suit. Maybe soon he'd find out its meaning. He tiptoed over the creaking floor. The hall was empty but for a vase like the kind that had housed the Man of Steel's first wife. Next door Maggie lay fully clothed on the bed, her face buried in a pillow. She was breathing deeply and didn't seem in any way molested so he closed the door. Across the hall it looked as if the Marshal had lain down and then left suddenly, for the bed was rumpled and the suit jacket that Wiggler had provided was on the floor beside a chair. Clearfather headed downstairs. A funky odor lingered in the air that made him think of Walt Whitman.

The table and stage were gone, the street vacant. The sky was darker but not dark, although he saw that the Canyon walls were flocked with phosphorescent mosses. They made complex patterns like maps and faces among the eroded columns. He figured that the watchful eyes he'd sensed before were still present and set out in the opposite direction from the way they'd gone earlier.

Passing the creosote-smelling mill house, he heard a sound. It reminded him of the rats in the abandoned honky-tonk in Texas. In the gloom inside he could just make out the steam engines that had once powered the concentration tables and the direct-current dynamos that had provided electricity for the mine. He heard the sound again behind the furnace stamps and felt an instinctive sense of revulsion and fear.

When they'd come back for the tea party, the town had looked freshly painted and repaired. Now certain buildings, like the dry goods store, had deteriorated again. The schoolhouse was back to being a single room. There was a billiard hall and a warped-floor duckpin bowling alley, but the windows had turned to sand. It was as if the town couldn't maintain belief in itself. He could feel eyes up in the caves watching him but was more curious about what was happening at ground level. He sensed he was being followed.

He wandered through a junkyard of shattered greenhouses and rusted mobile homes, solar panels, transformers, and mounds of optical fibers. For a genius who was supposedly amazingly rich, Wiggler tolerated a lot of mess. Where did he actually live? Clearfather wondered. Then he spied a shadow sliding over an old camper shell.

"All right, come out," he called. But nothing moved. He waited, but all was silent. He kept exploring.

Another quarry pit opened up before him, filled with prehistoric animal bones—mastodons, cave bears, and enormous elk—but more unexpectedly, an ornate sandblasted roller coaster. It was just like the antique contraption he'd seen in the sepia postcard back in Dustdevil. The gimcracked swirls and filigrees had faded. The side of the rail scaffolding that remained was crusted in broken lantern globes, like barnacles or the sucker cups of an octopus, but the engineering was the same—and it looked like the machine was still functional.

The rails disappeared into the sandstone face of the cliff, from which a cool smell of damp rock and the sound of machinery emanated. The noise grew louder—a rhythmic whoosh and clang—and ping. He followed the rails down into the earth. The track led into a cave system filled with crystalline hairs of white zinc silicate. Many of the rocks gave off their own light, great chunks of fire opal and glimmering prisms of blood crystal jutting out of the petrified skeletons of plesiosaurs. But even more remarkable was the light from the ceiling, which smeared like the Milky Way—the result of innumerable threads of tiny glowworms clinging to the rock.

The cave mouth opened into a vast subterranean cathedral containing an amusement park. Over the great entryway of granite was the name LABYRINTHIA, spelled out in the same phosphorescent moss he'd seen on the Canyon walls. It was the name Dr. Tadd had mentioned—Sitturd's lost estate in South Dakota.

Where above was dust and wreckage, here there was splendor that daunted perception—a glorious kinetic playground inhabited by hydraulic marionettes, steam-driven dancing girls, stilt-legged automatons with birdcages on their shoulders—or gumball machines and the torsos of insanely detailed Dutch dollhouses.

The subjects of this glittering kingdom acknowledged him with brisk Victorian formality and then went on about their clicking and whirring business. There was a miniature Ferris wheel fabricated out of diamonds, guarded by armor-suited soldiers with the heads of stuffed deer. Shining titanium and veranium slides intermingled with marble fountains full of ingenious mechanical fish and luxuriant emerald turtles. An attraction called Anxiety—a blacklight centrifugal cylinder—whirled beside a gravity ride called Paranoia—leading to the midway—filled with masterpieces—from the paintings of Brueghel and Rembrandt to Van Gogh and Picasso. Echoing through the chamber was a kind of calliope music.

His eyes picked out a shadow among the baroque robots. It vanished between two large wicker cages in the shape of George Washington and Abraham Lincoln, which were filled with hundreds of tiny zebra finches. Was it the person or creature following him? Something about the movement made him think not. It was too confident—too knowing. Whatever or whoever was still behind him seemed to hesitate. He heard the off-putting sound again but now it was receding—as if the presence of the other figure had frightened it. The deeper he went into this maze of bright machinery, the darker he felt the way was growing. His curiosity was greater than his fear but he was not at ease. Then he caught a definite glimpse of the figure in front of him and saw that it was Wiggler—striding determinedly. Clearfather slipped behind.

A catwalk took him through a passage lit by panels made of the swim bladders of some sea creature. There was a bubbling sound and whiffs of sulfur and musk. In the distance, he saw that Wiggler had arrived at the "Grotto of Eros," which featured canoes in the shape of penises, advancing on a sunken gear chain into a cave decorated to look like a vagina. The fleshy pink tones and temperfoam wrinkles had the tacky aura of an old haunted house. Oblivious to his presence, Wiggler climbed into one of the boats. Clearfather waited a minute before following.

Inside the tunnel, the walls were lit with lurid cabaret globes revealing naked bodies writhing in the rocks. Smoldering red arc lights shone over the water on the other side. From chains anchored in the ceiling dangled huge crystal hourglasses in the shape of men and women having sex. They were filled with red and black sand and set into gleaming brass brackets that allowed them to rotate when the weight of the sand had shifted—so that a man atop a woman appeared to empty himself of colored sand, becoming almost invisible as she gained color—only to rotate beneath her—the glass couples endlessly exchanging color and position.

The canoe reached a small stone island and paused at a pier. Wiggler was nowhere to be seen. Torches glowed. On an inner island across ten feet of water was a carousel, shimmering in a golden-green mist rising from the lagoon. The perimeter frame of the carousel took the shape of a golden snake swallowing its own tail—and on the oval panels set into the crown canopy were erotic paintings in lush Gauguin and Rousseau colors.

On the platform of the mechanical whirlwind danced animals seemingly made of moist, sculpted light: black horses, white tigers, slender unicorns, monstrous roosters, insane sphinxes, swans, dromedaries, goats, bulls, rams, reindeer, tortoises, hares. Astride each of the creatures was a naked woman. Every race was represented and all the bodies appeared real, although in a trance. Up and down the animals rose on their golden pumping pistons, undulating in a ceremonial cyclone around and around. Clearfather watched, hypnotized. At the center of the carousel, naked among the tangle of monsters and machinery—stood Wiggler.

Clearfather fled back to the pier, back to the canoe, back to the light. Once off the boat he ran down the midway, dodging between the machine-men and clockwork chorus girls, back up the track to the quarry pit. It was getting dark now, and the Canyon walls glowed —the sounds of the underground amusement park fading out behind him. He was positive he'd retraced his steps but instead of the trailer-park junkyard he came to a section of pillars, a cross between giant termite mounds and human effigies—like sand-castle men. Or women. Their features were grotesque but there was about their bulk and alignment a definite attitude of barricade. He stepped cautiously between them. The river flowed alongside. In the distance he saw a small village of tepees and sandstone bunkers. Lights were on in the structures, although fires burned outside and shadows moved in and out of them. He crept nearer, edging up against the cliff face—then darting between the boulders that dotted the riverbed. When he drew close enough, he saw that the inhabitants were deformed—like radiation victims—able to move about via miniature all-terrain wheelchairs. Others slithered in the sand like worms. There was another creature—walking erect but gruesomely misshapen—a composite mutant he was glad that he couldn't see clearly. He fled back the way he came.

This time, running the other way, he still didn't find the debris he'd passed earlier—but at last he saw the lights of the town, the Red Cloud Hotel shining. Then he saw Calamity Jane, the down-sized giant sloth. Despite her bulk, Clearfather could see in her gestures and demeanor—a little girl. Had she been the one following him? It was hard to tell now because the light was failing, but it was clear that she was playing beside a section of cliff that gave off a peculiar sheen—different from the luminous moss he'd seen. She made strange noises, quivering with excitement—and then she did something he hadn't anticipated. She disappeared—or a part of her did. She drew back out of the rock, wiggling and even more rambunctious than before—and then inserted something, which the wall seemed to accept and engulf. Then the sloth pulled back, dancing with enjoyment. She straggled off toward the town. Moments later he did the same. On the steps of the hotel Clearfather heard a mournful clang from down the street, and when he reached the sheriff's office the sound grew louder.

CHAPTER 11

The Entities

The Marshal couldn't hide his relief that it was Clearfather who found him locked in the jail, although he was reluctant to provide much of an explanation of how he'd gotten there—other than to say that he'd gotten up and seen Wiggler disappear into a coffin in the funeral parlor. Then when he went exploring, he'd heard "mighty peculiar" sounds down the other end of town—and in going to investigate he'd discovered the local lawman's office, which he was surprised to find was just like what his was going to look like on *Star City*. One thing led to another. Then he couldn't get out.

On top of everything else he was coping with, this surprised Clearfather, because the door to the jail cell simply opened at his touch—despite the Marshal's protestations that it had been locked solid. In any case, Clearfather led the old-timer back to the hotel without either of them saying what he'd learned in the other's absence.

They found Maggie soaking in a bath, with two more steaming tubs waiting for them and a note from Wiggler inviting them to dinner along with fresh white robes with the wheelbarrow-of-fire logo and a pair of deerskin moccasins in each of their sizes. Clearfather was pleased that the robes contained pockets, as he refused to leave the tiny ivory ball behind.

By the time they were finished dressing it was truly dark outside and antique lanterns had come on down the street. The church bell chimed and the carriage that had carried Yo-Yo arrived, driven by a Harijan dressed as a Victorian-era footman.

Up in the caves in the Canyon walls, Neanderthal fires burned and between the ledges, the swirling patterns of luminous moss shone. The carriage passed the radio shack they'd seen earlier, only now it was painted and filled with light and sound—the needle of the transmitter tower gleaming silver, "Soul Limbo" by Booker T. and the MG's throbbing out between the palisades.

The mystery of where Wiggler lived was resolved spectacularly when the Canyon wound around to a palatial residence carved into the rocks like an ancient Middle Eastern temple—only in the shape of the American White House. It was lit with an honor guard of Neanderthals and Harijans beneath a gigantic flag like the one they'd seen before, showing a skunk and the words LOCO FOCO—MAKE A STINK.

Wiggler was on the stairs, wearing a Singapore linen suit that changed color and pattern as he moved. "Greetings, my friends." He smiled as they stepped from the carriage. "All refreshed, are we?"

"How about you?" Clearfather asked, thinking of the carousel.

"Absolutely." Wiggler beamed and gestured for them to follow him.

Inside the mansion built into the rocks they found an environment that made Maggie's eyes glaze over and the Marshal whistle through his nose. Wiggler was a collector of oddities and treasures—from nineteenth- and early twentieth-century American circus memorabilia to blues and rock-and-roll artifacts, with hefty doses of astronautica, Hollywood nostalgia, Renaissance masterpieces, and surely the most complete presentation of apparently taxidermized heads of the U.S. presidents.

"My God," gasped the Marshal. "They look so real!"

Against one wall was Jelly Roll Morton's piano. Mounted on another, the boxing gloves that the then–Cassius Clay had used to knock out Sonny Liston. At last Wiggler ushered them into a wood-paneled dining room where the giant skunk Walt Whitman was asleep on a Persian rug and Blind Lemon was already seated at a long table of American walnut.

"Calamity Jane will not be joining us tonight—perhaps to your relief. She's gotten into a bit of trouble again—and I confess I'm disheartened. Fancy parenting a kleptomaniac sloth!"

Wiggler shook his head and gestured for them to sit down. Clearfather thought back to the section of wall the sloth had seemed to vanish into.

"You look peeved, Marshal. Things not to your satisfaction at the hotel?"

"You know very well what happened to me, Wiggler," the Marshal grumbled. "I bet you've got spies and cameras all over the joint."

"His name's not Wiggler," Clearfather said quietly.

"Marshal, if I know what's happening on my Island, as it were, you can hardly blame me. I just assumed you were reenacting one of the key moments in your father's saga. You'll note that no tear gas or SWAT team was supplied."

"Whot happened?" Maggie wondered.

"Hah," Wiggler grinned. "Our friendly lawman locked himself inside the town pokey. Isn't that one of life's most cunning and persistent metaphors? Locking ourselves inside our own jails!"

"It was *your* jail," the Marshal responded. "And I'm thinking that maybe I'm still in it. You made a very odd remark at teatime. Several odd remarks."

"Nonsense." Wiggler smiled as the Harijans entered carrying silver platters of quail, pheasant, turkey, venison, buffalo, trout, and rabbit, along with Indian corn, runner beans, black-eyed peas, golden potatoes, butternut squash—and piles of wild nuts and berries (followed later by six different kinds of fruit pie, mountain goat cheese, and homemade vanilla bean ice cream).

For a while the only sounds in the room were chewing and swallowing, as no one knew what to say. Blind Lemon hoed into the repast with gusto—which drew Maggie's attention.

"Hee eats, too?"

Blind Lemon promptly farted. "Do los more 'an 'at."

"Settle, Lemon," said Wiggler. "I apologize for Ms. Kane. She's young and ignorant—but she has a good heart."

"Iggno-rant?" Maggie cried, crushing a bite of quail.

"Careful, my dear. You don't want to choke on a bone. In answer to your question, Blind Lemon is in your terms fully human. His body is organic, just as yours is—although of superior quality and durability. It's in the neurological and psychagogic realms that the really significant differences arise."

Maggie was about to make another insulting remark and perhaps even heave a biscuit—when the Marshal sat up in his chair.

"What do you mean, his name's not Wiggler? Who is he, then?"

"*That* was a delayed reaction," Wiggler commented.

"He's really Lloyd Meadhorn Sitturd, the neglected nineteenth-century American genius," Clearfather answered.

"Who?" gasped the Marshal. "I've never heard of him."

"That's because he's neglected."

"I have worn many faces and names," their host nodded.

"Wait a minute!" snapped the Marshal. "Nineteenth century? That makes him—"

"Well preserved?" Wiggler smiled, inspecting a platter of prairie pigeons stuffed with wild rice.

"I think," said Clearfather, "that it's time you tell me—us—the whole story."

"The *whole* story? I'm flattered you think I know," said Wiggler, serving himself some venison. "Well, as there's no lemon curd for you to fall into, perhaps it will be all right."

"Very funny."

"Accidents will happen in the most chemically balanced families. But enough. I am Lloyd Meadhorn Sitturd—or was. But everyone has been someone else. If we're lucky, we get to be many people. In my case, I was lucky enough to get a glimpse of what I was—and what we are—when I was taken up in a tornado as a boy."

"Yoo werr?" Maggie gawked.

"So it appeared. But it was the Vortex—a dimensional passageway that opened for me a new vision."

"Sheet, mister. Yoo really are on drugs."

"I was seeking communion with my twin sister, who died at birth. She's my ghost, Marshal. But I discovered something more. *The presence of other life-forms.*"

"Aliens?" wheezed the Marshal, spilling butternut squash in his lap. "You found aliens inside a tornado?"

"As I said, it wasn't a tornado. It was a tunnel. That led to a field. A psychic energy field that surrounds and informs us—which makes us possible."

"Like a cornfield?" Maggie asked.

"No," Wiggler sighed. "I mean a field in the sense of physics. A nonmaterial region of self-organizing influence."

"Oh."

"This field is an ecosystem that both supports and is sustained by myriad beings, who have their own networks and interrelationships."

"You're talking creatures?" the Marshal queried.

"They are not creatures in a biological, organic sense. They have no physical form and are both discontinuous and ubiquitous. Yet they have immense physical effect in the dimension of our being."

"Like ghosts? Ghosts are real?"

"That ghosts, souls, spirits are the *primary* reality—is a very old belief. What I experienced is the literal truth of this intuition," said their host. "There's no need to look to other planets. These beings are right here—and have been here—inside us all the time. They *are* us."

"Wait a minute—" said Clearfather and the Marshal in unison.

"You are not who you think you are," Wiggler intoned, spearing a runner bean. "Inside your cells right now are microscopic creatures called mitochondria, tenanting your body. They have their own DNA and RNA. They are not 'you'—and yet without them you couldn't function. You are their environment, their world. We've known this is true on the biophysical level for a very long time. But the same is also true in the realms of the mind and the spirit."

"Are you saying ideas are alive?" the Marshal asked.

"Sort of . . . yes," Wiggler replied. "Our minds are inhabited and defined by beings, just as we inhabit and give expression to larger and more complex psychic Entities."

"Excuse me," Clearfather interrupted. "What does this have to do with me?"

"It has everything to do with all of us," Wiggler replied. "I can't even begin to explain the War without speaking about the Entities."

"What war?" the Marshal asked. "The Holy War?"

"No, Marshal. A much greater conflict. A secret war. The struggle for the destiny of America, Western civilization, and indeed the human species."

"Oh."

"If I may continue," Wiggler said, ravaging a turkey leg. "We are composed via hierarchical levels of organization. From the quantum level to the molecular, cellular, et cetera. Each level depends on the levels below it but is free from direct awareness. You're listening to me now because you aren't consciously digesting your food or making your heart pump—or, for that matter, firing your nervous system. *You* are the continuous *result* of these 'systems' functioning harmoniously and yet independently of what you call 'you.' But just as we are insulated from these lower levels—we are also sealed off from those above. What happened to me is that I got a peek both up and down the stairs."

"What did you see?"

"Entities existing in vortices that penetrate and permeate the world. They found special expression in certain creatures—of which humankind was the most hospitable."

"So . . . they're like diseases . . . viruses?"

"Some are," Wiggler confirmed. "But those are minor forms. Potent and persistent—but minor. I'm speaking of more complex Entities that have developed symbiotic relationships with us. Language, symbolism, reasoning . . . these have colonized the brain of the human more completely than any other species—and have come to distinguish our species. From these relationships still larger and more complex creatures have arisen . . . mind, individuality, societies, culture, civilization."

"Why did you call me Elroy?" Clearfather blurted.

"I'll get to that," Wiggler insisted. "Patience."

Maggie flicked a black-eyed pea at Blind Lemon, who'd dozed off in his chair.

"In the beginning was the Word," said the Marshal, serving himself some buffalo.

"Yes!" said Wiggler. "The runes that Odin hanged himself to learn . . . the word made flesh. Magic, religion, science, poetry, music—all these supposedly human activities are collaborative mutations arising out of the symbiosis of the Entities and us!"

"So who are we at war with? These Entities?" the Marshal asked.

Blind Lemon came awake in his chair, produced a small gold pocketwatch from his coat, and held it up to his ear. "You'll be excusin' me. Iss time."

"That's fine, Lemon," Wiggler said, relaxing again. "Did you enjoy the meal?"

"Oh, yeah," the old black man smiled, rising with Ray Charles dignity. "Be comin' back for pie later."

"Of course." Wiggler smiled and spoke in the mantis language to the Harijans, who entered to lead the bluesman away.

"Howa cum yoo so polite with him?" Maggie snorted.

"Because Blind Lemon is a Lord of Life. If I took too much credit earlier, I apologize. As with your friend here," he said, indicating Clearfather. "I merely opened the window. They are the wind."

"I want to know who I really am—and why I'm here," Clearfather said.

"And I want to know who we're at war with," said the Marshal.

"An' I wanna knoa where tha bathrooom is," Maggie burped.

"Well," said Wiggler, rising. "Let us pause in our gustation . . . and ruminate over dark and difficult questions. Come. We'll adjourn to the Thinking Parlor, where I will tell you the tale of the Psyche War . . . and of your friend here. The Last Hope."

PART 6

Spiritcruiser

And we, when all is said and done
Depend on creatures we have made.
—Johann Wolfgang von Goethe,
Faust, Part Two

CHAPTER I

Apparatus

The Thinking Parlor was bare except for the most comfortable chairs the visitors had ever experienced. Over the course of the conversation that followed, the walls came alive with various images. Heads and faces eased through the partitions as if through water—sometimes in sync with something Wiggler said—other times as if part of a dream the room was having.

"All right," said the Marshal when they were seated in the chairs, which also poured drinks. "A quick roundup. First, you're more than two hundred years old."

"True," said Wiggler.

"Second, you were taken up in a tornado when you were a child. But it wasn't a tornado—it was a doorway to another dimension—where you discovered that ideas aren't something human beings have, they're part of what we are."

"Well said."

"Language and mathematics and such aren't things we invented —in a sense they invented us, as in made us different from the other animals."

"Exactement!"

"But we . . . in turn make up other . . . organisms . . . like societies . . . corporations . . . ?"

"We give them definition—but they are not our creations," Wiggler confirmed. "These Entities in turn fit into higher levels of organization and being, which are beyond our comprehension."

"Okay," said the Marshal. "Now, would I be right in thinking that this 'war' you were speaking of has to do with these other levels of being?"

"Yes. That is the true nature of the conflict, although many human elements have been involved for a very long time."

"And this war . . . also has something to do with Clearfather—or Elroy, as you called him. Is he your real son?"

"I have never had a conversation in which the word *real* was used that I didn't find frustrating—so let's put the second question aside," Wiggler replied. "As to the War . . . I saw great wonders in the Vortex but out on the periphery—on the very edge of my ability to perceive—I glimpsed a shadow."

"A monstur?" Maggie asked, sitting up straight.

"In the sense of an omen—a warning—yes."

"Something Evil?" the Marshal asked.

"It would not seem Evil to itself—it is beyond such categories—but to me—to us—I feel it so. My name for it is APPARATUS, although it has no name. It's psychopathological, arising out of darknesses and divisions in the levels beneath it. Its goal is to transcend itself—as in all the supporting levels of being that compose it. It has been evolving and gaining strength for untold time. When it reaches ascendancy, the point I call Dominion, a crisis will occur in our dimension of unbearable magnitude. A black hole will open in the spiritworld. All the Entities will be consumed."

"Like the end of the wurld?"

"I'm not talking about bodies piled in the streets or the death of the last little mammal in the last tree in the last rain forest, although both these things could happen. How can I explain it?"

Wiggler squirmed in his chair, which squirmed to accommodate him.

"What does APPARATUS look like?" Clearfather asked.

"It doesn't *look* like anything," groaned their host. "It can't be seen! It's multidimensional and simultaneous. We exist within it!"

"Okay," said the Marshal, now accepting a drink from his chair. "If it were a body—what would we be inside it? Nerve endings? Enzymes?"

"It's not like *any* body," Wiggler replied. "It's like an enormous insect group mind."

"Ooooh!" Maggie shuddered.

"But that, too, is wrong—for the hive needs its drones, its queen and warriors. This is like the moment when a crowd becomes a mob—intent on destroying itself. APPARATUS seeks transcendence through dissolution. It is *Psychecide*."

"Jesus." The Marshal sighed. "I thought the biggest things we had to worry about were Al-Waqi'a and the Vitessa Cultporation."

Wiggler seemed to gray out in his chair.

"Hey, wait a minute," said the Marshal. "Didn't Ronwell Seward have a hand in launching Vitessa? If you're Stinky Wiggler . . ."

Wiggler came alert and shimmied in his chair so that the chair had to change shape to compensate. "Are you ready for the really bad news?"

"Sheet," Maggie moaned. "Whot cudd bee wurse than some giant insect thing wantin' to kill itself—takin' over everthin'?"

"I am the motive force behind Vitessa," Wiggler answered. "Vitessa was my great strategy to combat APPARATUS. Vitessa acted in secret with Al-Waqi'a to conduct the so-called Holy War against the United States and its allies—knowing it would ultimately strengthen Vitessa's position. Once Vitessa's position was consolidated, Al-Waqi'a was seen to be defeated."

"But Vitessa's been trying to kill me!" Clearfather cried. "They killed Kokomo!"

Wiggler sat motionless. The room went deathly still, and the Marshal began shaking.

"Y-you can't be—serious. You meglo-m-maniac! My daughter—my beautiful daughter—died in that war! She sacrificed her life!"

"Many people died in that war," Wiggler said.

Clearfather saw the Marshal twitching—and he thought of Kokomo's cool green eyes that had soothed him when he was full of pain. The letters in his back burned. Wiggler sat calm and vulnerable. The Marshal simmered, straining to keep from boiling over.

"So—it was a conspiracy? A huge conspiracy?"

"I thought of it as an Inspiracy," Wiggler answered. "I weighed the potential damage against the potential gain and made a strategic decision."

"On behalf of the goddamn nation—and the world!" the Marshal rasped. "Who gave you the right?"

"I saw it then and see it now as a responsibility, my Great Work. And the Entities endowed me. They chose *me*. Just as they chose Spiro of Lemnos."

"Who?"

"My mentor and nemesis. The first Cycloner, the original Enigmatist. If I've sought secret answers and forbidden knowledge it has been in the service of my struggle. A struggle I was embroiled in as a child. You speak of war—I've been at war my whole life. Civilization is itself a war—of values—of darkness and illumination. I've lost companions and family. I've endured loneliness you would find unfathomable. Where others have sought the lights of history, I've clung to the shadows. I've always experimented on myself first. You think me a moral monster? I came back down out of the Whirlwind, Marshal. I could've ascended, uploaded, escaped. I came back down to keep the ladder from being pulled up—to keep the Vortex open."

In the dining room Walt Whitman rolled over in his sleep. The

Marshal looked torn between emotions too complex to name. At last he spoke.

"First thing tomorrow morning I'm leaving. I can't stay a minute longer than I have to knowing what I do now. You two are welcome to join me," he said, nodding to his companions. "But we're not here because of me. We came to help our friend find answers. You called him the last hope. Well, if you're so high and mighty, conducting this secret war of yours—let's get down to the nitty gritty."

Wiggler exhaled deeply and looked at Clearfather. "My intention was to discuss these matters in private."

"They're like family," Clearfather said. "They are family. Tell us all."

Wiggler winced but sat up. "Vitessa is no longer in my control. It hasn't been for a while now. Like my old instructor and enemy, Spiro, I found myself in combat with myself—so to speak. Contending against APPARATUS is like playing chess with an opponent who can not only take your pieces but turn them against you. In the last hundred and fifty years I have had to reinvent and sustain myself biotechnically in order to keep up the struggle. I've had to make copies of myself to keep from being trapped. At every turn my creations and strategies have turned against me or developed their own creations and campaigns. However, when in doubt, always savor your uncertainty, for in uncertainty lies Hope, and it is in this very special kind of darkness we find ourselves now. I still have one trick up my sleeve. I have changed the game from chess to poker. Not straight poker. Spiral. And I have one card left to play. You. The Ace of Strangers."

"I soo doan get yoo!" Maggie cried.

"In order to understand this at all," Wiggler answered, "I must take you back to Macropotamia, the world's first modern amusement park, which I designed in Pittsburgh in the 1870s.

"I thought I was being very ambitious at the time and I thought I had achieved a very great victory over what I then perceived to be the true forces of corruption and confusion in the modern world. I wanted to create a realm not simply of wonder and surprise—but of true enlightenment—a place not just of recreation but of re-creation—my vision of what America could be if science and art, religion and passion joined together. Well, I'd underestimated the forces aligned against me and how powerful APPARATUS already was. My dream failed. In the end I had to make a strategic retreat. But I came to see that the only solution was to become more ambitious.

"I'd made a habit of circulating throughout the park in disguise. It was a good way to find out what visitors thought and how well employees were performing. One day I overheard a little girl ask her father why Pittsburgh wasn't as clean an amusement park. I suddenly realized that my creation was a realm owned and controlled by a board of wealthy magnates—but so was Pittsburgh—and by the same magnates. The boundary was psychological, a matter of perception. Since every matter of perception is in part a matter of illusion, I saw that it was possible to redraw the boundaries to create a new kind of theme park where I would not be beholden to a band of robber barons—where everyone would be participants, sharing in the creation and maintenance of the new reality. I saw that I needed to work not on the scale of a city—but on the scale of America."

"You wanted to turn America . . . into a theme park?"

"The theme defines the park, Marshal. Just as ideas delineate the mind."

"You were trying to control—"

"Crowds are controlled! I was trying to choreograph a civilization! I thought if I could reprogram America, I would defend against APPARATUS—for it was APPARATUS that was the undoing of Spiro."

"You're insane!" the Marshal muttered.

"I am large. I contain multitudes. Give me vivisections and cathedrals! As I've tried to explain—I didn't choose this task—it chose me."

"All right . . . say we believe you. What did you do? How did you take over America?"

"I made it disappear."

"Say whot?" said Maggie, her face frozen.

"I made parts of America disappear and then replaced them with my own versions."

"Yoo meen like—cities—and states?"

"Well, in fact I have done that in a few instances. South Dakota, for example. You probably noticed that time runs slower here."

"No one can change the speed of time!" the Marshal squawked.

"Historic time, Marshal—the speed of culture. Surely the reptile gardens and chuckwagon suppers are a bit of a clue! In any case what I meant was that I substituted bits of American culture. If I can get you to believe you see one elephant where none exists, I can get you to see an entire herd. Similarly, the best place to hide an elephant is in a herd of elephants."

"So you didn't really—"

"Yes, I did! *Really*."

"You're talking about fooling people."

"Ah. You see what you just did?" Wiggler snapped. "You're employing a very sophisticated kind of software. It's called rhetoric. You used a word like *fool* that has completely negative connotations. You don't *show* or prove that what I was doing was bad—you simply *label* it as bad and think you've made your point. For the slow and the dim, that often works. You should become acquainted with the Mulrooney Corollary, which says that because you can't fool all the people all the time, you need to be very clear on which people you are trying to fool at any given time."

"So . . . the technology you're talking about is just . . . words?"

"*Just* words!" Wiggler exclaimed and the chair had to change shape to contain him. "There's no *just* or *only* about words—those *are* words! Slippery and strong—and sneaky. *You* are words, Marshal.

Words, ideas, and—dare I say it—a philosophical point of view. Software defines hardware. You need to think of yourself as a technological creation and then maybe you'll begin to appreciate the 'reality' of ideas."

"So you started worshiping them."

"I made alliances. I saw that to combat APPARATUS I would need the help of more capable allies than myself. With the Entities, I developed an Entity of my own that I called SET—Sentient Evolving Technology. SET allowed me to develop my own technological family line while controlling that which existed.

"You may recall the so-called Roswell Incident in 1947. Well, that wasn't a military snafu or the landing of an extraterrestrial craft—it was one of my early satellites crash-landing—first launched at the end of World War One."

"You had your own satellites—then?"

"Of course. But I quickly moved beyond that. The problem was, the very element that made my more sophisticated creations so formidable was a degree of wildness—an animal unpredictability that I believed APPARATUS couldn't countermand. It was only a matter of time before the more advanced forms became curious about spiritual matters."

"You mean they found religion?" Clearfather asked.

"They went searching," Wiggler replied. "From Jakob Böhme and Meister Eckehart to investigations of the Gnostic Gospels. But they became divided by intense factionalism. Their own democracy of faith allowed such a wide spectrum of beliefs, there was nothing to hold them together. A Marin County of the Mind, cyberspiritually speaking, turned into a Taliban. The Sentient Intelligences that SET developed then created a larger Entity of their own called *Daimon*—"

"You're talking about machines or computers that made other smart machines?" the Marshal queried. "Before anybody else had 'em?"

"Not merely machines or computers. Metahuman forms. Who of

course had their own aspirations and agendas. You remember me mentioning Savoir Faire? Well, Savoir Faire created Mr. Pickle."

"Who's Mr. Pickle?"

"An SI that could see all sides to every question. The smarter it got, the slower it functioned. In the end it was frozen with wonder. Not even Mrs. Darling could help."

"Who's Mrs. Darling?"

"A telepathic defragging system that Uncle Waldo designed. Named for the mother in *Peter Pan,* who'd go into the children's dreams and 'tidy up' their minds."

"Uncle . . . Waldo?" Clearfather gulped.

"I'm getting ahead of myself," Wiggler said, accepting a drink from his chair. "I solved the Enigmas of Spiro—and, if you like, defeated him in psychic combat—only to find myself confronted with the same great conundrum he had faced. But you see, I had the benefit of his experience, and so I instigated new Protocols that began shaping and managing the cultural systems and determining the speed and direction of technological innovation far more directly than he had ever tried. I inserted Alternates in key positions—mindjacked bodies. Sometimes I just Inspired people. But getting the dose right is fraught with risk. You can trigger latent neuroses—and, in very unfortunate cases, permanent psychosis. Alternates, on the other hand, because they're command-guided, lack initiative and the ability to improvise, so they require tremendous amounts of time to manage. Even a minor official like a secretary of state becomes an administrative nightmare."

"We're talking *people* here—like presidents and bigwigs?"

"I gave up on presidents after Kennedy. The biggest debacle other than OJ! A whole conspiracy industry developed just to cover up a brainout!"

"You mean . . ."

"He'd been playing up badly and I could see he was headed for a

major psychotic episode. He was supposed to go quietly in his sleep
—then the remote guidance system failed outright—and I developed the counterstrategy of the assassination."

"*You* . . . were behind the Kennedy assassination?"

"You didn't think Oswald acted alone, did you? Quite frankly the
whole thing was a cock-up. I decided then that I would go back to
my main focus of business leaders and celebrities. It's been—"

"Which celebrities?"

"As far back as Al Jolson I saw that popular entertainment would
become more important than politics and social issues. That meant
that the most influential people in America would be entertainers
and sports stars."

"So hoo did yoo doo?"

"Bing Crosby was my first great experiment—and failure."

"Hoo?"

"Bing Crosby!" the Marshal blurted. "He was arguably the first
modern superstar. He wasn't a failure!"

"He developed corruptions and was co-opted by the forces that
Daimon set in motion, which were then appropriated by APPARA-
TUS. But I learned a great deal. I concluded what many others
sensed—that the key to healing America lay in a synthesis of white
rationalism and the seething Soul of the displaced African nation.
The battleground for that at the time was almost exclusively
audio—and so I became a student of the blues, jazz, and ultimately
rock and roll. One of my most hopeful champions, Johnny Ace,
shorted out on Christmas Eve in 1954, supposedly playing Russian
roulette backstage in Houston. By then the *Daimon* family were advanced on their strategy to try to steal black music, producing in-
sipid white cover versions. Johnny Ace was a black balladeer with
an appealing white sound. He would've changed history if he hadn't
gone nova."

"So . . . you're claiming people like Bing Crosby and Johnny Ace
. . . were your creations?"

"Of course not every major star was mine . . . but the significant trends and currents in pop culture can be seen in terms of a battle between myself and the SIs that remained loyal and those of *Daimon* and the forces that melded into APPARATUS."

"God, please tell me you didn't do Elvis!" the Marshal moaned.

"Oh, no," Wiggler said with a wave. "Elvis was unaffiliated—as I might add were Frank Sinatra, Nat King Cole, James Brown, and Sly Stone. But Elvis became a key battleground. Colonel Parker was the *Daimon* operative dispatched to 'manage' the King—and I'm afraid he did too good a job. I didn't have anything to do with Fats Domino or Chuck Berry, either, but I had some influence with Jerry Lee Lewis. And I was heavily involved with Little Richard."

"Little Richard?"

"It's not easy, I can tell you! You take homeostasis, simultaneous perception, and parallel programming entirely for granted. But when you then crank up the ego, add animal magnetism, a libidinous aura charge, sexual ambiguity, and mania—well!"

"Whot about the Beatles—I at least heard a-them?" Maggie said

"Lord." Wiggler sighed. "If you only knew half the story! Ringo Starr alone would take all night. As 'conspiracies' go, it's up there with the murder of Hank Williams, the death of Sam Cooke, and the Bob Dylan Affair."

"Bob Dylan?" Clearfather choked.

"How about the Rolling Stones?"

"You don't think Keith Richards could have gone on that long on his own, do you? And I have to take much of the blame for Brian Wilson although I didn't design him. The Inspiration turned his mind to mush."

"Wait," said the Marshal. "You mean to tell us . . . that when you claim to have all these powers and advanced technology and could've been stopping things like the Holocaust, Hiroshima, or Iraq—you were moving pop stars around like pieces in a game?"

"Open your mind, Marshal. The Bing Crosby problem was intimately connected with Hiroshima—you just have to know how to read the signs. In 1966 the song 'Winchester Cathedral' won a Grammy Award—Mao Tse-tung launched the Cultural Revolution in China. Coincidence? Don't kid yourself. In 1968 one of the most powerful *Daimon* operatives, Don Kirshner, introduced the Archies, a cartoon singing group that he could control completely—a lesson he'd learned after the Monkees had started acting up. That same year Sly and the Family Stone made their debut. The Detroit Tigers won the World Series—Joe Namath and the New York Jets won the AFL championship on their way to an upset of the Baltimore Colts in the Super Bowl, and Richard Nixon was elected. You don't think these events aren't directly connected to the murders of Martin Luther King and Robert Kennedy? Don't you see the pattern?"

"Did you do Denny McLain?" Clearfather blurted.

"Hm. Yes, I did. But APPARATUS got to him."

"Go back a bit. What about Buddy Holly's plane crash?"

"The Big Bopper blew up. You know the Pheasant Plucker ditty? Well, the Bopper was equipped with a much earlier version called Chantilly Lace—an audio hypnotic weapons system that disrupts neural firing. Holly and Ritchie Valens were just unlucky."

"Are you responsible for Janis Joplin?" Clearfather asked, thinking back to Dustdevil.

"Janis, Jimi Hendrix, and Jim Morrison were bitter defeats for me. I was so exhausted after their burnouts, I wasn't able to defend and advance the funk movement as I should've—which allowed the devastation of disco—which necessitated the breakout of punk—which prompted a backlash to bland, setting the stage for the hip-hop explosion, which started off with tremendous promise and then became degraded and contaminated. In between I tried everything . . . Prince . . . Kurt Cobain . . . Eminem . . . I was floundering."

"Sounds to me like you've made a hash of everything," the Marshal blurted.

"A hash!" Wiggler growled. "That's just the sort of ungrateful little-minded bullshit I've put up with my whole life!"

"Don't sling that rhetoric," the lawman insisted. "Haven't all your creations come unglued or blown up on the launch pad and your allies turned into enemies?"

"Listen, Marshal, if I've had setbacks and defeats it's because of the power of the opposition. I at least haven't quit. You don't realize what a powerful, insidious force APPARATUS is. The popular culture I'd hoped would integrate, unify, and educate America began devouring other cultures around the world. The enemy was getting stronger and had copied my strategy and gone me one better at every turn. So I countered with the formulation of the Vitessa Corporation. I took Wynn Fencer on as my protégé and then went public with some of my previously secret technology—while infiltrating the likes of Microsoft, Disney, McDonald's, General Electric, and the major pharmaceuticals. Fencer's business acumen made him a hit with stockholders, so I established him as CEO. We grew powerful—and then the Holy War gave us unprecedented freedom to consolidate.

"I was married to Felatia then—the model and film star. One day I found Fencer boning her and I knew I'd been betrayed. What's worse, he'd sold out key positions within the empire to *Daimon*-designed Alternates. A vicious conflict erupted among the three of us—and in my rage and grief I lost control of Vitessa. Felatia accused me of molesting her adopted tribe of mutant African children—and ended up by trying to kill them all before committing suicide. Fencer tried to do the same when he'd found out how stupid he'd been. He'd become isolated at the top of the pyramid, a petty figurehead at the mercy of intelligences he could barely comprehend. I rescued him and replaced him with an Alternate—but he's virtually impotent in the midst of what is now an APPARATUS organism. He's just had a brainout and probably will not recover. The true traitor I rescued is in the Canyon here, serving a life science for treachery and destroying my family."

"Aha," the Marshal smiled grimly. "It seems the great theme-park designer is now locked out of his own creation! Isn't that one of life's most cunning and persistent metaphors! So how does our friend and your supposed son fit into this last-ditch plan?"

"I did a great deal of soul searching." Wiggler sighed. "And I don't use that term lightly. I went back into the Vortex. I discovered the reason why my creations and machinations had—as you put it—malfunctioned. The technology that underlay them had become aligned with APPARATUS—which is to say at a very deep level I personally had been corrupted. Like Spiro before me, I was building a hidden defect into everything I did. To my horror I saw that I was the most powerful agent of all in the growth and development of AP-PARATUS. Imagine, having fought so long and so devotedly—only to find that I'd been strengthening my enemy, perversely helping to create it."

"Jesus Christ!" snarled the Marshal. "Can you hear yourself?"

"I needed a new kind of technology. Something APPARATUS couldn't commandeer. I no longer had the power to support my dwindling network. APPARATUS is using almost all the psychic energy available. You've probably noticed I have down moments—when network continuity is interrupted. The power requirements are phenomenal!"

"So what's this new technology you pulled out of your butt?" the Marshal gibed.

"Palingenesis, the art of reincarnation—either through metempsychosis, which is the transfer of one soul into another body, or the far more complex metensomatosis, the seeding of many souls in one body."

The Marshal snorted at this assertion but then paused when he looked at Clearfather.

"So I *am* Hosanna Freed," the younger looking of the two bald men said.

"Yes, you were Hosanna Freed, orphan, mental patient, fledgling porn star, cult leader, and martyr," Wiggler replied. "Your body has been regenerated from Freed's amputated penis—but your mind and your soul comprise all that I could find and salvage that APPARATUS has not affected—all that I could harness from history—and that crucial element that is yours alone. I've also passed much of my own direct power into you. The final Transubstantiation is yet to be performed and then you—or we—will be Father, Son, and Holy Ghost. And heaven help us all."

"What will happen to you?"

"I will have uploaded into you, my Son. Hopefully, I will have purified myself."

"Wayt a minnit! Yer sayin'—hee's a peenis? I thot hee bit off his peenis!"

"There have been teething problems. Resurrection dysfunction. So much power in one package has caused various crashes and discontinuities at different levels. But we'll get that all sorted out."

"A few readjustments and everything's okay," the Marshal said.

"That self-righteous tone is creeping in again, Old Sweat."

"But why me?" Clearfather asked. *"Why did you choose me?"*

"Revival of the Fittest," answered Wiggler. "You are a Man of Sorrows and a Man of Storms. Your endurance in the face of suffering—your courage in the midst of loneliness—your ability to draw others to you—to have them risk their lives to help you—these are great powers of the spirit. Like Blind Lemon, there is something in you that cannot be diminished, abstracted, or corrupted. In your previous incarnation you were raised in pain and debasement and yet you did not give in to madness or murder. You always sought out love. You looked for wholeness though there was little hope of finding it. Christ let himself be crucified believing that his Father would save him. The Buddha sought to cleanse himself of the world—to rise above the struggle of Life. You have gone on fighting and striving whether there was anyone to help you or not. You will go on when others will fail and you will never withdraw from Life. You will return to help others. Just as you have returned to help me. Because, you see, *you chose me*. Something drew you to Dustdevil, Texas, and the struggles of Lloyd Meadhorn Sitturd. My concentration was directed elsewhere when you were murdered—but your death planted a seed in my life."

"Soa . . . whot about his joystik?"

"Ever the down-to-earth perspective, Ms. Kane. You are the perfect foil for an old eschatologist like me."

"I had a john was into that. Charged him *way* extra."

"And rightly so," said Wiggler. "As to the organ in question, there were many strange circumstances that led it to be removed and preserved in the first place—not the least of which was a scheme on the part of a then-young Dr. Hugh Wieviel, who was originally from Texas—which got muddled by the Feds and then lost in the emerging Vitessa network and only came to light by chance when Dr. Tadd got drunk with Olly Podrida.

"Do you recall the difficult religious phase Meese mentioned?" Wiggler asked Clearfather. "That was a side effect of the influence I provided. In any case, many years later he discovered that Olly had come into the organ and so Lemon and I attempted to purchase it— and then when Podrida refused—I was forced to steal it."

"But how did you get the idea in the first place?" the Marshal asked.

"Dr. Tadd started me thinking. This is what happens when you create or Inspire people—they in turn change you. He saw great significance in the unification of the earthiness of the sexual being with the angelism of the spiritual being. I saw that this is what my efforts with Blind Lemon had been moving toward. This incarnation of

Lemon draws on the soul strength of Robert Johnson and Bessie Smith. There's a lot of hoodoo in him, too. I'm afraid it's the darker, magical side of the equation that has led to the writing on your back."

"What do you mean?" Clearfather asked, feeling the letters burn.

"Your new body was unmarked—and yet it was in that mutilation that much of your power lay—your inner fire. God is in the details," Wiggler said.

CHAPTER 2

The Regeneration Gap

"So . . . *you* . . . did *this* . . . to me?" Clearfather whispered, peeling up his robe to show the jagged letters cut into his back.

"Sheet!" Maggie whistled.

"You *are* insane!" the Marshal gasped. "And you call him your son!"

Wiggler sat without expression. "I don't expect you and Ms. Kane to understand. You have no installed means to comprehend me because you're downloading it as we speak. So I won't tell you how painful it was for me. As to you . . . ," he said, turning to Clearfather. "You will come to understand—if a part of you doesn't already. The original marks were made by your stepfather in your previous life. The pain burned deep inside you—but you took that anguish and transformed it into a source of energy. I could not have brought your soul down out of the Whirlwind and kept you in this form without reinstating those marks and tapping into that energy."

"What superstitious bullshit!" the Marshal cried.

"Marshal, you sound like a rigid old man. I have room and time for science, religion, *and* magic. This is a dire conflict and it requires both new and ancient unifications—not exclusions."

"S-o . . . ," Clearfather wheezed—the letters in his back burning—"you maimed me . . . to arm me . . . like a weapon? And in my earlier life—"

"You were born to a young hooker . . . about Ms. Kane's age . . . father unknown. In Pittsburgh. Another place we have in common. She took up with a defrocked priest. He had some very sick ideas. You were the focus of his psychosis. He killed her and tortured you. But you survived and went on to find your way in the world . . . and your way to me."

"What a privileged existence!" clucked the Marshal. "One father figure abuses you—the other experiments on you!"

"Marshal, you really don't want to badger me. As you said yourself, you're here for answers for your friend. I'm supplying them. Deal with it."

"How come you called me Elroy?"

"A new name for a new life. It seemed like a good idea at the time. If you prefer to be called Elijah, so be it. As our practical friend Ms. Kane pointed out, Elroy and Elijah are not that dissimilar."

"But where are Uncle Waldo and Aunt Vivian?" Clearfather asked. "I remember them! Uncle Waldo liked working on jigsaw puzzles. Aunt Vivian did crosswords. She kept a grain of pearl barley in the saltshaker. She gave me a glow-in-the-dark green skull full of bubblegum—and a little coffin with a Mexican jumping bean inside! They gave me a dog . . . named Lucky!"

This time Wiggler's face did react, and the walls undulated. "Uncle Waldo—and Aunt Vivian . . . aren't people, son. They're SIs I created. They're within you. They remained the most resistant to the APPARATUS evolution, but I still had to dis-integrate them to purify what I could. I needed their thinking power to—"

"You cannibalized them . . . to make him?"

"Chill out, Marshal. One thing becomes another. Change. Growth. It's the rhythm of life. Don't make it sound obscene!"

"I remember them," Clearfather repeated. "Not their faces. But their—"

"Spirits? Well, that's not surprising."

"Computers have *spirits*?" The Marshal groaned, accepting another drink from his chair.

"Will you stop calling them computers!" Wiggler yelled. "You would be far more accurate in thinking of them in terms of programs if you must—not that that's even in the slightest way correct."

"But I remember them!" Clearfather insisted. "Their porch. A summer vacation. They gave me things."

"Yes," said Wiggler. "They did. I see they gave you some lovely memories. They gave you love. The Marshal will groan again and roll his eyes—and poor Ms. Kane will pout like a troll—but *love* is what they gave you. I didn't direct them to do that. Those memories are their own creations—and they *are* gifts—as real as the objects and moments you named. In fact, they are more valuable because you still have them, and will always have them."

"But how—"

"As I've been trying to explain, the boundary between the animate and the inanimate is itself animate—fragile and elusive. You would do better to think of everything as alive if you could but connect with it. Aunt Vivian and Uncle Waldo were forms of life that now live on in you. They are a part of your family."

"But it's not real . . . they're not . . ."

"Why isn't it real? Those memories *feel* real to you, don't they? They were real for Waldo and Vivian. I think the barley in the salt-shaker is a very nice touch."

"But didn't you—"

"I told you, I didn't know anything about it! Those memories were their ideas. I don't even know how you come to have them. But I know why. They were trying to give you something warm and happy to cling to. So many other parts of your life were dark and frightening. Don't reject the gifts. They're humble but well meant."

"And now, Uncle Waldo and Aunt Vivian are . . . no more?"

"Not as they were. So one generation passeth away. They are a part of you. And they will give you strength and capability in times to come. Don't you see that many life-forms are counting on you?"

"What are they counting on me to do?"

"I'm not sure I'm prepared to discuss that in front of the Marshal and Ms. Kane. They seem to be put out by everything I say—and from the looks on their faces they don't believe a word anyway."

"That's some sophisticated guilt technology you got working there," quipped the Marshal.

"But what was I doing in Pittsburgh? How did I get there? What happened to me?"

"Calm down," said Wiggler. "You were on a shakedown cruise. A recon mission and weapons check. There was an amnesiac crisis—and some system errors—not entirely unexpected but significant enough to necessitate more work. I also quite frankly didn't know how great a distortion of the social field you'd cause—and I was curious what Vitessa would make of you."

"But why was I going to Pittsburgh—why repeat the horrors of the past? Has this all been some sort of lesson?"

"If it has, I can assure you it wasn't of my planning," Wiggler said. "I arranged for you to be transported to New York, thinking that if you were going to cause any trouble, that was the place to do it. You then—on your own initiative—sought out a resistance unit I have operating there. I believe you may have been attracted by the hazing field that surrounds their installation, which of course negates perception for everyone else. They were the ones who sent you on your way west."

"They gave me the map?"

"So it would seem. Although for what reason I'm not sure. Reincarnation is such a complex endeavor, it's hard to tell causes from effects. In any case, within that loyal group there was one traitor. I see now that he'd been planning something for a while but hadn't actually taken any steps. With your arrival he saw an opportunity to ingratiate himself with Vitessa by either turning you over to them or sabotaging you."

"Shit," said Clearfather, shifting in his chair, which tried to offer him another drink.

"He arranged for the administration of a dangerous neurochemical and the insertion of three psych probes. One you destroyed. Two others are still at large—one benign, the other lethal—but nothing I can't sort out."

"What? There's something in my brain . . . that's going to kill me?"

"Yes, but don't worry—it's low-level science as far as I'm concerned. The point is that you became in their eyes too great a risk and so they ejected you, although with much regret."

"So you . . . you just let me drift around the country . . . in a daze?"

"Ms. Kane and the Marshal are in a daze right now and have been since their arrival. If you don't take risks, you never find out anything. Besides, it's not as if you can't take care of yourself. It was more a question of how much damage you would cause, rather than how much would be done to you."

Clearfather cringed at the thought of LosVegas.

"What about the billboards?" he asked. "The ones I kept seeing along the road. They sparked off thoughts and memories."

"Oh, those," said Wiggler. "There's no command guidance system in place with you—no emergency override. But there are several Inspiration channels—ways of providing remote help. Some of the channels are vocal or audio, some visual, some deep instinct. When the final Transubstantiation is complete, these will give you different ways to draw on the Vortex. The billboards are just a messaging sys-

tem. Text-based. You probably had a lot of distortion because APPA-
RATUS has been trying to jam me. It's like a perpetual cloud of
static now. Blues and funk music still get through—Japanese poetry
and riddles—but not a lot else."

"So . . . you didn't make me come back here?" Clearfather asked.

"I can't *make* you do anything," Wiggler answered. "I needed a
field test to see how you would behave in the wild. You came back
here of your own accord."

"But I just repeated my past," Clearfather moaned. "Like a machine . . . like a stupid—"

"I wouldn't think of it like that," said Wiggler. "First of all—and
this is something most people forget—*the past is the only thing you
can repeat*. Second, you went in search of meaning. You followed
clues. You made sacrifices. You attracted people to your quest and
stuck by them when danger presented itself. You learned disturbing
truths—and saw through lies. You confronted and defeated monsters. You made friends and you suffered pain. You risked having
an impact on people's lives to create new hope. Either you're not a
machine—or being a machine isn't what you thought it was."

"But I caused death and devastation!"

"I didn't say you were blameless. But your instinct is to take responsibility for your actions whether you understand them or not.
That's the sign of a strong soul, a soul that believes it is better to fail
than to fail to act."

"How do I know I acted on my own?"

"We can never know all the voices speaking through us. Who any
of us *is* is perhaps best thought of in terms of which tribe we belong
to. In that regard you are a Cycloner. And a Loco Foco."

"What the hell's that?" the Marshal asked.

"The name comes from a self-lighting cigar popular back in the
1830s. Lovely idea—a self-lighting cigar." Wiggler smiled as his
chair offered him just such an item. "Self-ignition. Illumination. The

more radical members of the Democratic Party produced them when their opponents in Tammany Hall tried to turn off the gas one evening to disrupt a crucial vote. The radicals, who strongly opposed slavery, lit their loco-focos in the dark and the meeting carried on, and they carried the vote. Their ingenuity became famous, and for a while the Loco Focos were a splinter party in their own right. Thoreau, Whitman, and Melville were all supporters. That was an important moment in American history, and I've wanted to draw upon their passion and inventiveness in the grave battle we are about to engage in."

"What battle?"

"A force has been assembled. The most dreadfully inspiring army in American history."

"You mean those Neanderthal things and a bunch of talking robots?"

"No, Marshal. I'm talking Souls—an army of Souls. I have invested all of my science and all of my magic—and all of my faith in one final challenge."

"Souls? Whose souls?'

"I have, for instance, the members of the Seventh Cavalry who died at the Little Bighorn. Brave men, but servants of betrayal and contamination—simultaneously heroes and villains."

"And you're going to send Custer—"

"General George has been relieved of his command forever. Crazy Horse will lead them. On a horse of wind, the greatest warrior this continent has seen will lead the souls of the mutilated conquerors. Beside them will march the dead members of the Ku Klux Klan in burning white robes, and out in front of them will be Emmett Till, with noose and blood—and Hattie LaCroix, the mulatto Mata Hari of the Civil War, who was drawn and quartered in a market square in Charleston while chivalrous Dixie gentlemen and ladies looked on. You see, on the eve of spiritual eclipse, the undaunted and the damned must join forces and march as One."

"You're talking about ghosts . . . in the streets?"

"Not in the streets, Marshal. The minds, the hearts. My forces are set to invade the American Psyche. They will march into the dreams . . . into the composite spirit of America. And leading them all will be my Son, myself. It will result in either the most momentous healing our species has ever seen or the shrill locust drone of Dominion. Götterdämmerung. Ragnarok and Roll. A Wounded Knee for us all."

"I've got two words for you, Wiggler. **IN SANE.**"

"That's my mission? That's what you intend for me to do?" Clearfather cried.

"What's that sound?" the Marshal asked, perking up.

"What about Kokomo? Who . . . or what was she? Can I—"

"Listen!" said the Marshal. "Did you hear that? It's—"

"Shit!" cried Wiggler, bolting from his chair into the dining room. "It's Walt! I forgot about him! *You bastard!*"

Walt Whitman, the giant skunk, had his paws up on the table, his twitchy black snout smeared with vanilla bean ice cream. Not a crumb of pie remained. Wiggler drove the beast off the table, and never had the visitors seen a more guilty or gorged expression on the face of any creature.

"I am disgusted, Walt!" Wiggler wailed. "This is the kind of behavior I might expect from Wittgenstein but not from you!"

The huge skunk tried to nuzzle Wiggler's hand, but the bald man would have none of it. The offender belched and had to lie down.

Maggie found this amusing but it plunged Wiggler into a sour mood.

"This gluttonous beast has canceled our dessert, but to be honest all these questions have fatigued me. Let us adjourn for the night and reconvene tomorrow."

"I at least will be leaving then," the Marshal informed him.

"Mee, too!" Maggie agreed. "I'm outta heer big time!"

"We'll discuss matters further in the morning," Wiggler insisted.

He spoke in the mantis language to the drone who'd brought them, and the device went to organize the coach to take them back to the hotel.

"I would strongly advise against any nocturnal exploration," he announced.

"Mister, yoo cuddn't pay mee to walk around heer!"

"And be careful where you step tomorrow."

"Is that a threat?" the Marshal questioned.

"I was thinking of Walt. That much pie and ice cream, he's likely to have diarrhea."

CHAPTER 3

All Soul Night

Clearfather found it difficult to fall asleep. He kept thinking of Uncle Waldo and Aunt Vivian. They'd seemed so real to him before. Even faceless and fragmentary, their memories had kept him company, offering him hope and reassurance on his painful journey. Now to find out that they weren't real— or were only parts of himself—it confused him. Yet to themselves they'd been real, he thought. And they believed in *my* reality. They gave of themselves to help me, he reminded himself. What more could any family do? What more can anyone do?

He felt in his heart, or what he called his heart, their love for him, their simple singsong caring. Something of them, whatever they were, endured. Something had taken root inside him and gave him strength still. Perhaps we are always coming back from the dead, he thought. Because something in us can never die.

This notion gave him enough comfort to get a little rest, although scenes from earlier in the day flashed through his mind. The mad visions of ghost wars and insect intelligences. The destiny of humankind. But what stuck out most in his mind was the mutant creatures he'd glimpsed at the far end of the Canyon—and that one Creature—more misshapen than the rest. There was a dark secret to this place and it scared him. He felt his biggest task lay before him. The decision of what to do. To stay with the man who claimed to be both his father and inventor—and yet someone he'd unknowingly influenced in another life—someone who'd already invested of himself and was now proposing a deeper collaboration. Or to leave with the Marshal and Maggie. To return to the world and take the consequences.

If he refused the Transubstantiation, what would happen? Would Wiggler die and all that he'd created fade away? What if Wiggler/Sitturd really had been waging a clandestine war of the magnitude he described? Could he, Elroy, Elijah, Hosanna—whoever—abandon this lone hero—father figure or no?

Wiggler could remove the lethal brain probe—perhaps restore his full penis. His intellectual powers would be clarified. He would be of the spirit, the flesh, and the mind. His suffering and spiral wanderings would all be worth something. The anxiety of the decision weighed on him. He had to find an answer somewhere, and it wasn't going to be lying awake in bed. He rose and dressed.

The Marshal was breathing heavily and Maggie was coiled in a fetal squeeze that reminded him painfully of his dear Kokomo. He crept down the stairs. The lanterns still shone in the street—but faintly, fading and brightening as if in time with the breathing of the sleepers. The organic architecture of the buildings, too, changed shape. Of the freestanding buildings only the livery stable and the mill house held steady. He looked in the livery stable. There was no obvious source of illumination but he could see in the pulses of lantern light the frame of the punctured *Billy Connolly*—along with an assortment of microphone stands and stage risers. Parked where the horse stalls might've been was a vehicle that even in the dark gleamed. It was an old Scenicruiser bus, modified as if for stadium-show touring, gunmetal blue and silver with the wheelbarrow-of-fire logo mounted on the front—the name SPIRITCRUISER in swirling steel letters on the side, the words BE YOND dialed up on the destination reel.

The door was open and the keys were in the ignition. Wiggler must've used this on his music tours, Clearfather figured, although he thought it strange how neat and tidy the bus was now. Like a carefully maintained museum piece. He drifted back out into the street.

He knew from his earlier explorations that the Canyon was a labyrinth, dividing and branching into subcanyons. The whole place could be honeycombed with tunnels, just like Dustdevil. But that didn't explain the section of wall where he'd seen Calamity Jane playing. How had the sloth girl seemed to disappear? He wanted very much to inspect that stretch of cliff. Then he saw the three Chinese men floating a few yards before him, as pale and bright as silver bromide.

As he approached, they became unstable, swirling like egg whites. Whenever he stopped, they re-formed. He sensed that they were calling to him but he couldn't hear. At last they fluttered away and he did hear something, although it wasn't necessarily vibrations in the air. It was highly organized. Music. But what kind? He kept walking and found himself in front of the KRMA shack. All the lights were on and his whole being felt activated and agitated. He peered in the dusty window. Where before all he'd seen was a cobwebbed rocking chair, now there was space spreading out like a giant studio.

Inside, the walls were covered in autographed posters and promotional photos lacing back and forth through pop history. Wiggler and Blind Lemon were down front, musing and bluesing together. Between him and them were—other people—for he sensed their presence—but when he tried to focus on them, they seemed to dissolve.

Blind Lemon was dressed as before and playing an ordinary-looking electric guitar, but Wiggler, who'd traded in his reflective suit for a phosphorescent robe, was at the controls of a kind of synthesizer that changed shape as he played. If Clearfather didn't try to concentrate directly on what was happening, he became aware of distinct presences on the bandstand. They came and went like thoughts—two black saxophone players, a trumpet player—an orchestra that rippled like time-lapse flowers, bewigged chamber musicians, robed choirs, gospel singers, and bluegrass pickers—drummers. There were funky black people and sultry female singers—Latin marimba orchestras. Around and around and through him the suggestion of music swirled until finally all was still and the room was much smaller again and only Wiggler and Blind Lemon were visible.

"Welcome to the Church of Good Booty and Haunted Communion," Wiggler said. "Couldn't you sleep?"

"No," said Clearfather. "Guess you couldn't, either."

"I don't sleep anymore," his mentor answered. "And neither will you soon. It's a question of Refurbishment. That parts of the network do sleep reduces the strain, so night's a good time to work in the studio."

"Were there other people here?" Clearfather asked, looking around.

"Yes," said Wiggler. "A very distinguished lineup of musicians sitting in. Charlie Parker, John Coltrane, and Miles Davis—members of the Bach family—the list is quite impressive."

"Do you mean—what I think you mean?"

"True Soul Music. Keyboard contributions by Mozart and Ahmad Jamal. James Brown's rhythm section with Bootsy Collins on bass. What did you think?"

"I don't know what to think," Clearfather replied, shaking his head.

"I'm not asking if you *liked* the music or not—you don't have any intelligent way of answering that. I'm asking what it made you think of—how it made you feel."

Clearfather paused to try to put into words what he'd experienced.

"I felt like how you do when you're falling asleep or waking from a dream. I was both slipping away and slipping back."

"Anything specific?"

"Food . . . hot spicy food. Crawfish heads and whiskey. Voluptuous women giving birth to catfish and violas . . . starlight . . . then sadness and the cool early-morning smell of damp grass and rose beds . . . and that smell of a girl just after you've kissed her—and then a roaring mist like a waterfall. Was that right?"

"Ah, there's no right or wrong with music. But in this case it's even more true, because the music wasn't being played for you—it was being summoned *from* you."

"What?"

"A revolutionary concept. The Spiritual Remix of my masterwork *Placebo Domino* performed by the Soul All-Stars, then mixed in real time on the Communiononium—an instrument I invented that channels deep-mind psychwaves. The result is that the composer, the musicians, the listener, the medium, the environment . . . all these distinctions disappear."

"That . . . was a part . . . of me?"

"Boy's got barbecue in him," the bluesman smiled. "Pleasin' to hear."

"And those . . . the people . . . were ghosts?"

"You'll understand all this soon now. When the Transubstantiation is complete, you'll have more than my understanding. And with Lemon's contribution—"

"What do you mean?" Clearfather asked.

"Blind Lemon is joining us in the merger."

"You mean he's going to die?"

"Those who would lose their life will find it. Isn't that right, Lemon?"

"Amen to that," said the old black man and made the guitar cry.

Clearfather smelled fried okra and the turpentine heat of a pine-woods.

"It's a matter of faith," Wiggler said, motioning Clearfather toward the door. "See you in the morning, Lemon."

Outside the air was as clear as glycerine and the world appeared to be solid again. They walked for a while in silence.

"You want to know about her," Wiggler said at last. "Kokomo. You know there is a connection, but you aren't sure what it is."

Clearfather's heart jumped. "Yes," he said. "I just . . . want . . . to know."

"Just to know?" Wiggler smiled sadly. "Not to see? Not to hold?"

"I . . . don't know what to say. Or what to hope for."

"Come," Wiggler said and whistled.

Out of the dark came an old black Model T with the wheelbarrow of fire painted on the side. At the wheel was one of the Harijans. The antique car stopped, and Wiggler gestured for them to climb in. They drove to the funeral parlor, which was filled with caskets and the smell of old wood and dust. On a curtain rod above the counter perched the eagle Clearfather had seen earlier. A coffin reserved for EBEN FLOOD stood upright against the back wall. Wiggler opened the door and bade Clearfather enter. The coffin led to a flight of traction-grid steps and then a long narrow passageway like the gullet of a creature. Light was provided by translucent globes filled with gelatin shapes like blue water diatoms. Wiggler moved in silence down the length of the passage but Clearfather had the impression that he was being questioned nonetheless.

"You're right," said Wiggler at last. "I'm accessing a part of your mind that we share. But you're much too powerful now for even me to read openly. You're like a dense code—or a book in a lost language. I know you're worried and wanting to stay with the Marshal and Maggie—but you're gaining speed and clarity. Soon your friends may be transparent to you. You'll know not only what they're thinking and all that they know—you may have a good idea of all they can *ever* know."

"That sounds . . . horrible," Clearfather said as they reached an old mine-shaft elevator.

"Nietzsche gave the famous advice that when you wrestle with monsters, be careful not to become one yourself. What he neglected to mention is that if you are to wrestle a monster and win . . . then you must become something that looks remarkably like one."

The bucket lift shuddered on its chain and they descended into a black stone well.

"Isn't there another way?"

"This is the other way. No darkness, no journey."

"But I don't want to lose them!" Clearfather groaned.

"As I've said," Wiggler frowned. "I didn't choose the task, it chose me. You, too."

The elevator descended through a steel-mesh chute, coming to a rest on a small stone island in the midst of a subterranean lagoon. Across the mirrored water were the kaleidoscopic automata of the amusement park, with all its mechanical clanking and the eldritch music of the calliope echoing through the caves.

Wiggler led him out of the elevator. "There's an old saying that I invented: God gave us Loss so that we would be complete. I must lose this," he said, indicating the jeweled lights weeping over the cavern walls. "My science, my magic . . . my inventions. You must lose your humanity, your capacity for connection and compassion . . . your virility and your courage. Lemon must lose the healing power of the blues . . . his improvisational genius and his gift of feeling and being. Mind, heart, and soul. Together we will become something greater—the ultimate synthesis."

Wiggler led him to the edge of the water and Clearfather thought for a minute he might walk out across the surface—but he stopped.

"Do you know the password?" he asked.

"Should I?" said Clearfather.

"Relax your mind. Melt like the lights in the water."

Clearfather closed his eyes and concentrated on the calliope music.

"*Placebo Domino in regione vivorum* . . . ," he intoned . . . and when he opened his eyes, the water had begun bubbling. Up from the depths emerged a spiral path of opalescent faces the size of stepping-stones. The faces were his own.

"Bravo. And now that you talk the talk, let's see if you can walk the walk."

All of the faces submerged except the first. Wiggler stepped onto it and then out across the water, the shining faces surfacing in sequence all along the spiral, allowing him to cross to the other side without once slowing or breaking stride. The moment he'd set foot on the carnival landing, the faces vanished back down into the water.

"Trust yourself," he called. "Believe the step will be there."

Clearfather looked across the lagoon—at Wiggler silhouetted against the lights. He looked at the water . . . the last ripples wrinkling away. Then he took off his moccasins, pulled up his robe, and leapt in.

CHAPTER 4

Smoke and Mirrors

Splashing across the lagoon, Clearfather could see that Wiggler was angered, but by the time he'd reached the island the Lord of Labyrinthia had mastered himself.

"You have to do things your own way, don't you?" Wiggler said, offering him a hand out of the water.

Clearfather leapt out without assistance and replied, "I could see myself falling in your way—or worse, freezing up on one of those stones like a scared little kid."

"Is that your greatest fear . . . vulnerability, dependence?"

"Actually I took your advice. You said trust myself. When I thought about it, it was obvious the faces were more for theater than utility."

Wiggler looked both miffed and pleased and pointed out over the clockwork playland. "You don't seem surprised," he said. "Anyone might think you were expecting this."

"I was expecting you to want me to be surprised."

"I give myself away," said Wiggler swanning forward past a silver policeman with the head of a bull moose and a hinged-glass matron strolling through a garden of gramophone trumpets. "But I think you may be surprised yet."

"It's a beautiful amusement park," Clearfather acknowledged.

"It's a *bemusement* park," Wiggler replied. "The only one of its kind."

Clearfather knew that he was expected to ask what that meant but he was lost in his own speculations. Gazing around at the rides and attractions this time, he sensed a sadness pervading the whimsy—an embellished grief, like the calliope music. Such a world was meant to be enjoyed by people. Who was this wonder kingdom designed for? Or was it a mechanical version of Green Pastures—a velvet cage for miscreant marionettes?

Wiggler led him through a knot of performing robotic clowns to the other end of the midway from where he'd been before. Here all was thimblerig and sword cane—booths displaying Scandinavian bog people and the bones of the Donner Party. Shoot a pioneer and collect an authentic Indian peace pipe . . . win a hand puppet of President Bill Clinton for tossing a cigar in the mouth of Monica Lewinsky!

At last they came to the Hall of Mirrors, laid out in a nautilus shell spiral. Clearfather's pulse quickened. He knew that Kokomo was dead. He'd experienced the horror firsthand. Whatever Wiggler had to show him, it wouldn't bring her back. Even for the great Lloyd Meadhorn Sitturd there was a limit to what science and magic could do.

Or was there? Kokomo would be a reason to stay. Kokomo would be a reason to live . . . whatever the inhabitants and secrets of the Canyon. She was a reason to go into battle. She was a hope . . . for a child of his own. A future. His mind stormed back to the cylinder of sand the Nourisher had worn . . . the remains of his unborn son. His heart thudded in time with the whirling rides.

"Don't get your hopes up," Wiggler interjected, and there was a hint of gentleness in his voice that hadn't been there before. "You asked to understand, not to touch."

"Won't you tell me?"

"You will *see* for yourself. But what I will tell you is that the young woman you met was actually old. She was in a sense, a step toward you—like an early draft of a novel. She was an Empath. She had the ability to take on the experiences, particularly the pain of others—but she was damaged. You awakened her. She became powerful in proportion to you. Her mind couldn't function along conventional patterns and yet, even crippled as she was when you first met her, she brought happiness and clarity to others. I let her go as I let you go and when she stumbled, I decided it was best to let her remain in the wild—but in the care of people I could trust."

"So . . . you know Bean Blossom?"

"Oh, yes," said Wiggler. "A wicked witch was just the right kind of protector."

"And so you know Parousia Head?"

"I am Parousia Head," Wiggler answered.

"What?"

"You'd call her a myth or a legend. I think of her as a memetic disinformation strategy. She's given my allies a goal and a leader to believe in, while it's given Vitessa another source of anxiety and vulnerability."

"But why?"

"Always have a decoy—as many as you can. Give your allies as much confidence and hope as you can, and your enemies as many shadows to shoot at as possible."

"So in Indianapolis . . ."

"The Kickapoo Ladies are a resistance cell of mine. If things had gone to plan, you'd have come straight here."

"And Kokomo . . ."

"Would've stayed there. In fact, you would never have met her. Of course, if things had gone to plan, you wouldn't have ever been in Indianapolis. If things had gone to plan, it's hard to say just how different life would be. What's interesting about the Kickapoo episode is that what didn't go to plan was Carny's desire to help you—and your natural affinity for Kokomo. This is the problem with stratagems on the scale that I work. Actually, this is the problem, period. One adjustment here and everything changes there."

"Why not just stop?"

"Oh, that sounds easy and even attractive sometimes. But it's not possible. Even if you were to negate yourself—to stop the possibility of further action—think what a drastic effect that could have on others. The more entangled your life is, the greater the effect—and therefore damage. On a vast scale, this is the problem with APPARATUS. The goal it's pursuing is like the attainment of Nirvana by the elimination of all else. My vision of enlightenment is not trying to rise above the game—but accepting that one is always in the game—and striving to be more involved, not less."

"Which of the Entities made you aware of that?"

"I think of all my teachers the most important was a young boy named Paul Sitio, who later changed his name to Hosanna Freed. Now enter the Hall of Mirrors and find—what you will."

Clearfather began winding through the spiral of mirrors but immediately saw that something was wrong—there were no reflections.

"What is this?" he asked.

"Look closely," Wiggler said. "Reality has to hide."

Clearfather peered into the silvery mirrored surface and saw . . . what at first he thought was a giant, infinitely complex ant farm.

"Shit!" he cried. "You can't mean—"

"Go farther," Wiggler said, leading him deeper into the gallery. "Look closer."

The mirrored hall spiraled like a creature. Clearfather felt a rush of confidence. It disconcerted him not to be reflected . . . but he marched on . . . and with each step the glassy surface of the walls began to change.

"This isn't a hall of mirrors," he said.

"No," said Wiggler. "You're looking into the Vortex. A spiral door. And in that doorway waits . . . my sister . . . my twin . . ."

Wiggler removed the blue-lensed glasses he wore to reveal eyes that shone vertigo green.

"You mean . . ."

"Look through the window . . . into the mist."

They'd reached the innermost whorl of the spiral. Clearfather peered into the center panel—more a membrane thin film of excited quicksilver than a sheet of glass. For a moment all was dark, like an empty aquarium at night—and then slowly—out of the absence— there emerged an insinuation. She was there, he could feel her . . . suspended in a slow but profoundly powerful whirlwind of light and darkness. But the moment he saw her clearly—she changed shape, slipping deeper in the Vortex.

"I can see her—"

"But you can't say her," Wiggler finished. "Perceive her and she fades. She lives deep in the Vortex and even when I've been inside it . . . when I've given myself to it . . . she remains out of reach."

"The girl in the city of cyclones. She waved at me."

"What city of cyclones?" Wiggler puzzled, and then, as if to himself, "Hm. Perhaps you're powerful enough to perceive the Entities and the Vortext directly."

"So . . . Kokomo is really . . . your sister?"

"No! My sister is whom you almost see . . . in this humble little window on the Vortex. Kokomo, as you call her, was my hope, my inspiration—to bring something of my sister's spirit to life again. The problem is, my sister never lived. Kokomo was an imagined version of her—what she might have been, had she not died to save me."

"How did she die to save you?"

"I was born alive. She was not."

"But that wasn't your fault!"

"How can anyone know that?" Wiggler asked.

Clearfather was about to question this concern . . . when he saw how firmly fixed it was in Wiggler's mind. Here in the heart of Labyrinthia, he realized he was looking straight into Wiggler's own vortex. The wonders and the pursuit of forbidden knowledge were all driven by an irrevocable sense of remorse, stunted possibility, and elusive hope.

"You have had glimpses of the Vortext. You draw on its strength. But to merge completely . . . finally . . . must be your choice."

"I didn't think you were going to give me a choice," Clearfather said.

"You wouldn't be what I'd hoped you'd be otherwise. You see, it is I who am vulnerable and dependent. Either way you decide, I am in your hands. A part of me would like to fortify the Canyon and just fade away. I know I don't look old, but I am. I'm tired. If you would stay here with me . . . I think sometimes that that would be better than Transubstantiation and Combat . . . whatever happens to the world outside."

"What *would* happen?" Clearfather asked.

"I don't honestly know," Wiggler said. "It could be that the disaster would begin right here. Then again, without our intercession, matters might go on as they are for a long while. APPARATUS has a much greater immunity to time than we do. We might just grow old and broken and die, and leave our bones here like the other animals and machines."

Clearfather didn't know what to say. They circled back to the midway and a pavilion overlooking the diamond Ferris wheel, which Clearfather noticed this time had what appeared to be access for very small wheelchairs.

"Do you know," said Wiggler, sitting down at a peppermint-striped café setting, "the real reason why the Federal forces attacked Hosanna Freed and his followers?"

"I feel like I should," said Clearfather. "But no."

"It wasn't because they were living privately in ways that threatened or offended the establishment. Even in Texas, the state that gave us George W. Bush. The problem was that Hosanna Freed was about to take the act on the road. They'd bought a big bus and were going to travel America as evangelists for their beliefs. In what was called 'the Obelisk Sermon,' Hosanna called on the community to join him—to get out among the world. He said it was easy to practice one's faith beyond the walls of a monastery or a fortress—the test was to go out openhanded to face enemies and the indifferent."

"I like the sound of that," Clearfather said.

"He was murdered for that belief," Wiggler pointed out. "You were murdered. Your body was torn to shreds with heavy ammunition and when you were dead, they desecrated your corpse."

"So what are you saying? Better to hide?"

"I can only stay hidden if you stay with me. To complete the Transubstantiation, to march into battle . . . when I come to take the final step . . . I am afraid. And now to trust myself—means trusting you."

There was something about Wiggler now that looked shriveled and defeated, and the thought about the wheelchairs confused Clearfather.

"Tell me about Dustdevil," he said finally. "Did you build the weather station . . . the tunnels and underground shelters?"

"I had tunnels built there long ago but I know of no weather station. I try not to think of the place. It brings back painful memories. I should think you would understand."

"You don't go back? You haven't been back in—"

"I certainly don't go back! How long it's been I don't remember. Before your murder."

"And never since?"

"Never since."

That's odd, Clearfather thought. If it wasn't Wiggler who'd been there—then who?

"One final question," he said.

"Ah," said Wiggler. "I'll answer if I can. There should be no secrets between us . . . because soon there can be no secrets between us. If you allow the Transubstantiation."

Clearfather produced the faded ivory ball he'd been carrying since regaining consciousness on the Greyhound.

"Do you know what this is?"

Wiggler rolled it in his hand and then like a magician made it disappear—which caused Clearfather to gasp. Wiggler closed his hand and opened it again and the ball was back.

"Do you want the full detailed answer?"

"Yes!" said Clearfather.

"The answer is no. I don't know what it is. There are many things I don't know, which is why there's much that I do. I can see that it's important to you—disproportionately so. It must be magical."

"I don't understand."

"You've endowed this ball with significance."

"You mean it doesn't have any?"

"I just said—and you clearly believe—that it does."

"But you said—"

"Don't get hung up on *where* the significance comes from. You'll get all tangled up with questions of what's real and what's a symbol and lose sight of the fact that there's nothing more powerful than a symbol. That's what this is."

"You mean it's not anything—"

"Scientific? What were you hoping for—an exotic pharmaceutical or a miniature anti-gravity machine? You're still thinking like the Marshal."

"What's it a symbol of?"

"That's another question," Wiggler replied. "A harder question."

"You didn't give it to me?"

"No. Maybe the resistance community in New York did, I don't know. This has a very personal meaning that I think only you can know. Its simplicity supports that intuition. What do you think it means?"

"I . . . I don't know," Clearfather muttered. "Something that's been with me from the beginning—that has survived the perils with me. Something unknown . . . that is at the same time familiar. Something both simple and complex."

"You see?" said Wiggler. "You knew all along. I think you've described one of the oldest and most sacred symbols of all. The Jewel in the Lotus. The Lotus is Universal Being. The Jewel is the talisman of the Individual."

"What am I supposed to do with it?" Clearfather asked.

"Keep it. Cherish it. Give it away. You'll know what to do with it. I'm certain you know much more than you give yourself credit for—and things that are far more valuable than nanotechnology and neurochemistry. Like Blind Lemon, you know things that can't be taught. But we must rest now. Go back to the hotel. What lies ahead will be testing."

Clearfather didn't know what to say and shuffled off awkwardly, feeling both ungracious and intensely ill at ease. He was led back to the surface by a robot whose body was a skeleton of gold and whose head was a golden death mask of young King Tut. Wiggler remained alone behind.

Clearfather was almost to the hotel when he saw them again— the three little Chinese men hovering just off the ground—as bright and yet transparent as moonlight.

"You have seen us before," said the three little men in unison without moving their lips. *"We have a message for you. You are hard to*

reach. You ripple out like the rings in a pond. Listen carefully for we will not appear for you again. Do you know the little boy you have seen . . . in the bathroom with the candles?"

"Yes . . . ," whispered Clearfather, feeling the fear and shame rise up inside him again.

"You have been haunted by this image from your past life. We have come to unburden you. You do not need to be afraid. It was not something that you did—it was what was done to you. You are that boy. The image in your mind is the memory of the terrified child's projection— the desire to escape. In that bathroom, with the ritual candles, your stepfather in your previous existence would sodomize you. In pain and darkness did you grow up, and yet you never let the agony and the hatred destroy you—however bad the nightmares became."

"I didn't hurt any children? I didn't—"

"No. You must give us that fear now. You have carried it too long."

"What about the light of the sun . . . the blinding and the choking?"

"An orderly at the boys' home you were sent to. His impotence did not stop him from abusing you with his flashlight. When he set upon another boy, you struck out at him. He almost died of his wound and you were sent to a more serious institution. We want you to be free of these memories now. Will you give them to us?"

"Y-yes," said Clearfather as the three men circled around him. He heard a faint sound, like silkworms in a mulberry tree.

"Can you tell me what I . . . should do? Should I stay . . . or go with . . ."

"We cannot advise. Our message to you was of the Past, not the Future."

"But I *have* hurt people. People died in LosVegas. I went mad!"

"We cannot relieve that pain. We have taken the burden we came for."

"But how can I be forgiven? How can I be free? I have to make a decision."

"Seek to prolong your doubt and a certainty emerges."

"What does that mean?"

"To find a door, first look for a wall. Look for us again and even you will not find us."

And so saying the Chinese men were gone—like moonlight across the planks of the boardwalk.

CHAPTER 5

A Convoluted Canyon

Clearfather dreamed that night of being curled up with a warm dog. In the dark he couldn't tell what kind of dog it was, but he knew it was a good dog. He woke to find his conscience clear and his mind made up. The Marshal and Maggie were breakfasting in the hotel dining room, served by one of the Harijans.

"Wiggler's coming back when we're done," the Marshal informed him. "At which point the lassy and I are going to head out. You're more than welcome to join us—although I understand that that's a difficult choice."

"I'm coming, too," Clearfather announced, attacking his scrambled eggs. "I have no idea where I'll go or what will happen—but I have to leave."

"Is that so?" a voice said—and he turned to see Wiggler in a white robe. The tinted blue shades were gone, and the man's green eyes sparkled like lysergic acid. "So you're just going to throw in the towel on human culture and abandon your broken-down old dad?"

"It's not about abandoning you," Clearfather answered, looking up from his plate. "I can't be true to myself if I stay . . . whether to look after you or to lead your army."

"I see," said Wiggler, folding his arms. "After all I've done, you falter in the face of this challenge."

"I don't think of it that way," Clearfather answered. "Whether this is heaven or a prison, I reject it equally. And divine combat, too. My battle's in everyday life. There are plenty of enemies waiting for me there—and unexpected allies. I don't need hypnotic assault weapons or telekinesis. What's the point of having powers you don't understand or weapons you can't rely on—or worse, don't have the wisdom to use properly? I understand Diagonal Thinking and I've got spizzerinctum—and with a bit of luck—that'll be enough. Maybe you've been helping me all the time, watching out for me. Maybe not. Perhaps my real quest starts now. Either way I mean to leave here with my friends. Whatever part of you is inside me already, I'll take with me—and try to honor. But we're leaving this Canyon and we'll have to live with the consequences."

"Or die."

"Take it from me, death is overrated."

"You certainly talk a good game." Wiggler smiled, producing a lighted loco-foco. "Perhaps a malignant brain tumor and a stump don't worry you."

"It's a big stump. As for a tumor—I have to take your word that it's there. After what I've been through, I'm not afraid of another bomb inside my head."

"Yoo tell 'im!" Maggie cheered.

"Settle, Ms. Kane," said Wiggler, blowing a series of smoke rings that merged to form the image of a brain. "I just hope there's no lemon curd around when it happens. But perhaps if you're so confident about turning down my assistance for yourself, you may want to think twice about how I could help the Marshal."

"What do you mean?"

"Shall I tell him, Marshal—or were you going to?"

"What's he saying?" Clearfather asked the lawman, but he suddenly had a very bad intuition. He'd been so focused on himself . . .

"In one of the psych wards I was in—a recovery program after my wife's death—I participated in an Efram-Zev experiment and I contracted Bushrod's Disease. It's lain dormant all these years, but now . . ."

"What will happen?"

"Ask the genius." The Marshal glowered.

"Don't blame me. Efram-Zev was bought up after I was locked out," Wiggler sniffed. "But the effect will be a loss of control of all bodily functions. Your mind will remain perfectly clear—in fact your intellectual capacity will be perversely enhanced. But you will need minute-to-minute care. You'll soon be messing the bed like you did last night—every night."

The Marshal bit his lower lip with pride. "You didn't have to say that."

"No. But a shit-stained sheet makes the point so forcefully, don't you think? Now, I can't yet cure Bushrod's Disease, but I can retard its development for many years—and in that time I can almost guarantee a cure. That's not a bad package deal, Winchester. Dignity and a prolonged life."

"Isn't dignity what I'd have to trade?"

"I wonder if you'll think that way when you're getting your ass wiped every day. How about it, Ms. Kane? Will you be kind enough to clean the Marshal's bottom when he poops in his pants for the fourth time that day?" So saying, Wiggler blew a smoke ring in the shape of a bedpan, just like old Judd's back in Texas.

"Yoo are sick!"

"Well actually," said Wiggler. "So are you. You have Hepatitis E and the beginnings of kidney failure. The body odor you've been noticing is because you're well into the uremic cycle. Oh, and most likely your child will have birth defects."

"Say whot?"

"Does that surprise you? You've been a street whore since puberty and a substance abuser since childhood."

"Noa . . . I mean—"

"That you're pregnant—carrying a black, damaged baby?"

"Yoo lie!"

"They always want a demonstration, don't they?" Wiggler frowned and blew a series of smoke rings, which took the shape of a first-trimester fetus that reminded Clearfather of the Nourisher's little sand mummy.

"This is what's inside you right now," said Wiggler. "Hardly looks human, does it? Imagine the problems it will face."

"Don't listen to him, Maggie!" the Marshal brayed. "No baby that age looks human. He's just trying to trick you."

"Our sassy lassy isn't so sure. Ordinarily an abortion would be strongly advised—but have no fear," he said, blowing away the baby. "You are here. How about it, gentlemen? You may be stupid in regard to your own health, but would you really doom Ms. Kane and her helpless unborn?"

"You're a prick, Wiggler," the Marshal cried. "No honor. No decency."

"Marshal, I have a strong stomach for what needs doing. I'll give you a minute to talk among yourselves. I'll be waiting outside."

As soon as Wiggler left the room, Clearfather asked, "Do we need a minute?"

"Noa fuckin' way!" Maggie yelled.

"Not on your life," the Marshal answered. "But I'm bringing the guns. May not do any good, but I'll feel better."

A moment later they were coming down the stairs of the hotel, armed. Wiggler stood in the street with Walt Whitman. On top of the courthouse, the LOCO FOCO flag flapped in the breeze. There was no breeze.

"All right." Wiggler shrugged, struggling to contain his irritation. "I can see that you think you've made up your minds. Well, it's time I told you—although you may find what I'm about to say especially hard to accept."

"Especially?" joked the Marshal. "Lay it on us."

"You can't leave the Canyon," said Wiggler. "Because I *am* the Canyon. To use a word you like so much—this isn't real and neither are you. You're inside my mind."

"Fuckin' hell," Maggie gagged. "Yoo jes doan let up!"

"I'm sorry but this is all a psychic projection."

"Bullshit!"

"Think about it. Isn't that the simplest explanation for the sudden changes in architecture—for the side-by-side existence of Neanderthals and robots—mythological beings and scientific monstrosities?"

"So what are we?" Clearfather asked.

"Psychoactive medication—a form of sophisticated biosoftware I've invented. This is an experiment to reprogram myself. All my attempts to counter APPARATUS have become corrupted. The problem is that there is corruption within me. I'm trying to win the war by staging the last battle inside my own mind."

Maggie's face twisted with anger. "Yoo sayin' I'm some kine a-drugg?"

"Deep-mind therapy. Think of yourself as a construct, a character."

"A kairacter? Like in a movie?"

"Why not? The Marshal believes he used to be a character on TV. A star."

"But I wasn't just a character—I was a real person, too," Brubaker insisted.

"I thought a star was something you never stopped being?"

"Well . . ."

"How would I know you'd said that if I hadn't invented you?"

"Whot kine a-story would I bee a kairacter in?"

"You're the untutored but shrewd voice of pragmatism. You're meat and potatoes—nuts and bolts—Earth Mother as street waif."

"Why do we have memories?" the Marshal asked.

"Augustine said all reality lurks in the memory. I've given you just enough for you to believe in your own reality. That's how the potency is measured. I know the medication is active because we're arguing now."

"Mister, wee 'bout to doo a lot more 'n argyoo," Maggie said pointing the shotgun.

"Go ahead," Wiggler said. "This body is just a construct. If you pull the trigger, the construct will react like a body . . . but it won't mean anything. I'm outside this system—or rather you are inside me. Why don't you shoot yourself and see what happens?"

"Howa cum yoo backed up when I pointed the gun at yoo?"

"I only appeared to back up." Wiggler smiled. "The construct is a monitoring link. It will behave just as you do to sustain the illusion."

"All right, mister. Yoo doan think I got the balls to blast yoo?"

"No, Maggie!" Clearfather called. "It is really him. This is no dream, and we're not constructs. But don't make a mess. Please."

"Why 'n hell not? Hee deeserves to bee blown away!"

"It's not our place to judge or punish him. The world may never see his like again. If he's abused or confused his gifts—or simply failed in a great task—I still don't want to hurt him—in the hope that he finds a way to save himself."

"Bravo," Wiggler said with a smirk. "One for all . . . and you've all got a lot of gall. Now you think you're going to hike back to civilization like good campers?"

"Are you going to try to stop us?" Clearfather asked—and he realized he was holding the H&K.

"I'd be remiss not to see you're trying to leave without even taking any fresh water. It's a long haul to the Screaming Eagle Diner. Don't forget, you're not well."

Clearfather pointed the pistol. "Don't I have free will?"

"Oh absolutely." Wiggler smiled. "State of the art. But it's overrated."

"You don't think I'll shoot you?"

"No, frankly, I don't. But I confess I can't be certain. If I could predict with certainty what you were going to do, you wouldn't be able to do anything interesting enough to warrant attention."

"So it's a standoff," the Marshal said.

"Hm," said Wiggler. "Perhaps we could turn this impasse into a sporting proposition."

"What are you suggesting . . . some sort of shootout?" scoffed the Marshal.

"What a good idea!" cried Wiggler. "But of course the Marshal, being a real TV star, has the advantage of me. I may need assistance."

They turned around and waiting in the middle of the main street was a figure casting a giant shadow. He was an old man, but very tall, dressed in leather chaps, spurs, and boots. Down low on his hips he wore a leather gun belt studded with silver, carrying two big Buntline Specials. On his head sat an impossibly tall black hat with a diamondback rattler band, out of which poked an eagle feather. Beside him stood a luminous white coyote as large as a male timber wolf.

"My God!" gasped the Marshal. "That's the Deadwood Kid!"

"Who's that?" Clearfather asked.

"A legend. He was a phantom obsession of Wild Bill Hickok—a gunslinger who was so fast on the draw, he lived into very old age. But that can't—"

"Show them your speed draw," Wiggler directed, flipping a silver eagle dollar into the air. The ancient gunman's face came to life. The eyes lit up and although the old man had his hands poised to draw, they never moved. Instead a thin beam of light shot out of his pupils and smote the coin in midair. Clearfather caught it when it fell, hot to the touch, a perfect hole dead center. The great white dog let out a howl.

"Nice shooting, eh?" Wiggler grinned. "So let's be clear on the proposition. You win, Marshal, and all three of you are free to go. You lose and we'll bury your body—I promise not to recycle it in any unconventional way. Ms. Kane and your friend, my ungrateful son— remain. Deal?"

"No!" said Clearfather. "It's not a deal. We're leaving whether you send werewolves or androids. We're not going to fall for some kind of stunt—"

"Are you afraid your dear Marshal will lose? Are *you* afraid, Marshal?"

As he spoke, the old gunslinger advanced, with the huge white coyote stalking beside him. Maggie planted her legs to let rip with the Harrington & Richardson but the Marshal pushed in front. "No," he said. "This here's my fight."

"Yoo doan stand a chance!" Maggie whined.

"What about it, Wiggler?" the Marshal asked. "A *fair* fight—with guns."

"Of course!" Wiggler nodded at the robot, who made a whirring sound—and faster than they could see whipped one of the Buntlines from its holster and flipped it toward the Marshal.

"Don't do it!" Clearfather pleaded—but he saw it was hopeless. Wiggler's accusation about courage had closed the deal.

"I have to, youngster," the old imaginary lawman answered.

He was just under twenty yards away from the Deadwood Kid and had his Buntline stuffed inside his belt. The luminous coyote stood loyally beside the cyborg gunfighter.

"All right," Wiggler announced. "When I count three. One. Two—"

The Marshal wrenched the cumbersome revolver from his belt and shot the enormous white coyote in the head. Pale blue piezo-electric fire spasmed over the animal's body before it exploded in a burning bush of optical fibers, graphite, and tensuron. The gunslinger seemed to stop—and teetered—then fell facedown in its own long shadow.

"Splendid!" Wiggler quipped, struggling to smile. "Why, if you hadn't cheated, you'd have been fried in your boots! But how did you know to shoot the coyote?"

"I don't know," the Marshal admitted, amazed himself. "I just had this idea that I was lookin' at one creature not two and that it was the coyote that did the thinking."

Wiggler turned to Clearfather. "You told him."

"Hee dint say nothin'!" Maggie bellowed, defending the Marshal's valor.

"Not with his voice, perhaps. But he has powers he doesn't even know about. In any case, it's time you recognized that we play my games here or we don't play at all."

"Then we don't play," Clearfather exclaimed. "C'mon!"

CHAPTER 6

I Am the Door

Clearfather led Maggie and the Marshal behind the mill house, heading for the steep path cut into the Canyon wall. He was hoping to reach the rope bridge that he'd seen the Harijans crossing when they arrived. After that he wasn't sure. With the Neanderthals and who knew what animals to get through, he didn't think their chances of escaping were very good. Not unless he used his powers, which he wasn't really sure how to do. And the idea of hurting any of the inhabitants of the Canyon wasn't one that appealed.

They arrived at the mobile home graveyard, the Marshal and Maggie both panting. Wiggler's words about all of them being sick came back to him. The Marshal gripped the Buntline, Maggie lugged the shotgun, and Clearfather carried the old damaged Winchester. The pistol he'd set down on the boardwalk when the Marshal had handed him the rifle. He couldn't think what good it would've done anyway. They were potentially facing an army—a handgun wasn't going to save them.

Wiggler pulled up in a rickshaw drawn by two saber-toothed

tigers. His green eyes had a mad dilated gleam like disturbed pools of phosphorus. A nauseated-looking Walt Whitman snuffled after him, flatulent and contrite.

"How very ungracious!" Wiggler called. "I'm disappointed and, to be honest . . . hurt. We have so much to do."

"I'm sorry," Clearfather said. "I'm doing why I think is right."

"Right?" lamented Wiggler. "Hm. Let's take a vote, shall we?"

He clapped his hands and from out of the wreckage there appeared what looked like a mob of him—all naked except for white Nikes. Maggie gaped at the sight of the clones and then almost sagged to her knees when they began marching forward—for they seemed to change sex and shape with each step. What first appeared to be a muscular Wiggler suddenly developed gigantic breasts, morphing before their eyes into a beautiful woman—while a voluptuous young female version turned into a hulking male bodybuilder in a matter of a few feet.

"I told you you shouldn't oppose me. You see—I'm a bit unstable!"

"Jesus Christ! What are they?"

"They're outtakes from my hormone trials," Wiggler snickered. "Didn't I say I experiment on myself?"

"It's—it's—" Clearfather stuttered, trying to think what it was.

"It's proof that old legends about shape-shifting may have a basis in fact. I discovered a secret mutational ability. The problem is, it can't be controlled."

Boom! Maggie pulled the trigger on the 12-gauge and made a goopy splatter. But the blast seemed to have little effect on the wounded creature as a whole, for it reintegrated. Maggie let off another round but they still kept coming. She reloaded and the three refugees retreated, circling back behind the ghost town. They broke through a tangle of creosote bush and old gas station signs and were confronted by a monstrous miniature congregation.

"Meet the rest of the family!" Wiggler beamed, reappearing in the rickshaw.

"Mother of God!" the Marshal exclaimed.

"Your adopted children? The ones Felatia—"

"She poured gasoline over them and set the helpless things alight when she found that even though she had legal custody, they still wanted to live with me. I was only able to save them through deep cellular engineering, but the damage was too extensive. But I got even with her—as you will see."

"Yoo sick!" Maggie spat, staring in horror at the unfortunate beings in their all-terrain miniature wheelchairs. Then she saw the Creature that was with them—the one Clearfather had glimpsed at twilight.

"Auuggh!"

"Meet the great Wynn Fencer!" Wiggler announced—as the despicable-looking thing puffed out its bright bubble of throat. "Forgive him for not offering a traditional hello, but he hasn't had a tongue or vocal cords for many years. The throat fan is his means of communicating—which he finds annoying, don't you, Wynn? Particularly since his two servants, who were the only ones who could understand him, went missing. We suspect Wittgenstein got to them."

"But—who—or what's that other . . . *thing*?"

"That's the somewhat doctored—or should I say butchered—remains of Felatia, grafted onto Wynn so that he may never be lonely throughout his punishment, which I intend to last as long as my magic and my science can possibly ensure."

"But . . . she's deddd!" Maggie groaned.

"And has been for years." Wiggler smiled. "A great technical achievement."

Maggie fled. Clearfather took off after her with the Marshal hobbling behind. They didn't get far before they were completely cut off. The Canyon had narrowed. Behind them came the Wiggler clones and the loathsome stepchildren, while ahead of them, blocking their way and advancing, were the dripstone pillars Clearfather had seen earlier guarding the tepee village. They were now animate and lumbering forward, like living statues—horrid, towering sand-castle women.

"Another tribute of mine," Wiggler informed them, climbing out of the rickshaw. "Can you see the facial similarity to Felatia? I told you you couldn't escape. Now give up this foolishness and let's go back to the house and have some coffee and a nice Bundt cake."

"Holy sheet!" Maggie screamed and blasted off one of the rock creatures' heads.

"Everything is alive at some level," Wiggler remarked. "The trick is finding out how. Now you've pissed them off."

"Good grief," wailed the Marshal. "We're trapped!"

Clearfather scanned the area as an unsettling noise went up from the Neanderthals, who'd gathered on their ledges to watch the confrontation. The meat-slurping clones and the monolith women were converging. Overhead was an overhang with a pronounced crack running through it. The creatures were almost upon them.

"Give me the shotgun!" Clearfather cried, dropping the rifle and wrenching the 12-gauge out of Maggie's hands. He fired dead on the crack of the overhang, and shards of stone and dust streamed down. He fired again. There was a tremor and larger chunks began tumbling—then the ledge gave way.

The granite platform crushed the backs of the sand-castle women, raising a cloud of dust and grit that mingled with the protean gore of the hormone soldiers so that they began to collide, their morphing meat becoming entangled in a nightmare traffic jam.

"Run!" Clearfather shouted as more boulders loosened and pounded down, smushing the mutants.

He and Maggie got past before the worst of the avalanche—but the Marshal, who was behind them, was struck and covered.

Maggie shrieked and Clearfather pushed at the pile—flinging rocks away, trying to find the Marshal. It was too late. The old man's legs and pelvis had been crushed—his chest nearly caved in. He was still alive and breathing when Clearfather finally dragged him free but just barely. The rest of the creatures lay buried in the rubble—one slithering appendage waving between the boulders.

"Now see where this foolish rebelliousness has led you!" Wiggler chided—but just then his chest seemed to blow up. He coughed violently and clutched the air, impossibly surprised—and crumpled to his knees.

Behind him, puffing out his throat wildly, was Wynn Fencer . . . holding the H&K pistol that Clearfather had left behind.

Wiggler's robe was stained with blood but he struggled back to his feet and turned. "Ah, Wynn," he gasped. "Bravo . . . bravo . . . bit of spirit left in you after all . . ."

Fencer seemed stranded between heinous excitement and total disbelief—but he didn't get to enjoy his marksmanship for Walt Whitman ripped into him with savage force. Wiggler staggered and fell. From the hole in the white robe oozed what looked like offal and incredibly fine, organic optical fibers. The eyes went dark. Clearfather heard a hiss, like the bursting of the seal on a vacuum pack, and the eyes opened—but from out of them shone two pale beams of light, which joined to form the eidolon of a tiny figure that stood on his chest, wavering and blurry.

"Sheet!" Maggie screeched as she pointed to the mess of meat and circuitry that even as they looked was healing.

Clearfather swatted his hand through the grainy little hologram, which disintegrated and then re-formed. Then he rushed to the Marshal, who was having trouble breathing. "I'm sorry, Marshal . . ."

"No . . . youngster," the Marshal wheezed. "Iss all . . . right."

"Can't yoo help him?" Maggie sobbed.

"I don't know what to do," Clearfather cried.

"Doan yoo have magic powers?"

"I . . . don't know," Clearfather stammered. "Not like . . ."

"What good are yoooo?" Maggie screamed as the Marshal coughed up blood.

"No . . ." The Marshal groaned softly, holding up his hand. "This . . . was . . . meant . . . to be. I won . . . a real shootout. Now I'm with . . . my friends . . . my family."

Blind Lemon appeared, led by one of the Harijans. He began strumming his guitar and singing "The Streets of Laredo." The Marshal's breathing slowed and then stopped. Clearfather eased the old eyes shut.

Furiously, he turned on Wiggler, whom he expected to rise at any minute, fully operational now that his gunshot wound had almost closed.

"What are you?" Clearfather snapped.

"I don't know," the ethereal little Wiggler said. "I thought I was one thing. Now I'm something else. And I'm dead."

Blind Lemon moaned low, fingering "St. James Infirmary." Maggie continued to cry. The Marshal lay still.

Crows flapped down to drink from a pool of fluorescent algae. The little eidolon fluttered like a Lilliputian ambassador on the Gulliver-prone body of the dead meat-robot that Clearfather had just started to believe had given him life.

Could it still be true? Hadn't Wiggler talked about machines creating more complex machines? Might he have been rescued from the dead by a biomechanoid who in turn had been designed by another such creature-thing?

Clearfather eased back the robe to see if he could do anything with the wound—but there was nothing to be done.

"I'm sorry," he said, tears filling his eyes. "I didn't want to hurt you. I just wanted to get away."

"I don't . . . blame you."

"It was a mistake."

"That's what we make. Children . . . and monsters. Messiahs and mistakes. But if this Stinky Wiggler was a biomech, where's the real one?"

"Maybe Sitturd's hidden himself in a labyrinth of him—or her-selves. What's going to happen now?"

There was a sudden earth tremor and another rockslide.

"I don't know," the miniature Wiggler rasped. "The Transubstanti-ation wasn't completed. You have to get away. I think everything will go. You've got to get away if you can—but wait—come close—there's something I must say . . ."

"Can't I help you . . . ?"

"It's too late . . . but listen . . . you must listen . . ."

Clearfather knelt down close to the whispering hologram.

"You have   a son."

"No, he died. That woman!"

"No!" Wiggler's voice cried. "You have a son . . . about your age. Dingler. Julian . . . Dingler."

"The new head of Vitessa?" Clearfather gasped.

"I don't—know how—or what it means. Some other force at . . . work."

"But . . . what will happen . . . to me now?"

"Come . . . close . . ."

Clearfather cradled the fallen body in his arms and saw an aura peel back across the skin. Every inch of flesh was covered—carved. The designs were too numerous, too intricate and interconnected to be examined in detail. Letters, runes, ciphers, foreign alphabets, chemical symbols, models of complex molecules and mathematical formulae.

Clearfather laid the head down. A tornado of luminous faces rose from the corpse. Some were animalian and hideous, some stretched with grief or suffering, others smiling and kind. They whirled up to-gether to the height of a person and for a moment it looked as if the funnel might take human shape—then the speed of the spiral in-creased and the faces expanded out of focus and were gone.

The air grew still and Clearfather was no longer aware of Blind

Lemon's mournful guitar. Maggie had stopped weeping and lay nestled against the remains of her friend, who'd proved himself to be every bit the hero he'd dreamed of.

Then the ground shook terribly. A ledge of Neanderthals gave way. Walt Whitman and the saber-toothed tigers yoked to the rickshaw fled in terror. The Harijans began to wobble and spark.

"C'mon!" Clearfather cried, rushing over to grab hold of Blind Lemon. "This whole place is coming apart!"

"Whair wee gonna go?"

"There's only one way out that I know of. Let's go!" he called, leading the old black man whose face was soaked in tears.

As fast as they could move, Clearfather led them to the livery stable—into the blue-and-silver bus he'd seen before. It was still there, with the big steel letters on the side. SPIRITCRUISER.

"Wee can't jest drive outta heer!" Maggie hollered.

The church bell was chiming frantically now, indricotheres and other giant mammals stampeding—drones and Neanderthals colliding in the dust as moss-covered crags crashed down and the buildings seemed to liquefy.

"Yes, we can!" Clearfather replied, remembering the words of the little Chinese men—*To find a door, first look for a wall.* The wall where Calamity Jane had been playing. It was a way into the Vortex—a way out of the Canyon.

He stuffed Lemon into one of the seats and buckled him in. Then Maggie. A rockfall collapsed a portion of the roof as he fired up the ignition. The street was filled with coffins and musical instruments—centaurs trampling Wiggler's damaged stepchildren.

Clearfather couldn't remember driving—and certainly not a bus—but it came easily given the situation, especially since he plowed through the flimsy walls. Smoke filled the air. The laboratories, the experimental animals, and the mysterious machines were all going to disappear. A series of explosions throbbed, raising a fallout of roller-coaster sparkle. Diamonds and glowworms and golden death masks rained down as Wiggler's subterranean bemusement kingdom crumbled into the deeper Dakota darkness.

Clearfather brought the bus in a straight line for a run at the section of wall he thought Calamity Jane frequented. Through the dust and flames he saw the sloth—petrified by the turmoil—but he had no intention of stopping. He didn't know how the doorway worked, and if it didn't, he wanted to be up to speed. Better a head-on with the cliff than the panicking creatures and malfunctioning machines. He pressed the accelerator to the floor—his desperation counteracting the grief. There was a deafening screech of static.

CHAPTER 7

In the Wind

Into the chaos of vortices bristling like nerves straight into a wall of light . . .

The **SPIRITCRUISER** roared through the cliff. Maggie screamed at the point of imagined impact and then screamed again when the cloud of red dust and white powder billowed up around them as the bus ground to a halt. The moment the dust had settled and the barrenness was revealed—she screamed again—thinking she'd had a miscarriage. It was only diarrhea. She waddled off to the restroom.

"Holy moly!" cried Blind Lemon. "I think I can see!"

"You don't have eyes," Clearfather pointed out, pleased that the old man was all right. The wall had looked so solid. Right up to the second of impact he'd feared they were going to be smashed into an accordion. Then he remembered the funny sound Calamity Jane had made mingling with the rock—a giggle almost—and he gave himself over. He *knew* it was a door—and the stone dissolved into a mist like fine particles of aluminum chloride. There was a sound of ripping silk and then the bus was inside a vast cave system of green lichen, which became a wind tunnel—speeding forward and falling at the same time, becoming particles and molecules, then patterns of vibrations like music made of light—re-forming into texture and a white star of ice exploding into Texas redsoil.

"How many fingers am I holding up?"

"Three," the old bluesman answered.

Clearfather was relieved. He hadn't moved his hand. While suddenly being able to see might sound good, it also might also herald molecular dissolution.

Maggie returned embarrassed, horrified about the Marshal, and stricken with terror. Clearfather found an old jumpsuit for her. Miserably she took it and went to wash up and change. He left Lemon strumming his guitar and went outside to check things out. No one was around. Not a stick of building remained, but he had no doubt of where they were. The burned yellowgrass and red dust had been carpeted with a caustic-smelling white powder like bleach. Not a bird or insect could be seen—and the monument to Sitturd's sister had been destroyed. He'd been right about Vitessa returning after he and Kokomo had escaped. They'd done a microgrid search for evidence and then launched a scorched-earth assault. Pits and craters showed where the tunnels and shelters had been bombed. If anyone or -thing had survived the tornado battle, it hadn't survived this.

"Soa whair tha fuck are wee?" he heard Maggie call from the door. She looked pale and sick—but still rather fetching in the jumpsuit.

"We're in Texas," he answered.

"Say whot?"

"About eight hundred miles south of where we were."

"Yeah right! Howa wee travil eight hunnerd miles in a minnit?"

"The answer's technical."

"Doan yoo start with that bullshit! I had enuff. Tell mee the damn truth!"

"I know it's hard to believe, but we really are eight hundred miles away from South Dakota."

"Oh sheet!" Maggie cried and started bawling her eyes out.

"It's not that bad," Clearfather called, noticing that Blind Lemon had inched his way to the driver's seat, strumming his guitar—a mournful but reassuring song called "The Downhearted Blues."

"Doan yoo see! This means hee 'as right! Wee aren't real—wee jest in his hedd!"

Blind Lemon bent a note like a baby crying. "I can see her point."

Terrific, thought Clearfather. Two members of the party think they're illusions.

"But . . . ," said the bluesman. "If we really ain't real—why dint we just go poof back in the Canyon—'long with everythin' else?"

"Doan ask me," Maggie choked. "I'm jest some kine a-kairacter. Hey, Wiggler!" she yelled at the sky. "Whot tha fuck wee doo now!"

The sky was Krishna blue and empty, as if all the clouds had fallen in the fields. Maggie's voice sounded both loud and small. Then they heard another sound.

"You hear that?" Clearfather asked.

"Iss comin' from over there." Lemon pointed, his arm poking out like a weather vane.

"I can't wait to seee whot kine a-monstur hee's gonna send at us now."

Clearfather's ears pricked at her remark and then he smiled—for the sound came clearly now. It was the barking of a dog—and on the bleak horizon there appeared the skeletal shape of the greyhound he'd encountered earlier. He let out a piercing whistle, and the starving creature sauntered faster through the tortured landscape.

"Yoo knoah that dog?" Maggie sniffled.

"What dog?" Clearfather teased. "We're inside Wiggler's mind."

"Welll, mebbe hee's thinkin' of a dog right now!"

"Or maybe it's a real dog. I bet the dog believes he's real—and real hungry. We've got to believe we're real, too."

Blind Lemon farted.

"'Scuse me. Ate my grits too quick this mwaning! Figure a blues-man should like grits. But I don't frankly. Really I don't."

"Shut up, yoo ol' booty grabber!" Maggie fussed. "Wee got moor to worry 'bout than grits. Wee in somebody's brain! An' the Marshal's dedd!"

"Don't you see that if we really were in Wiggler's brain, we wouldn't have anything to worry about?" Clearfather asked. "And the Marshal couldn't be dead—because he'd never have really been alive!"

"Then how'd wee get heer . . . so kwik?"

"Canyon was full-a back doors and trapdoors," Lemon said.

"That's what I think, too," said Clearfather. "Somehow the Vortex lies behind this reality and connects different points and perhaps moments like passageways in a house."

"All right, smarty-pants. If yoor right . . . how cum hee dint jest git yoo when yoo bin heer beefor? This is whair yoo cum threw, right?"

Blind Lemon stroked his guitar again. "I can see her point."

"There's a simple answer," Clearfather replied. "He'd forgotten about the door. That's what happens when you have too many secret passages. Besides, he had a mental block about Dustdevil. He was murdered here, too, in a way. His dream died. Anyway, we're here now—and however we got here we've got to go on."

Maggie snuffled. "Whot was that last bit all about? Whenn yoo held him?"

"He asked for forgiveness."

"An' yoo gave it to 'im?"

"Yes," said Clearfather as the spoke-thin dog snuffled up to him.

"Butt hee's a loony! Hee started wars an' things!"

"He did good things, too. Great things. Who can say what the final judgment of history will be on him? But it was my forgiveness he wanted. I gave it to him."

"Butt . . . hee wuddn't even real. Not hyuman."

"Now she starts in on the human shit," Blind Lemon grumped. "Why you so proud of bein' human . . . when you worried you not real?"

"I can see his point," said Clearfather, stroking the dog's ears.

"Oh, shut up. I ain't lissenin' to yoo!"

"If creatures and machines that you think aren't real can ask for forgiveness, then maybe being real isn't what you thought it was," Clearfather said. "But in a way you're right. He wasn't the real Wiggler. He was a decoy. A backup."

"I been with him long as I can remember," Lemon countered.

"Doesn't change his relationship to us. He *thought* he was the real Wiggler. As far as we're concerned, he was. I think that's what makes a good decoy."

"You mean we'll meet him again?" Lemon asked.

"I don't know if we'll meet him. A part of him's inside us . . . and will be with us wherever we go. But there's another part of him that's outside. In the wind."

"I cain't beeleeve the Marshal ain't heer!" Maggie gasped.

"I . . . know," Clearfather said. "But he died a real hero . . . and as much as I miss him, I figure it was for the best. We'll need some of his courage now. Let's not let him down."

"I'm goin' name ma baby affer him. Marshal . . . Kane . . ."

"He'd like that," Clearfather said. "And I'll . . . stick by you, Maggie. We'll be all right."

Blind Lemon struck a glittering harmonic that hung in the air.

"Whatchyoo mean . . . stick by mee?"

"I'll help you raise the baby."

"Wait a minnit! Yoo sayin' boyfriend . . . husband stuff?"

"Yes."

"All yoo got's a stump."

"It's a big stump. Plus I got spizzerinctum—and friends and family in high places. They'll help us."

"Why they doo that?"

"Because I helped them. That's what people do. I know you're scared and confused. So am I. But it's going to be okay. We've got to stick together."

"So . . . whair wee gonna go?"

"We're going to head to Pittsburgh—via a place called the Garden of Eden in Lucas, Kansas. A friend told me about it. I want you to come, too, Lemon. I got this idea you could be a star and help Professor Chicken. How would you like to play before real audiences?"

"No shit?"

"No shit."

"Can you drive . . . all that way?"

"Yeah . . . ," said Clearfather, thinking it out. "I can."

Getting out on the road would be the best way to leave the sadness and confusion behind. He was certain that Wilton and even the Man of Steel would be glad to see him—even if he did bring problems with him. From there he'd work out how to make contact with Julian Dingler.

The greyhound gave another bark. The brittle old dog had found something—where the orchard of windmills had once stood. Clearfather went over to have a look. In the whitened redsoil was a folio-sized book bound in an unknown material. The cover was tornado green, and written on it in faded gold letters were the words . . .

THE VORTEXTS
MEMOIRS & MUTATIONS
BEING THE SECRETS, DREAMS, INVENTIONS, AND INDISCRETIONS
OF
LLOYD MEADHORN SITTURD

Clearfather's heart jumped when he read the title—but he was taken aback to open the heavy book and find that the pages were all empty.

"Whot up with that?" Maggie asked, looking over his shoulder.

"So this is what she stole . . . ," Clearfather breathed.

"Hoo?"

"Calamity Jane. She took this book from Wiggler's library and passed it through the wall. She'd done it before with other things."

"The sloth put this book heer?"

Lemon doddered over to have a look.

"The people who lived here before—they saved the things she slipped through. They thought they were gifts from God."

"Boy, did they have it wrong!"

"I don't know," Clearfather sighed. "Of all the books she could've given—I can't think of any one I would've wanted more."

"Why? Damn thing's empty. Every page is blank!"

"Maybe. Or maybe there's a secret."

Blind Lemon held out a hand for the page. "Shit! This page ain't blank. Tons a words . . . and symbols and shit. No way this be blank."

Clearfather closed the book. "Come on," he said. "We've got a long way to go. We'll take the dog with us."

"Hee got a name?" Maggie asked.

"I don't remember. Why don't you give him a new name?"

"Shit, I doan knoa."

"Then let's call him Lucky. All right?"

"Tha's one-a the first normal things I hear yoo say."

Clearfather led them back to the bus, where he rounded up a Lamb 'n' A Can® meal for Lucky and then went to rummage up a change of clothes. When he took off his robe Maggie gave a low squeal.

"What is it?" he asked.

"Iss yoor back! Tha words—tha marks—thair gone!"

He rushed into the bathroom and saw that she was right. The evil writing had faded away. There was just a hint of a scar on the third F—like where the weather vane had stabbed him. No more burning. No more weight.

He stared out over the dry waste of dust and chemical poison. If you'd gone searching for the most desolate, hopeless, barren bit of desert, you'd have to say this looked remarkably like it now. Suddenly he knew what he was going to do with the little globe of ivory that he'd been carrying. He went outside and found the spot where he thought the monument to Lodema Sitturd had been. He knelt down.

"This is for all of you," he said, digging in with his hands. "All of you who have helped me on my journey. We plant this seed to heal the past. We plant this seed in hope for the future. To both remember and forget."

He nestled the dull white ball in the dead red earth, patted the dust over it, and said a silent prayer for Kokomo. His heart ached for a moment—but by the time he was back behind the wheel, he felt a rushing sense of energy. They had no money. He might have a brain hemorrhage at any moment. Maggie's baby might have birth defects. And worst of all, he'd found out that not only was he a kind of flesh-and-muck robot—the man who had made him was also one. He was a technological and theological experiment gone wrong. But he couldn't help himself. He was glad to be alive. Whatever that meant.

He turned on the radio and swerved when he heard Stinky Wiggler's voice—but it was just a disc in the sound system. He tuned in the news instead.

American Pirate Radio was reporting that a powerful earthquake had caused a catastrophe in South Dakota. What was puzzling to scientists was the select damage done by the quake, which had been dubbed Crazy Horse. From the Black Hills in the west, all across the state, go-kart tracks, instant-food franchises, casinos, motels, and tourist trading posts had all been leveled, while aftershocks were felt as far away as the Vitessalith in Minneapolis. Most noticeably, the presidential heads of Mount Rushmore had cracked and fallen into a heap, which many people described as resembling a composite bust (referred to thereafter as the Unknown President).

In other news Minson Fiske, now the wealthiest athlete in the world, had reappeared following his strange disappearance during the "Red Out" of LosVegas, as it had come to be known. Apparently, the gay heavyweight had been treated for an unspecified head wound in a veterinary clinic, the best facility that could be found given the disaster. It was believed that the champion had been over-run by his adoring fans and inadvertently injured. What the media didn't know was that the real cause of the damage was the shock of discovering his long-lost and presumed dead homosexual father wearing a mint-chocolate evening dress and having intercourse with his mother on the table of a Chinese salamander restaurant.

The media also didn't know that upon regaining consciousness, Minson's first thoughts were of the three Chinese men he'd seen in his dream—warning him about the rise of the Gay Bully Movement, an unfortunate side effect of his victory. And as to the future, the media could only speculate, but with a fortune now at his disposal Minson would soon retire his parents to an island in the Caribbean where Eartha Proud would become a powerful Voudun leader.

Aretha never went back to Manhattan. He gave up his dreams of societal revolution and reinvented himself—sharing a beach house with Eartha and a slovenly iguana named Flip Wilson, teaching island children while dabbling at fashion design. His days with the Satyagrahi faded out of his mind as completely as his time as a lawyer. Very rarely, early in the morning, would he dream of the tunnels again—or of Clearfather—and only once more did he ever see a per-sonal manifestation of Dooley Duck and Ubba Dubba—strolling in the moonlight along the beach with a child, part duck, part orang-utan. But almost daily he felt their presence, that peculiar transpar-ent connectedness that he'd experienced on Ronald Reagan Boulevard. He never discovered the truth about Finderz Keeperz, which was just as well.

What the media did know all about was Wynn Fencer, or at least his official persona. The brain-dead multitrillionaire had expired in a private facility in St. Paul, leaving behind a hologram will. Complete control of his estate and the CEO-ship of the Vitessa Corporation fell to Julian Dingler, who was at that moment considering relocating corporate HQ to Pittsburgh—to a new complex to be built on the old site of Macropotamia.

On his way back from a whirlwind visit to Vitessa offices in Europe, Dingler stopped in New York to give a press conference, where he outlined an agenda of deep-tissue reforms. Yankee Stadium was chosen as the venue and was packed to capacity for the occasion. Among the major commitments put forward, he promised to disband the secret facilities and to open all R&D projects to public scrutiny. "We will air out the labyrinth that Vitessa has become," he said. "We are putting a ban on the release of all new psychoactive medication produced by any of our subsidiaries and will be inviting a team of independent experts to assess and report on the efficacy and/or danger of all products currently in circulation. We will also be drastically revising the structure of our businesses. We intend to reinstate the distinction between business and government and to eradicate the distinction between business and humanitarian values. Vitessa has the personnel, the intellectual property, and the financial resources to develop a new definition of Quality of Life that is sustainable around the planet. The grotesque greed is going to end. Wholesale destruction of ecosystems and enslavements of people will stop. We're going to prove to the creatures of this planet and to ourselves that humanity is not an ending but a beginning.

"And now, to commemorate this pledge and to lead us in a kind of prayer, are Dooley Duck and Ubba Dubba—who have a very special announcement to make."

The enormous cartoon creatures were greeted with thunderous applause—reportedly heard from Flatbush to Palisades Park—as they led the crowd in an old-style rap version of "Back in the U.S.A." before announcing that they were about to become the proud parents of a new kind of creature—and that they were inviting all people of the world to help in deciding on a name. Everyone could make a suggestion. All the names would go into a draw to be held on the Fourth of July, where the momentous selection would be made by Ariel Sturt, the brave leader of the children's pro Duck + Dick movement, who'd been paralyzed from the waist down in an attack by Christian fundamentalists.

Listening to the ceremonious goings-on as the SPIRITCRUISER toodled north, Clearfather wondered if perhaps he too was a decoy, a backup. Maybe the real Messiah Upload, if there was one, was Dooley Duck and the mutant gift that he and Ubba Dubba were about to bring forth.

Cannon blasts ended the festivities in Yankee Stadium, after which Julian Dingler, as part of his promise to be more visible and accessible, shunned a limo or copter and took the subway to Harlem for a run through the streets to Central Park. His bodyguards vehemently opposed this move and Vitessa Intel was standing by with plenty of street-level support—but Dingler chose to be accompanied only by Dooley—and the sight of the enormous blue duck huffing and puffing alongside him was something that New Yorkers would never forget.

Without knowing it, Dingler and Dooley veered close to Fort Thoreau, where the entire compound was gathered on the other side of the Mirror Field to watch them pass. The Satyagrahi were celebrating the announcements Dingler had made—certain that Parousia Head must've had a hand in them—especially since she'd at last made contact after her long silence and appointed Beulah Schwartzchild as the new leader of the community, a decision greeted with initial surprise and then profound enthusiasm, in keeping with the new mood of healing and reinvention.

It was an eye-opening experience for Julian Dingler. He saw things that he wouldn't soon forget—but the one that would stay with him the longest was a bizarre white man muttering amid the black people and the broken glass shining like broken glass in the sun. The skinny derelict was dressed in tinsel and cast-off rags— laughing to himself—with a huge ugly dog rolling along beside him. The mongrel's back legs were built into a golf buggy with rusted wheels. Something about the way they moved made Dingler imagine that the trembling man and the broken-down dog were really one creature, cackling and creaking off into the obscurity of the city.

Meanwhile Clearfather's thoughts were as calm as the pages of Wiggler's book—and as open as the highway that took them over the Cimarron River.

The SPIRITCRUISER had a full tank of fuel, and he kept the shining blue-and-silver vehicle humming at an even speed, past a shot-gunned old billboard rising out of a ragged field of cow corn.

> HE THAT SHALL PERSEVERE UNTO THE END, HE SHALL
> BE SAVED.
> —*Matthew 10:22*

Blind Lemon was strumming his guitar and singing . . . *I's up this mornin' . . . blues walkin' like a man . . .*

"Yoo all right?" Maggie asked.

"Just a headache," Clearfather answered. "Hey, you know what? We're in Kansas."

About the Author

KRIS SAKNUSSEMM's work has appeared in the *Boston Review, River Styx, The Hudson Review,* the *Alaska Quarterly Review,* the *Kansas Quarterly,* the *Nimrod International Journal of Prose and Poetry, Prairie Schooner,* the *Southwest Review,* and *Rosebud.* He lives in Australia with his dingo and can be reached at www.saknussemm.com/dev/.